SNAP

BANNISTER'S MUSTER: BOOK ONE

BARBARA GASKELL DENVIL

Cover design by
It's A Wrap

ALSO BY BARBARA GASKELL DENVIL

Bannister's Muster Series

SNAP

SNAKES & LADDERS

BLIND MAN'S BUFF

DOMINOES

· LEAPFROG

HIDE & SEEK

Also available in Audio and soon to be Spanish editions too

For more info please go to https://bannisters muster.com

FOREWORD

Hello everybody, and welcome to the world of Nathan, Poppy and their medieval friends.

In medieval England, people spoke a little differently, and even today the English language has differences in America, Canada, England and Australia.

Spelling is often different in different countries. In England, they talk about a 'lift' whereas in America it is an 'elevator'. In England, one word is spelled 'colour' whereas the exact same word is spelled 'color' in America. What a muddle!

But wait – there's more. Because in my series BANNISTER'S MUSTER, there are a few old-fashioned words that aren't used in any country anymore. For instance, 'braes' which is the old, old word for men's underpants. Try telling your mother you need a clean pair of braes this morning to wear to school.

John and Alfie are important characters in these books, and both speak old 'cockney' which is a simple distortion of the common language. 'Ain't' instead of 'isn't' – well, most of us say that from time to time. But also 'tis' (for 'it is') and 't'weren't' instead of 'it wasn't'. They also make some major mistakes in grammar, such as 'me old man' instead of 'my father' and 'it were me' instead of 'that was me.'

I have kept this sort of language to a minimum because I don't want to make my book hard to read for anyone, but these characters all speak a little differently, and I hope you don't find it confusing.

I do hope everyone from all countries enjoys my books and do let me know if you have any problem with the language.

Best Regards,

Barbara Gaskell Denvil

CHAPTER ONE

I t was the laughter that woke him. With a jolt, Nathan sat up in bed and stared into the darkness.

"What was that? Who's there?" he said loudly, startled.

At first there was no answer. Half befuddled with sleep, Nathan almost lay back down, thinking the laughter must simply have been part of his dream. But just as he was ready to go back to sleep, someone said, "Well, Bumble-Bee-Head. Are you ready for an adventure? Or not?"

Nathan blinked, hiccupped, and sat straighter. Rising up from the corners of his bedroom the huge balloon rocked, its striped colours as bright as the sunshine, even though now it was past midnight. It seemed to burst through the ceiling, huge and beautiful, bigger than his room and yet completely visible, bobbing on its moorings. Below the balloon in a neat wicker basket rather like a shopping bag but much larger, was a thin man, his knees poking up to his chin as he sat squashed into the limited space. He wore black and a top hat as tall as his shadow. His laughter was like water gurgling down the plug hole, and it seemed to be Nathan he was laughing at.

"This," said Nathan to himself, "is a very stupid dream."

"This," answered the laughing man, "is no dream at all, my young friend. So climb in with me, and I'll show you just how stupid it is. Or perhaps how stupid it isn't." He nodded and the top hat tilted. "Unless, of course," he added, "you're too frightened to risk an adventure you'll never forget."

Nathan rubbed his eyes and said, "You're a mad man."

"Just a mad wizard."

"It's the middle of the night and I don't want to go anywhere." This wasn't entirely true, but having been taught not to talk to strangers, getting into a magic balloon with one seemed definitely unwise. So Nathan added, "I don't even know your name."

The thin wizard leaned forwards, half out of the basket, until his top hat slipped right over his eyes. He said, voice high and thin, "I'm Brewster Hazlett. The one and only Brewster Hazlett. And you, Bumble-Bee Head, are Nat Bannister."

"I'm Nathan Bannister. I hate being called Nat. It sounds like an insect." He wrinkled his nose. "And I'm not a bumble-bee either. I don't buzz and I don't bite."

"Then you'll make a good companion," the thin man said, stretching out one long-fingered hand. "Come on, Nat. Don't make me wait. There's an adventure that's itching to be born and it's all yours for the taking."

His bedroom was starting to fade. One wall with the pictures of him and his grandmother with his sister when she was a baby, had completely faded away. His small white wardrobe was gone. The spotty wallpaper, and the bedside table had entirely disappeared. Nathan was sitting on his bed with the quilt still up to his waist, but everything else around him was turning into a colourless haze, until all he could see was the huge bobbing balloon and the odd man leaning out from it. The stripes on the balloon's sides became brighter and bigger and beyond the top curve, Nathan could see the moon. It was a dark night and the moon was just a thin sliver. Nathan rubbed his eyes, but that helped nothing and now the bedroom ceiling had gone and the floor and walls were fading fast.

"Quick, quick, stupid boy," Brewster called. "Hurry before the bed disappears and you fall into empty space."

The wizard's voice was high and a little squeaky and Nathan wasn't sure he liked it, but there was nothing else to do except obey. Only his quilt remained. Nathan gulped, took the strange man's hand, and found himself pulled straight into the balloon's basket. The wizard's hand was thin and bony with long scratchy nails like claws. Nathan tumbled in and plopped onto the wicker bottom, where a bright red velvet cushion broke his fall. So he sat on the cushion and peered out.

His bedroom had now entirely gone. His house no longer existed. Even the garden couldn't be seen anymore. All that could be seen was the huge black night sky and a thousand blinking and flickering stars with the thin sickle moon high above.

Brewster said, "Well, Nat. Hang on. We're off."

Nathan stared. "And I'm not dreaming?"

"Are you cold?" demanded the thin wizard. "Do you feel the wind? Yes, of course you do, Bumble-Bee Head. And you know that doesn't happen in dreams."

"I'm not a Bumble-bee Head and I hate being called Nat and this sort of thing doesn't happen in real life either." Nathan was hanging on to one of the ropes that attached the basket to the balloon. He could certainly feel the cold wind, and he was sorry he hadn't had time to put on his dressing gown and slippers. He was only wearing his fleecy striped pyjamas and was shivering as the wind whistled through the ropes. But the excitement was far greater than the discomfort, and as he gazed up and around, Nathan could smell something sharp and spicy.

"Smell that?" Brewster Hazlett seemed to guess what Nathan was thinking. "When that scent comes spinning up your nose any time in the future, you'll know I'm nearby."

"But," said Nathan at once, "does that mean you'll be visiting me again and again? What if I don't want you? Can I tell you I don't want to see you anymore?"

"You'll want to see me alright," cackled Brewster. "First of all, you'll want me to come back and take you home."

"What?" yelled Nathan, turning around abruptly. "You mean you're taking me to some strange place and then you're going to leave me there all alone in the middle of the night?"

"No." The thin man shook his head. "I'm not taking you some *place*. I'm taking you some *when*." Still laughing, he added, "Look down."

Both hands holding tight to the wicker lip, Nathan looked down over the edge of the basket, and gasped. Spread out below was a great city, but it was nothing like any city he had ever imagined. There were no skyscrapers and no motorways, but the hundreds of houses were small and clustered together either side of narrow lanes and twisting alleyways. There seemed to be very many churches with high steeples and one great cathedral with a huge spire and massive pillars rising from the raised entrance. Through the dark sleeping city ran the twists and loops of a river, which was wide and shining silver in the starlight.

"Where is this?" asked Nathan. "Is it still England?"

"Foolish Bumble-Bee Head," sniggered the skinny wizard. "This is London, of course. Don't you see the River Thames? Can't you see St. Paul's Cathedral? And there, in the distance, is Westminster Palace."

"You don't know what you're talking about," Nathan objected. "It can't be London. St. Paul's doesn't look like that at all. It hasn't got a spire, it's got a dome. Some of those little houses have thatched roofs. London certainly doesn't have little thatched cottages, or any funny old houses like this at all. And I can't see Big Ben nor Tower Bridge."

"But you can see the Tower with a hundred turrets," Brewster said, pointing. "Look, stupid boy. The Tower of London. So where could we be except London itself. Look, Nat, look, and use your little brain."

Nathan was cold, tired, confused, and extremely excited, but getting annoyed. "Don't call me Nat," he objected. "Gnats are horrid little flying insects that bite and there's nothing wrong with my brain. And yes, there's the Tower. But where's the bridge?"

"The Tower bridge," grinned the wizard, "won't be built for nearly four hundred years. This, Nat, is London when King Richard ruled England, and the city was a very different place."

The wind was howling like a wolf, and the basket was shaking, buffeted by the growing gale. The smell of magic, which Nathan had first found exciting, now seemed rank and too strong. Nathan shook his head, trying to get his hair out of his eyes. "My name isn't Nat," he mumbled. "My name is Nathan. And King Richard who? We haven't got a King Richard."

"Ah, but we did in the year 1485," said Brewster, pulling on one of the cords. "And that's where you're going, boy. Richard III. He was a king some people hated and some people loved, and you're going to meet him, if you use what little sense you have."

Nathan took a deep breath. "I still don't know if this is a real adventure or just a dream," he said, "but you're rude and I want to go home. I want my bed. And I don't want to be made to walk around a lot of old houses in the cold just wearing my pyjamas. I haven't any idea why you chose me for your crazy adventures and you can't leave me here against my will."

And Brewster Hazlett laughed again, very loudly. "Well now," he cackled, "as it happens, yes I can."

The basket began to tip. It rocked in the stormy wind and Nathan hung on, screwing up his eyes to see. The stars were bright but now the thin slice of moon was hidden behind clouds. As the balloon began to hover lower and lower, so the huge stone walls of the Tower rose up to meet them. Looking up, Nathan saw the bright balloon roll and shake, while looking down all he could see was menacing darkness, mossy stone walls and the stars reflected in the water of the river nearby.

Then the whole balloon and the basket too began to twist as if caught in a tornado. It spun around and around until Nathan was dizzy, but he could still see Brewster Hazlett laughing at him. The thin cackle seemed to pierce through the howl of the wind, and even though Nathan continued to hang on tightly, he felt he was falling.

One minute there was the velvet cushion beneath him and the clutch of the basket safe between his palms, and the next moment the wind was whistling in his ears, he felt a terror he had never known in his life before, and the whole world went topsy-turvy.

With a bang and a clunk, he landed on hard cobbles. Bruised and shocked, he sat there a moment, watching as the balloon sailed away from him, up into the night sky. The wizard was peering down, laughing again, and waving. His fingers were long and skinny and they shone pale in the darkness, but what showed brightest was his mouth, open in laughter, red lipped and full of long white teeth. His tall black hat was askew and his skinny pointed knees were shaking with enjoyment. And then, within minutes, there was nothing more to be seen and the whole balloon and Brewster with it had disappeared into the clouds.

Nathan sat very still. For a very brief moment he felt like crying. All alone and completely confused, he had no idea what to do next. He wanted, very much, just to wake up. But by now he was sure that he wasn't asleep at all. He was very much awake, and very frightened. He wondered what his Grandmother would do in the morning when she came to wake him up, and found an empty bed. Granny would shout and little sister Poppy would come running in to see what was wrong. But Nathan would not be there to explain.

Looking around, he realised that he was sitting in a very narrow lane. The ground was cobbled and a thin gutter ran wet down the middle. There was no pavement and the windows of the houses either side were dark and closed with wooden shutters. There were no street lamps and no lights in any of the houses. Right next to him there was a set of old broken steps leading down into deepest shadow, and at the end of the lane, the huge soaring stone walls of the Tower of London blocked his view. Next to the dark and broken steps was a smithy, but it was closed, although through a crack in the doorway where the hinges were rusty, he could see the deep red embers of the smith's furnace. Then he heard a church bell which seemed to come from the other side of the stone wall. It tolled five times and although it sounded nothing like Big Ben, Nathan thought that might mean it was five o'clock in the morning. And then suddenly there was a flicker of light in an adjacent window, and a grating and clank as someone within the house took down the shutters.

Nathan struggled up and began to walk down the alleyway in the opposite direction to the walls of the Tower. And at that moment there was the sound of running feet and five dark figures bolted from the shadows, came racing around the corner, and ran straight into him.

6

Winded, everyone stopped, and one small child fell over with a grunt as he banged his small elbow.

The fallen child began to cry and Nathan reached out a hand to help him up. They all stood, looking at each other and finally Nathan said "Hello. You must be – cold."

It was true. He was conscious of his own weird looking pyjamas and bare feet, but what the other children were wearing was even more odd. The tallest boy wore a long grubby shirt to his knees and under this his legs were bare and so were his feet. At least over his shoulders was a heavy cape of thick sheepskin, clipped tight under his chin, but his feet looked blue and icy. The next tallest was a girl with very long tousled hair and she wore a long tunic dress in some dark heavy material, but peeping beneath the skirts, she also had very dirty bare feet. A dark haired boy wore a torn shirt and was also bare legged, but a small blue cape covered his shoulders. The other two smaller boys were wearing even less, just ragged and dirty shirts.

Hesitant, and gazing at him in surprise, the small group seemed unsure whether to push past and run on, or stop and talk. The eldest boy was staring at Nathan's pyjamas. "Well, we're used to the cold," he said. "But where did you get them funny things? You look chilly too." He shook his head of light brown curls. "My name's Alfie. Who are you?"

Nathan sighed. "Nat," he said, accepting the inevitable. "Hello Alfie. Do you live here?"

"'Course we do," Alfie said. He pointed to the girl at his side. "She's Alice. And the little one you knocked over is Sam." He nodded to his right. "He's John Ten-Toes," then nodded to his left, "and he's Pete." Alfie waited a moment, but when Nathan didn't say anything because he couldn't think what to say, Alfie added, "So where do you live?"

"London," Nathan sighed again. "But not this London. Another one. A different one… In a house in Hammersmith."

The girl Alice, frowning, said, "Hammersmith is a little village way out West beyond Westminster. That's not London." She was hugging herself and shivering. "And if you've got a proper house to live in, then that's where you should be on a cold morning like this. Are you lost?"

"Oh yes," admitted Nathan, "very, very lost."

7

It was John Ten-Toes who smiled suddenly and said, "Then reckon ya better join our gang. The best, we are, the very best. Reckon there ain't no better in all London. We'll look after ya till you finds your way home again." He put his hand protectively on Nathan's shoulder, ten very dirty fingers with ten very dirty finger-nails. "Ain't no one bests us," he grinned. "We'll keep ya safe."

CHAPTER TWO

It had begun to rain and a silvery sprinkle of drizzle was soaking them all as they stood huddled in the alley. People had started waking in many of the houses. The shutters were being lifted down and windows showed the flickering light of new lit candles as people rolled from their beds and prepared for work on the new chilly day.

"Folks will shout and wave brooms at us if they see us," said Alfie. "They think we're thieves and cut-purses, 'cos sometimes we sleep in the streets. So come on. Let's go."

He turned, and not knowing what else to do, Nathan followed. The rain was in his eyes and dripping from his hair onto his face, while the shoulders of his pyjamas were soon soaked. They hurried down the alleys until they ran into a much wider road, and finally stood on a grassy bank looking across at the river. The shadows were gradually lifting and a pale hint of light hung over the river's darkness.

Alfie was grinning. "Now we usually bunker down in this old warehouse," he said, nodding towards a ramshackle building beside them. "Gets a bit cold sometimes with the wind coming upriver, but it don't feel too bad and there's no one to bother us."

John muttered, under his breath, "Ain't no one dares."

Nathan stared at the warehouse. Tucked between larger buildings, it seemed to be toppling over, and was kept up by wooden beams crossing its walls. Nathan had heard of the old buildings made of plaster and lathe, and here, where the plaster was cracked and broken, he could see the lathe within. There were no windows at all and the roof had big gaps in the tiles. "Looks draughty," he muttered.

"Used to be a storage for wine kegs," Alice said. "But not anymore so we sneaked in and made it home. There's places where the rain and snow comes in but there's nice warm corners too. We've all got straw beds and real blankets. We're luckier than some."

"I wanted to be an apprentice once," nodded Alfie, "but they wouldn't have me 'cos I got no mother nor father and they threw me out. But I don't care, we look after ourselves."

The three younger boys were pushing Alfie from behind. Sam said, "Quick. Tis still raining. Let's get back inside."

Inside it was as big and empty as a deserted barn. The drizzle had puddled the dirty old floorboards, and it was dark and dingy, but it was better in than out. Alice pointed towards the side where the back wall leaned inwards, as though buffeted by wind. There were several piles of dry straw, and a squash of colourless blankets. In the middle of the space near these beds lay a slab of stone and on top was a pile of twigs and ashes, with a little black iron pot sitting on the floor nearby. "I'll light the fire," said Alice, "and boil some pottage. Are you hungry, Nat?"

Nathan was about to complain and say his name wasn't Nat, when he remembered that he had himself said that was his name. "Hungry?" He thought a moment. "Not really. But I suppose it's time for breakfast. Though I usually have a boiled egg and toast. What's pottage?"

Alfie laughed, but it was a much nicer laugh than Brewster Hazlett's. "I don't know what toast is," Alfie said, "but pottage is the best after a cold night. Come sit near the fire."

The boys were running around in a bustle, playing with each other and chasing. The two younger ones pulled up their blankets to wrap around their shoulders and finally they all sat to watch as Alice lit the fire with what she called a tinder box, put an iron trivet over the flames and sat the pot on top. She began stirring the pot's contents with a large wooden spoon. "Won't be long. But we've got no platters so you'll have to share straight from the pot like everyone else."

The small fire lit the space and Nathan was able to look around and see more clearly. Not that there was much to see. The little flames seemed hesitant at first, just a golden hiss and dither. Then they flared and a real welcoming heat swept out. Smoke puffed up. Nathan gazed up at the high ceiling, held up by dark beams, and at the walls which were flaking their grubby plaster. Then he jumped as something brushed past his bare feet. He had been wriggling his toes, trying to get warm again, but now he quickly moved away. "What was that?"

Alice giggled. "Just Mouse."

"You've got mice here?" Nathan stared down, but the shadow was far too big for an ordinary mouse. "Not rats, are they?" he said with dislike.

Alfie had leaned back on the floor, his sheepskin cape as a cushion beneath his head. "'Course we got rats," he said. "Every place along the river's got rats. They come in on the big ships, but it's Mouse that frightens most of them away. Mouse is our cat. Look."

Mouse now sat at Nathan's feet, looking up with a complacent smile. She had only one ear, and her fur was mottled black, grey and white in a hundred curled stripes. She was purring, whiskers aquiver.

"Likes you."

Sam, who had been reaching for Mouse, now quickly leaned back with a pout of disappointment. Everyone now sat in a circle around the fire, their blankets over their heads and snuggled over their wet shirts, bare feet poking out and dirty toes wriggling in pleasure as the fire began to blaze. Only Alice stood, stirring the pot.

The pottage, when heated, was far more pleasant than Nathan had expected. They all passed the pot around, drinking from the same big wooden spoon. Nathan discovered it was a sort of stew so full of chunks and lumps that he didn't know what it all was. But it tasted good. He wished there had been more of it, but after only a few gulps, Alfie yawned. "We bin up all night and now reckon tis time to sleep," he said. "But not on the straw, we don't want to risk sparks from the fire. So we cuddle up here on the floor next to them hot ashes, and we sleep." He grinned at Nathan. "I got two blankets. You can have one."

Nathan was thankful for that. Even next to the fire, it was chilly and his back was caught in a draught. There was no chimney and not even any windows, so the smoke from the flames just puffed in big grey clumps, very hazy and bad smelling. It made Nathan cough but everyone else seemed accustomed to it.

Within moments each of them had curled up, snuggling under the blankets, legs spooning one behind the other to share body warmth. Nathan found himself squashed between Alfie and John Ten-Toes, with the cat pushing up beside his face. Mouse's whiskers tickled Nathan's nose, the cat purred and dribbled happily on his ear, and gradually one by one they all went to sleep.

Nathan was the last to close his eyes. He had already slept that night, but his sleep had certainly been very much interrupted and he was now exhausted. Even cat dribble couldn't keep him awake. But he hoped beyond hope that when he awoke again, he would find himself back home in his own bed with his grandmother bringing him a glass of hot milk, telling him it was time for school.

But that's not the way it happened.

Nathan opened his eyes to the gaze of bright blue eyes looking back at him. He could feel cat dribble down his neck, the fire had gone out and he was cold, the blanket covered all of him except his feet which stuck out like chocolate ice lollies although it was dried mud and not chocolate, and he was most definitely not back snug in his own home. He sat up, stretched, and dislodged mouse, who meowed a complaint. They were Alfie's eyes staring down at him, and Alfie lurched back.

"Just wanted to know," Alfie explained, "if you was awake."

Well, "I am now."

"Then it's time to move," Alice called. She was stamping out the last little sparks from the fire, and trying to tie back her long tangled hair with a ribbon at the same time. "We're late," she said. "We slept in. Now we have to get to work."

Once again Nathan was confused. He rubbed the last grains of sleep from his eyes and mumbled, "Work? Don't you mean school?"

Alice giggled and with a sniff, Alfie said, "We can't pay for no schooling. You got rich parents or something? And we gotta work or we can't eat."

Alice had stamped out the hot ashes but now she was rubbing the little burns from her bare feet. "Down the market," she explained. "We need to grab what we can from the stalls, and then run like mad."

The gloom inside the warehouse was unchanged and no sunlight crept under the closed door. Nathan scrambled up, the blanket still around his shoulders. He wasn't sure whether to laugh or complain. "You mean you steal things? Last night you told me people take brooms to you because they think you're thieves. But you really *are* thieves."

John Ten-Toes rubbed his nose, which was as wet as mouse's, and snuffled, "Ain't no need for insults. We ain't thieves. We just take stuff. We's just hungry."

Nathan looked down at him. Yes, the boy certainly had ten toes, very dirty ones, but then so did he, so Nathan said, "So you steal food?"

"We get what we can," said Alfie, a bit crossly. "Food, money, clothes, blankets. You think we just ortta sit in the gutters and die?"

"Sorry," said Nathan, reluctantly giving back the blanket. "What time is it anyway?"

Alfie looked astonished. "How should I know?"

But when they pushed open the wide wooden warehouse doors, the sunlight flooded in. Beyond the grassy verge, the river was calm and seemed spangled with reflections, glittering in the brightness. All along the river there were little boats full of people being rowed up and down the Thames. The narrow road leading to the warehouse was also glittering, for the night's rain had left the ground wet and now the sunshine lit the puddles. Nathan stared, amazed. He suddenly realised how beautiful it all was.

The splash of the oars was constant from what seemed like a hundred little boats of different sizes going in different directions and their occupants shouting as they passed each other. "Mind, you're too close." "Watch out, idiot, you just bumped me." "It's a bright morning, Elsie, are you off to the market?" "'Tis busy on the south side. See you in Southwark later." And, "Have you heard about the queen? They say she's sick."

There were gulls and ravens wheeling in the sky above, swooping down for fish or raking through the rubbish in the gutters. People were bustling through the streets too, dogs were barking, there were huge puffs of smoke spiralling up from all the chimneys, and the sky was bright blue with just a few hazy clouds. Although the sun was bright, the air was still frosty and Nathan guessed it was still morning.

"Come on," Alfie yelled, "Keep to the shadows. Don't make too much noise, and when we get to the shambles, we separate."

Not ever having heard of the shambles, Nathan kept close behind Alfie, running away from the river and into the long dark lanes leading north. He tried to see everything as he ran, for the busy city was nothing like the London where he lived. These streets were far narrower and the houses were smaller and closer together. There were hundreds of little shops where the front window had been opened into a wooden counter, and the shopkeeper sat outside on a stool, inviting passers-by in to see his wares. The smell of new baked bread was delicious, and there were perfumes of herbs and spices, hot pies, new cut reeds for weaving, simmering porridge and sharp rich cheeses.

But there were bad smells too, with tanned hides, sacks of coal, and the bloody stench of raw meat hanging in the butchers' shops. Worst of all was the stink of sewerage. Nathan realised that the wet slippery central gutters were full of nasty things that he didn't want to step into.

His bare feet were sore, but he wasn't cold anymore and he was fascinated by everything they passed. Buildings were all made of plaster with thick wooden beams on the outside, and windows were small and the glass was held in tiny diamond shapes within leaden frames. Most different of all were the clothes the people were wearing. Women wore long dresses and cloaks, with their hair covered by hats and cloth headdresses. The men wore fancy doublets over tight stockings that hugged their legs, with short capes and grand feathered hats. Nathan was embarrassed to be wearing just his striped pyjamas, but he thought all the other people looked even stranger.

Then watching from a short distance, Nathan saw Alfie grabbing two apples from an open stall and then turn to run away. But he had been seen by the stall owner, who shouted, "Stop thief," and then there was chaos.

Alfie ran full speed in the opposite direction, with John Ten-Toes close at his heels. Nathan made a split-second decision and followed fast behind. They ran along a huge road full of shops and open stalls, ducking behind awnings and whizzing around the clumps of people. The stall owner who had lost his two apples was running hard too, and in his heavy shoes his footsteps vibrated and echoed. He continued to shout, "Stop thief," and soon other people joined in the shout and the chase.

Nathan, John and Alfie turned quickly and ran into a dark lane with a squelchy mud filled gutter, and from there into an even narrower lane where the little houses seemed to be tipping together with their roofs touching and blocking out the sky and the light.

Bang, bang, the stall owner's shoes clomped past. The shouting and calling disappeared into the distance. Nathan felt safer. The boys huddled together, keeping very still in the dark shadows. Alfie put his finger to his lips and shook his head when Nathan started to whisper something, but he began to eat one of the apples hungrily, and handed the other to John. Nathan didn't want to eat a stolen apple but there was not enough anyway.

Very gradually and quietly they began to creep from their hiding place when suddenly a loud voice boomed over their heads. "And what do we have here?" said the voice, gruff and deep. "Three grubby brats trying to hide from the law, it seems. I heard the cry 'Stop thief' and now I see I've found the thieves."

Nathan shivered, peering up. A very wide shouldered and exceedingly fat man was staring down at them. He was dressed in the most amazing clothes Nathan had ever seen, with a shining coat of scarlet velvet down to his knees, and open to show gleaming taffeta and satin beneath. His legs were muscled, held in tight black stockings over short blue boots. The man had red hair to his ears, cut straight, beneath a huge red hat with a peacock feather blowing in the breeze.

"Oh, no," muttered Alfie. "It's him."

15

John glared up at the grand man. "You've no right ta stop us, nor touch us. We ain't done nuffing ta you."

But the big man ignored this, saying, "And where's the rest of your nasty little gang? Run off and left you, have they? So, now, tell me where Alice is, and I'll let you go. Otherwise it's off to gaol with you." He was staring with evident interest at Nathan's pyjamas, and frowned, ginger eyebrows lowered. But Nathan said nothing, and squashed back against the wall behind him.

"I ain't telling," Alfie said, stepping forwards. "Alice can go where she likes and you can't stop her. Besides, I don't know where she is now. Run off, she did, wiv the others."

The large, richly dressed man grabbed Alfie by his raggedy shirt collar, and hauled him closer. "Then you come with me, thief, and we'll have a nice cosy word with the Constable."

Struggling and cursing, Alfie was hauled away, and Nathan and John Ten-Toes were left alone, gazing at the disappearing shadows. "Don't tell Alice," wailed Alfie's voice, trailing off, and was gone.

"What do we do now?" whispered Nathan.

"Dunno. Go kick the wall. Jump in the river. Curse," suggested John with a sniff. "But I reckon we just get back home."

CHAPTER THREE

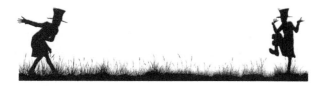

John Ten-Toes, still munching on his ill-gotten apple, led Nathan back to the warehouse and found that Sam, Peter and Alice were already there waiting impatiently for them. The sun had slid behind a cloud and the day seemed colder.

Alice was sitting on the boards beside the stone slab and the pile of cold ashes, looking up, worried. "Where's Alfie?" she asked as soon as Nathan walked in. "The Constable didn't get him, did he? They haven't dragged him off to Newgate?"

Nathan plopped down beside her and shook his head. "He told me not to tell you."

"Stupid," Alice complained. "Of course I have to know. Tell me quick."

Shrugging, Nathan said, "Someone came and took him away. Someone you all seem to know who was very grand and very nasty as well. He was asking after you, but Alfie wouldn't tell him."

John ten-Toes was finishing his apple and the juice dripped down his chin. He said, mouth full, "That mean Baron Cambridge, it were. Big fat pig-man he is and I reckon someone should chop his head off and sling him in the Tower. But says e's taking our Alfie ta gaol."

Alice groaned. "That's the worst – the absolutely worst possible news. That vile man won't take Alfie to the Constable, nor to gaol.

He'll take him back to his own house and lock him up and whip him till he tells where I am." She looked around, white faced. "If they beat Alfie and he tells about this place, the baron will send the law against all of us. So I'll have to leave here and so will you too, and we'll all have to go somewhere else, but first of all I have to rescue Alfie."

There was a short shocked pause and then Nathan sat down, began scraping the mud from his feet, and said, "I'll help. I'll help with anything you like. But first of all," he looked up directly at Alice, "you have to tell me what all this is about."

Sam, a blanket half over his head, said, "And I reckon you has to tell us all about yerself too, 'cos you's a right pokey puzzle. Them clothes. And living in Hammersmith and going to real school. And just turning up in the night all ready to eat our pottage and come thieving with us. So, who is you, then?"

Nathan couldn't imagine how he could explain, so he said, "There's no time for that. We have to rescue Alfie first."

"No." It was Alice who spoke. "We need explanations and then we can make a proper plan. Just running off into the city won't help Alfie at all. I know the baron and he won't bring in the sheriff yet. I have to think carefully. So –," and she frowned at Nathan, "let's start with you. Who are you and where do you come from? Are you secretly working for the baron?"

"Gracious." Nathan was startled, and stared back, forgetting about cleaning between his toes. The little flakes of dried mud scattered on the floor like exhausted ants. "I don't know anything about your horrid baron and I'm not working for anyone." He gazed at Alice. "Look," he said, "I'll tell you about myself but you won't believe me. Because either I'm a weirdo from the future, or," and he gazed down at his striped pyjamaed knees, "you're all weirdos from the past."

It was John who said quickly, "I'll believe ya, Nat. I reckon you're alright. Anyone brave enough ta wear them horrible clothes, gotta be all right."

"I, on the other hand," said Alice, sitting very straight with her hands clasped tightly in her lap and a deep frown on her face, "will have to wait and see. Just tell the truth."

The warehouse door had been left a little ajar and the entering breeze was whispering in the ashes. In the slanting beam of light, Nathan saw a huge cobweb hanging down from the roof's beams, and the little yellow spider sitting in the middle, just as if it was listening to Nathan's explanations too. So Nathan sighed, and stared back at his feet, and said, "I'm Nathan Bannister. Some people call me Nat. One horrid person called me Bumble-Bee Head but I don't know why."

"'I know. It's cos your hair is brown with lots of sunny streaks in it," interrupted Sam from under his blanket. "So it's goldy stripes on brown, just like a bee. Do you like honey?"

Nathan ignored him. "I'm twelve," he said. "Nearly thirteen. And I go to school but I don't like it very much and I live in my Granny's house in Hammersmith." His voice dropped to almost a whisper and he added, "I haven't seen my father or my mother for ages. Years. They went away when I was little and they didn't come back and no one knows what happened to them. My little sister Poppy was only three and she doesn't remember them but I was five, so I do." The spider seemed to be bored and had gone to sleep. Then Nathan realised that Mouse had crept back and was also asleep, curled up on his toes, keeping them very comfortable and warm.

Nodding, Alice said, "I don't have any living parents either but it makes no difference. Go on. Where did you come from so suddenly and why don't you go back home to that fancy school of yours?"

"Because I don't know how to get home," said Nathan looking up suddenly with a scowl. "I live in the future. This is the past. I was brought here by a mad wizard and I can't go home until he comes to get me."

"Oh, rubbish. Impossible," said Alice at once.

"I believe you," insisted John. "I reckon there's wizards up in them cold northern lands."

"Well, it's true," said Nathan. "And I know it must sound crazy but I'm no one's spy and I don't know anything about your funny past world and daft clothes and the whole city looks so different. I can't prove it, but it's true and I come from the future."

"Go on," mumbled Sam. "'Tis a good story."

"Why did ya Ma and Pa go away?" asked John, licking the last apple juice from his fingers. "Didn't like Hammersmith?" He thought a moment, smiling. "Didn't like you?"

Nathan shook his head. "They went on holiday but they said Scotland and I don't think that was true because they didn't have a car crash or got sick in hospital or anything like that. They just never came back. So I went to live in my grandma's house with Poppy. Granny October is really nice. I don't know why we call her Granny October, but we always have. Poppy's not too bad though she gets annoying sometimes."

"That has no relevance at all," said Alice sticking her chin up. "So how did you travel from the future back here?"

"Brewster Hazlett," said Nathan abruptly. "And don't ask me who he is because I don't know. Says he's a wizard. I didn't believe in wizards before either, but he appeared in my bedroom and whizzed me here in a balloon. So that's that."

"What's a balloon?" asked John. "Sounds daft. Must be magic." He was wiping his mouth with the back of his hand. "Bag-loon? So some loony fellow wiv a bag?"

About to shake his head, Nathan suddenly smiled. "Yes – sort of."

"And of course wizards are real," said Sam.

"I was excited," admitted Nathan, "but he wasn't a nice wizard and he didn't explain how he chose me for his weird adventure and then he tipped me out the balloon and disappeared and I'm stuck in the past."

"So what year do you come from?" demanded Alice, disbelieving.

Nathan took a deep breath, knowing it would sound ridiculous. Rather apologetically, he said, "2017."

They all stared and even John said, "That can't be true. The world gotta end before then."

"Well, it hasn't," Nathan muttered with a hiccup. "And it's a lot nicer with good houses and proper toilets and shops and kitchens and pavements. And there are computers and televisions and phones and even school isn't too bad."

This was too much for all of them, so John turned to Alice. "Well, now," he said, widening his smile. "Reckon that tale will take some beating. Now tis your turn. I only knows a bit of ya story, so it'll be good ta listen. Tell us all about everything and Baron Cambridge and your real Da."

Alice took a deep breath and unclasped her hands. Then she leaned over and picked up Mouse, cuddling her, fingers sinking into the thick fur. Mouse now purred and dribbled cheerfully. Alice's voice sank low as she began.

"Well," she said, "your story is quite impossible to believe, but I must tell my own story anyway, now that Alfie's been taken." Mouse was snuffling sleepily into Alice's lap. "My parents are dead too," Alice said sadly. "My father died when I was little, and as I was his only child, and he was the Lord David Parry and a very wealthy man and friend of the previous king, I became an heiress. None of the property was entailed, and my Papa left it all to me with just a portion to my Mamma.

"Then, when I was seven, she married again. I don't know why because we were happy together, just the two of us out in the manor house in Devon by the Tor. Of course I don't suppose she knew how horrible her future husband was capable of being, and she expected to be happy. But she was not. Baron Cambridge is a devious brute and a cruel man.

"Poor Mamma died just three years ago when I was ten. I'm not sure how she died, but I sometimes wonder if my step-father killed her. He took her money, and gambled most of it away. Then he tried to take control of me. Already he's my legal guardian, and if I die, all my wealth will be taken by him."

Alice definitely did not look rich, so Nathan blinked. "So you ran away from your step-father?"

"I had to." Alice looked down into her lap, where Mouse was curled. "I was very unhappy after Mamma died and I hated the baron but I was still living in the same house, when Alfie came one day. I was out by the stables and I saw him, all raggedy and shivering, going to the back doors. I was sorry for him, so I followed. He was asking the steward for a job. He said he wanted to be an apprentice cook, or at the very least a scullery boy, and he promised he'd work very hard if they let him sleep on the floor by the kitchen fires with the other scullery boys. But the baron's

21

steward was angry and told Alfie he was a dirty little beggar, and to go away.

"I ran over and said the steward should give the boy a chance, but the horrid man said the baron hated homeless beggars, and would never agree to employ such a one.

"Poor Alfie looked so cold and hungry. He hung his head and went away, looking back over his shoulder with a sniff. So I ran after him and took him one of the new baked pies from the kitchen. He was so grateful and said he hadn't eaten for three days. So we got talking and I told him about my horrible step-father and how unhappy I was too, even though I was rich and had a good bed and ate three times every day."

"So you ran away with Alfie?" Nathan shook his head. "Why didn't you bring your money with you and buy a house?"

"I reckon you really does come from the future," sighed John. "Ya sure don't know nuffing."

Alice was frowning. "My money is held in trust for me until I'm eighteen, or until I marry," she said, staring in confusion at Nathan. "I hope you don't think I have lots of gold coins in a money chest in my bedchamber or something silly like that. Most of it is in property anyway, and I don't really know how much there is. But I know I'm an heiress and the baron has been trying to make me marry his younger brother. But I won't. They'd take everything, and the brother is just as horrible as the baron."

Nathan was shocked. "You said you were only thirteen," he objected. "How can you get married at thirteen?"

Alice was equally confused. "Why not?" she demanded. "Lots of girls marry at thirteen or fourteen. Except I don't want to. So I ran away with Alfie and all I managed to bring with me was a sheepskin cape and some blankets. We found this abandoned warehouse and sneaked in to live here. Sam and Peter and John are all beggar children too and we saw them cold and hungry and invited them to join us. So now we have a gang."

"Well," exclaimed Nathan with a shocked stare, "That couldn't ever happen in England in my time. It's horrible."

"But you understand?"

"I suppose I do," Nathan said, suddenly standing up. "You don't believe my story but I believe you and I'll help rescue Alfie. You were all nice to me and shared your breakfast even though you don't have much of anything, and I think I know what to do." He smiled. "Listen." And as they all crowded around, Nathan began to explain. A pale trickle of sunshine was leaking in through the open doors again, and he could hear the splash of boats on the Thames outside, and the calls of the people. No one had relit the fire, so there was no smoke left in the hall, even though the warmth remained. A seagull was wailing outside and Mouse was purring.

"I'll believe your story if you want me to," sighed Alice. "I just have to get Alfie back safe before my step-father hurts him."

"You said Alfie went to the kitchen doors for work long ago," Nathan said quickly. "And you say you know where the baron will have Alfie locked up?" Alice nodded. "Well," Nathan continued, "we can all go to the kitchen door and ask for food and make lots of noise and beg for jobs and get your steward angry again. And we'll refuse to leave until the steward calls for your step-father. Then you creep in the front door and go and set Alfie free."

"Not that easy," Alice said sadly. "The steward will just throw boiling water at you all. And I'd never get in the front door without someone seeing me, and I wouldn't be able to unlock the cellar door anyway. The baron will have the key with him."

Peter put his small hand up and waved it in the air. Nathan couldn't remember Peter saying anything at all ever since he'd met him, but now he whispered. "I can do that."

"Do what?" asked Alice.

Peter blushed, looking down, his brown curls flopping into his eyes. "I know how to undo locks," he said very softly. "My Dad taught me when I was little cos he was a locksmith afore he died. Reckon I can unlock your cellar 'lest it's a real complicated padlock."

Everyone stared at him and Alice said, "Oh, how wonderful," and jumped up. "Come on then, let's go. "

"What about the other problems?" interrupted Nathan, staying where he was.

Alice was happy and almost dancing, standing on her bare toes and skipping, holding up her long swirling skirts. Mouse had tumbled back to the floorboards and now stalked off, head in the air and the fur of her neck bristling. "Easy," Alice said. You and Sam and John all go to the kitchen door like you said. You make a big fuss and cry and say you're starving. One of you will have to pretend to faint inside on the tiles, so the steward won't be able to throw boiling water at you. In the meantime, Peter and I will smash the pantry window, which is quite big and hidden behind a bush. We can climb in and go down to the cellars to rescue Alfie. Then we'll all meet up back here."

It didn't sound too safe to Nathan but he was quite excited at the idea of rescuing someone and he liked Alfie, though he wasn't so sure about Alice because she was bossy and a bit older than him. But he grinned, and said, "I'm ready."

By now it had slipped into late afternoon and a steady dusk was descending across the city. Above the tips of the little pointed roofs, the light sank into a soft grey and with a last wail, the seagulls flew back downriver. Without street lights the lanes and alleyways were quickly shrouded in shadow. Alice, peeping out from the doorway, beckoned to the others. "Follow me," she said softly, "and I'll lead you to my home. It was my father's city house before the baron moved in, so I grew up there and I know it very well and I'll explain exactly what you all need to do." She looked down at Peter. "You stay close to me. And if there's any trouble, just run like mad and don't worry about anyone else. Just save yourselves."

A last big black crow was poking into the fish scales lying on the river bank. It looked up as Nathan passed, and flew off with a squawk. With Alice leading, the boys tiptoed past and entered the dark lane to the side of the warehouse.

"Hope we don't have to walk all the way to Devon," muttered Sam.

Alice ignored him, but said, "My London house is up past Crosby Place where the king used to live. It's not so far."

Folk were hurrying home, shopping bags full. Market stalls were packing up and the shops were closing, pulling up their counters to cover their windows, and locking their doors. The Shambles, which Nathan discovered was the butchers' street, was all shut up now and a few of the shop-owners were throwing buckets of water to clear the blood and scraps from the cobbles. A wandering dog, looking hungry, was darting to avoid the water but grab the scraps of meat and a large meaty bone.

It was growing darker and the first stars peeped out from the glowering sky. The wind had dropped but the darkening night was chilly and the moon was hidden behind the clouds.

Alice led the others on past handsome houses with spreading gardens and trees, their branches still bare silhouetted. A few steps along on the other side of the road was another large house, not quite as grand but impressive with three storeys and a big garden stretching to either side. "That's my real home," muttered Alice, staring up. "Look, that window on the second floor right in the middle. That used to be my bedchamber."

Nathan mumbled back," You must miss it now, living in a dump."

Alice turned. "I'm happy living with my friends and not my cruel step-father. But one day, if I can get some help from someone, I may be able to get my home back again. Then you can all come and live with me in comfort."

Smiling, Nathan didn't answer. He was beginning to like everyone in the gang, even bossy Alice, but there was no way he wanted to live here. He missed his own home and family far too much. But eventually, as they walked slowly forwards, he said, "I'll help. Don't worry. I'll think of something."

And then suddenly a thin gleam of light seemed to shine down from above. Thinking it was the moon escaping from the clouds, Nathan looked up. Then he stood stock still, amazed. Far away above them he saw the bright striped colours of the balloon which had brought him here, and just a glimpse of the tall skinny wizard in the top hat leaning over the side of the basket, waving. Nathan started to wave back, hoping that Brewster Hazlett had come for him. But when he looked again, the balloon had disappeared and all Nathan could see were stars.

CHAPTER FOUR

They entered the grounds of Baron Cambridge's house by a small side gate, and tiptoed towards the rear. The gardens were not extensive but they seemed somehow bigger as night fell and the shadows merged. Hedges, bushes and pebbled paths converged. "Hush," Alice whispered, "the pebbles clink."

Peter whispered back. "Where's that pantry window?"

Alice pointed, then turned to Nathan, John and Sam, saying, "Look, there's the kitchen doors. It's supper time so they'll be busy, which means they won't watch you so closely. The cook is quite nice, and the horrid steward will be in the main hall with my step-father, organising the meal. You know what to do." She paused, smiled and blinked back tears. "Good luck."

Then she and Peter ran around the back into the darkness, and Nathan turned to John and Sam. "Alright," he said. "Time to start."

Stepping briskly forwards, Nathan banged loudly on the doors. He could hear the bustle and noise from within, with the clang of pots and pans and the shouts of the cooks and the scullery boys.

"My fingers is burning," yelped a young voice.

"Get on with it and turn that spit," came a man's gruff reply.

Nathan knocked again, banging hard with his fists until the door shook. Then it opened so wide and so abruptly that Nathan nearly fell over. He quickly poked his head into the kitchen and pushed past the young boy who had swung the door open. A burst of hot white steam blew in their faces, and for a moment that was all they could see. Then the haze lifted and the three boys peered forwards.

Nathan, looking around, was astonished at what he saw. This was not anything like any kitchen he had ever seen before. It was huge and along the far wall were two enormous fireplaces, with fires blazing and crackling. On each, a boy was turning the handle of a spit, with large meat carcasses roasting on each over the flames. Juice from the cooking meat dripped onto the logs below and the fire spat. Now Nathan understood why one boy had complained of his fingers burning.

There were several long wooden tables all covered in platters and pots with food steaming and bubbling. Clouds of smoke filled the whole place, dark smoke from the fires and pale condensation from the hot plates of food.

For a moment, utterly amazed, Nathan was speechless. Then he heard John Ten-Toes saying in a sad voice, "Please, mister, we's ever so hungry. Ya got any scraps fer us? Can we hav' some supper too?"

"Get out of here," called an irate cook from near the fires. "I'm busy. Come back later when the master has finished eating, and you can have what is left over."

It was John who marched forwards. "I's hungry right now," he shouted over the noise. "And all them lovely things on them plates is making me faint." 'Tis agony. Reckon I'll die right here and now."

One of the scullery boys ran past, grinning, but another pushed Nathan out of the way as he rushed out carrying a huge platter of sliced beef, oozing gravy and surrounded by baby onions. Three older men seemed to be the cooks, and the head cook wore a very bright red apron, whereas the other two wore white. It was the head cook who looked over and waved his big wooden spoon at the boys. "I've no time for this," he said. "Oliver, get those urchins out of here."

A short burly man in a dirty white apron hurried over and grabbed Nathan's arm, but Nathan shook him off. He had suddenly realised that it was quite true, he really was hungry. The food smelled wonderful and he hadn't eaten anything since a few spoonful's of pottage early that morning. Then the cook grabbed John, and with an exaggerated sigh, John collapsed on the tiled floor. With a dramatic moan, his knees buckled, he staggered from side to side, flung out both arms, and tumbled hard to the ground, nearly tripping up another of the scullery boys who was trying to clean up some spilt custard.

Sam, with a squeak, bent down beside John. "You done made my friend sick," he complained. "He's gonna die."

With a faint howl of agony, John added, "Gonna die. Gonna die. Almost dead."

Another under-cook peered over. "If that brat is sick, get him out of here. We don't want any nasty diseases to spoil the supper."

Nathan was tempted to run to the nearest table and grab some food. There were savoury and sweet things all mixed up together with plates of jellies, fruit, custards and cakes beside other plates of meat, vegetables and pies. But instead, he bit his tongue and went to kneel beside John. "He's not sick," Nathan yelled. "Just starving. Give the poor lad some dinner."

John was twitching on the ground, pretending to be in pain with his eyes firmly shut. He managed a few groans, which Nathan thought were probably genuine since now the three boys were all dreaming of good food. Sam darted around the feet of the cooks and approached one of the spit boys. "Give us a slice," he asked.

The spit boy grinned, shaking his head. "Watch out, loony. You'll get burned." The fires belched more flame and smoke, spitting vivid scarlet sparks. One of the cooks pushed Sam out of the way and Sam immediately cried out and fell over.

Exasperated, the head cook called out," throw hot water at those idiots. Get them to go away or this supper will be ruined and the baron will be furious."

"You can't do that," Nathan yelled back. "These boys are already about to die from starvation. You'll kill them if you're not careful and then I'll accuse you of murder and run and tell the judge." He didn't really know what he was saying but was desperate to make time for Alice and Peter to go and rescue Alfie.

John, his dirty shirt up around his thighs, was writhing and squirming with exaggerated suffering. Those filthy ten toes were curled in pain.

"I shall tell the master," said one assistant cook. "If this supper is spoiled, I don't intend getting the blame for it."

The commotion had certainly echoed into the main hall, and it seemed the baron had heard the shrieks and shouts. Quite suddenly the inner doors were thrown open and the baron appeared in the entrance, looking absolutely furious. His face was as red as his bright red hair and his scarlet satin doublet. He stamped both feet and roared, "What's going on in here? Where's the rest of my supper?"

All the cooks stared, and bowed while the scullery boys and the spit boys immediately stopped whatever they were doing and began to apologise. The head cook pointed at the heap on the ground where both John and Sam were lying, and where Nathan was bending over them pretending to be worried in case they were dying of starvation.

And then as the baron marched forwards towards Nathan, yelling, "You nasty little beggar brats, I'm going to whip you red raw and haul you off to the Constable," his voice suddenly trailed off. His soft indoor shoes, unused to the slippery steam-damp tiles on the ground, began to slide. He waved his arms in the air but could not regain his balance, and with another roar of fury, he whooshed from doorway to fireplace, his feet as if on ice, and everyone dashing to get out of his headlong panic. He slid almost into the flames, until the chief cook had the common sense to stand right in front of him, calling both spit boys to hurry beside him. The baron hurtled into the human barrier and everyone collapsed in a frantic heap, the baron cursing loudly and pummelling with both fists.

"Idiots," screamed the baron. There was gravy on his gleaming expensive doublet, pink jelly on his nice white shirt cuffs, and squashed peas on the knees of his hose. He punched the spit boy on the nose, and the spit boy began to cry, since it seemed most unfair after he had helped save the baron from being severely burned. Undeterred, the baron kicked out, then stomped over to Nathan, Sam and John Ten-Toes.

John was trying to stay on the ground with his eyes shut, and not to laugh, but the sound of his snigger turned into a gurgle and a half-choke. Sam was sitting up and giggling loudly and couldn't stop, and Nathan had his hand over his mouth to stifle the laughter. The various cooks and scullery boys were either gasping in shock and fear, or cackling so much they had tears in their eyes. The one spit boy who was actually still crying, sat down in the ashes of the fire, and then got up with a yelp and his tunic scorched.

"Quiet, all of you," screamed the baron. "You brats, get over here this instant."

John was still pretending to be unconscious although he was still convulsed with silent laughter, but both Sam and Nathan marched over to the baron, and stood staring up at him. Sam poked John in the side with his own bare toes, and John wheezed, staying still.

"It's not our fault you went flying and made yourself look really silly," said Nathan with a smirk. "And we're still hungry." He knew the baron would be so angry that they would soon all have to run, or would be caught and beaten. He just hoped that there had been time already for Alice and Peter to rescue poor Alfie. So he stood tall, hoping to take just a few more minutes before leaving at speed.

There was a hushed silence except for the crackle of the fires and a quick swirl of smoke which made John Ten-Toes cough loudly.

Then the baron, brushing the peas, jelly and gravy from his heavy calves, legs, and bony knees, strode to the second spit boy, pushed him out of his path, grabbed a towel from the table nearby to wrap around his hand, and proceeded to grasp the handle of the long metal spit, wrench it from its hooks, and point the sharp end towards Nathan. Then he leapt forwards holding the spit like a lance in a tournament and sprang.

There was still a large joint of beef pierced by the spit, hanging there in the middle, and as the baron waved the metal pole, so the roast beef rolled and danced and flying drops of boiling hot fat and meat juices were thrown from floor to ceiling, scorching everything they touched.

Looming through the swirls of hot steam and the clouds of smoke from the fires, the point of the spit came straight at Nathan's face. Above, the baron's face was dripping sweat, and his mouth was open in a snarl.

30

Nathan yelled, turned, and danced behind the big central table. The baron raced around after him but Nathan was quicker, and the baron was still slipping a little on the damp tiles. Meanwhile John Ten-Toes had scrambled up, and he and Sam were edging towards the door. "Come on," John called. "Reckon we've done all was needed. Let's go."

Now burned by spots of hot fat, one of the under-cooks was shouting, "That's it, my lord, skewer the dirty little brat," which Nathan thought was most unfair since the cook himself was wearing a filthy apron with spilt grease on his tunic. Nathan ran around the table again, avoiding the baron, and wishing he had his phone with him and could take a photo of this big bulky man, flushed and glaring, slipping and sliding while waving the metal pole but unable to catch his prey.

As the spit, the roast beef and the baron's furious snarl came rushing at them, more juice and fat dripped to the tiled floor and the baron slipped once again. At the same time one of the scullery boys was burned by the flying grease which was so hot he began to howl. Then seeing that both John and Sam were half out of the door, Nathan followed them, pulling the door hard shut behind him. He heard the wallop as the baron hurtled against the door, probably bruising his nose, but there was no time to wait and all three boys ran fast back into the main street.

"This way."

Bishopsgate was the wide road beyond the baron's gardens, and was a principal thoroughfare leading to one of the main entrances into London. But it was not towards the gate that the boys ran. They raced back down towards Cheapside in the direction of the Thames. Now very late into the dark evening, there was no one around and the street was empty but there was flickering candlelight in many of the house windows. Nathan looked up again as he ran, hoping to see again the balloon and Brewster Hazlett hovering and ready to take him home. But all he saw was the bright crescent moon and some stars, blinking like the candles, and peeping from the clouds.

"Be careful," whispered John as they finally slowed their pace and began, out of breath, to trail along the cobbles. "We needs ta avoid the Watch."

"Watch who?" demanded Nathan, confused. "What's wrong with watches. And I don't wear one anyway."

John stared at him, completely puzzled. "You don't talk no sense sometimes," he muttered. " 'Tis the Watch I'm warning ya of. They walks up and down all the main streets at night, holding big flaming torches and looking out fer thieves and murderers and folk getting drunk when they ortta be in bed."

"Big flaming torches? Well, we'll certainly see them coming then," said Nathan in astonishment.

"They calls out too," explained Sam, who was rubbing his chin where the fat had scorched him, "saying all's right or who's there."

Nathan thought he'd seen something of the sort in films, and just nodded. He was tired, but he was also very worried and hoped they had given Peter and Alice enough time to rescue Alfie. But it was not until they finally arrived back at the warehouse, bedraggled and exhausted, that they found out.

Alfie, Alice and Peter were sitting next to a bright welcoming fire, with the little logs and twigs flaming merrily. Peter was curled up with his thumb in his mouth, half asleep but Alice was sitting behind Alfie with a big bowl of water. Alfie, crouched in front of the fire and half bending over, had his head in his hands.

"Thank goodness," Nathan said, hurrying over. Then he stopped as he saw why Alfie was so quiet. His shirt, which was all he had been wearing, was ripped several times down the back, and beneath it his skin was bleeding.

Alice looked up, and seemed to be trying not to cry. "Thank you," she mumbled, biting her lip, "for giving us the time to get away. But poor Alfie is badly hurt. My step-father whipped him and punched him too. See, Alfie has big bruises on his face and his flesh is torn in big stripes down his back."

"We should go to the police," said Nathan at once, before realising that this was impossible and no one would understand what he was talking about anyway. Alfie said nothing, but he sniffed a couple of times and Nathan was sure he was in great pain. His back was raw and the marks of the lashes cut deep. "We need ointment and bandages," he sighed, "but I don't suppose you have anything like that."

"No, we don't," said Alice. "But I'm washing the blood away, and in the morning, I'll go to the apothecary and ask for a herbal cream."

"They say butter's a good ointment," suggested John. "Not as we got any."

"Alfie's not a sandwich," said Nathan, although everyone stared at him once again, not understanding his words. "Where's the nearest doctor live? Alfie needs proper help."

"We ain't got the money ta pay a doctor," objected John.

Alfie looked up, inching back his shoulders and trying not to wince. "I'll be all right," he said, a catch in his voice.

Nathan shook his head. "No you aren't and you need a doctor." Then he looked at the others with a sudden smile. "And I've got enough money for a doctor, I think, and for some good food too when the shops open in the morning."

John stared. "Balloons and schools and now real money? Reckon you ain't no normal person neither. P'rhaps tis you is the wizard."

Astonished, Alice said, "You never said you had money before."

"Because I didn't have it before," said Nathan, rummaging in the pocket of his pyjamas. And he pulled out a fat purse, round and bulging, made of soft leather with a little metal clasp at the top.

"You nicked it?" demanded John, clearly impressed.

Nathan was still grinning and didn't feel guilty at all. "First thing I ever nicked in my life," he answered. "And I would never have done it, under different circumstances. But when the baron came marching into the kitchen, he was wearing this strapped to his belt. Then, when he fell and slipped across the floor, this came off and landed right beside me. I didn't know what it was but when I picked it up, it jangled and clinked so I hoped it was money. Nobody saw me because everyone was staring at the baron so I just kept it hidden in my hand. Normally I would have handed it back, but the baron was trying to kill me with the spit, so I thought – well, I'll keep his money. You say it's all rightfully yours anyway." He cheerfully passed the purse over to Alice, who, wide-eyed, opened it and emptied it into her lap.

The gold and silver coins came spilling out in huge handfuls. "You are wonderful," she exclaimed. "Well done. Just what we desperately need. First of all a doctor, then food, and finally new clothes for Alfie because his shirt is all ripped and he hasn't got anything else to wear."

"Maybe some for me too," muttered Nathan under his breath, "so people will stop staring at my pyjamas."

Alfie heaved a sigh of relief and managed a very small smile. "I thanks you all," he said. "you saved me and I never thought that were going to happen. I thought I was a gonner. Now I even gets bandages and pay fer some bread and cheese."

"We can pay for a lot more than that," said Alice, scooping the coins back into the purse and waving it in the air, which disturbed Mouse. She had been peacefully sleeping but with the clank and chink just above her head, she jumped up in alarm, and then stalked off to curl up on the other side of the fire. Alice kept a tight hold on the purse as she spoke to Nathan, John and Sam. "You all did a brilliant job," she said. "And so did Peter. He got that padlock on the cellar door open as easily as blink. Clever boy. Rescuing Alfie will make the baron even more angry, but I don't care about that." Then she opened the purse again and began to count the coins, smiling up at Nathan as she counted. "Five, six, seven – Nat you are a miracle, truly. This is more money than we've ever had before. You are so clever."

Nathan looked sharply at Alfie. "Did you tell him anything? Being whipped must have been dreadful, so did he make you say where Alice was and about this warehouse."

"No." Alfie shook his head and then grunted, because it hurt. "Reckon I would have told in the end if he'd done it again, but you got me out in time. So he don't know nothing, but he'll tell the Constable and the sheriff and they'll come looking. I reckon we need to move."

Nathan was gazing at the gold coins in Alice's lap as she picked them up one by one and dropped them back into the purse. Many of the coins were small and silver while others were big and bright and heavy and Nathan had never seen any money like it before. He knew it had been luck when it fell from the baron's belt and landed at his feet, but clearly the others were very proud of him and thought it a wonderful act of skill and courage.

"I seen a doctor what lives nearby," said John. "Tis late, but I can go there and see if e's awake." He thought a moment. "And if e' ain't, I'll wake him."

"Here," Alice handed him a big gold coin. "Show this to the doctor so he'll know we can pay. And tell him it's urgent."

Alfie was scowling. "Too much fuss," he muttered. "I ain't dying."

Alice ignored him, and nodded to John. "Tell the doctor to hurry," she said, "and we'll pay extra."

CHAPTER FIVE

The doctor had arrived almost immediately, and had spread ointment all over Alfie's back, and had then bandaged him all around so that John said poor Alfie looked like a sausage ready for the pot.

They slept by the fire, their blankets pulled around them, but woke early, ready for action. It was time to move.

Very quickly they were able to buy a hot pie each, and their desperate hunger immediately faded. But buying what they needed was not as simple as Nathan had expected. They ran from the old warehouse and the muddy banks of the Thames, up through London's narrow streets, some cobbled, some just dried earth, with their central gutters shining as folk emptied their night's chamber pots out of their bedchamber windows.

Alice led the group to the shops and stalls of Cheapside, where the noise and bustle of a hundred shoppers became quite a squash. Nathan was interested to see that shops selling the same sort of things often huddled together in the same street, which made prices more competitive and the goods for sale were easy to compare. The street names echoed what was for sale and Bread Street was full of shops selling bread, their little ovens hot and the smell of baking delicious. Friday Street was full of fishmongers for no one was supposed to eat meat on a Friday, but The Shambles was full of butchers' shops. Yet Nathan was even more amazed at the prices, for a single penny was the price of many good things and even the big readymade pies only cost three or four pence.

Alfie, his bandages showing under his torn shirt, went straight to a large apothecary's shop, which Nathan guessed was like a chemist's. But the owner frowned at Alfie.

"Where you get that money from?" he demanded as Alfie held up a silver coin. "You stole it, I reckon. You're all dirty little beggars."

"The money is from my father," said Alice loudly. "We need good ointment and can pay a fair price."

The apothecary was still shaking his head when his wife hurried over. "Give the poor boy what he needs," she scolded her husband, holding out a little pot of white creamy paste which smelled of parsley and other herbs. "Here," she said, handing it over and accepting the coin. "We make the best salve in London. This works a treat and you'll soon feel better, young man."

The same difficulty arose when they went to a haberdashery, a large shop filled with linen shirts and petticoats. A sharp-nosed woman swooped upon the group as soon as they entered. "I want no beggars in here," she said. "This is a respectable shop."

This time Nathan stepped forwards. "We're not beggars and we have money from our employer to buy new clothes."

"From our master," interrupted John.

"From my father," said Alice.

"Lies," objected the woman. "You can't even get your story straight."

"My father is their master who employs them," said Alice quickly. "They all need proper clothes so they can work in my father's kitchens and stables. Good shirts, warm tunics and hose, and proper braes too." She showed the large gold coin in the palm of her hand.

The shopkeeper immediately changed her attitude and smiled. Five shirts, five tunics, five under-braes and five pairs of hose would be very good business. Everyone sat in the middle of the shop, Alice and Alfie on stools and the others on the floor. John Ten-Toes was dancing around, poking his nose into cupboards and pointing at the piles of warm knitted hose and lacy shifts. The sharp-nosed woman fussed around them, showing items of clothing and assuring the boys that these were the right size and the best she had. Nathan sat a little apart, watching intently. He thought everything looked well made, but it was all plain undyed linen, which was not pure white, and a little thick. Nothing seemed to be made of fine cotton, but no one appeared to mind and one by one they were dressed in long white shirts which tied under their chins, black hose which looked like tights to Nathan, but were knitted woollen and very snug, and over-tunics in various colours. His own was dark blue, broadcloth and he thought it most uncomfortable, but at least this way he ended up looking like everyone else. The braes were white linen underpants and he didn't like them either because they were rather baggy, but it was better than nothing.

Alfie's sheepskin cape had been taken by the baron, but in the new shirt and tunic he seemed warm enough. He threw away his ripped and dirty shirt, bloodstained and very old, but Nathan insisted on keeping a tight hold of his pyjamas.

Next they moved on to the shoe-makers and ordered a pair of leather shoes each. The cobbler measured all their feet, including Alice, but it was clear he didn't like touching them. Their feet were exceedingly filthy from running around barefoot, and many had sore and grazed toes with broken nails. Nathan's were just as bad as the others because there had been no way to wash at all.

"Well, lads," said the cobbler, "I'll make you good shoes with strong bottoms you won't wear out, and good strong leather on top. But I'd advise you all to take a bath before you ruin the shoes as well." He took their money, but said, "Come back in three days, and they'll be ready."

Nathan certainly wasn't used to having his shoes made for him, but he realised everything was different in the past, so he said nothing. He just wondered, if Brewster Hazlett came to collect him and take him home soon, how he would explain his very strange and old fashioned clothes to his grandmother and sister. Poppy would laugh at him, he knew, but he rather thought he would also be laughing at himself.

Buying food was easier, and no one at the stalls questioned their pennies. They were able to buy leeks and pees, slices of raw lamb and kidneys, flour, honey, and even a tiny screw of paper with salt inside.

In the meantime, with packages of food and their old clothes under their arms, and gravy from the pies on their chins, they hurried back to the warehouse.

Now past midday, the city was at its busiest and not a street nor a lane was empty. People in large hats pushed in and out of the shops, and most of the houses had their doors open with the housewives sweeping out old rushes and dirt from their doorsteps. Some were cleaning their windows in the pale sunlight but many of the houses did not have glass in their windows at all, and the space was covered only in thin polished bone, or in translucent parchment. The chimneys puffed smoke for it was still chilly, and the smoke hung heavy over the rooftops, some tiled and some thatched. It was a bright day in mid-March, only partially clouded with little wind except for a slight breeze.

The stall-holders were shouting their wares, calling, "Come buy," "Best steel knives," and "Cheapest cabbages in the country." Stray dogs were wandering the lanes, their noses ferreting out scraps from the gutters, and two stood wagging their tails desperately beside the butchers' shops, and Nathan felt very sorry for them. There were chickens too, pecking outside the houses, and a little scrawny pig running fast into the shadows. One house had three goats tethered outside, and another had a donkey, asleep on its feet. There were many birds, ravens, kestrels, seagulls and crows, with little flocks of sparrows sitting on rooftops.

Alfie had been keeping up with the others, yet it was clear that he was experiencing some difficulty. He limped a little, and hunched over. His eyes were half shut in pain and his face was so badly bruised, it looked almost purple.

"Thank goodness, we're here," he gasped as they arrived back at the warehouse.

"For the last time," sighed Alice.

"So where will we go next?" No one liked the idea of losing the only home they had known for a long time, and Nathan was dubious too. Creeping into some new hole sounded both uncomfortable and dangerous. He said, "We ought to work out a proper plan for getting rid of the baron, and then we can all come to live in that grand house."

"Oh, I wish we could," Alice said, promptly sitting down on the floorboards beside the slab where the few remaining ashes were a memory of last night's warm fire. "By rights, I have two homes. The grand house in Bishopsgate, and an even bigger manor house in Devon. But the baron has taken them both."

"Haven't you got any uncles or aunts or people who would back you up?" Nathan asked. "Isn't there any important person who would help?"

"I have an aunt," she replied. "Aunt Margaret. But she's frightened of the baron too, and her husband is crippled. He was wounded in battle and only has one leg. He can't fight anyone anymore."

"The Constable?"

"Gracious, no." Alice smiled. "He wants to put me in gaol for being a wicked girl and not doing what the baron tells me."

"Humph," John interrupted with a loud sniff. "That there Constable is a pig-man. Just wants to haul us off to the clink. 'Siff we was thieves or something."

Nathan lay on one of the straw mattresses, hands behind his head. He felt very smart but rather crazy, dressed in tight black stockings tied up around his waist with two long ribbons, over a pair of loose linen pants. No shoes yet, but he had a warm although rather scratchy linen shirt which came down to his knees, and a dark blue tunic on top. He stuffed the package with his pyjamas in under the straw, and gazed up at the high beamed ceiling. He noticed that the little yellow spider had built itself an even bigger web.

It was Alfie who interrupted. "Future plans is for the future. Right now we needs to find a new home."

"And I need a wash," sighed Nathan. "Perhaps I can jump in the river."

John Ten-Toes chuckled. "You'd come out even grubbier than when ya went in," he said. "Our river ain't no bath."

"But there's a bathhouse up near the Tower," Alice said. "Folk go there to wash clothes and themselves too. Once we have a safe home again, then I'll show you where it is. I'd love a hot bath."

"All that can wait," Alfie said. "T'will be dark soon. That's when we start looking. Collect all our stuff, blankets, pots and clothes. Then we get going."

They crept out as the sun sank in the west, disappearing down behind London's tall chimneys and smoky roofs. The busy shoppers were already scurrying home and the markets were packing up. Even the river traffic was diminishing as the last few little rowing boats landed by their wooden piers, with people climbing out, women holding up their skirts and men with their hands flat on their heads to keep their hats from blowing off.

For one moment as Alfie stood on the river bank, looking downstream, Nathan saw the great bridge which he had barely noticed before, since it had just seemed to be another road. This was certainly not the Tower Bridge he knew from his own home. Such a crowded and cluttered bridge certainly did not exist in his own time. It had houses and shops all along the sides, and stood tall on many stone pillars with the river water surging beneath. There seemed to be a church in the middle, and a huge gate at the southern end.

"They'll lock that gate soon," Alfie nodded. "No one gets in or out o' London once it's dark." Nathan could not imagine anything so strange but he said nothing and just stared at the busy bridge and the people rushing to cross before the gates were locked against them.

With no street lights, the night fell quickly and even the little candlelight in the windows of the houses was soon blocked out as the people put up their wooden shutters. Alfie, Alice, John, Sam and Peter crept out into the narrow lanes, and Nathan walked beside Alfie and John.

Alice had hidden the purse of money by tying it to the waistband of her shift, and she was careful not to clink as she walked. But they made little sound, since none of them yet had any shoes, and they padded softly in their woolly hose as the stars peered down at them from behind the soaring stone of the Tower. Church bells were ringing but there were few other sounds and gradually London sank into silence. Even the dogs wandered off, their tails between their legs, and the last birds flew away into the clouds. There was a hush which Nathan could not ever imagine happening in the modern city, but in the past, without cars or buses, sound was muffled or non-existent. They did pass a tavern with a flaring torch lighting the open doorway, but even here the men were leaving and staggering out into the cold darkness.

Nathan noticed that Sam, although he was the smallest of them all, was carrying a large bulging parcel, wrapped in his old shirt. Then he heard the snuffles and purrs from inside, and knew it was Mouse, not forgotten and certainly not left behind.

"I reckon I knows a good place," John whispered, "up by the Tower wall."

"And I knows an attic, over the top of a storage shed," Alfie said. "It ain't far. Follow me."

Keeping to the shadows, the group crossed a small churchyard and crept through the cobbled lane between the long sheds of a communal stables. They could hear the horses kicking at their stalls, and neighing, but one by one even the horses were going to sleep. Alfie waited by the end of the lane where there was a shed for hay and storage of saddles, bridles and rakes.

"There's a place in there," Alfie pointed. "Above where they keeps the hay and straw. 'Tis real warm."

"But no place for cooking, I reckon, wiv all that straw," guessed John. "T'would catch fire un burn us out."

"Let's have a look," suggested Alice, tiptoeing forwards. She pushed open the double doors and peeped in.

A ladder was balanced against a high ledge above the stacks of hay. Up there," whispered Alfie, sneaking towards the ladder. There were no windows and the space was cosy but dark. But Alice frowned, keeping her voice low. "So where do the stable boys sleep?"

"Dunno," said Alfie. "But I bin here five times, night and day, sleeping up there when I was worn out and hungry afore I ever met all of you. I never saw no one, and when folk came to rake up some of the hay, I just shut me mouth and hid far back."

"Oh dear," murmured Alice, "it's not the best place for so many of us. No way we'd be able to creep in here unseen during the daytime, what with the men coming to fetch their horses, and all the bustle and cleaning out. Besides, we couldn't even light a fire or cook."

"Reckon my place would be better," sniffed John.

But Alfie was halfway up the ladder when another tousled head poked out for the straw on the top ledge. The boy yelled. Then two more boys scrambled from the straw and glared at Alfie and the others below.

"Who are you?" demanded the first boy. "What you doing here?"

"None o'your business," Alfie yelled back angrily.

"We're cold," Nathan said quickly, "and need a place to sleep. There must be plenty of space here."

"No there ain't." shouted another boy, swinging his legs over the side so he sat beside the top of the ladder, staring down. "We work here. We're stable lads and we got every right to sleep here. You ain't."

"You never used to," glowered Alfie. "I've been here when it were all empty."

"That's cos the owner changed hands," explained an older boy. "But now tis our home. You better go quick afore the big man wakes."

Alfie was about to argue but Alice tugged at the bottom of his new tunic, and mumbled, "Quick, before they call for the Watch."

Yet as Alfie climbed down and the group turned to leave, three of the boys jumped down after them, two holding knives and the other brandishing a long-handled rake.

Sam and Peter ran, but Alfie faced the angry boys and kicked out, swinging his fists. Alice quickly stuck out one foot and tripped the tallest boy as he ran past, and he fell in a heap with his knife lost in the hay. Nathan didn't like fighting but there had once been a bully at his school, and he'd had to fight him several times, so he knew what to do. Grabbing the second boy around the neck, he swung him out, twisting him so he was dizzy and fell.

As the boy scrambled up again, John ran to wrestle him back down and Nathan ran to help Alfie who was grappling with the boy brandishing the rake. It was sharp pronged but Nathan managed to grasp the handle and twist it free as Alfie kicked the boy and sent him running.

"Quick," yelled Alice. "Let's get out of here."

43

They turned, racing out of the big shed into the cobbled lane outside where Peter and Sam were waiting. Once out of sight, they stopped, bending over to catch their breath and brush the spikey stalks of straw from their woolly hose.

Alfie grinned. "I admit it," he laughed. "Not such a good idea."

"So now I reckons tis time to look at my place," said John with a smirk.

CHAPTER SIX

J ohn took them to a disused cellar down below a storeroom in a
narrow cobbled alley which was almost closed at one end by the
great moss-damp outer wall of the Tower. This kept out the
light from the east, but there was a large ironmongers, closed now, on
one corner, opposite a smithy, also tight shut for the night.

When they all stopped, staring up and down the alley, Nathan tried
to brush off the last of the straw sticking to his legs. "I must look like a
haystack," he muttered, but at that moment, Nathan realised this was
exactly where he had first arrived, pitched from Brewster Hazlett's
balloon and sent tumbling to the ground of the same city where he
lived, more than five hundred years into the past. He recognised the
place in detail, as it had also been dark then. Just three nights ago, yet
so much had happened since.

Wondering whether there was some special meaning to coming
back to precisely the same spot, Nathan started to tell Alfie. But John
was pointing to some dirty broken bricked steps leading into black
shadow, saying, "There." It was next to the smithy, but underground in
the cellars.

John led, with Alfie hurrying after. Clearly he could no longer
walk well after the long night, and needed to rest. Alice hurried
behind him, then Sam and Mouse, Peter, and finally Nathan. Being

exceptionally narrow and steep, with several steps broken into rubble and others missing entirely, they had to be extremely careful and stare at their feet as they clambered into the deep darkness. They jumped the bottom step as it wasn't there at all, and Sam grunted as he landed with a bump and a jolt. Nathan heard Mouse hiccup with a sort of frightened wheeze. Then they found themselves peering into a tiny empty space.

"Squeeze in, fatties," John told them, "and get around that corner."

They all did as they were told, turned the little corner, pushed open a door hanging half open on its hinges, and suddenly found themselves in a wide open space.

Against the far wall, which was all bare brick, it was extremely hot. "Next to the Smithy furnace," nodded Alice. "Now that's just what we need. But we'll have to find more straw for beds."

"Should've brought some from that rotten barn and those nasty stable boys." Alfie was still annoyed with them.

"Too far, sniffed John. "We'd ave lost the lot. Dropping stalks from there ta here, so's any idiot could easy follow right where we come."

"Like breadcrumbs Hansel and Gretel," muttered Nathan, but as usual no one knew what he was talking about.

"Never mind," Alice was delighted and smiling wide. "The wind will blow it all away by morning. We have our blankets and it's so warm, we'll sleep well anyway. Tomorrow we'll try and find some better bedding." But then her smile turned to a frown. "What will the ironmonger and the smith say if they see us creeping down here. Are they nice people? Do you know them?"

"Not really," admitted John, "but they seen me plenty in the past and they never cared. Busy, they are. Too busy ta poke their noses into the old cellars."

Now even Mouse was smiling and with a pull and a heave, they wrapped themselves in their blankets and curled up by the glorious heat of the wall next to the smithy's furnace.

"Reckon I'll wake up already smelted," grinned John.

"Smelted and melted," agreed Sam with a snigger. "But this floor's mighty hard. We needs straw for pallets."

Nathan saw that Alfie was having trouble on the hard floor, which was just dried earth and quite lumpy, so he spread out his pyjamas as a mattress, and his blanket as a folded up pillow. "Won't help that much," he said, "but it'll be better than nothing. I'm not cold. I don't need them."

Alfie was thankful and he was so tired that soon he was deep asleep, but Nathan found it harder to doze off. He was still puzzled as to why they were back in exactly the place he had fallen from the balloon. He sat up, leaning back against the hot wall, and stared out into the darkness. Mouse was dribbling on his toes, and it was sinking in through the wool. Peter and Alfie were breathing heavily and Sam was snoring a little bit, and even muttered through his dreams. Then, unexpectedly Nathan realised that Alice had crawled up beside him. She put her finger to her lips and beckoned. Nathan followed her until they were both sitting against the opposite wall, far away from their sleeping friends.

"I wanted to talk to you," Alice explained. "First of all I have to thank you so much for everything. You're not really part of our gang but you've done so much to help us. You're a real hero."

Astonished and somewhat embarrassed, Nathan mumbled, "Not. Never. I mean, I haven't done anything."

"Yes you have," Alice insisted. "You kept everyone in the kitchens while I got Alfie out, and John says you really faced up to the baron. Then there's all the money."

"Luck," Nathan admitted.

"Yes. But you were quick-witted, and generous. You could have kept quiet and all the money would have been yours." Actually, that had never occurred to Nathan, so now he just kept silent and blushed a bit. Alice continued in a hushed voice. "And then you said about making a plan to get the baron out of my house. I've been thinking about that ever since and just how we could do it. So tell me what you had in mind. You seem to be good at plans."

Nathan was still blushing. He used to think he was never any good at anything and had never been considered much use at school. Poppy usually called him stupid. Now he was being called a hero and a mastermind of plots and plans. "Well," he said slowly, but trying to think fast, "You said your step-father wanted you to marry his brother. So I

47

thought if you went to the brother, and said you'd marry him if *he* gets rid of the baron, I mean, so you and the brother could keep all the money. If he's as nasty as you said, then he'll want to do it. Then of course, once the baron is out of the house, you refuse to marry the brother after all."

"That might be tricky." Alice smiled wide. "But I could try. It would be fun."

"I'd help." Suddenly Nathan realised he was also having fun. "But I might have to leave suddenly. Go back to my own time. I've no idea how that could happen but it will one day, I hope."

"There was something else I wanted to say," Alice whispered, her voice even more hushed. "See Alfie doesn't want anyone else to know, but he admitted to me that he had told the baron we lived by the river, so that's why I said we had to move house. Poor Alfie. They dragged him off and tied him to a table, and they whipped and whipped him till he was bleeding, and he said the pain was terrible. They kept on and on until he told what they asked. He still wouldn't give details, but I think the baron would be able to find the warehouse quite easily. I don't blame Alfie for telling. They said they'd keep whipping him until he died, if he didn't tell where I was."

Nathan shivered. "I don't blame him either. That must have been awful. And they didn't even call a doctor for him."

Alice shook her head." I wish I could whip the baron. He's a pig. He was horrible to me while I still lived there, and now he's stealing all my money."

"Then the plan's important," nodded Nathan. "We can sort it out tomorrow with all the others."

It was the sounds from the smithy and the heating of the furnace that woke them all early the next morning. As the smith and his assistant began work, there was the huff and puff of the bellows, then a mighty clang and bursts of flame, all echoing through the wall to those sleeping in the cellar below. Nathan woke with a start and Alfie moaned. John Ten-Toes jumped up, as if expecting an attack. Sam and Peter grumbled about still being tired and Alice yawned, stretched and said she would go out, buy some bread and bacon, and bring them all a hurried breakfast. Nathan offered to go with her and she nodded.

It was quite a hop and a leap up the old steps, and when they reached the top they were surprised to see the lane was already busy with business. A tall man in smart livery was leading a horse to the smithy for new shoes, and opposite at the ironmonger's shop there was a queue of customers waiting for service.

The front of the smithy was opened up, and the smith watched intently as Nathan and Alice appeared from the cellar next-door. He was busy twisting metal in the roaring golden flames before him, but he chewed his lip, and nodded as Nathan caught his eye.

'Tomorrow we might get our shoes,' Nathan said hopefully to Alice. "My feet are getting soggy and sore and I don't want holes in my brand new hose."

"I've got so used to being barefoot," Alice smiled, "I don't care anymore. But these stockings are lovely and warm and I don't want holes in them either."

"Must be strange," decided Nathan, "being so poor after you were rich before."

"Freedom and friendship," Alice explained. "It's worth everything else."

Even without shoes, they no longer immediately looked like beggars so when they held up two silver coins, they were able to buy exactly what they wanted, and Alice put the rolls of dark bread, the slab of smoked bacon and the wedge of cheese into her basket. But as they hurried out from the bakers and turned towards their new home, they were stopped abruptly.

"You," roared an angry gruff voice, and a large hand clamped down on Nathan's shoulder. Alice, startled, moved aside, keeping a tight hold on the basket and the purse of money.

At first, struggling against the grasp on his shoulder, Nathan had no idea who the man was, but then he remembered. This was one of the assistant cooks from the baron's kitchen, whom the head cook called Oliver. He no longer wore his greasy apron, but Nathan recognised the snarl, the beady eyes and the tufts of white hair.

"I don't know you. You've got the wrong person," Nathan yelled, still struggling. But the assistant cook had him in an even stronger grip, with one arm twisted up his back, and Nathan could hardly move. It hurt badly, and he yelped.

"Yes, you cry, little pest," said the cook. "It'll be a good deal more painful once I get you to the Constable. I'll have you thrashed and thrown in the stocks for a week."

Nathan had heard of the stocks, but had certainly never thought one day he'd be locked in them himself.

He was being dragged off, and the crowds of customers nearby were all calling and shouting, some taking Nathan's side but most taking the side of the cook. "Let him go, you bully," yelled a stall-holder. "He's just a boy, and he paid the price asked. He didn't nick anything."

"I expect he's a runaway apprentice," an elderly woman said, frowning. "Leave the man alone to do his job."

"All them brats is thieves," objected another man.

Nathan tried to kick back at Oliver's shins, but step by step he was dragged off. He waved wildly, trying to ask Alice to get help, but Alice had completely disappeared.

Back at the cellar, Alfie was deeply asleep, wedged up hard against the heated wall of their new home. Exhausted and still in a great deal of pain, he didn't even hear the sounds of the smithy next door. Sitting with his back to the wall, just a short distance from Alfie's feet, Peter had his thumb in his mouth, eyes shut, waiting patiently for Nathan and Alice to return with food.

After a long wait, John decided he should go and look for them. He was well aware that anything could happen. "Might be arrested as thieves," he pronounced gloomily.

"But they got money," objected Peter, thumb still in his mouth.

"Then maybe some rotten thief done nicked their money," John said with an even deeper frown. "There's some rotten folks out there, dangerous robbers and such."

Peter returned to the concentration of his thumb. "Go look then," he murmured.

John turned immediately and ran towards the steps. "I will," he said over his shoulder. "Ain't no one gonna hurt my friends."

But Sam was crawling across the uneven brick floor, peering into dark corners, and calling softly. He was worried. Mouse had gone.

He poked Peter in the stomach and Peter opened his eyes again with a jerk. I think poor Mouse went out to catch mice," he said softly. "But this is a new place and she don't know her way around. I think she's lost."

"Cats don't get lost," Peter decided.

Sam was not convinced. "She knows the way back to our old warehouse and the river. But she don't know here. I'm going to go and look for her. There's stray dogs out there. They could tear her to pieces."

"Mouse is too quick for hungry dogs."

"She might be sick. She might be lost. I'm going to find her."

"Suppose I'll come too," Peter removed his thumb from his mouth and wiped it carefully on his new tunic. "But should we leave Alfie all alone?"

"Poor Alfie's got a black eye and purple cheeks and a squashed nose," Sam said, looking with sorrow at his friend. "Needs to sleep. Reckon we'll be back with Mouse before he wakes."

They crept from the old cellar, clambered up the steps and started to run south towards the river, keeping to the shadows. The day was mildly sunny but the narrow lanes with houses that bent over, almost meeting roof to roof, blocked the sky and made more shadows than sunbeams.

The river was still lost in morning haze, with a fog blowing up from the estuary far beyond the Bridge. Curls of soft white mist hung over the water, creeping along the banks and hovering in damp shrouds. The little river boats, already busy, could hardly be seen as they rowed both up and downstream, some almost bumping into each other, finding it hard to peer ahead through the mist. But Peter and Sam knew exactly where their old warehouse stood and were able to scurry through the fog without difficulty. However, they were not able to see the two men waiting just outside until large damp hands reached out and grabbed them.

"That's them," one man shouted, grasping Peter by his collar. Meanwhile the other man grabbed Sam.

"Well, you rascals," the first man said, holding fast as Peter tried to wriggle away. "We're the assistant constables, sent out by Baron Cambridge himself, to find the urchins and thieves living in the warehouse by the river. Seems we got you."

"Not us," squeaked Peter. "We're not thieves."

"Nor urchins neither," said Sam. "And we've done nothing wrong. We don't know no barons."

"Well, he knows you," said the assistant constable. "Says you and some others abducted his step-daughter."

"Abducted?" said Sam, irate. "Poor Alice, she ran away. The baron were horrible to her."

"Ah," grinned the assistant constable. "So you *do* know the baron. You're brats and liars and you're both coming with us down to The Poultry Gaol."

"And I'll inform his lordship, the baron," said the other.

Marched from the riverside through the winding streets to the small local gaol at the Poultry, Sam, who was still more worried about Mouse than he was about himself, and Peter, who whispered that he'd be able to pick the lock on the door and escape anyway, both suddenly jerked around as they saw Alice talking to John Ten-Toes just past the market. They were both clearly upset, and when they turned as the assistant constables pushed past, and saw Sam and Peter, they gasped and began to follow. Trying to keep out of sight, but determined to see which gaol was the destination, everyone avoided bumping into each other, but whispered messages as the heavy boots of the constables echoed on the cobbles.

The Poultry gaol was a small one, often keeping only those who would be thrown into the stocks the next morning, taken straight to the judge, or others who would be released after they paid a bribe. Just one heavy barred doorway led to the single dark dungeon, and here Sam and Peter were pushed, each with a clip around the ear, and a warning to behave while they waited for the baron to be informed and make his decision regarding the prisoners.

But it was also here that Sam and Peter made the astonishing discovery that the young boy huddled alone and miserable in the corner, was in fact their friend Nathan.

"How did you get here?" demanded Peter.

"Thrown in. Just like you."

"Because of the baron?"

Nathan sighed. "Yes. That same revolting man. Actually it was one of his cooks who recognised me from the kitchens." He shrugged. "Was unfortunate he saw me so soon, but I suppose it was bound to happen one day." He paused, wondering, then asked, "What about you? Thieving?"

"Certainly not," said Sam, affronted, as if he had never stolen anything in his life. "We gone back to the old house to look for Mouse, and them assistant constables were waiting for us there. I reckon that baron somehow guessed where we lived, and they were there waiting."

"I wonder if Alfie told him after all," mumbled Peter.

"Impossible," said Nathan at once. "Though I wouldn't blame him if he had. Did you see what a terrible state his back was in? He must have been whipped twenty times or more."

"That mean baron's gotta pay for this," Sam said, stamping his foot, and then hopping, holding his toes since the stamp on bare concrete had hurt.

"Well, if we ever get out of here," said Nathan through gritted teeth, "I've got a few ideas. But Alice will have to help too, and she ran away when I got arrested."

"None of us ever runs away," objected Peter, his usually soft voice growing loud. "We saw her out there, she was talking to John, and both of them followed us here. They must have a plan too."

The cell was bitterly cold as no light entered. The walls were stone without windows, the ceiling very low, and the floor broken slabs of concrete. Nathan shivered. He was glad he wasn't wearing just pyjamas anymore.

Sam started to speak, but his voice dropped to a whisper as they heard noises outside. "Can you pick the lock, Peter?"

Peter was nodding when the door opened wide with a smash and a slam, and two guards entered with a wooden platter and three rough wooden cups. "Here," said the first guard, banging the platter down on the ground so that half the bread scattered and one of the cups of water spilt. "Tis all you're getting, lest you got money for more."

They shook their heads. Alice had the purse and all the coins.

But when they were gone and the door clanged shut again, Peter leaned forwards. "I can do it," he said.

Unknown to Nathan, Sam and Peter, John Ten-Toes and Alice were standing outside the gaol walls, just a few steps away, whispering to each other. "Perhaps," wondered Alice, "I can pay to get them out."

"No luck," John said at once. "The pig-brain baron will pay more than what we can. And I bet e's promised a purse full ta the Constable if he gets you back in e's talons."

"I expect you're right," Alice sighed. "How horrible if he spends my own money to trap me and force me back under his guardianship."

John leaned against the outside of the gaol wall. "If we waits a bit," he suggested, "P'raps Peter will be able to pick that lock."

On the other side of the thick stone wall, Peter was saying, "I got my penknife hidden in my belt and I can use that. I know what to do, it's just a quick twist with the point. We'll be out afore nightfall. I just need a bit more light."

"Well, I ain't got no candles," Sam pointed out. "Night is better for escaping anyway, I reckon. Can you do it in the dark?"

CHAPTER SEVEN

Meanwhile, once more back at the cellar, Mouse landed with a cheerful thump on Alfie's chest, having just found her way home. She was plumper than usual, having eaten three mice for breakfast, and she was delighted to be back with her special friend.

Alfie rolled over with a yelp. "What's happened?" he muttered. "Who's dying?" Mouse meowed with a happy dribble. "Oh, it's you," winced Alfie, closing his puffy blackened eyes. "And where's everyone else?" But this was a question Mouse could not answer. So Alfie climbed slowly to his feet, staggered over to the doorway, peered around the corner and up the steps, and realised that it was still day, but no longer early morning. The half-hearted sunshine wafted down into the opening, and Alfie could hear the hearty bashing and clanking noises from the smithy.

Still weak and wobbly on his legs, Alfie sat down again for a moment, and then quickly made up his mind. It was unusual for him to find himself totally alone, and it seemed likely that something had gone wrong. So he managed to climb the broken steps to the outside world, and began to walk towards Cheapside and the centre of the city. Trying to keep his back straight and stride along instead of shuffling, he arrived at Cheapside and asked the first stallholder if there had been any trouble that day, and if anyone had been arrested.

The stallholder turned away from his bright rows of polished red apples, and grinned. "Friend o' yours, is he?" he sniggered. "That brat was arrested. A boy in a blue tunic with brown hair and yellow bits, striped like a wasp."

"Like a bee, not a wasp," said Alfie crossly. "Where did they take him?"

The stallholder waved a disinterested hand. "Gaol, I reckon. The Poultry, I'd guess since tis the closest."

"And a girl too?" Alfie asked, but the stallholder shook his head.

"No females. Just the wasp boy."

Dusk was falling and shopkeepers were beginning to lock up for the night, but the sun, peeping low over the rooftops, was still sending out enough light for the last shoppers before hurrying home. Alfie, trying to ignore the pain in his back, skirted the main shopping area and made his way to the small gaol at the Poultry.

Alice and John saw him coming, and ran towards him. "Were you worried?" said Alice. "I'm glad you came."

John pulled a face and sniffed. "Tis a day of accidents," he said. "Nat got arrested first. Out with Alice, but she got away. He were bundled off ta the clink. Then seems them silly urchins, Sam and Peter went back to the warehouse and got arrested too. Lucky they got slammed into the same slammer. I bet they're having quite a feast in there."

"I bet they're feeling terrible," sighed Alice. "Poor things." She smiled at Alfie. "And there's you, still in pain. I feel so guilty because most of all the trouble is everyone trying to help me. So it's all my fault."

John grinned. "Reckon you'll make it up ta us, when you's rich again, and that pig-brain baron is the one in gaol. We can all live the high life for free in your big grand 'ouse."

Alfie grinned too. "You'll be Lady Alice."

Giggling, Alice said, "I am already because my father was a lord. But it sounds silly while I'm barefoot and live in an abandoned cellar."

"Ain't abandoned no more," John pointed out. "Tis a good home wiv better heating than I reckon they've got in the palace."

"And we can go get our knighthoods off the king, fer helping the lady in distress," Alfie laughed. "Then we'll feast on roast beef every day."

"Reckon we'll need shoes first," John said. "Just two more days and I won't be John Ten-Toes no more."

"You'll still have ten toes. They won't fall off, they'll just be hidden inside the leather," laughed Alice.

John stuck out his foot. "Gone already," he pointed down, "wrapped all warm in them woolly hose."

And that was the exact moment that Peter, wriggling the point of his little knife inside the keyhole on their locked cell, said, "I got it. Listen," and they heard the loud click as the lock sprung open. Then with a creak of huge hinges on old wood, the heavy door swung wide.

First peeping nervously around the half open door, the three boys crept from the rank stone prison and into the narrow passageway beyond. They saw no one and tiptoed ever closer to the world outside. First there was the archway over the annexe, which was the guards' chamber, with a table and stools standing in the gloom. They feared seeing their gaolers seated there, but the guards had gone to get ale and supper and the way out was unwatched. Still careful and peering into the growing darkness, Nathan led the way to the main entrance, and within moments they were outside staring around and blinking. After the lightless confinement of their cell, even the dusk outside seemed bright and they had to squint to see anything at all. The chill of the wind hit them full in their faces, making them shiver again, but brought a wonderful feeling of relief. They didn't dare laugh yet, but they knew they had achieved the impossible.

They were free.

It was Alfie who saw them first, waved frantically, and rushed over. Alice was so excited, she hugged each of them, which Nathan and Peter found most embarrassing, but Sam rather enjoyed it and hugged her back.

"Quick," John said, "we gotta get outta here afore them guards come back. Run. Back home, fast as we can."

"Looks suspicious if we run," Nathan objected. "We should walk. But walk fast."

So that is what they did, keeping to the smaller lanes and cutting across several churchyards. The faint echo of candlelight through windows and the muffled sounds of householders preparing supper was all they could see and hear of the folk living there. Nathan recognised many of the street names, but none of these places and roads looked remotely the way he remembered them from his own time. Through the back lanes cutting into Lombard Street, then down the winding alleys approaching the north side of the Tower, Down Nicholas Lane, into East Cheap, across to St. George's, on over the Lower Lane and into Thames Street, up again and Tower Street before finally Harp Lane and Beer Lane. Then at last, their own small street. They made straight for the steps to the cellar. Bandy Alley, as it was called, was deserted with both the smithy and the ironmongers closed for the night, so everyone hurtled down into the dark cellar, flopping down by the heated wall, with tremendous relief. Alfie was out of breath, and lay down flat, easing his back against the rising heat, but the others were eager to exchange stories.

Sam was comforted to discover Mouse curled in a cosy corner, purring gently to herself, well fed and content. He sat close, head back against the wall, and yawned. "Never been in gaol afore," he said sleepily. "Don't like it. Won't go again."

"Nasty and chilly and damp and dark," agreed Peter. "The ceiling was only just over our heads."

"Well, I hope we're safe now," nodded Nathan. "It's all thanks to you, Peter, and those clever fingers of yours. Those guards are going to be mighty shocked when they come back and find the cell door wide open."

"They had no right to arrest any of you," said Alfie. "None of us did anything wrong. You didn't hit anyone. You didn't steal anything."

"Well, I stole the baron's purse," Nathan pointed out.

"I don't reckon 'e even knows about that," said John. "Reckon he's got so many purses, 'e ain't even realised 'e dropped one. Asides, that weren't what they nabbed Nat for."

Alice said at last. "You're right, and it's time to do something serious, or we shall all end up in gaol some time over the next days. Nat and I have a plan."

It took a long time to explain.

"Not a very good plan," murmured Nathan after Alice had described their idea, "but we have to try and do something."

"Because," added Alice, "every time we go out, we'll be trying to hide – frightened that someone will recognise us – that we'll be arrested. That will drive us crazy. So I'm going to try."

They prepared. It began with Alice describing the baron's younger brother, who she was supposed to marry. "He's short and fat and ugly," she sighed. "He has a stomach that pokes out and doesn't fit properly under his doublet. His hair is bright red and he uses a hot iron to try and make it curly. But that usually singes so he has funny burnt curls. I hate him."

"Not the sort a' person anyone would want' ta marry," said John, pulling a face."

"You can't cuddle a pig man," observed Sam from his corner, where he was happily cuddling Mouse.

"His name is Edmund Darling," sniffed Alice, looking down again, as if she couldn't bear to talk about him. "And there's no one I've ever met who's less of a darling. Except maybe the baron himself."

"You don't want him, but what if he don't want you?" asked John doubtfully.

"New clothes," decided Alfie. "Look pretty."

"He doesn't care about that," Alice shook her head. "I could be a dragon. He'd still want to marry me just because he wants my money and property."

"He sounds like a dragon himself," muttered John, "You didn't ortta go anywhere near him."

"I have to." Alice stared down into her lap, where she was clasping and unclasping her fingers. "I know I'll be frightened and I know it's a risk, but I have to stop us getting arrested for no good reason. And I don't want new clothes. I've got plenty at my house. But I suppose the one thing I ought to do first, is have a bath."

Nathan looked down at the dirt on his hands, and he could feel the sweat under his arms from all the running. "That's what I want too," he said at once.

"Not me," John turned away. "All that nasty hot water, and then being horrid and damp and cold."

"Cold toes?" Nathan laughed. "Why are you called Ten-Toes, anyway? Don't we all have ten toes?"

John sighed, leaning back against the heat of the wall. "I never had no parents," he said. "I were just a tiny baby when they found me on a rubbish dump." He grinned to hide the sadness in his eyes. "Proper place for me, I reckon. Anyways, I were given ta the monks at Blackfriars and they brung me up more or less, just like they does with all abandoned children. I reckon I was pretty stupid and them monks didn't teach me too well neither and learning to count took me ages. But I never had no shoes so when I couldn't count on me fingers, I used me toes. Seemed easier cos I had to use one finger to do the counting and it seemed like I only had nine left. So them monks called me John Ten-Toes, laughing at me. I were a cheeky little brat and I don't reckon they liked me much. I ran away when I were about eight, though I ain't sure exactly how old I is."

"You'll be a lord soon," Alfie smiled, and Sam, almost asleep in the corner, looked up.

"Sir John Ten-Toes. You'll fight in tournaments and go to battle with the king and hold his banner."

"More likely end me life on the scaffold," muttered John, half to himself as he lay down to sleep.

CHAPTER EIGHT

B aron Cambridge surveyed his brother. Edmund was stretched out in a comfortable chair, his feet reaching towards the blazing fire on the wide marble hearth before him, his hands loosely clasped over the swell of his large stomach. The stomach rose and fell gently as he breathed as if it had a life of its own. His three chins wobbled as he licked his lips, relishing the taste of the last meal he had eaten. As guest of his elder brother, he ate a good deal better than he did alone in his own small home.

Hugh, the baron, was a stout man but being a little taller, did not seem quite so wide. He managed to keep his stomach under control with a big leather belt, and his doublet had padded shoulders to try and seem more muscular instead of just fat. He also spent a considerable sum of money on special clothes tailored to make him look slimmer, grander, and even a little bit handsome.

The Baron said, "Get on with it, Ned. I'm not going to wait forever."

Edmund snorted. "I'll do it in my own time. And don't you go thinking you'll get all the property rights afterwards either. Share and share alike. Three quarters for me and a quarter for you."

The baron went pink. "Half and half, Ned. May I remind you of our original agreement."

But Edmund sneered, curling up one corner of his thin mouth. "I've got to put up with the stupid girl as my wife, not you. So, I deserve the largest share. Otherwise, I'll not do it."

"And may I also remind you," said the baron loudly, "that if you don't do it, you'll get nothing at all. I have control of the girl's wealth until she turns sixteen, and that's still three years away. As long as no interfering judge comes along to poke his nose into my business, I can continue to eat my way through that money. And you'll not get a penny, brother dear."

Edmund sat bolt upright and glared back at the baron. "You be careful, Hugh," he shouted back, going even pinker than his brother. "You try stealing the lot and I'll be the first to go running to the king." He calmed a little, sinking back in his chair again, and his chins settled. "Besides, you know you can't take the lot without me marrying the wench. If you did, as soon as she turned sixteen and found out what you'd done, you'd be thrown straight into Newgate Gaol."

Both men glared at each other.

They were interrupted by the baron's steward, who sidled in, obviously having heard what the conversation had been about after eavesdropping outside the door. "My lord," he said softly, "forgive me for interrupting, but I wish to make a suggestion."

The brothers turned their stares onto the steward, waiting for the next words. "None of your business, Lacey," huffed the baron crossly. "But tell me anyway."

The steward bowed. "If your lordship were to invite the young lady to a little chat, over dinner perhaps to put her at her ease, and then discuss the difficulty of her inheritance. Tell her that she is not as wealthy as she might have thought, that most of the money was entailed. Tell her that the only way she can live comfortably in the future is to marry Mister Edmund Darling." He smiled. "Naturally, the young lady cannot possibly understand all the complications of her inheritance. She is only a female, after all."

"Very good idea," said Edmund at once. "Well done, Lacey. I shall not forget your help once I get my hands on all the property."

Once again the steward bowed, and quietly left the room.

62

It was a large, grand room with painted scenes on the walls, a huge fireplace, and comfortable cushioned chairs. The window was not shuttered but it was bleary with the pouring rain outside. It stayed warm, however, as the high flames across the hearth crackled scarlet and golden.

"Well, that's a good idea," said Edmund, looking cheerful again. "You do that, Hugh, and once the wedding is done, then I'll share halves with you like we originally agreed. Otherwise the blasted female may never agree to marry me. You could try forcing her, but you can't even catch her."

"Have to find out where she is first," grumbled the baron, flicking the satin ribbons at his cuffs. "It's more than two years she's been hiding. But I'll find her sooner or later."

"Better be before she turns sixteen," Edmund pointed out.

The baron turned pink again. "I'll get Lacey to send out most of the servants tomorrow morning, to start searching the city. And I'll alert the Constable too. I already told the silly old fool she's been abducted, so it's about time he started searching for her himself."

Meanwhile back in the cellar at Bandy Alley, Alice yawned, stretched, and stood up, ready to face the new morning. "Blast," she said, pointing towards the opening in the brick wall, where the little broken door hung ajar, leading to the steps. Rain was slopping down and had trickled from the passage to the middle of the cellar floor. "There must be a real storm outside. If we go out now, we'll be drenched."

"Don't matter if we're just going to the washhouse," said Peter, staggering to his feet and tripping over Mouse. "Wet inside. Wet outside."

"I ain't coming to the baths," Alfie said. "Me back is too bad and I don't want ta wash off all that special cream. Reckon I'll go to the apothecary instead and buy some more."

"Nor me," Sam said in a small voice. "I don't want to get cold."

"Baby," sniffed Peter. "There's nice hot water, you know, and real nice smelly soap." But Sam shook his head.

John grinned, "That bathhouse soap don't smell nice. Tis made for scrubbing dirty linen and it stinks. I'm off ta the cobbler's to see if he's got our shoes ready."

"No." Alfie frowned. "None of us should be alone. There's too much risk now and if you got arrested we might not find you so easy. What if you got slung into Newgate? Nobody ever escapes from there."

"So just me, Nat and Peter will go to the baths, as soon as the rain stops a bit," Alice said, collecting up her shopping basket, "and the rest of you stay safe here. I'll bring back something nice for dinner."

Because the cellar was so well heated both day and night, Nathan slept only in his shirt and braes, as did all the other boys. They used their tunics and soft woolly hose as pillows. Now Nathan sat up, feeling very stiff and aching from sleeping all night on the bare cement floor. He tied up the neck of his shirt, which was now all creased, but he didn't care about that. Then, shrugging into his dark blue tunic, he looked down and wriggled his toes, laughing. His feet were absolutely black, and looked as though they had been painted with tar. He certainly wanted that bath. Back in his own home he hadn't been that keen to shower every day as his grandmother told him, but now he thought he'd do anything for his own bathroom and a lovely steaming hot shower.

He pulled on the hose and stood up. There was a growing puddle of water in the middle of the floor. "I don't mind getting a bit wet," he said, pushing his fingers through his bright brown and yellow streaked hair. "Peter's right. Wet inside and wet outside. So it doesn't matter."

"Well, I haven't got a cloak," Alice said, "and none of us have shoes yet so we'll be soaked. But I've been soaked before and I don't really mind. Alright. Let's go."

"We could put the blankets over our heads."

"Oh yes, and then have dripping wet blankets to sleep with tonight."

"Just go stand in the rain," John grinned. "Best bath you'll get, and free too."

"And get splashed with mud from every passing horse and cart."

"Oh, stop complaining," said Alice. "You cowards stay here, and I'll be back soon."

Nathan laughed. "I'm coming."

And Peter ran after them as Alfie waved goodbye calling to them not to get drowned.

Out in the street it was pelting with rain. Nathan decided it felt as though someone had emptied a bucket full of water over his head, but he liked the sudden fresh chill after the clammy heat of the cellar. And quite suddenly, after all the horrid chill of the gaol, and the fear of being locked up, and the worry about peering through the shadows for guards and enemies, and wondering what the baron would do with him, Nathan felt completely happy. After all, this was the greatest adventure anyone could have, and he realised that he was exceedingly lucky. He shouldn't be frightened. He should be laughing.

Alice was bossy but he liked her very much and felt sorry for her too. Alfie was brave and smart and terribly kind, while John was really funny and kept everyone cheerful. As for Peter, he was a genius with locks, and Sam was sweet and loving. Nathan looked around, opened his mouth and swallowed a great gulp of cold rain. It tasted like magic. He smelled the heavy spice that had hovered around Brewster Hazlett's balloon, and with a hop and a skip, Nathan ran ahead.

Alice and Peter looked at him in amazement. "You gone daft?" inquired Peter solemnly.

But Alice laughed too. "Yes, we ought to be happy," she agreed. "We're off to have a lovely hot bath, we can afford it and some good food afterwards, and we have a great plan, thanks to you. Just wait and see! By next week everything will be solved and I'll be back at home. You'll all come with me and have your own comfy bedchambers with feather mattresses and candles by the bedside."

It was not the sort of thing Nathan had ever wanted in his life, but now he loved the sound of it. He almost hoped that Brewster had not yet come to take him home. He stared up into the thick clouds as the rain dripped down his shirt collar but no balloon sailed there and he saw nothing except clouds and rain. Alice stretched out her arms, palms up, and danced in a huge circle, laughing. So Peter joined in and ran around them both, jumping in the puddles so they splashed everyone.

The washhouse was on the banks of the Thames near the Bridge, and as they approached the low lime-washed building, with its bustling queues of women hauling great bundles of clothing and sheets with them, ready for the boiling tubs, Nathan took a long look at the Bridge. The only one over the river, it was the busiest street in all the city. The shops all along were doing a great business and folk were squeezing through the roadway, trying to cross to the other side. Beneath it, the river waters surged between the many pillars, and the boats were as busy below as the shops above.

Then, startled, Nathan noticed one boat in particular, rowed by a tall skinny man dressed all in black, with a long slim top hat tilted over one eye. Nathan stared. Surely it couldn't be – but he was sure that it was. These were not the sort of clothes everyone else was wearing, and Brewster Hazlett was not someone you could easily mistake.

The man dropped one oar into the boat, and waved. Nathan stepped back, confused. Did he want to go home? He knew he didn't, but he couldn't risk being stuck in the past forever.

The smell of magic was very intense and it swirled from the little boat and around Nathan's head so strongly that it almost shut out the rain, making him dizzy. Alice and Peter had skipped ahead and didn't seem to have noticed that Nathan remained behind. He turned to run and catch them up, but the rowing boat sped towards him with a great churning wave of river spray, and bumped hard into the bank where Nathan stood.

"Well now," said the man, with that same high squeaky voice that Nathan remembered, "how nice to meet you, Nat. I've heard a lot about you."

Nathan was even more mystified. "But we've met before," he said. "It was you who brought me here."

"No, no," said the man with a gurgle of high pitched laughter. "That was my twin brother, Brewster. I'm Wagster Hazlett. Nice to meet you." His large white teeth gleamed as the heavy rain bounced off his top hat and cascaded over his shoulders. And yet, as Nathan suddenly noticed, the man did not seem to get wet at all.

"Why are you here?" Nathan muttered. "And how can you take me home in that little rowing boat?"

"Oh dear, dear," said Wagster with an annoying waggle of his long thin finger. "Who said anything about taking you home? You've got a lot of work to do first. Oh, yes, Bumble-Bee Head, starting tomorrow. You'll see."

Nathan wasn't sure if he was pleased or not. "So why did you come?" he asked.

And then the laughter stopped.

For a moment the world turned to ice and a huge shadow loomed, blocking out everything else. Nathan couldn't see the river or the boat, and not even the Bridge. All he could see was this growing darkness and the huge mountainous shape of Wagster Hazlett swallowing the light. The shadow darkened until it was blacker than night, and as tall as the disappearing sky. Two great thin legs, like stilts, towered up and then the body hunched over, peering downwards to where Nathan stood, stunned. Then within the shadow glowed two great piercing eyes, narrow and hooded, golden like the eyes of a snake.

Shivering and quickly hurrying backwards, Nathan shouted up," What are you doing? That's horrible. You're not a wizard, you're a monster. What do you want? If you're not taking me home, then I need to go and catch up with my friends."

"Friends?" And again, "Friends," boomed the enormous shape of Wagster with a very different voice than the one he had used before. The word echoed and repeated, and then abruptly he squealed with laughter. "No grandson of Granny October can have real friends," Wagster said.

Staring up and silent for a moment, Nathan wondered if he had heard right. "What has this to do with my grandmother?" he whispered.

"Everything, absolutely everything," Wagster sneered, shrill-voiced again. "You'll find out, stupid Bumble-Bee Head."

Nathan could not look away. The serpent eyes seemed magnetic, and through the knife-like pupil, Nathan thought he could see wriggling maggots and tiny worms slithering away into the distance.

As Wagster began very slowly to shrink back to normal size, he finished speaking, his tongue flicked out, and Nathan saw it was dark red and forked. A cockroach, its antennae alert, walked the underside of the tongue, travelling back into the gaping slime of the throat. As he sighed with relief, thinking the wizard had gone, he heard one last hiss. "I'll be back soon," came the voice through the clouds. "Be ready for me, boy. You have no idea – no idea at all – what is coming."

Nathan yelled out, not caring who else heard him, "You can't threaten me. And you can't say horrible things about my grandmother."

"Save your courage, Bumble-Bee Head," whispered the final distant murmur. "Danger, boy, beyond anything you can imagine."

The last cackle echoed, then faded. And in a blink, he was gone. The light came back, the clouds began to clear, and the pouring rain began to ease. There was no sign at all of the little boat rowed by the tall skinny man, and life had returned to normal. Except that Nathan did not feel normal at all. His knees were weak and his head spun. Then unexpectedly Alice was facing him.

"Come on, snail." She was still happy and laughing. "We're waiting for you. Why did you stop?"

"Didn't you see?" whispered Nathan, still not able to think clearly.

"No. Nothing. What? Was there an accident on the river?"

"Sort of." He didn't understand how she could have missed something so dreadful and so huge, but he certainly wasn't going to tell her about it. "But it doesn't matter," he managed to say. "Let's get into the bathhouse."

Staggering to the bathhouse, although it was very close, seemed an agony to Nathan, but once sitting up to his chin in hot steamy water, he cheered up. It felt positively wonderful. All his aches, pains and problems seemed to drift away. He even began to wonder if the whole nightmare of Wagster Hazlett had occurred only in his imagination. All nightmares were dreams after all. He smiled to himself, leaned his head back on the rim of the tub, and closed his eyes.

There was one huge communal room for men and another for

women, each with long rows of wooden barrels, bound in copper hoops, just like the old barrels of beer. These were cut in two, and set to stand close together, waiting until someone paid for a bath. Then the bathhouse staff would boil kettles over the fires and then pour the bubbling water into the tub. Although surprised at the way it was done, Nathan had immediately undressed and climbed in, sitting quickly with his knees bent up under his chin.

And it was after a little while that he remembered this was how Brewster Hazlett sat in the basket below the balloon, and also how Wagster had sat in the little rowing boat. But he brushed away the thought. He knew Brewster was real after all, because otherwise he would not have been there. True, he had not liked Brewster. In spite of the excitement and the adventure, Brewster had been rude and offered no choice. But his twin brother Wagster was far worse.

Once again pushing away such thoughts and smiling to himself, Nathan watched the dirt dissolve from his body, and rise to the top of the water in a muddy scum. He laughed softly. He had never before been so dirty, but it was most relaxing now to feel clean, warm and comfy.

When he clambered out, waving to Peter who was in another barrel tub nearby, he hoped to grab a clean towel and rub himself hard. Then, once dry he hurriedly dressed, and with Peter trotting behind he went outside to wait for Alice.

She came quickly, looking rather different, Nathan thought, than she had before the bath. Her face was shining and her skin was soft and pretty. Her long hair was not so dark anymore and it hung in long attractive blond curls down her back. It had stopped raining and the sky was bright. The streets sparkled with raindrops, each reflecting the sunlight. There was no more spicy perfume of magic, and instead there was a fresh smell of spring leaf and blossom on some of the little trees beside the river.

"We can buy hot pies," said Alice, "at the Baker's, and take some home to the others." She was pointing her toes, dancing along the wet cobbles. Without shoes, she knew her woolly stockings would soon be damp again, but that would help keep her feet nice and clean after the bath.

"A hot pie." Nathan suddenly felt his stomach growl with hunger. "That's a brilliant idea. Yes please." He hadn't even realised he was starving until pies were mentioned.

"Not far," and Alice led the way.

The shop was small with a big oven and glorious smells sweeping out into the bright air, far nicer than the smell of Hazlett magic.

It was on the way out, clutching the shopping basket crammed with six big fat pies oozing meat from crusty hot pastry, that everything changed again. First out of the shop, Alice bumped hard into a protruding stomach tightly wrapped in a blue satin doublet, sleeves slashed in turquoise velvet, and a coat of cerise brocade. Alice looked up, ready to apologise, and found herself staring into the bloated but widely smiling face of her guardian, Baron Cambridge.

CHAPTER NINE

First a frown, eyebrows connecting over his nose like two small ginger rabbits shaking paws, and then a smile as the eyebrows snapped apart. "Well, what a delightful coincidence," said the baron, his fat hand clamped hard on Alice's shoulder. "I was just thinking about you, my dear."

But this was no delightful coincidence as far as the others were concerned. With a gulp, Alice struggled and turned to Nathan. "Help," she called out. "Grab the basket and hit him."

"Now, now, my dear," said the baron with calculated friendliness. "I merely wished a small word with you. An invitation, in fact. I've no desire to hurt you, I assure you, and won't insist that you come back to your home with me. You are quite free, my dear lady, to go where you wish."

Standing stock still in surprise, Alice regarded her guardian with considerable doubt. "Then let me go now," she said, ignoring the other shoppers who were crowding around. "I have to take these pies back to my friends and Mouse. I don't want to talk to you."

"Not very polite, my dear," said the baron, with the wide pink smile still stuck firm to his face. "And you have a pet mouse. How – sweet. Never been very fond of mice myself. But no matter. Keep pet rats and toads too if you wish."

One woman shopper, her face partially disappearing into the hot pork pie she had bought, called out through drops of gravy, "Don't you go making pets of them nasty little black rats, girl. Dirty, they are, and leave their poop all over my floors."

"Mouse is just a cat," explained Alice, but her voice was lost beneath the cackle and gossip. Everyone around started to argue with everyone else about the value of mice, rats and toads, and whether or not they should be kept as household companions.

"Vermin," complained a young man. "Stick 'em with a penknife."

An elderly gentleman shook his fuzzy white head. "How would you like to be stuck with a knife, young man? Think of others. Do no harm to no man. That's what they say in church."

"But 'tis the priests what does harm too, all them crusades and such," muttered a woman wiping her hands on her apron.

As another man began to exclaim at length concerning the wickedness of toads, the baron moved quickly away, pulling Alice with him. Peter and Nathan followed closely. Nathan had already taken the basket as asked, and was ready to pummel the baron's stomach with it, should that seem necessary. But the baron was saying, "My dear Alice, I simply wish to put a generous proposition to you. I suggest you come to the house for dinner at midday tomorrow, and I will explain. I swear I shall not keep you there after we have talked and eaten. You will be free to leave and go to your own friends, wherever you now live, and think over what I have said." He patted her shoulder, even though he still kept a vice-hold on her other one. "So shall we say midday tomorrow at my house?"

"*My* house," said Alice, with a scowl.

"Indeed, indeed," chuckled the baron. "And you are free to return and live there whenever you wish. I did not force you to run away. That was most certainly your own idea, and definitely against my own wishes."

"Can I bring my friends to this dinner?" Alice asked after a thoughtful pause.

"Ah, no," the baron said at once. "My apologies, Alice, but what I have to say is private. But your friends may come and collect you afterwards by all means. Come at midday, and tell your friends to turn up and collect you at – let us say, two of the clock."

Alice nodded, unsure and hesitant, but prepared to see what the baron would offer. "Yes, I'll come," she decided. "I promise. At midday." He let her go at once and she walked quickly away.

The baron watched her go, and his smile widened until it almost cracked his face in two. This was exactly what he wanted.

Back at the cellar, this most unexpected invitation was discussed at length. Alfie was against the plan.

"But don't you see," Alice explained, "it's all working in my favour. I can go to dinner tomorrow, and pretend that I really will agree to marry the baron's vile brother. But only on condition that he moves out of the house, and gives me back control of my property. I'll say it has to be that way, or his stupid brother will starve, because I'm fairly sure he hasn't a penny. I want my house back. I want him to give up his guardianship, because that stops being legal; once I'm a married woman anyway. Then, when I've got everything back, I will go to the lawyers at St. Paul's and say they have to help me keep what is mine, because I refuse to marry horrible Edmund Darling."

"No. He won't let you go." Alfie was adamant.

"'E's still your guardian," muttered John. "'E' can keep you there and make you marry the man."

Alice looked worried. "But he said you could all come later and collect me from the house."

"He'd set his dogs on us and never let us near you," Alfie insisted, leaning forwards. "I reckon you don't even realise just how cruel that pig-baron really is. He had this big cold table in the wine cellar, and he had his steward chain me to it, wrists and ankles. Then he leaned over me and punched me over and over in me face till I were sick. All I could do was squeeze me eyes shut and try not ta cry out. But then the steward turned me over, and started to whip me across the back. I yelled and yelled and cursed them all but the whip kept slashing. I could smell me own blood. Finally they unchained me and threw me on the ground. They locked the door and just left me there."

Now Alice was crying and Sam looked very wet-eyed. John threw one of the pieces of broken brick against the far wall in frustration. "That's terrible. That vile man ortta be executed."

Nathan was shocked. Even though he already knew this had happened, the story was painful to hear. He began to wonder if he could get the monster Wagster Hazlett to do something awful to the baron and frighten him away. Nathan said, "Look, Alice needs to get her home back, and her money, and be free of the baron and his brother too. I think if she promises to marry this Edmund person, then they'll be nice to her. They have to pretend to be nice in case she runs away again. They need that marriage."

"Marriage," mumbled John gloomily. "Must be a right horrible thing. Weddings and everything. And ta someone like that. Waking up and seeing that fat red face and stringy red hair staring back at you. Ugh. I wouldn't be able to eat any breakfast. And now I can't bear thinking about it so I'm going to sleep."

Nathan, lying close to the hot brick wall, wondered desperately if he was making Alice do the wrong thing. Not that he was making her do anything really, but it had been his idea and if something terrible happened then he'd be to blame. He almost got up to go out into the street and call to Brewster Hazlett to come and help, but he didn't. He knew the others would follow him and think he was even more crazy than they did already.

They all awoke the next morning, stiff and sore. Alice had made pottage from the leeks, onions and bacon they had bought, and now she built a little fire and heated the pot. No one was speaking very much and they shared the stew in silence.

Alice had no comb but she carefully pulled her fingers through her knotted and tousled hair, trying to make it look neater. Eventually she stared at the others sitting around the fire and watching her. "So what am I to do?" she demanded suddenly.

"Stay here," said Alfie at once.

"Go buy a big carving knife and take it with you," suggested John.

Sam hiccupped and grabbed at Mouse who was trying to wriggle away. "Be safe and stay with us," he said.

But Peter stood up suddenly. "I think you ought to go," he mumbled. "But we should all come too and hide in the garden till it's time for you to leave." And then he flopped down again, blushing slightly.

"Excellent," said Nathan at once. "We'll all go, and wait outside, but we don't have to hide. If the baron is trying to be nice to Alice, he can't be horrible to us. We won't try to go in, but we won't go away either."

"First we go and get our shoes," said Alfie. "I need shoes on when I kick that vile steward and the baron too."

"Yes, shoes, and a comb as well," agreed Alice. "I'll feel less embarrassed if I don't look like a beggar girl."

It was a cold morning with a little frost in the air, as the sky was almost cloudless and the sunshine was bright for an early spring morning. The church bells had rung nine times for Prime when suddenly, as they all walked carefully through the lanes towards the cobbler's shop, it became quite dark. They all stopped, staring up at the sky, and immediately Nathan thought it must be Brewster and the balloon blocking out the sun. But then he realised that everyone else in the street was standing still and staring up as well, and many were frightened, pointing and calling.

Gradually something like a great black ball was sliding across the surface of the sun and little by little, the light blinked out. Within only a short time, the sun had gone utterly dark, with a strange pale halo of yellow haze surrounding the black ball above them.

Now people were running home, and one woman sat down in the middle of the street with a squeak and began to cry, her little white hat fell off and she managed to wipe her eyes on her fur trimmed sleeves.

A group of people were running to the nearest church, begging the priest to protect them. But the priest, in his long robes, came out to the church porch with a calming wave of both hands, to tell everyone that this was nothing terrible. It was an eclipse of the sun, and had been predicted by the wise.

"Tis the day of St. Abraham, the sixteenth day of March," he said reassuringly. "I have known this would happen this morning, and have been waiting to see it. Most interesting."

"Eclipses," said a small man, "I heard of them. Folk says they bring evil tidings."

Nathan was smiling at his friends. "Honestly," he said quickly, "it's quite safe. These things happen every now and again. Eclipses are quite normal."

The darkness was strangely disquieting, and everyone was pleased when very, very gradually the black ball moved away from the light of the sun once again. The light began to flood back. Oozing out like water from a badly plugged hole, the sunshine returned.

"Gracious," muttered Alfie. "I didn't like that."

"What were that round black devil thing?" asked Sam with a shiver. He had been clinging to Alice's arm.

"The moon," said Nathan, looking around. "It's just the way the planets move and everything. Sometimes the moon goes past the sun and blocks it out for a little while. It's not a devil."

"The moon only comes out at night. Now it's day," complained Peter.

"And the moon is a pretty silver with light too. It's not black. I never heard of a no black moon," objected Alfie.

"I don't know all the details," Nathan shook his head, a little vague. "But it's not a bad sign or anything. I think it's black just because of shadows or something,"

"A portent," said John quickly. "I reckon Alice don't go to see the baron today. Wouldn't be safe."

Alice looked at each of her friends, and finally at Nathan. "You're sure it's safe? Not an evil sign?"

"I promise it isn't." But he wasn't even sure himself. Everyone around them was rushing home, rushing into the church, or standing as if mesmerised, still staring upwards. It had left them all a little shaky. "Come on," Nathan said, "let's get to the cobblers. Alice can make up her mind afterwards. There's plenty of time before dinner."

Their shoes were ready for them, sitting in a gleaming row on the cobbler's counter. There were soft brown leather boots for Alfie and John, with strong flat soles and black cord to tie them up around the ankle. Sam, Peter and Nathan had shining black leather shoes, tied with ribbons, and fitting perfectly. Alice had little blue leather shoes, which closed with turquoise cord.

Everyone sat and tried their shoes on, which cheered them up considerably. The feet of all their hose were already quite dirty, but once hidden inside their shoes, they all appeared very smartly dressed.

It was sunny now, and they all seemed to have forgotten the eclipse. Alice bought a comb, and Alfie bought two bright new blankets, thick and woolly, and a small pillow of feathers in a linen case. Sam thought it would be nice to have a pillow too, and even suggested they buy one for Mouse, but John said no, it was only proper for Alfie because his head and back were badly injured with all those bruises and whip slashes. "Don't be a baby," John told Sam. "You's nigh growed up."

"I'm nearly nine," sniffed Sam. "Don't mean I can't have a pillow, does it?"

"We could try and get pallets with a load of straw again," suggested Alfie. "Would be nice against that hot wall."

"Tomorrow, perhaps," Alice answered him. "We don't have time today. I have to walk up to Bishopsgate. Are you all coming with me?"

"For sure," said Peter, who was jumping up and down on the cobbles, enjoying his new shoes.

"I still reckon you shouldn't go." Alfie was hobbling a bit. Even his new shoes didn't help his injured back.

But ignoring him, Alice led the way north towards the grand wide road of Bishopsgate. They grouped together, no longer feeling threatened nor risking arrest. The temporary accord with the baron had at least brought a day of peace. Alfie dragged a little behind, partially because of the pain in his back but also because of his doubts about the invitation, but Nathan walked with Alice and tried to reassure her.

He was saying, "We'll be watching, both the front door and the back," when four liveried guards, riding fast with a thundering pound of the horses' hooves, pelted down Bishopsgate and into Cheapside with their heads low across the horses' necks

Alice, Nathan, and the whole group pressed back against the edge of the road, escaping the gallop, and other folk hurried away, clamping their hands to their hats and looking worried.

"Kings men," said one woman. "Livery of the Tower."

"Something's amiss."

With the horses and their riders disappearing into the distance, people stood a moment, staring, and discussing what might have happened.

They found out when they reached Alice's house where the great front doors stood wide. The baron, his bright red hat askew on his bright red head, came charging out, almost bumping into Alice.

He waved plump hands in the air. "No time. Have to go. Is my horse saddled? Where's the groom?"

"It would be nice to think," muttered Nathan, "that those Tower guards want to arrest the baron and he's trying to run away. But," and Nathan shook his head, "probably not."

Realising that his step-daughter was standing startled in front of him and at his own invitation, the baron managed a lopsided and unconvincing smile. "Ah, my dear girl, I have to rush. So sorry. But go in, my brother is there waiting to meet you and will present my proposition. He knows all the details. You can trust him entirely."

"I doubt it," said Alice loudly, stamping one beautifully shod foot in its new blue shoe.

"Start dinner without me," insisted the baron. "It's all ready. Edmund is waiting for you." His horse was being led up to the front door from the stables, led by a sulky groom, pulled away from his own dinner. The baron took the reins and struggled to raise one foot into the stirrup. He turned angrily to the groom. "Fool. Give me a hand up," and the groom reluctantly obliged. Once mounted the baron turned back to Alice, saying, "I see you brought your maggoty little friends even when I told you not to. They can't come in. I'm not giving them dinner. Tell them to wait in the kitchen. I shall be back as soon as I may." And with a sweaty wave, the baron clamped his large fat knees to the horse's rump and trotted off.

Alice and the others stood staring after him. It was the groom, scratching his head, who explained. "The Queen," he muttered.

"The queen has invited the baron to dinner?" asked Alice, disbelieving.

"Lord no," mumbled the groom, sidling back towards the stables and his dinner. "Poor lady's been sick for a week or more. Now dead, she is. A lovely gracious lady she was, tis a shame. Will be hard for his majesty. I reckon they were a good pair."

Nathan, who had no idea who the queen was, did not feel much interested, but clearly the others were moved. Alice gazed, mouth open, and told Nathan, "That's horrible news. Queen Anne was a wonderful queen and much loved in the country. Poor lady, she lost her only son last year. Now her. The king will be devastated."

John, making the most of his new shoes, kicked at the cobbles. "Rotten news," he complained. "Tis the good people what dies and the pig people what goes on living."

"Well, I won't die yet," said Alfie, catching up and leaning heavily on the hedge. "But tis good news if the baron ain't here."

"His brother is just as bad," Alice said. "But I'd better go in and face him."

CHAPTER TEN

E dmund Darling greeted his visitor with a delighted swaying of chins, stomach and hands. The news of the queen's death did not affect him since he had never met her and had no court position, but he was secretly pleased that his brother had been called away, and he could therefore make his own private declarations to his prospective bride.

"Ah, my dear young lady, this is such a pleasure." He bowed slightly, although it made his knees twinge, and it seemed absolutely absurd to bow to a raggedy female in a dirty old dress, no fur cape, and her hair in tangles.

Alice frowned and said nothing.

The dining table was set to impress. Goblets of shining pewter, platters of painted earthenware, spoons and knives of polished steel, and huge wooden trenchers of white bread rolls and piled marzipan candies. The tablecloth was spotless linen, and a dozen perfumed candles were lit in the chandelier above. Pages stood behind the two high chairs, and Alice sat, looking around her with suspicion. She recognised all the linen and cutlery, plates and grandeur, for each and every piece had once belonged to her father, and by rights now belonged to her. But she took a deep breath, saying, "It is extremely sad about her majesty. Now the whole court will go into mourning."

This was not what Edmund wished to talk about. He reached over and patted her hand, and Alice quickly took her hands from the table and tucked both neatly on her lap and out of sight. The steward Lacey open the doors from the kitchen and half a dozen young servers brought in the platters heaped with food. Perfumes of roast suckling pig and venison, pickled onions, custards and honeyed tarts filled the large dining hall. Alice had eaten pottage that morning, but after a couple of years eating next to nothing, this feast made her mouth water.

She permitted the boys to serve her, shook her head at the wine and accepted light cider instead, and, keeping her eyes firmly on her plate, began to eat.

Edmund Darling watched her in annoyance. "We have a lot to talk about, my dear lady," he said, mouth full of venison. "I'm delighted to see that you enjoy my choice of platters, but our discussion is the most important subject." She ignored him and he sighed. Meat juices dribbled as he spoke. "Come back here to live, and you shall eat like this every day of the year."

Looking up for the first time, Alice's eyes glittered. "Then I'd be as fat as you," she said.

Edmund spluttered, wine goblet to his lips. "Very humorous," he managed to say, quickly wiping his chin with his napkin. "But my offer is quite serious, my dear Alice. I have long – admired – and cared for you. From a distance of course. And because of your age, I felt it wrong to proclaim my ardent sentiments too quickly."

Alice giggled. "I think we should talk about the possible agreement, without pretending anything else," she said at once. "I know quite well that you don't care for me, Edmund, and you know that I really don't like you at all." She was now so full of marzipan and roast suckling pig that she could hardly move, so she sat a little forward and smiled. "But I realise that we can both benefit from a marriage, and I'm willing to think about it."

Immediately Edmund's chins waggled and he smiled widely. "Delightful, my dear, how honest. And how true. It's agreed then?"

"On several conditions," said Alice, "And I'm not willing to negotiate. It's all or nothing." She looked over her shoulder and waved away the page who was waiting to refill her platter. "Privacy first." And once all the servants, including the steward, had left, she continued. "This is my house, not the baron's," she said quietly, leaning forwards again. "And if we marry, then it will be yours too. And all my wealth and property. Yes, I know I'm an heiress, and I know you want my money. Well, we can share it, but only once your revolting brother has left and stopped being my guardian."

"Your mother made him your legal guardian before she died," Edmund grumbled. Not my fault, I should point out. And not something in my power to change."

"Oh, yes it is," Alice insisted. "Tell him I'll marry you only once he leaves this house, surrenders his guardianship, stops stealing my money, and leaves me free to marry you as I intend."

She was aware that a small nose under blond curls was pressed to the long window in front of her, and tried hard not to laugh. Edmund Darling had his back to the window, but she worried that he might look behind him. The little face at the window bobbed up and down, and suddenly stuck its tongue out with a smirk. Alice clamped her hand over her mouth.

Edmund was talking. "It's an attractive idea, but I doubt my brother would agree." He lowered his voice. "Lacey will be listening at the door, you know. Have to whisper." Which is what he did. "Have to discuss this with my brother. But pretty sure he won't agree."

"Tell him," said Alice very loudly, "That it's the only way I'll agree to marry you."

With a sneer, but still in a whisper, Edmund told her, "He can force you, you know. Not too hard, under the circumstances."

"Wrong." Alice lifted her chin and glared back at him. "I'm not as weak as you seem to think, and not as stupid either. And if you threaten me again, I shall walk out and go directly to the sheriff."

Sam and John were hovering beside the front doors to the house, peering in at the windows, while Alfie, Nathan and Peter stayed alert at the back where the doors to the kitchens were also firmly shut. The steward was certainly not permitting entrance to any of the dirty urchins his master had told him to chase away. But chasing away seemed impossible since there were five of them, all faster on their feet than Lacey. Besides, the steward knew very well that both the baron and his brother were trying to appear friendly to the Lady Alice.

Nathan, sitting on the back step with his head in his hands, elbows on his knees, was feeling gloomy. "Everybody thinks there was an evil omen and then the queen died. What's worse than that? But if something horrid happens to Alice, then it'll be my fault."

"It'll be that baron's fault." Alfie was sitting next to him, hunched over and trying to ease his back.

"If Alice isn't out to meet us by two o'clock, we should try and break in," suggested Nathan.

"And how do we know when it's two of the clock?" Peter asked. "There's no big clocks around here, not even sundials."

There was certainly nothing wrong with the sunshine now, and it spread a hazy golden light over the paths and hedges, bushes and trees at the back of the house, leading to the stable courtyard where some of the horses were snorting and kicking at the doors of their stalls, clearly restless. Presumably, all the grooms were having dinner, probably in the hayloft.

Alfie said, with a snort rather like the horses, "Bet Alice is having food fit fer a king. And I'm proper starving. I can smell that roast meat. I can just imagine them slices of pork and crunchy crackling."

"Bet the king's not eating food fit for a king," mumbled Peter. "Bet he's sobbing his heart out."

Had they heard what Edmund Darling was saying at that moment, they would have been considerably more worried.

Back in the lofty dining hall with its high beamed ceiling, Edmund was sitting at the table, his chair pushed back and his legs stretched out as his stomach swelled, belching and overflowing with venison and pork, leeks in cream and onions in butter, marzipan and jellies, flavoured custards and honey syrups. "Have to admit," he said, still keeping his voice extremely quiet, "my brother wanted me to keep you here today, you know. Was going to drag you and me straight into the chapel. Has a priest waiting. His own personal confessor, Father Michael, I expect you remember him. All ready to pronounce us wed. Has a special permission from the priest not to call the banns. With witnesses, being him and the priest. No secret wedding, but not what you might call a public ceremony."

Standing in a hurry, Alice scraped back her chair so fast, it tumbled over with a crash. Lacey, eavesdropping outside, was startled and got the hiccups. Furious, Alice said, "That's disgusting. How dare you."

"Him, not me," said Edmund complacently. "I'll not do it, don't worry. I don't want no prisoner for a wife. But I expect a proper promise from you, and one you'll keep."

"I've told you," Alice said, throwing down her napkin and walking towards the main doors. "Get your horrid brother out, and I'll agree to marry you. If you like I'll promise and I'll promise to keep my promise. But no baron! Not here, not anywhere close. I want no guardian and no Lacey either. He's nearly as bad as my step-father."

There was a slight bang from beyond the side door to the kitchens, as if someone had tripped over and Alice guessed who it was.

But she did not step to the kitchen door, she marched to the front. Opening the double front doors, the sunshine streamed in and both John Ten-Toes and Sam were waiting there, grinning. "Quick, round the back to get them others," John said. "Go call them, Sam. Then we can run home again afore more big black balls go messing up the sun."

"Run."

"No need to run," said Alice. "Edmund couldn't run as far as the privy. But I'm leaving at once."

The difference in comfort between the little empty cellar with its tiny central fire and one meagre pot of stew, no beds, no chairs and no table, and the contrasting grandeur of the Bishopsgate house, its cushions and carpets, huge fireplace and chandeliers, was too obvious to ignore. Alice flopped down on the bare floor and sighed.

She said, "It was lovely being in my old home again. It reminded me of my happy childhood. But I'm not sure it's going to work." She turned to Alfie. "And you were right, the baron planned on keeping me prisoner and dragging me to the little chapel to marry his brother against my will. Our old priest Michael had agreed, and if I ever get home safely, I shall tell him to leave and go back to his monastery."

"I expect the baron threatened him."

"Or bribed him."

"It doesn't matter," Alice said. "I'm lucky the baron had to gallop off to court to pay his respects and condolences to the king, and be dutiful like all the nobility. But I've agreed to marry that loathsome Edmund if he gets rid of the baron." She sighed again, looking down at her shoes. "Perhaps, if he does what I've asked, I should really do it."

"Never." Alfie shod up with a lurch, and then sank down again. "They'd plot together ta kill you, so they could have all the money and everything. Once he were yer husband, you'd really be in their power."

Looking very close to tears, Alice groaned and lay back flat on the concrete slabs. Mouse immediately cuddled up, purring.

"We need to talk everything over in detail," said Nathan, very determined. "We need to agree on what to do next. And clearly you can't ever go back to that house until we get rid of the baron."

There was a short pause, and then, "Aunt Margaret and Uncle Henry," said Alice, sitting up again and rubbing her eyes. "We'll have to go and see them. They have a little house away out in Hammersmith."

"Well, what a coincidence," smiled Nathan.

Cuddled against the heated wall, his pyjamas back as his soft striped pillow, and the blanket to his nose, Nathan dreamed of his grandmother, and little sister Poppy. Throughout the dreaming he was convinced that he was awake, thumping on a magical window, determined to tell his Granny that he was still alive.

He saw her in the bright cosy kitchen baking scones, light, fluffy and tinged with vanilla sugar, just the way he liked them. But Poppy, who was sitting beside the kitchen table watching, was telling her not to make so many.

"After all," sighed Poppy, "there's only two of us now."

Granny October shook her head. "He'll be back," she said. "Just you wait and see."

Poppy, slumped in her old pink fluffy dressing gown, brown and golden hair in a ponytail, said with dramatic exaggeration, "He's having an adventure. He'll never want to come back to boring old home. He'll never leave all the excitement."

"Then," his grandmother said calmly, not looking up from her rolling pin and flour covered fingers, "We shall have to start making adventures and excitement happen here too, shan't we. And then he'll come hurrying home."

"I want to come home anyway," yelled Nathan, thumping on the window and then kicking at the kitchen wall. "I miss you so much." But no one in the dream heard him.

He was, however, most disconcerted to discover that everyone in the cellar had heard him clearly. He had woken them all up while yelling his head off in the middle of the night. Alfie had thrown his new pillow at him. But Nathan had continued sleeping until sunup. He eventually opened his eyes to five glaring faces.

But after finishing off the last of the pottage, which Alice prepared for them all but did not eat herself having eaten more the day before than she had in a month previously, everyone sat around to plan the day.

"Hammersmith is too far to walk."

Well, Nathan certainly agreed with that. From close to the Tower of London and back to home, he would normally have taken a tube train, or perhaps a bus. But there was no chance of either here.

"I'll go and hire a horse and cart," said Alfie, scrambling up.

"I'll go," John said quickly.

"No." Alfie straightened his shoulders and walked to the doorway. "My back feels a bit better. I ain't no invalid and I don't want no fuss." His face was still swollen and discoloured with large darkening bruises, but one blackened eye was now fully open and, Alfie assured them, hurt less. Once he had climbed the steps outside, taking two large coins with him, the others, sharing the one comb, began to prepare themselves. There was water in a small barrel by the outer doorway which collected rain, and they used this for drinking and cooking, and also to briefly wash their hands and faces.

"My Aunt Margaret," Alice was explaining when Alfie came skipping back down the steps, jumping the last one to prove he was feeling well, "is rather shy. She is my mother's younger sister and we saw a lot of her when my father was alive. But when Mamma married the baron, he frightened everyone away."

The horse and cart was tethered outside and they already heard the wheezing of the horse. "A bit tired, I reckon," Alfie admitted. "But tis a good cart with space for all of us. No awning though so it better not rain."

"How long you paid fer?" asked John dubiously.

"Till sunset. Come look."

They eyed the horse as the horse eyed them. Slightly shaggy with a raggy black mane and a wispy tail, it was small for a sumpter horse, rather hungry looking, and bleary eyed. "Pimple." Alfie introduced the horse with a grin. "I hired the cart from a big fellow in Beer Lane. Says they used to carry the beer tubs and deliver all over the city. But now Pimple's too old and he don't like pulling anything too heavy." Alfie was patting Pimple's neck, and the horse narrowed its eyes in suspicion.

"Reckon it ain't used ta much affection," decided John.

"We shall buy nice fresh turnips and good hay," said Alice at once. "But with all of us in the cart we'll surely be as heavy as the beer."

They clambered, one by one, into the cart and tested Pimple's capacity to take them all the way to Hammersmith. Alfie sat on the front bench and took up the reins. Pimple sighed. Shook his mane, and set off with a slow clomping amble. Alfie shook the reins and muttered a few choice expressions aimed at the back of Pimple's head, but the horse adamantly refused to walk any faster. As for a gentle trot, clearly it was not going to happen.

First they headed towards the stalls in East Cheap where they stopped, much to Pimple's appreciation, and Alice hopped out of the cart and approached the first market stall selling root vegetables. She bought a basket full of turnips and went straight to the horse's head. Offering a turnip, Alice said, "How about a little bribery, Pimple? Two turnips first, and if you manage a nice little trot then I shall give you two more."

She barely had time to clamber back into the cart, grabbing John's hand to help her in, when Pimple, chewing merrily, set off again at a far more acceptable pace.

CHAPTER ELEVEN

The cart, wooden planks on small wooden wheels, bumped across the cobbles and bounced over the gutters. Everyone sitting in the back bounced too. First they made their way down to the river, as this would be the easiest path to Hammersmith which followed the Thames almost all the way with few deviations. They passed their old home in the warehouse, and Pimple, still slurping on turnip, decided to vary his diet and munched on the grass as they clomped along the sloping banks.

Lower Thames Street gradually led to the Ludgate, where Nathan had his first look at the ancient stone walls of the old city, and the huge gateway through which everyone had to pass when travelling west. It was a bottleneck, and crowds merged, pushing and shoving to get through. The gatekeeper shouted at some, and when a flock of squawking geese appeared coming in the opposite direction, he insisted they wait until Pimple and the cart had squeezed through the gateway first. The goose-boy, who was guiding the flock with a long stick, shouted out that he was in a hurry, but the gatekeeper ignored him. As Pimple trotted through, the goose-boy yelled, "Them birds keep pecking at me legs. I gotta get to market."

Nathan felt sorry for him, as his bare legs and feet under a dirty old shirt to his knees, were bruised. The geese flapped, complaining and hissing. Their large webbed feet were painted black with tar so they could walk long distances along the rough unpaved road to the market. Nathan shook his head. He decided he never wanted to eat roast goose as he felt sorry for the boy and the birds too.

The cart crossed a small bridge over the River Fleet and soon trundled along the grand road of the Strand. Here were enormous palaces and huge manor houses with large gardens full of trees and flowering bushes. Their high roofs were topped with a multitude of great brick chimneys puffing smoke, and liveried servants stood grand beside their front doors.

"Is that where the king lives?" whispered Nathan.

"Not likely," said John. "Don't you know nuffing, Nat? The Strand is where all them rich nobles live, and bishops and earls and stuff. Wealthy traders an 'all When I gets knighted as a hero, reckon I'll buy a house here too."

"That one." Peter pointed, first removing his thumb from his mouth. "I like that one." It was four storeys high and a hundred windows reflected the pale sunshine. Above the front door was a huge coat of arms.

Nathan said nothing. He just wanted his own home back in Hammersmith and was curious to see what the old village looked like, but it was taking a long time to get there. Although delighted with his turnips, slobbering with newly found happiness, Pimple was certainly not capable of a smart swift canter. The cart tipped, rolled and bumped to such an extent that Nathan felt bruised as he hung on tightly to the rackety wooden sides and wondered how on earth Alfie must feel since his bruises were already far more serious.

Westminster was at least partially familiar and Nathan recognised the Abbey, which had changed very little, and part of the old palace which he knew in modern times was now the home of government. But the old palace was only very slightly similar, and he asked, "The king? The court?"

"King Richard's palace," nodded Alice. "Poor man. He'll be missing his queen. He has other palaces too, but this is the principal one."

And then the countryside began to change entirely. Open fields, little muddy pathways, old farm houses and tiny scattered villages stretched around them. Sometimes they still glimpsed the river, winding and glittering in the sunbeams. Occasionally a little boat would row past but there was no busy river-traffic such as had been continuous in the city. Mid-March and many of the trees were only just budding new fluttering leaf, and there were spring bulbs growing from the scraggy grass along the roadsides.

Along the hedgerows, some folk had spread their washing to dry and sheets, tablecloths and shirts were lying, caught in place by the twigs and twists of the hedges. They flapped in the breezes but did not fly away. Beyond in the fields some farmers were mowing, spreading seed and raking away old clover, leading huge farm horses by their bridles.

"Look there," John Ten-Toes laughed, pointing, "you should be ashamed, Pimple. Look at them great big farm horses, going twice as fast as you."

Pimple ignored him with disdain and trotted on down the country lanes.

With no seats, and nothing except the wobbly sides to hang on to, the bare planked interior of the cart was extremely uncomfortable. Everyone bounced, rolled, lurched and rebounded over every rut and hole in the pathway, and there were many hundreds of those. By the time they reached the outskirts of Hammersmith, everyone was sore and aching but were delighted finally to have arrived at their destination. At a pretty cottage with a thatched roof, tiny windows and early bluebells by the door, Alice hopped down, saying, "Well here we are." She gave Pimple the last turnip, tethered him to the branch of a birch tree, and waved to everyone. "Come on, I'll see if Aunt Margaret and Uncle Henry are at home."

"Well, I certainly hope so," said Nathan, rubbing his backside, "after coming all this way."

But as she reached out to knock on the little door, there was a sudden peel of unexpected noise. Several voices were yelling with high pitched excitement and there was the vibration of pounding feet on the street of beaten earth. Scrambling and pushing, figures in the distance were running at each other and yelling. "Is it a fight? What's wrong?" asked Nathan, quite worried after the long peaceful drive where the only disturbance had been from a few squawking crows being mobbed by magpies protecting their nests.

Laughing, Alfie and John both pulled faces at each other, indicating that Nathan was being daft as usual.

"Football," said Alfie.

"Calcio, as some folk call it," said John.

"*Football?* In the *streets?*" asked Nathan, confused.

"Well, where else is they supposed to play it?" said Alfie with a slight snigger. "On the rooftops?"

The rules had definitely been quite different, thought Nathan, and soon decided that actually there had been no rules at all. As he watched from outside Aunt Margaret's little cottage, a hoard of young men and boys came hurtling down the street, cheerfully insulting each other, grabbing at arms, tripping up legs, and generally brawling to get at the ball. This was an inflated pig's bladder, covered in mud and wet grass, but was the desired aim of at least thirty players, who were each fighting for themselves, and not for any organised team.

With elbows stuck out to poke at anyone trying to pass, the men of all ages raced from street to street, eventually aiming for the village green. They crossed the little church courtyard, covered in worn grass and daisies, much to the annoyance of the priest, who hurried out from the church's shadows.

"Get off my holy grass," shouted the priest, his long robes swirling out behind him as he danced in fury. "And the queen dead too, and the country in mourning and you ungrateful fools desecrate other folk's graves. Shame on you. You should all be locked up until you apologise for your behaviour."

But in spite of the priest's rage, no one appeared to care or even notice, and ran on regardless. John and Sam started to run after them, excited and eager to join the game. Alfie clearly would have loved to do the same, but did not yet have the energy, and Peter, thumb back in his mouth, said he was too sore. Managing to get close enough to kick the ball, men laughed, whooped and called, yelling, "I got to it, I got a touch."

Then the whole crowd disappeared with gleeful shouts up into the centre of the village where the green, filled only on market day, lay ready for play. John and Sam ran with them, kicking out proudly with their new shoes.

When Nathan stopped watching, and turned back, he realised that a tall man supported by a wooden crutch was standing in the open doorway. Alice hurried forwards and flung her arms around the man's muscular chest, and smooth brocade doublet. "Uncle Henry. It's lovely to see you again after so many years."

"Good Lord," exclaimed the man, swaying slightly on his crutch. "My dear niece. It's an age, to be sure, but what has happened to you?" He was looking at her clothes.

Nathan nodded. "You go in and explain everything. Peter and I can wait outside until you've finished all the private stuff." He turned to Alfie. "You don't mind, do you?"

Alfie said, "I'm staying out here. I don't reckon on being in the way and shall sit on the doorstep."

At that moment, as Alice skipped happily inside the shadowed interior, John reappeared, hugging the large misshapen ball. Then he set it on the ground, turned, and with a mighty kick he sent it flying backwards into the following crowd, which whooped and cheered and went bustling to catch it.

Nathan stared in surprise at John. "I thought this was *foot*ball? That's feet, not hands."

Laughing and flopping down next to Alfie, John grinned up at Nathan. "Don't know much about football, do you, Nat? Reckon you don't know much about nuffing!"

Nathan sighed, then looked around. This was certainly not the Hammersmith he knew. The small village with its little lanes and pretty thatched cottages, was clustered around the large open green. It was larger and less defined than the modern green, and was filled with men running and laughing as the ball bounced and flew.

Only a few moments later, a small pink face appeared at the open door, and the woman smiled, beckoning. "All Alice's friends are welcome here," she said. "Do come in. I have warm Perry and oatcakes with honey. Come in by our little fire."

Inside the rooms were tiny, low ceilinged with whitewashed beams supporting the ceiling, and a little central fireplace on a stone slab. There was a cushioned settle and several stools, but no comfortable furniture, and no proper chimney. Nathan felt they were more comfortable in their dark cellar, and at least they weren't so squashed. As for the grand house in Bishopsgate, there was no comparison. He sat politely on one of the stools, and accepted the little cup of Perry, which he realised was cider made with pears instead of apples. Warmed and smelling of cloves, it was a very pleasant drink on a slightly frosty day.

Aunt Margaret and Uncle Henry sat together on the settle, and listened to the explanations as Alice, sitting in their midst, told all about the baron, the baron's brother, and the possible marriage arrangement.

"You cannot marry that man," murmured Aunt Margaret, quite horrified at the prospect. "Those brothers would take everything once you were in their power, and you might end up being locked in the attic."

"Or killed," sniffed Alfie.

"But," explained Nathan, "this is just a ruse to get the baron out of the house. Alice doesn't want to marry anyone."

Uncle Henry stood up, balancing on his crutch. "I shall go to the sheriff, and the mayor too," he announced. "In your dear Mamma's last testament, Alice, she never named your step-father as your guardian, you know. She stated your next of kin and closest living relative. And that is most certainly Margaret and myself. But on the parchment after that statement, where surely the name would have been spelled out, there was a huge ink blot. I was convinced at the time that this had been added afterwards by the lawyer in the baron's pay. I tried to claim guardianship at the time, but my poor dear Margaret was frightened off. The baron threatened us, you know. And because he was already living in the house, it would have been extremely difficult to get rid of him."

"Still is. That's the problem," Muttered John.

"We need people in authority on our side," said Alice at once.

"We needs them lawyers near St. Paul's," said Alfie, sitting eagerly forwards. "Them grand judges, and p'raps a bishop or two."

Jumping to her feet, Alice clapped her hands, delighted. "I'll come with you, Uncle Henry, and we'll go to every official in London."

It was exceedingly crowded, dark and smoky in the cottage and Nathan kept coughing as there was only a hole in the thatch and no proper chimney, so the fire spat all its smoke in a swirl. Each time anyone moved, it swirled again. Having finished his Perry, Nathan got up, apologised, said he needed a little fresh air, and hurried out of the front door to stand in the street and breathe deep.

Once outside, with the sky frostily blue above, Nathan patted Pimple who stood patiently and began to wander down the lane towards the green. The birds were singing, he heard the call of the cuckoo and the sweet twittering clicks of the courting starlings. Then something caught his eye down a side lane, he stopped and turned, expecting to see the continuing game of strange football. But it was not that at all.

Brewster Hazlett was sitting in the middle of the pathway, on what could only be described as a throne. His long thin black trousered legs were crossed, one bony knee sticking high into the sunshine. His arms rested on the chair arms, whilst his head, leaning back against the padded throne, was half in shadow from the tall top hat. The scrawny long fingers on both hands, nails like dark claws, grasped the golden balls of the chair arms, and as he gazed back at Nathan, his smile revealed a row of white pointed teeth.

"Well, Nathan," he said with a high pitched cackle, "how do you like my adventure?"

"Nat, not Nathan," said Nathan, glowering. Already he could smell the drifting, twisting stench of spiced magic. "And what do you want now. Taking me home, are you? Or just teasing, as usual? And where's your horrible twin brother?"

"What a lot of questions," grinned Brewster. "Let's start at the beginning, shall we? No, it's not time to go home yet, but it's adventure, not tease. And there's a lot to be done before you can go back to your Granny."

It seemed so ludicrous to see this peculiar man sitting in the middle of a village lane on a grand chair like a royal throne, that instead of asking anything more important, Nathan said, "Where did you get that silly chair? And where's the balloon?"

"The state throne of wizarding ranks, highest grade," Brewster announced with a rather proud lift of his pointed chin. "Known, in my world, as the Throne of Lashtang. A great honour, it is." Frowning slightly, he uncrossed his legs and stood. Nathan noticed that his little tight boots were golden leather, with bright red ribbons, although every other thing he wore was black.

"A throne?" Nathan stared, his voice challenging. "Thrones are for kings."

"Kings. Wizards, Those with great power." He was cackling again, each squeal of laughter finishing on a high squeak. "Look, look," he chortled, "see what those with power can do." And with a flick of one long fingernail and a twist of his wrist, Brewster pointed upwards.

The lane was narrow and only a slit of sky shone above. Now the slit opened, as though cracked like china. Jagged edges split away and through the break suddenly flooded a moving vision of ice tipped mountains. It was snowing over the peaks, and the glitter of falling snow crystals contrasted with the sunny blue sky over the village. Then the icy vision expanded, and Nathan could see a great ruined building, its stone walls crumbled and falling, its towers in collapse and its gateway blocked with broken stone, crushed pillars and the rubble of a ruined palace.

Once again twisting his wrist and clicking his long curled nails, Brewster smiled. With a crack and a gust of cold wind, the sky closed into its natural blue and pale sunbeams.

"Lashtang. A glimpse, a gift, and a reminder."

Nathan stood, open-mouthed. "Where is it? What is it? Is it truly in the sky?"

"My country, Bumble-Bee Head, not yours." Brewster peered, frowning, before his expression returned to its usual menacing laughter. "Now to more important matters," Brewster continued. "I have come to tell you that you must never speak to my brother. Never. On pain of death. Never open your mouth to Wagster under any conditions."

Blinking, Nathan couldn't think of anything to say. Brewster towered over him, the top hat slightly tilted, but the wizard's eyes brilliant and angry stared from the shadows of the dark brim. Finally Nathan said, "I don't want to talk to him. He's horrible. But I'm not sure I want to talk to you either."

Brewster cackled. "No choice, Nat, no choice, if you ever want to get home again. But I'm off to Lashtang, where you can't go."

The throne was beginning to fade. Its tall golden back and arms, padded in crimson velvet, were disappearing into the pale sunshine, and the wriggly golden legs and stubby feet were disappearing into the gravel of the lane below.

Worried that Brewster was about to fade too, Nathan called, "So when can I go home, then? I need to see my family again."

Brewster began to skip, kicking up dust from the gravel, his extremely skinny legs like a couple of black knitting needles. "This year, next year, sometime, never. Wait and see, Bumble-Bee Head, just wait and see,"

Angrily, Nathan called back, "So can you help with Alice and the baron?"

"That's what *you're* here to do," chortled Brewster, still dancing in a circle. The throne had quite gone, and now the man was starting to fade too.

"Don't go. Come back. Can you help?" yelled Nathan.

"Ask nicely and anything's possible," the wizard called from the mist that gradually surrounded him. His little golden boots were kicking higher and higher, his knees like spikes bent almost up to his chin. His dance twirled faster and faster, and he began to rise into the air.

"I'm asking as nicely as I can," Nathan called after him.

But Brewster was gone. Just a little breeze of swirling dust was left behind.

CHAPTER TWELVE

Back in their shadowed London cellar, the group sat with their backs against the heated wall, and everybody talked at the same time.

"Uncle Henry will see important people and fix everything."

"Bet there ain't no important folk will listen to a country bumpkin, when there's a mean-faced baron to listen to instead."

"Well no one's gonna listen to raggy dirty children, will they? Better an intelligent man, even if he hasn't a title."

"He's brother-in-law to a Lord. My Papa was a knight."

"And you's just an orphan without no proper clothes."

"Uncle Henry is clever. People will listen to him."

"Even if he ain't got two legs."

"That's a sign of courage," interrupted Alice. "He was a hero and fought for the last king at Tewksbury."

"And ought to be your proper guardian, 'stead o' that nasty pig-man the baron."

Alice turned to Nathan, who was sitting pale-faced and a little numb. "You're the only one saying nothing," she said. "Did you like my aunt and uncle?"

Nathan sat up with a jerk. "Of course. Lovely people." But he was thinking of Brewster Hazlett. "If your uncle can get a good lawyer and show that parchment with the ink blot that he was talking about, then I think we might get luck on our side again."

They had delivered Pimple and the cart back to the grumbling owner, and it was already late when they finally settled for sleep. The discovery that the baron's guardianship of Alice was not even legal, had shocked and excited everyone, but the solution was not so obvious. They all went to sleep puzzling out the situation, and only Mouse dozed off without difficulty and troubling dreams.

They were woken by the crash and clank of next door's furnace cranking up, the heave of the bellows and the hiss of the flames. They could hear the cheerful song of the smith as he began his daily work. He sang, and although the words were indecipherable from the other side of the thick wall, they could hear the voice and the rollicking tune.

Sore from all the travelling in the bouncing cart the day before, Nathan crawled from his blanket and rubbed his eyes. But Alice was already up and busy, gathering water from the barrel outside and washing her hands and face. The water was icy from the cold night air but this, she told the others, helped wake her up.

"As you know, I've arranged to meet Uncle Henry this morning," she said. "And I want Peter to come with me in case we need to get past any locked doors. Does anyone else want to come?"

"I will," said Alfie at once, pushing back his hair from his eyes. "I don't trust no one and I ain't gonna risk you getting caught by that pig man. After all, your uncle ain't gonna be running fast, is he?"

"Tis raining again," said Sam, watching the trickle of water come sliding down onto the floor. "Reckon I'll stay here and look after Mouse."

Nathan stood and stretched. He didn't really feel like going out in the rain, but he didn't want to stay in and just stare at a blank wall all day either. "Not sure," he admitted. "Maybe I'll just go for a walk and visit the market."

"Reckon I'll come wiv ya," said John. "Or you'll be lost soon as turn the corner, or picked up by one o' them angry cooks from the other day." He laughed. "Or go whizzing around in that balloon you was talking about."

"Well, take some money and buy some food and another larger cooking pot while you're out," Alice suggested, "and we can all meet up back here later on."

"If it keeps raining, I might buy a coat," decided Nathan.

"A cape," John corrected him.

Nathan could not imagine himself wearing a cape, but he didn't want to get soaked either. Meanwhile Alice was explaining her own plans. "Uncle Henry and me, we're going to visit the baron's solicitor. He may refuse to show us my mother's last Testament, but Peter may be able to get at it if I cause a diversion. If we can get it, then we'll take it straight to another lawyer, and try to prove that the baron isn't my guardian and shouldn't be living in my house."

"Humph. Good luck wiv all that," John snorted.

"I'll look after her," Alfie nodded. "Ain't no one gonna put her or her Uncle Henry in the Clink."

It wasn't long before Alice, Alfie and Peter hurried off, and Sam curled up in the warm bed with a sleepy purring Mouse. John turned to Nathan. "Ready, Nat?"

They wandered out into the rain. It was just a silvery drizzle but the daylight was hidden behind glowering clouds. New shoes clomping on the cobbles, keeping their feet nice and dry, Nathan and John hurried up the broken steps and into Bandy Alley, up to the end and then west towards East Cheap.

"All ten toes nice and dry and comfy?" grinned Nathan.

John sniggered. "Only bit o' me what is dry and comfy. This rain is chilly."

The market stalls were already crowded and it seemed that a little drizzle was not going to deter London's housewives from their shopping. Both shops and stall-keepers were shouting their wares and their prices. The bright striped awnings were flapping in the wind and dripping their collected rain in sudden bursts. One man, holding up a pair of bloodstained pliers and a short length of thin rope was calling for, "All you poor folks in pain, and fellows with yer teeth hanging out. I's the best tooth puller in London, I surely is. Come see me."

One man in a heavy hooded cape was holding the side of his jaw, clearly suffering, but he answered the tooth puller shouting, "You pulled the wrong tooth last time, Bert. I'll not risk it again."

"Will do it for free, and get the right tooth this time," offered the man, waving his bloody pincers. "Ain't no time fer being a coward."

Another stall was set up with an anvil, and a stone wheel that turned as the owner was sharpening knives, sparks flying. Rows of shining vegetables and fruit were shining, protected by the awnings, and one woman was selling hot pies. The fruit smelled fresh, the pies even better. There were painted wooden puppets for sale, whistles, little coloured drums, and another stall where a quiet man sat mending the strings of lutes. A small man in bright ribboned clothing was juggling with three wooden cups and a young girl was singing softly, sitting on the wet ground and collecting pennies in her lap from any kind passers-by. A large brown and cream duck, head high and proud, was leading her cluster of six tiny fluff-puff ducklings across the muddy ground, and Nathan hoped no one would grab them for dinner. A goat was being milked by an elderly woman hunched on a stool, with a wooden bucket at her feet. Then she ladled the milk into cups, and sold the contents to thirsty shoppers while the goat tried to eat the cabbages on sale at the next stall. The milk smelled sweet and rich and warm.

A clammer of shrieking and shouting echoed from the edge of the market street and Nathan looked up, curious. "What's all that? More football?"

John shook his head. "Probably a cockfight," he said, "or a dog fight."

"That's a horrible idea." Nathan stepped away.

John shrugged. "Good fer a wager," he said. "But it don't interest me."

They walked in the opposite direction, and Nathan stopped at a shop, its doors wide open behind the stalls. "Looks like they sell capes and stuff," pointed Nathan and he squeezed past the awnings and hurried in out of the rain.

It was warm inside, and an elderly man was serving a young woman, showing her a variety of different cloaks. "I will tailor one to suit, mistress," he told her. "To your measurements and your choice."

"I want it now," the young woman complained. "My hat is already horribly wet."

"Then if you care to wait just a moment while I serve these young gentlemen," said the tailor, smiling at Nathan and John, "then I will undertake to alter whichever cape you choose, mistress, to a suitable length." The little woman was very short, and clearly the capes already made and on view, were all too long for her.

Nathan knew he wasn't very tall either, but he asked, "Is there a short cape, with a hood, I can buy right away?" He pointed to a cape lying over the back of the counter. "But not too expensive," he added quickly. John was examining another much longer cloak with a luxurious fur lining, and Nathan hoped he didn't intend to steal anything.

"I do indeed," young man," the tailor smiled. "For your age, sir, about thirteen years, I presume? Yes, there are several young gentlemen's' styles already on show. Let me suggest –" and he held out a short blue broadcloth cape, hooded and lined in pale blue knitted wool. "Oiled and ironed, sir," continued the tailor, "to protect from the bitter ice and the strongest storms."

Without the slightest idea whether the price was fair or not, Nathan looked to John, but John had disappeared. Quickly Nathan paid the price asked, grabbed the cape and pulled it around him, flipped up the hood and ran out of the shop.

Gazing around, he saw no sign of John but after scurrying a few steps into the market, John came up behind him and startled him with a clap on the back of his shoulder. He was proudly wearing a fancy long cloak of scarlet with a patterned edge and a rich fur lining. Nathan gulped. "You nicked it?"

"Had to," said John without any sign of guilt. "Can't you tell it's a fancy female cloak? Tis fer Alice. Poor lass, she ain't never warm. This will suit her a treat." He pulled it off, laughing, and folded it up under his arm.

"I'm not sure it makes it any better if you steal for someone else," frowned Nathan. "But let's get moving before someone calls *stop thief* again."

They bought hot chicken pies and finally wandered back to Bandy

Alley, where they stopped at the ironmongers' on the opposite corner. Here Nathan examined the pots and platters on the long shelves with interest. Most were iron, although a small cluster of pewter cups were displayed on the top shelf. The ironmonger did not seem to recognise them as the ragamuffins from the cellar on the other side of the alley, and he cheerfully sold them two pots, one large, one small, and assured them that none of his work would ever leak.

Clattering their heavy pots together, Nathan, in his new cape, skipped back across the lane and its small central gutter, and John, hugging the stolen cloak, followed. But then both stopped for a quick pause, listening to the smith still singing deep in his shop as he poked up the furnace.

John was not much interested, and called, "Come on. These pies is going cold and will be soggy if they gets wet."

But Nathan was standing stock still outside the cellar steps. For the first time he could hear the words of the smith's song, and something definitely wasn't right. Over the roar of the furnace flames, the voice rose deep and strong. Nathan clamped his hand over his mouth to stifle the gasp, and almost dropped his pie and pots. This tune was slow, deep and sombre, but it was the words that made him gulp.

"Lashtang Tower, dark as night with no moon,
  Lashtang Palace, blazing with flame.
  One whispers soft the Hazlett name,
  The other roars. Both hide your tomb.

Come taste the flames, come taste the ice.
  Nightmare beckons, dreams of death.
  Enter. Now breathe your final breath.
  Peace at last, but Lashtang claims the price.

Nathan felt his heart stop, then he jumped down the steps with a stumble and a leap, rushed into the cellar and flopped down as far away from the hot brick wall as the space permitted. He stared open-mouthed and silently as John hung up the cloak he had stolen on an old nail sticking out of one corner wall, and sat to eat his pie. A second pie had been brought for Sam, who woke with a sniff and a mumbled thanks, and stuffed half the pie into his mouth, dripping gravy which Mouse began to lick directly from his chin.

But Nathan sat for some time before he ate. His brain was whirling and he did not know what to think. Eventually as John pushed the last crumbs into his mouth, Nathan asked, trying to sound casual, "Do you know a place called Lashtang? Is it an old story or a song or something?"

"Never heard of it." Shaking his head, John was only interested in sucking the gravy from his fingers.

"I like them stories of King Arthur and Lancelot," said Sam, offering Mouse a tiny piece of meat. "I like all the stories. Songs too. But I ain't never heard of Lam-Tangy."

"Lashtang. And Hazlett." Nathan could still hear the faint murmur of song from the smithy as it echoed through the wall.

"No." Sam curled back down, stroking Mouse. "That's not a story I know. It must be one of your funny future ones."

The rain stopped with a last slurp and just as Nathan had decided he must accept the inevitable, go outside, and face the smith to ask where the song came from and what he knew about the Hazlett twins, when Alice, Alfie and Peter came racing down the steps, flung open the little broken door, and danced into the cellar, beaming with success.

"We did it," shouted Alice, clapping her hands.

"We got the parchment," said Alfie, dancing too in spite of his bad back. Even the bruises on his face looked cheerful.

"I did it," Peter jumped up and down, pointing his new shoes. "I unpicked the lock where the old fraud keeps his secret papers."

"Now my uncle has the document," explained Alice, "and he's going to take it to a lawyer he knows. Mister Weeks, Uncle Henry says he's very good and very honest. It will take time and they'll have to take it to court, but I think it's all going to work out. I shall be free,' and Alice clapped her hands again.

"We just finished all our pies," apologised John.

"No matter. We had food at the Ordinary," said Alice, unable to stop dancing.

Nathan grinned and congratulated her, saying, "We'll put that horrible baron in prison yet, just wait and see." But it was the smithy next door he was thinking of, the Hazlett twins and the strange country of Lashtang.

CHAPTER THIRTEEN

Percival Weeks sat, straight backed at the small table, with a very creased piece of parchment spread in front of him.

Watching him from the other side of the table, the one-legged man, balancing on his wooden crutch, tapped the parchment with a firm fingertip. "There," he said.

The lawyer Weeks nodded. "Using some form of liquid bleach," he murmured, "urine, perhaps, I hope to remove the ink blot and discover what is written beneath."

Uncle Henry looked dubious. "But you might also remove the word underneath by mistake. I fear urine would be too strong," he said. "Is there no way of seeing through the inkblot?"

"Not as far as I know." The lawyer peered closely at the parchment for some minutes but then shook his head. "I have heard of a special glass made in Italy, which magnifies some things. It is a globe, filled with water, and looking through this enlarges the vision of what is seen. So exciting. There is, however, nothing so magical in England I believe. But I shall do my best. I intend to visit the Constable himself, and I also am well acquainted with one of London's most respected judges. You must accompany me, if you will, Mister Fallow."

Returning to the inn at the London end of the great Bridge, Uncle Henry settled in for the night. He had an appointment for the following afternoon with the Constable, and was practising exactly what he would say as he fell asleep, his bed warmed by a brick heated in the inn's downstairs fireplace, and his pillows fluffed up to muffle his satisfied snores.

It was not so far away to where Alice was excited both by the developments and her uncle's success so far, but also by the glorious red velvet cloak with its thick martin lining. She pulled the cloak over her shoulders and swirled, turning circles on the cellar floor, encouraging the velvet to billow out around her.

"I shall wear this to meet the lawyer and the judge tomorrow. I'll feel so grand. It will certainly help my confidence."

"You're not going to see the Constable too?" Nathan asked.

But she paused, shaking her head. "No. You see, he already has a warrant for my detainment on suspicion either as a thief, or the victim of an abduction. Silly, isn't it? But I can't risk being held in detention for a week or more."

Once again they were able to curl by the heated wall and sleep soundly, excited for the morning. This time Alice used her new cloak as her blanket, and gave her own blanket to Alfie.

Nathan had intended to go and face the smith next door, to ask him questions and keep asking until he understood the mystery. But it had not happened that way. Instead, listening avidly to Alice's explanations of the events that day with her uncle, Nathan had stayed where he was. Eventually he had heard the smith lock up, let his furnace sink to a low burning heat, put away his tools, and leave the building, plodding out into the damp shadows.

There had been no more singing.

Nathan had not dreamed, but it seemed that Alfie had. He woke the next morning as dawn rose over the city in a pastel pink promise behind the heavy clouds. Alice was up early as always, and as happy as the dawning sun. But Alfie woke with brick dust in his eyes and a frown more like the clouds than the dawn.

"I bin thinking," he said.

"Now that's a flaming miracle fer a start," John grinned.

But Alfie was not joking. "What if," he addressed Alice, "Yer Uncle Henry just wants yer money too?"

Alice turned at once, her frown as deep as Alfie's. "What are you suggesting? You think my uncle's a thief?"

"Well," interrupted Sam, still curled up with Mouse, "there's plenty of proper nice people what steals when they must."

But Alice was staring at Alfie. "That's very rude. You're talking about my uncle, who is just trying to help me."

"But he ain't a rich man," Alfie pointed out. "There's no poor man what don't dream o' having more coin. And I reckon he'd love to come and live in your big house, 'stead o' that teeny cottage miles away from the city. And if he's so good and honest, why did he leave you alone all them years, knowing you was in that pig-man's power, but didn't do nuffing to help?"

"If he wanted to steal my property," Alice said crossly, "he would have done something, wouldn't he! Knowing he was my real guardian, if he wanted to steal – well – he'd have gone straight to the Constable."

"Yet he weren't no help at all."

"Because Aunt Margaret was frightened. The baron threatened to have them both thrown in gaol if they interfered."

"And how does we know this lawyer is a good man too?" Alfie had started to march around the cellar, hands clenched at his sides.

"Because he's trying to find what's under the ink blot on the testament," Alice sighed, sitting down and slumping her shoulders. "Don't lose your temper, Alfie. Just come with me and you can see exactly what happens."

"Oh well." Alfie stopped, glared down at his feet and kicked his new pillow into the corner of the room, which seemed to relieve his anger. "Reckon I can watch and wait," he said, "but I'll protect you, and if yer uncle don't do the right thing, then watch out."

Alice stayed sitting where she was. "You're my best friend, Alfie. But don't go thinking everything is a risk. I've known Aunt Margaret ever since I was little and she was always so sweet when Papa was alive. He was usually off at court so I never saw that much of him, but Aunt Margaret often visited my mother, so I trust her now." She was cuddling her grand new cloak, and the fur lining tickled against her cheeks. "We'll go together to see Mister Weeks the lawyer, and you can wait outside when Uncle Henry and I talk to the judge. Then we can both wait together when Uncle sees the Constable." She nodded earnestly. "I'll tell you everything, I promise."

This appeared to please Alfie, who looked relieved. Nathan mumbled, "You have to trust some people sometimes, after all." But his own distrust of the smith next door had been troubling him all night. He knew he had to face the man sooner or later. He sat quietly, watching as Alice combed her hair and swung her cloak around her shoulders. Alfie then took the same comb and pulled it through his dark hair, which made Nathan smile. It was the very first time Nathan had ever seen Alfie make an attempt at looking respectable.

'Right," Alfie said. "We goes to meet yer uncle first at the inn. Then the lawyer to see if he done seen through that ink blot."

Alice nodded, then looked around at the others. "I'll be back later on to tell you all about what's happened," she said, excited and happy again while looking very ladylike in the expensive cloak. "There's enough money for all of you to buy food. Alfie and I might be late back." She stroked the velvet cloak. "This is gorgeous, but don't go stealing anymore please?" she pleaded. "If you get thrown in gaol, it will make everything so much harder."

"I'm staying here with Mouse," Sam said, still wrapped in his blanket. "She's got all fat and purrie, so she won't need to go hunting today. Her tummy's all full."

Peter pulled his thumb from his mouth with a plop. "And I'll be here in case you want to come and get me for unlocking anything."

Nathan was about to say he would be happy to stay in too, when John stood up with a grin and looked over at Nathan. "If this lot is off ta lawyers and such like, then reckon you and me, Nat, should go visit Pimple. I got mighty fond o' him. He can't work at them beer tubs no more, so's we could buy him. We got enough money if I talk that mean old codger into a good price."

Alice and Alfie were already bustling up the steps outside, and Nathan could hear Alice laughing so he guessed Alfie had cheered up. He looked back at John in surprise. "What on earth would we do with a horse? How would we feed it? Where would we put it? "

John frowned. "Buy hay. Tether Pimple outside like they do wiv goats. And ride a horse in ta market when we wants to, and not always walking."

"What's wrong with walking?"

Shrugging, John looked at Sam and Peter. "Dunno. I likes walking meself. But Alice is gonna have a fine house and shouldn't be walking everywhere. And them," nodding at Sam and Peter, "only has little legs."

"I'm not that little," Peter objected. "I'm ten."

"I think I'm ten too," added Sam. "But I might be eight. Or I might be ten. I could be anything at all."

'You're too little for ten. Reckon you're eight."

"Oh, come on then," sighed Nathan, not admitting that visiting Pimple would make a good excuse not to have to go and talk to the smith. "Let's go there and see what happens. At least we can think about it."

It was a slow morning wander, with both John and Nathan thinking more about Alice and the baron than they were about their own business. As the errand to see Pimple was certainly an excuse and a diversion for Nathan, so he was fairly sure it was serving exactly the same purpose for John, helping him not to think constantly of the threat and the danger.

They discovered Pimple, head down into a small scatter of old hay, standing in the yard outside the barn where the owner was loading two carts with great heavy barrels. Two other horses, bigger and smarter and certainly younger, were also waiting in the yard, munching on their hay, turnips and clover, ignoring their small and shabby companion.

Hearing John's voice, Pimple looked up. His eyes brightened and he trotted over to the fence, where a large turnip was waving temptingly. "Here, poor old Pimple," John called. "Look what I brought ya."

The horses and cart's owner trudged out from his barn, wiping his huge hands on his apron. "You want to hire my cart again?" he asked hopefully.

"Not today." Nathan shook his head. "We thought we'd visit Pimple. We like him."

"Aah." The man appeared disappointed. "Well, you won't be liking him for much longer. He goes down this evening when I close up."

"Down where?"

"Down the floosie," said the man, with obscure meaning and a tap to the side of his nose. Seeing the puzzled faces staring back, he added, "Horse meat."

John yelped. "You can't do that, Fred. E's a lovely old horse."

Yawning, Fred appeared unmoved. "I ain't feeding that useless plodder forever, now he can't work proper hours, but he'll make enough meat for a few pies. I'll skin the body and sell it to the big pie shop out by Cripplegate."

"They sell horse pies?" asked Nathan, horrified and wondering if any of the pies he'd eaten recently had been made of horses or dogs or cats."

"I'll buy im," said John suddenly. "But alive, with his bridle."

"Well," Fred scratched his head. "How much you got? You can't have the cart."

Nathan thought a moment. "Sixpence." He had not the slightest idea how much an old horse might be worth.

"More," Fred scowled. "That ain't half enough."

"One shilling."

John was patting Pimple's neck. "Them bullies wants ta cut yer poor little throat? Well, I shan't let em. Reckon you'll be happy living wiv us."

"I'm sure Alice and Alfie will be delighted." Nathan was quite sure they wouldn't at all.

"Two shillings," said the horse's owner. But John turned, pulling a furious face.

"Greed and cruelty," said John very loudly. "You should be giving that poor old thing fer free. He done worked fer you all his life and now you reckon on slitting his throat."

"Hush, keep your voice down. You'll upset the customers."

John raised his voice even louder. "You slaughter all yer animals, does you? You fill them beer kegs wiv blood, no doubt. Poor horses, chained and flogged."

"Alright." Fred shrugged, surrendering. "One shilling and sixpence, if you take the horse and leave quietly."

Led by his bridle and still slobbering on turnips, Pimple almost pranced his way along the two streets back to the cellar doorway.

Then everything happened at once and Nathan didn't' have time to think, didn't understand everything that was happening, and was so confused he nearly ran around in a circle.

First of all Sam, having heard the noises of hooves and John's voice, peered up from just inside the crooked cellar door, calling, "So pleased you're back. Quick. There's something wrong with Mouse. I think she's dying." Then he looked again. "And what's *that?*"

Pimple nudged John's arm with his nose, hoping for more turnip, but John was hurriedly tethering him outside.

"Our new horse," John said, jumping down the steps and disappearing into the shadows. "Now, what's wrong wiv Mouse?"

And as Nathan turned to follow John, the smith from next door wandered out, his bellows in his hands. He was a huge man, with shoulders as wide as any furnace. He looked searchingly at Nathan, said nothing and quickly turned back to his doorway. But he was singing.

Pausing at the top of the cellar steps, Nathan, one foot in the air, heard the first words of the song.

Over the horizon, to where the mountains soar,
Wander Lashtang snow and ice,
Explore the forests and the fields,
But see your world no more.

He nearly fell down the steps, heard his own heartbeat race, and turned back with a gasp.

And that was when he saw the fat man with bright red hair under his large pink hat, walking up the alley towards the Tower wall, talking cheerfully with three other men. It was the baron. Seemingly, chatting loudly, Baron Cambridge had not seen Nathan, but it was inevitable that he would, any moment. Unsure and dizzy, Nathan could not decide whether to rush down to hide in the cellar, or to run in the opposite direction. It took just one blink for him to realise that he could be seen leaping down the cellar steps, and then the baron and his friends would have all of them cornered. So Nathan took one very deep breath and began to run as fast as he could down the alley away from the baron.

"Hey, brat," the baron yelled. "I know you." Nathan kept running. "After that urchin," the baron urged his friends. "He attacked me, the wicked creature, and nearly killed me in my own kitchen. He's one of the felons that has kept poor Alice prisoner for more than a year. Catch him and I'll have him flogged." And then he raised his voice even louder, screeching, "Stop thief."

Feet pounding, up one lane and down another, rushing past intrigued shoppers who turned to stare, pushing them aside, with no time even to breathe. Nathan's hair was in his eyes but he couldn't stop to shove it away, and all he could hear were the footsteps of the baron and his friends coming closer. He felt sick but he didn't stop, and although it was a clear and frosty day, Nathan was sweating. He had never run so far nor so fast in his life before.

Very soon as Nathan rounded the corner towards the market stalls, he realised his mistake. As he ducked between the flap and flutter of the awnings, avoiding the fruit sellers and the baskets of the green and fragrant bunches of spiky rosemary, parsley, sweet thyme and sage outside some of the stalls, he also ran past a narrow doorway, tucked between a counter selling pots of treacle, and another with clusters of nettles and dandelions for a medicinal broth.

He did not recognise the little shop at first, but then he did as the shopkeeper came lurching from the doorway, pointing an accusing finger at him.

"There he is, rotten little thief," yelled the man. "He's wearing the cape I made."

Nathan stopped, mid-street. "But I paid what you asked for it," he said, extremely upset.

"But whilst I was serving you, your friend stole the most expensive cloak in my shop," shouted the man, furious.

"That wasn't me." Nathan whirled around, looking in all

directions, and saw many of the stall owners and shopkeepers converging. His knees began to shake.

"It was your friend," accused the tailor. "You bought a cheap cape so he could steal the best in the shop."

With a gulp and a groan, Nathan began to run again, this time backwards and away from the market street and the hoard of angry men striding towards him. "Hue and cry," he heard someone shout. "Stop thief." "Thieving brat." "Call someone in charge."

Now he was frightened. Everything was happening at once. Head down, Nathan hurtled onwards, he slipped and wobbled over the uneven cobbled lanes and skidded in the dips of the long central gutters, splashing in the dirty water flowing there.

Ridiculous visions flashed through his mind as he ran, of Pimple eating Mouse and Mouse yelping as she disappeared into Pimple's gaping mouth, Sam crying, and the smith next door dropping Pimple and a whole basket of turnips into his furnace while he sang of Lashtang and Brewster Hazlett.

Over the horizon, to where the mountains soar,
Wander Lashtang snow and ice,

And then, not watching where he was going, he hurtled headfirst into a large man's fat stomach, and the baron yelled, "Got you."

CHAPTER FOURTEEN

Podgy satin-clad arms grabbed him, sweaty hands groped for his neck, but Nathan kicked out, wriggled away and kept running. He felt considerable satisfaction when he knew his hard soled shoes connected with a hefty thump against the baron's woollen covered calf. The baron's three well-dressed friends stood back, unwilling to touch the grubby boy, or risk being kicked by his muddy shoes.

So, panting for breath, Nathan ran for the river. The baron roared, "Stop that boy. He's a felon, a thief and a vicious criminal."

The market crowd was far behind, but their calls of "Stop thief," echoed down the winding alleys.

The wobbling and breathless baron could not run as fast as Nathan. His woolly hose began to slip and soon were hanging baggy at the knees and his face was flushed scarlet. Dodging and twisting, Nathan fled into a darker passage between tall houses. He could hear the river traffic before he saw the water, and stumbled along the bank, falling to his knees in the scrubby grass. He was exhausted, but he couldn't stop now. He had aimed for the Thames with some hope of hiding in the old abandoned warehouse where the group used to live. But he quickly remembered that the baron knew all about that place now, and there would be no safe shadowed spot where he might hide in there after all.

He had a moment to stare down into the water and for one crazy half-second of absolute desperation, he considered jumping in. The water was sluggish at low tide, and the muck and dead fish lay swept up on the bank. It looked freezing and Nathan shivered, telling himself how stupid he was being to think of such a thing.

The little boats were plying their trade as usual. River taxis, thought Nathan, considering whether he could jump aboard one, and pay to cross over to the south side. But he realised that even rowing hard, no boat would be able to move as quickly as a man running. That made him look over to the great bustle of the Bridge, not too far away.

With no time to think, at once he started to run towards it. Nathan had never even set foot on the Bridge before, but he could see how crowded it was, and how filled with shops and just hoped he could get there and merge into the crowds before anyone saw him.

Gasping, wondering if his legs could keep up the speed, onto the roadway leading to the bridge's rise, with the sounds of the boats below, the thud of wooden planks bumping against each other, the splash of oars, and the slop of the gradually incoming tide, then the first hop onto the bridge itself and its cobbled street between shops – but then almost at once he saw the very last thing he would ever have expected to see. For just a moment Nathan stopped, and thought he would be sick.

Up beyond the rooftops where the shop owners lived over their businesses, where the chimneys were billowing their dirty smoke into the heavy grey clouds, was a distant shape of a balloon, sailing high, its bright colours winking out from the cloud cover, with the tiny silhouette of a top hatted man sitting, knees squashed up, in the basket below. Caught in the wind, the balloon swerved and then began to descend.

Something else was crammed into the basket, but the other shape was smaller. Nathan, gulping, was hoping beyond hope that it wasn't both brothers together coming to hurt him. He wouldn't mind escaping home right at that moment. Now that, he thought, would give the baron a shock, to see him snatched up and carried away in a magical balloon. But Nathan feared it would be something far less helpful.

The whole hovering contraption was still too high to see properly, and no one else on the Bridge seemed to see it at all. Even the swooping seagulls did not appear to see the great flying thing in their midst.

Shoppers were scurrying from open doorway to open doorway, chattering and laughing. "Look, Lizzie, this is the best milliner I know." 'Look at the fine bleached linen. I must buy that delightful veil." Also through the centre of the street folk were hurrying, trying to cross to the other side in both directions. There were angry collisions and raised voices., although everyone avoided those on horseback, who cantered past uninterrupted. Other folk were not so lucky. One man heading north led a small frightened lamb, and another heading south was accompanied by a large boarhound. The dog saw the lamb and strained on his rope leash, barking loudly while the lamb bleated. The hound's owner pulled his pet away, and both men were quickly separated by a group of black-gowned monks, pushing through the crowds.

None appeared to see the balloon, and yet it bobbed and bounced in the cold wind, whizzing lower, then blowing higher.

For that moment, the baron no longer worried him. The Hazlett twins seemed to be all that mattered. He stood quite still staring upwards. Several people pushed him out of the way, but he continued looking up. The second shape was no longer visible, but the eager wizard was unmistakable.

Nathan turned once. There, at the beginning of the Bridge, was the baron. Heaving, bent over with his hands to his knees and his head down, he seemed to be feeling even worse than Nathan. He was puffing and wheezing and clearly could not regain his breath and his crimson satin and shining ribbons were all limp and sweaty, and the baron's companions seemed to have deserted him.

Looking back, then up, then back again, Nathan shivered, not knowing what to do. The balloon worried him most but he could not entirely ignore the baron's determination. At least it seemed as though the tailor and the market folk had given up the chase and were no longer calling after him.

And then everything changed all over again.

The clouds darkened further until they were as black as night. They rolled over the city in sweeping waves, as though huge mountainous shapes were collecting and merging, and finally swooping downwards in jet black torrents. With a crack and then a roll of thunder, it then started to pour with rain. Like the opening of the skies, the rain pounded and roared, slashing down onto the water and all the boats, and pelting onto the crowds along the Bridge. Everyone screamed or shouted, pulled up their hoods over their fancy hats, and rushed into the chapel or the nearest shops. Others ran for the gateway to Southwark or back into London for cover.

Unsure where to go or what to do, Nathan stood where he was and within half a blink, was absolutely soaked. His new cape and shoes kept him dryer than otherwise, but his bumble-bee hair was drenched and dripped rivulets of water down his neck. But he was still staring upwards and the balloon was still there, buffeted by the storm, and looking behind him he saw the baron, still heaving and now as wet as the river.

With a determined step forwards, the baron attempted to close the gap between himself and Nathan but at the exact moment, a terrifying stab of white lightning arched and forked from the sky and cut, arrow sharp, towards the baron. With a horrified screech, he stumbled backwards, falling with another squeak straight into a wheeled barrow which had been left outside a shop when its owner had rushed in to escape from the storm. The baron could not extricate himself. Too fat to climb out and too exhausted to wriggle, he sat there staring, mouth open, plump legs swinging, as the barrow where he was wedged began to roll backwards.

Rumbling as it gathered speed, the barrow aimed straight for a gap between the shops, where the river could be seen. The lightning strike was followed quickly by a huge bellow of thunder, and the baron's yelps for help could not be heard.

Then the barrow, now whizzing backwards at top speed, bumped into the bridge's low wall, came to a hurtling halt, and the baron was thrown, feet over astonished head and flailing arms, straight into the river below. There was a very loud splash.

Nathan bit his lip, and looked up again. He could imagine the baron sinking under water and down into the river mud, and wanted to laugh. But everything was too serious. The balloon was descending. There was no one else on the bridge to watch, and even from the shop doorways, the blinding sleet would close off all visibility. Nathan waited.

Bump, bump. Onto the cobbles, the heavy basket, perfectly dry and without even a gleam of rainwater, landed with two tiny bounces, and settled on the cobbles. The tall skinny man grinned over the wicker edge, his black trousered knees tucked right up under his pointed chin. The top hat was, as usual, tipped a little askew by the windy descent. His long knobbly fingers and long curved fingernails were poking at something now unseen in the bottom of the basket.

"Well now, Bumble-Bee Head," cackled the wizard, his voice squeaking over the noise of the rain, even though the rain did not appear to touch the balloon. "Such a pleasure to see you again."

"Brewster or Wagster?" demanded Nathan, thinking that one would be bad news, but the other would be worse.

"We Hazletts," said the wizard, "are identical. But entirely different." The laugh was a squeaky snigger. "You must learn which is which. That is of extreme importance and you may live to regret mistakes."

The strong stink of magic spiralled through the wet air like sodden burned curry. "You're in the balloon," Nathan sighed, wiping rain from his eyes, "so I suppose you're Brewster."

"Wrong!" chortled the skinny man. "I am Wagster, and you must never, ever, under any circumstances, speak to Brewster again. It will be the worst for you if you do."

Nathan took a worried step back. "Don't threaten me. It's Brewster who's supposed to take me home soon, so I have to talk to him when he comes." Wagster was still grappling with something hidden down by his feet. "And what have you got there?" Nathan asked, puzzled.

"A gift," Wagster said, bending over into the basket. "A special present for you, young Nat. You will, I am sure, be overjoyed." And he cackled again.

Suddenly Nathan was positive that he wouldn't be overjoyed at all, and he feared it would be something horrible. He looked around, wondering if he should run, now that the baron had gone. But he knew the basket could overtake him, and he was exhausted. So he looked up, glaring at Wagster. "Have you done something horrible? Is it a trapped animal? Or a trapped person? Is it – Brewster?"

"My adorable twin?" the wizard giggled, high pitched, showing his long pointed teeth. "Would I ever hurt my dearest brother, or spoil his pretty face when he looks so exactly like me."

And he began to chant.

"The first and then another,
   Snap.
   Wagster and his brother,
   Snap.
   Snap comes the first cut, snap comes the second.
   But still more poison to discover,
   Snap.
   Choose the ice or choose the fire,
   Snap,
   One takes you lower, one spins you higher,
   Snap.
   Both burn, both - kill.
   And if one doesn't get you, then the other one will."

Then, with an abrupt flourish, Wagster hauled up the large bundle he was holding within the basket's depths, made two attempts to grab it more firmly, gave it a pinch and a wallop, and tossed it, writhing and wriggling, onto the bridge's hard cobbles. It slipped and slid a little, then came to rest. As Nathan stumbled backwards away from the thing, the basket started once again to rise. A small flame sprang from the base of the balloon, it gave a warning whoosh, as it streaked upwards. Wagster was waving. His hands, like thin sharpened knives, both flapped in the wind, and his squeaks of pleasure echoed down. Disappearing into the clouds, the balloon's colours faded and Wagster, basket, balloon, top hat and all, were gone.

The rain stopped.

One final echo of thunder and all was still. A vivid stripe of glowing rainbow rushed across the sky, as though in relief. The remaining rainwater trickled into the central gutter and oozed away. People began to peep out from shop doorways, wondering whether it was safe to go out, or whether the rain was only having a hiccup and would start again any minute. Untrusting, they muttered to each other and then moved back into the warmth, shaking their heads.

Nathan was alone, standing on the middle of London's great Bridge, staring down at the bundle thrown there. It had stopped moving, and was still, but there was something that troubled Nathan considerably, and something that he found strangely familiar. Even though the thing was wrapped in a mess of black ropes, cords, and rags, there was a flicker of hair at one end, and a glimmer of shoe at the other.

With growing horror, Nathan moved closer, bent down, and prodded. The parcel gave a tiny squeak. Then, with a gasp, he began to untie the bindings.

It took a very long time, for he had no knife and there were a hundred knots, all twisted and extremely tight. His fingers shook from tiredness and worry, and slipped from the water dripping from hair and chin. Yet it soon became obvious that a small person was imprisoned there, with the hands tied behind the body, and roped to the ankles. The eyes were shut and the mouth was gagged with a black rag wrapped several times around the head. The person was certainly breathing, though seemed, thought Nathan, half dead.

But Nathan, struggling without pause, now knew exactly who it was.

The rain still dripped from his hair and shoulders and he was kneeling in a puddle, yet he noticed none of this. Only undoing the bindings mattered now, and one by one, as the ropes fell apart, the small shuddering figure began to emerge. It was sometime before she was absolutely free, and it was even longer before she managed to speak at all.

She snuffled, crying uncontrollably, the tears rolling down her small round face, but Nathan put his arms around her and hugged her very close, whispering, "It's all right now. You're safe. I'll explain soon. It's all right now."

Not yet able to stand, she sat on the wet cobbles with Nathan beside her.

It was Poppy.

CHAPTER FIFTEEN

As sweeping wisps of coloured light tinging the puddles with reflections of the rainbow, Nathan's sister sat in a world that had existed more than five hundred years before her birth, and gazed around.

She said, "Is it a dream? It's a nightmare, isn't it?"

Feeling quite guilty, as if it was all his fault, Nathan mumbled, "Sorry. No. It's real. Haven't you missed me? Was Grannie worried? How long have I been gone?"

Poppy shook her head, her ponytail coming undone, and stared at Nathan as if he was quite mad. Which, naturally, he thought he was too. "Gone?" she asked, dazed. "Well, we didn't see you this morning, which surprised me because you don't usually rush off to school that quickly. You usually take ages and moan and pretend you're too tired to go." She smiled faintly. "But I saw you last night just before you went to bed."

"Crazy." Nathan began helping his sister up, supporting her as she stood uncertainly on the uneven cobbles. "I've been here for days. More than two weeks, I think, though I've lost track of time. And it was a balloon that brought me here, just like the one that brought you. Only a different wizard and he didn't tie me up. He offered an adventure and when my bedroom sort of started fading away, I said yes. Then he tipped me off here."

"And where's *here?*"

Nathan took a deep breath, knowing he wouldn't be believed. "London. In 1485." He waved one arm, adding, "And this is London Bridge. Changed a bit, hasn't it. Where we live in Hammersmith is just a pokey little village, and now I live in a cellar with four boys and a girl."

He was gazing at Poppy's clothes, just as she was staring at his. She whispered, as if she didn't have the courage to speak aloud. "You've got the strangest things on. You're not even wearing trousers. That tunic thing looks like a short dress and you're wearing woolly tights."

"They're called hose and all the men wear them." Nathan sighed. "Trousers don't seem to exist yet. I arrived wearing pyjamas, but I had to change that. And you're wearing school uniform. That's worse. All the women here wear skirts to the ground and they'll think you're really shocking wearing that little dress."

They stood together looking back over the Bridge to where old London stretched, glistening in the aftermath of the storm. Roofs still dripped water and every street was bright with the pale sun's reflections in a thousand puddles, and above, as the seagulls started to reappear, the rainbow still arched in dazzling colours.

"So how do I get home?"

"When the balloon comes back for us," Nathan said. "I don't know when. The wizard who brought you is called Wagster and he's horrible. His twin brother brought me, and that's Brewster but he's horrible too. One day, I think Brewster will come back for us."

Poppy nearly fell down again. "You mean it could be days and days? Weeks?" gasping, looking glassy-eyed. "Months? Years? For ever and ever?" Her shoulders slumped in dejection. "So what happens now?"

"I'll take you to our cellar," said Nathan. "And try and sort out some new clothes."

Dazed, Poppy followed Nathan, her school shoes thumping along beside him. At one point between the shops, Nathan peered over at the river, seeing the boats continuing their busy trade while baling out water. The tide was rising fast and the water churned around the bridge's pillars, but there was no sign of the baron. Hurrying back into Lower Thames Street, they passed an inn, noisy with custom. It was The Whistle and the Wherry, where a crowd of men were standing outside, pleased that the rain had stopped.

Then quite suddenly Nathan realised that amongst the cheerful crowd stood Alice, Alfie and Uncle Henry. He turned away and gulped, really not ready to face them yet. But clearly they had seen him and Alfie rushed over, the others behind him.

He was grinning. "Did you do that? Incredible! Genius."

With his head in a whirl, Nathan was even more puzzled than ever. "Did what?"

"The baron," said Alice with a beaming smile. "We saw it all. He went hurtling into the river with a yowl. When the rain started, we hurried inside, but hearing that scream, we looked outside again. I realised it was my vile step-father at once. He disappeared into the water but we saw lots of bubbles."

"Did he drown?" asked Nathan hopefully.

But Alfie shook his head. "Wish he had. But them boatmen pulled him out. Brought the pig-man ashore and he sat on the bank pulling faces and heaving and coughing up water. A few people came over to see if he was alright. Not us. Watched from the window, wiv big smiles, we did. Then at last he just staggered off hugging his fat belly. Reckon he'll be rotten sick. That river water ain't clean. Did you push him in?"

Although speaking to Nathan, Alfie's eyes had wandered to Poppy, standing shyly in Nathan's shadow. Ignoring this, Nathan said quickly. "Well yes, that was me, sort of. The baron was chasing me, calling me names after what I did to him in the kitchen. He deserves to drown after what he did to you."

"He'll be in the Tower when we done finished," Alfie assured Nathan. "But fer now, reckon he's had a mighty good lesson. Dumped in the river, wiv all them fancy clothes ruined. Came out in a proper mess, he did, one shoe lost and his silly hat gone. Wish them fish had eaten him." He snorted. "Wish I coulda' gone and pushed him in again. You done well, Nat."

Alice clapped her hands, "Oh marvellous, Nat. Look, Uncle Henry," looking back at the smiling man, "see how great my friends are."

There was a silent pause as everyone became more aware of Poppy and she blushed, saying with an embarrassed squeak, "I'm Nathan's sister."

"This is Poppy," sighed Nathan. "She's from the future too. My little sister, Poppy Bannister."

Alice blinked. "I think," she said at last, "we should find you some new clothes, Poppy. This is all very peculiar."

"This is her school uniform," nodded Nathan. "Like a sort of livery."

"It's more like being naked," frowned Alice. "She' showing her legs and too much of her arms too. Very odd. If she walks around like that, she'll be arrested."

"I reckon," grinned Alfie, "we better get back to the cellar. Then we can tell you what happened today – and you can tell us."

With much interested attention from the crowd outside the inn, they said goodbye to Uncle Henry who hurried back inside for a strong beer after the day's many appointments, and Alfie, skipping ahead, led the long winding way back to Bandy Alley. He seemed surprisingly buoyant for someone recently so badly injured, and Nathan presumed the day must have gone well for him. In the meantime, Nathan was not at all sure what he was going to do about Poppy.

Bandy Alley was as alight with reflections as all the other streets, but here it seemed as though the rainbow arched directly overhead. Nathan felt as though he was walking under a brightly coloured doorway, and straight into another adventure. Pimple, shaggy hair still wet, was standing at some distance, his tether at full stretch. He was blissfully asleep on his feet, eyes closed, lashes drooping, as his mane dripped rainwater.

Not expecting Pimple's appearance, neither Alfie nor Alice seemed to notice him, and made straight for the cellar.

It was outside the cellar steps that the smith was standing, holding up a shining axe to the bright sky. He nodded when he saw Alfie, Alice and Nathan approach. Nathan stared at the axe, with its clear silver metal and gleaming sharp edge. It reflected the rainbow as well, as though polished in glitter.

"Pretty thing, ain't it?" smiled the smith proudly. "My own work. Best in the city. Swords, axes, and armour fit for a king. I specialise. You ever need a good knife, you come to me." He winked suddenly, emphasising the word 'knife' "You need a knife, boy? I have one just right for you."

Nathan hesitated. He had to get Poppy undercover, but he said quickly, "You were singing yesterday. You sing about a strange place. Lashtang. What is it?"

"Just a song." The smith frowned.

"And the Hazlett brothers. You sang about them too."

The smith's frown deepened. "'Tis a long story. Come back another day, lad," he said. "I'm busy now. But one day just come over for a talk and I'll tell you some things you'd be better off not knowing."

"But I need to know." One foot on the top step, Nathan turned, nodding. "It's important," he said.

"Then come talk," repeated the smith. "Ask for me. My name's William. Will to my friends. But most folk call me Grandpa October."

Nathan almost fell down the steps, and felt himself choke. Behind him, Alice hissed, "Hurry up, Nat. We need to get inside and sort out what to do next."

With a hop and a jump everyone burst into the cellar, avoided the huge puddle which had trickled down the steps in the rain, and pulled off their capes.

Sam and Peter, both curled in the far corner, looked up, and Sam whispered, "Hush." Peter did not remove his thumb from his mouth, but was looking tired.

"Oh gracious, yes," Nathan remembered with a jolt, "Mouse. How is she? You said she was dying."

Everyone quickly crowded around the shadowed corner, where Sam and Peter sat protectively. Peering into the semi-darkness, they saw a muddle of shapes squashed up on Alfie's pillow, which he had kicked there that morning. Mouse, her distinct patterns of grey, black and white like a maze as she lay complacent, was sheltering three little balls of scrawny fur, each attached to her teats as they fed and snuffled. One was white, one was black and one was grey.

Peter removed his thumb, and whispered, "She was doing strange things and making funny noises. Then out popped a baby. Then another. And then the third. First we were worried for her. Then we got very excited."

"She's had babies," said Sam in whispered delight. "Now we got four cats."

Poppy, immediately transfixed, knelt down and stroked each kitten with a careful finger. Mouse did not seem to object, and purred loudly. The kittens quivered and continued sucking. Her hair in her eyes, Poppy kneeled lower and bent to kiss Mouse on her little moist black nose.

It was John, marching in from outside, who stuttered, "Who's *that?*" He pointed at Poppy. "I just bin to feed Pimple," he said, "and I comes back to find some undressed female kissing our cat."

"It is," smiled Alice, sitting on her folded blanket, hands clasped in her lap, "time for an explanation."

So Nathan began. With Poppy sitting uncomfortably, a little frightened and very timid beside him, he said, "You all know I said I come from the future. I live with my grandmother and my sister in a big house in Hammersmith, and it's the year 2017 and London is completely different. *Everything's* completely different. I was brought by a wizard called Brewster Hazlett, who never explained a single thing. He just picked me up in a flying balloon, brought me here, and tipped me out."

Poppy shivered. "And that's what happened to me too. Except it was Wagster Hazlett who is another wizard, and he tied me up and wouldn't let me go until he tossed me out on London Bridge. He was mean. And thank heavens Nat was there, or I think I would have died."

"*Two* wizards?"

"They're twin brothers," said Nathan. "And it was hard enough for me to understand when I found myself in the past, but now my little sister is here too and it must be so peculiar and frightening for her, and I can barely look after myself but I'll have to look after her too."

"Reckon we'll all look after her," said John, smiling down. "Tis saving you wizard-loving Bannisters is what I likes most. Bring 'em on, the more, the prettier."

"Oh, indeed we will help look after your sister," Alice assured both Poppy and Nathan. "And as for looking after yourself, Nathan, you're a real hero. Saving Alfie when the baron had him locked up –"

"Well, just helping."

"– and getting all that money, and now pushing the baron off the bridge. I loved seeing that."

"We all did." Alfie grinned at John. "You don't know what you missed."

Poppy, still uncomfortable, was at least now looking intrigued.

"Poppy," Nathan said as an introduction, and pointed at each member of the group, giving their names. "Sam. Peter. John Ten-Toes. Alfie. And Alice. Alice is the eldest." He looked around. "And Poppy is only ten."

"I'm ten," said Sam. "Or I might be nine. I could be eleven. Suppose I could be eight."

"So now we got another girl in our gang," said Alfie.

"And three kittens," smiled Sam.

"And an 'orse," added John.

"And we had a good day with Uncle Henry," nodded Alice, "and the Constable and the judge and Mister Percival Weeks the lawyer, and I'll tell you all about that after supper. But now I'm starving." She nodded to Poppy. "You must be hungry too."

"No thank you." Poppy shook her tangled yellow and brown curls. "Granny October made me a good breakfast before I set off to school, and it was after that when the horrible wizard snatched me into his balloon."

"Still don't know what a balloon is," muttered Alfie to himself.

But it was Granny October Nathan was thinking about, for it had reminded him that the strange singing smith next door had called himself Grandpa October. Which didn't make any sense at all.

On a tiny fire of collected twigs, Alice began cooking pottage, watched with both interest and suspicion by Poppy, sitting close. Poppy looked closer and recoiled. "Cabbage stew?" Trying to look polite, "I'm really not hungry." Then, as an afterthought, she reached into one of the large pockets in her school blazer, and pulled out a sticky and partially melted bar of chocolate. "Anyone want a piece of Mars Bar?" she asked, looking around.

Six pairs of eyes stared back at her. Even Mouse looked up.

"They don't know anything about chocolate," Nathan grinned. "It hasn't been discovered yet."

Alfie's face told the story. "Future food?" he asked, as if sure he was being offered poison. "Better not. I ain't got a future stomach."

"Just taste a tiny bit," Nathan suggested, laughing.

John reached out. "Try anyfing once," he nodded. "But it looks funny and 'tis wrapped in weird stuff."

"Just shiny paper." Poppy handed a broken slice to John and watched with interest as he popped it in his mouth. "But you should have taken the paper off first."

He spat the crumpled paper out, but held it in his palm as if precious as he sucked slowly on the sliver of Mars Bar. "It's – gorgeous," he managed to say. "Like honey only better. And reckon that paper don't taste good but it looks proper gorgeous too."

Alfie sniffed the small piece he had been given. "Smells good."

"It's – wonderful," mumbled Peter, thumb out and chocolate in. "Best I ever ate in me life."

"Shall I give some to Mouse?" asked Sam, sucking on his own little square piece.

"Not good for cats," Nathan shook his head. "But very, very good for people."

"Where can we buy it," Alice was excited, eyes bright as she swallowed her last little bit.

"Sorry." Poppy gave the remaining sliver to Nathan. "Tesco. A sweet shop. But nowhere in 1485, I don't think."

Finally trusting the melting corner in his hand, Alfie shoved it in his mouth, and closed his eyes in bliss. "Magic."

"Well, it is, isn't it," said Alice eagerly. "I have to admit I never really found it easy to believe the story about coming from the future, and all these balloon things and so on. But now I believe it, and it has to be magic, doesn't it. And ever since you arrived here, Nat, life has changed. It is *so* much better." She licked her lips with pleasure., leaned over and took Poppy's hand in hers. "Your brother is amazing. And so are you. Now my uncle is involved in my problems and he is helping so much. The Constable has promised to look into the matter, the judge says he is sure we have been badly treated by the baron, and our lawyer thinks he has scraped off enough of the ink blot to see my aunt's name underneath. It is all so exciting. My life has changed ever since Nat came to stay. We even have money for food and shoes and capes and pillows."

"And a horse ta take us ta market," added John.

"And kittens," said Sam.

Nathan sniggered slightly. "I don't think the kittens have much to do with me," he laughed.

"But it's all happening now," said John. "Wiv that pig-baron in the river and now this! Bars Mar."

"Mars Bar."

"Heaven. Magic."

"Which reminds me," said Nathan. "Does anyone know anything about the smith next door?"

But no one knew anything at all. Only that his furnace kept them all comfortably warm.

CHAPTER SIXTEEN

They stayed up late, curling against the heated wall, but still murmuring to each other, too excited to sleep at once. Alice had given Poppy her thick new cloak, fur up, folded on the ground for a mattress. But even with this, Nathan's sister found it hard and wretchedly uncomfortable. She had never had to sleep on the floor before, and although she squeezed her eyes tight shut, both fear and discomfort kept her awake.

"He says it can be proved beyond doubt. He says he can prove it. He says he won't charge me until I have my home back, with my aunt and uncle as guardians," Alice murmured.

"Percival Weeks," mumbled Alfie. "Lawyer. Silly name. But reckon he's alright."

Half muffled under his blanket, John said, "So you trust this uncle fellow now, Alf?"

Alfie paused. The silence echoed. Then he muttered, "S'pose so. But I ain't sure o' nuffing. Reckon I won't be sure till Alice is back in that grand house."

Mouse, one kitten at a time held by the scruff of its neck, brought her babies to snuggle up next to Alice. Repeated squeaks and purrs were reassuring through the darkening shadows.

"I expect the baron will fight back," sighed Nathan. "He won't just accept what the lawyer says."

"There's the judge and the Constable too," Alice reminded him as she cuddled all the balls of dappled fur.

Poppy had little idea what they were talking about, but on the following morning, Nathan explained in greater detail. Horrified at the idea of being forced to marry a cruel and fat old man when she was only thirteen years old, Poppy immediately felt particular sympathy for Alice, but all she really wanted to do was go home again.

Sitting on the top step leading into the cellar, with the wind whistling down the back of their necks and Pimple having an occasional chomp on their dishevelled hair, Nathan spoke quietly to Poppy. "This is serious," he said. "If we want to do anything to help get ourselves out of here, then you have to remember everything. What did Granny October say this morning before you left for school?" Poppy bit her lip, trying to remember. "She can't just have ignored it all," insisted Nathan. "She gets up early. If I wasn't there, she must have been surprised."

"No." Poppy studied her shoes, sturdy school fashion. "I sort of rolled out of bed as usual and went downstairs in my nightie and Granny was already at the table reading the newspaper. My plate was on the table with scrambled egg and toast all steaming."

"Only one plate? Nothing prepared for me?"

She suddenly realised the relevance. "Nothing put out for you. Not even a bit of toast. So I asked Granny where you were. Gone to school already, she told me." Poppy stared up at Nathan. "Now that must have been a lie."

"Granny doesn't lie."

"Pooh. Everyone lies."

"Not Granny."

"She just did." Poppy shook her head. "Maybe she went in your bedroom and found the bed empty, and guessed you'd gone to school."

"With my pyjamas gone, and my school stuff still around the room? Did she think I'd gone to school in my pyjamas?"

"Well you came here in them," and Poppy sniggered.

"So Granny lied. I wonder, does she know about Lashtang?"

"Now you're talking rubbish again, Nat," Poppy complained. "What on earth is Lashtang?"

"Probably not on earth," Nathan sighed, "and that's the whole point."

The smith had not arrived to open the shop next door. Impatient, Nathan waited outside while Poppy went in to cuddle the kittens. It was already way past the time most shops opened. Confused, he wandered up and down Bandy Alley.

Alice and Alfie had once again met up with Uncle Henry for a final day of discussion, and a last talk with the lawyer. There would be plenty more to be done before the situation was ready to go to court, but for that they would have to wait. John, Sam and Peter remained in the cellar, sleepy after the late night. John was muttering in his sleep with incomprehensible words such as, "*Similty,*" and "*Go'way plonkfish.*" Sam was back with Mouse and the kittens, and Peter was examining his crinkled scrap of Mars Bar paper, wondering how it got so shiny and patterned."

Poppy, admiring Mouse, looked over. "It says *Ba,* cos that's the bit of Mars Bar I broke off," she explained.

"I can't read," Peter looked up, smiling. "But you go to a real school. That's mighty special. Did you get taught to read there?"

"Well yes, years ago," nodded Poppy. "I could teach you some letters if you like."

But Peter pulled a face. "No use to me here. Nothing to read anyways, 'cept your bits of funny paper." He ironed the scrap with his wet thumb. "Was it ever so expensive?"

"Not really."

John said, "Wiggish hollik."

Peter said, "But paper is much too expensive just for wrapping things. Comes all the way from Italy, and it's mighty rare. Even parchment is expensive."

Poppy sat down with a plop. "That's weird." She didn't have the beautiful cloak to sit on anymore as Alice was wearing it, but she was getting used to the hard ground. "Wish I could go back to my house for a day or something, and collect paper and clothes and chocolate and stuff, and bring it all back for you. But then I'd want to go straight back to Granny's again. It's much, much nicer. I think living in a cellar is dark and horrid and boring."

Peter looked quite hurt. "I'm happy here. It's warm and secret. I like it."

"Pooh," Poppy exclaimed. "Wait till you go and live in Alice's house. It sounds big and grand and comfy."

At that same grand house in Bishopsgate, the baron and his brother glared at each other over the huge dining table.

"The brats have brought some fool lawyer into the business, and a judge too, by the sound of things. This blasted lawyer came to visit me this morning, officious little idiot. Now you're going to have to marry the Alice girl quick and smart. No time to wait."

"You don't tell me what to do," objected Edmund. "I started to negotiate with the young lady, and I believe she'll comply willingly. I'm prepared to wait."

"No, you're not," roared the Baron, refusing to be contradicted. "Tried to fool you, did she? Probably said she'd wed you if you got rid of me. Oh yes, I know you, Ned. Bribed you, did she? Well, you're a fool to believe any of it. She'd run out on you at the church porch just as soon as I was gone."

Edmund blushed since this was exactly what he and Alice had arranged. "Said she'd be happy to marry me."

"Lying brat."

With exaggerated shock, Edmund said, "She's the daughter of a lord. I'm quite sure she wouldn't lie."

"Nonsense," retorted the baron. "Everybody lies. *I am* a lord, and I lie. You're an idiot and *you* lie too. You've been lying now, to cover up the plan you've had with that lying child."

"What did the lawyer say?" demanded Edmund, hurriedly changing the subject. "And I hope you sent him packing."

"Humph," snorted the baron, settling back in his chair. "Of course not, fool. I was exceedingly polite, gave him good wine and pretended that all I hoped for was the truth to be discovered."

"So you lied." Edmund smiled into his wine cup.

"Naturally." The baron clasped his hands over the extensive rise of his stomach. "They've discovered my wife's last testament, though I've no idea how. I shall make my own lawyer pay for that, since it was supposed to be kept under lock and key. And this new lawyer has seen there's an ink blot over the name of the proposed guardian. He believes the blot covers that idiot Margaret's name, and her husband Henry, who are Alice's next of kin."

"We know that."

"Of course we do," glared the baron. "But we don't want it brought into court. I'd be thrown out without a penny. And you, dear brother," his glare turned to a sarcastic smile, "would have even less. You might even have to go and get a paid job. I can just imagine you cleaning the privy."

"No judge would uphold a decision against you, Hugh." Edmund's face was flushed bright red. "You've bribed or threatened every judge in London."

Sighing, the baron slumped down, shoulders hunched. "It could happen, Ned. There's new court rulings under this blasted king Richard, and new judges with absurd ambitions to do the honest thing. As if the country needs honest judges. We could end up in no end of trouble with such an absurd idea."

Edmund's scarlet cheeks suddenly turned white. "You mean we might actually lose."

"I mean we find the silly girl as soon as possible, force her into the chapel with my priest to stand witness, and marry her."

"She'll squeal."

"I don't care," said the baron. "With a priest and a baron as witness, including her legal guardian, no one would question it. Then we keep her quiet for a year or so until the scandal dies down, and we kill her off."

Edmund smiled widely. "Good," he said, the colour reappearing in his cheeks. "So I don't have to put up with her forever. I can find someone as a second wife. Someone I like. Nice and pretty and plump."

"And rich."

"Of course, Hugh. You and I will live comfortably and wealthy for the rest of our lives."

The baron stood suddenly, tossed aside the skirts of his satin coat, and stomped to the door to call for a page, more wine, and some quince tart, which was his favourite. "But," he said, "we have to find the brat first. She and her urchin friends were living in a warehouse down by the river, but they moved. I've no idea where they live now. But I want her, and I want that nasty brat of a boy too."

"The one who pushed you in the river?" Edmund tried to hide his smile, but the snigger burst through, and the baron eyed him with a grimace.

"Yes. Him," said the baron through gritted teeth. "I'm going to abduct that loathsome boy, tie him in the dungeons, and thrash him till he begs for mercy. But he'll get no mercy from me."

"I shall come and watch," offered Edmund. "Most diverting. And I shall beat Alice too, but not until I have her safely as wife. Then I can do what I want."

'So we spend the next week searching for this wretched female. There's no time to wait."

Edmund stood with a smug smile, his thumbs tucked into his belt. "Well now, dear brother. Not as clever as you think you are, are you! Let me tell you exactly how we catch her, and no need to wait a week. You know this lawyer she's visiting? You know his name and where his chambers are? Well – that's where we go. Alice will visit there often, I imagine, and we'll be waiting just around the corner."

"With a sack to throw over her head."

"And a horse and cart to bundle her off and out of sight."

In Bandy Alley, the smith had finally turned up. Nathan was still waiting, and immediately hurried over. He did not live above his business, but arrived marching through the long shadows, appearing from the Tower end. Since the alley was remarkably narrow, it was almost constantly in shade from the rooftops on either side, but Pimple had managed to find one small angle of sunshine, and was standing, pulling on his tether, outside the smithy.

Grandpa Octobr, smiled at the ramshackle horse, and patted its neck. "Well now," he said, looking over to Nathan, "reckon you both have questions for me, then?

Nathan was much too intrigued to laugh. "It's urgent," he said, half under his breath in case of arriving customers. I really need to know about the Hazlett twins and Lashtang. And about your name too."

"Now that, laughed the smith, "is no secret. My name is William October. My Pa was William October and his Pa was William October. But now I've a parcel of little grandchildren, and they call me Grandpa October, so everybody else has copied it. What's so mysterious about that?"

He strode into the shop, flinging wide the doors and heaving up his enormous wood and leather bellows, while Nathan stood back, watching. The explanation of the name seemed a little disappointing, but Nathan was sure there was something missing. October was not a common second name, but he wondered if it could have passed down over the centuries in just this one family. That would mean that the smith was his own great, great, great, great grandfather, with a lot more greats thrown into the title. But it didn't quite fit. Nathan scratched his head as his sun-streaked hair fell into his eyes.

He said, quite suddenly, "I live with my grandma. She's called Grandma October."

The smith turned, squinting in the smoke of his furnace. "Fancy that," he said, rather softly. "Maybe we're related." But he winked, and Nathan knew something more was being kept secret.

"Alright then," he said, "what about Lashtang?"

And once again the smith began to sing. His voice was deep, and the tune he sang was slow and mournful. As he listened, Nathan felt dejected, as if the song made him miserable.

"Over the horizon, to where the mountains soar,
Wander Lashtang snow and ice,
Explore the forests and the fields,
But see your world no more.

Over the horizon to where the cliffs rise white,
Lashtang valleys call to you,
The moors and boggy streams,
But this is nightmare, not delight.

. . .

137

The throne of Lashtang standing cold,
  Is occupied as ever,
  Its brilliance is forever bright,
  But blinds you, binds you, all freedom sold."

"That's – sad," mumbled Nathan. "So where is this place? And why do you sing of it?".

"If you have to ask," smiled the smith, "then you'll never find it. 'Tis those that know already, will find the land in their dreams. But you visit once, and you'll never want to go back again."

"Dreamworld? Only dreams? But the Hazlett twins are real. I've met them both and they weren't dreams."

Grandpa October frowned, looking back over his shoulder. "Ignorant boy. Don't you know that all dreams are real?" Then he grinned suddenly. "Though, of course," he added, "that depends on what you mean by real."

It was John hurrying up with an armful of hay for Pimple that interrupted the conversation. "Gonna help me?" John asked.

Nathan reluctantly followed him, but as he looked back, he saw that the smith was standing still, gazing after him. "Fancy a balloon ride one day?" called the smith. "Oh yes, I know what they are. I'll take you on a trip you'll never forget."

"That's exactly what's already happened. Nathan paused, frowning. "Could you take me to Lashtang?"

Cackling, the smith shook his head. "Fire and ice, lad. No one survives Lashtang."

"What was you talking about?" enquired John, frowning. "Sounded mighty queer."

Nathan thought a moment. "I need a knife," he said. "That baron is dangerous, and after falling in the river, then he'll hate me even more. I might have to protect myself."

Grinning, John began laying down the hay for Pimple, adding a fat turnip to the top of the heap. "Too right," he told Nathan. "You needs a good belt and a good knife to stick in it, and I reckon the rest of us could do wiv that too. Go back and tell that smith what we wants."

"I will – tomorrow," muttered Nathan.

At the Whistle and Wherry, Uncle Henry had walked to the inn's stables with Alice, ordered the horse saddled, and had ridden off towards the Ludgate on his journey home to Hammersmith Village. Bending down to say goodbye, he assured her, "I shall be back, my dear, and will bring your Aunt Margaret with me next time. We need to finalise this business, and Lawyer Weeks wants us back in his chambers in three days from now. He thinks he'll have good news by then."

"I shall certainly come with you, uncle," smiled Alice. "I shall look forward to it. You, uncle dear, and Lawyer Weeks are both so good to me. I feel so much better, almost as though I am back home already. Nothing can go wrong now."

CHAPTER SEVENTEEN

Having been so determined to dream of Lashtang, Nathan was startled to dream instead of his grandmother.

"Nathan, Nathan, Nathan, answer me."

"Yes, Granny. I want to come home. Help me come home."

Her eyes were wide and desperate. "You don't realise your own danger, Nathan. Do as I tell you and come home."

"But how do I do that?" the dreaming Nathan begged. "Without the balloon, how do I come back to my own time?"

Granny October banged both hands flat down on the kitchen table, which shook. "Don't be a fool, Nathan. You turn around three times, click your heels and wish yourself back here. And make sure you bring Poppy with you. She's too young to look after herself. Remember, *there's no place like home.*"

It was after he had woken up that Nathan realised the dream was just silly. Clicking heels and wishing himself home was just what happened in the films. He didn't believe it at all, but he told Poppy all about it. She laughed. "So let's try, just in case."

They stood together, holding hands and laughing, as they clicked their heels. "We want to go home. There's no place like home. We want to go home. There's no place like home." Nothing happened. Taking a deep breath, Nathan said, "It was just a dream. And Granny said you were too young to look after yourself. She'd never say that really. She always calls you the practical one."

Poppy changed laugh to glare. "Of course I can look after myself, and you too. I'm the sensible one and I'm top of my class and you don't even go to school if you can help it. I'm the clever one in the family." She looked quite cross, but Nathan just grinned.

Although his dream had not been a serious one, Nathan couldn't get Granny October's voice out of his head. He kept thinking about her and the smith, and wondered what significance there was to October.

But now it was April, and spring was the one thing that seemed the same across the centuries. The weather was erratic, with some days sunny and mild, but others wet and windy. The trees were fluttering their new leaves, wildflowers were growing along the hedgerows and blossom budded thick and perfumed on many bushes.

Alice bought new clothes for Poppy, which caused much laughter and much excitement. Eventually, as all the boys were ordered to wait outside in the street, Poppy stripped off her school uniform and Alice stared at every piece of cloth that Poppy was dropping on the floor.

"What's that?" Alice gasped.

"A zip. And that's elastic. Don't you have those things?"

"Not at all," Alice was amazed. "They're magical." She pointed at Poppy's school blazer, now lying in a heap on the ground. "What's that coat of arms?"

"The school's arms," Poppy said, holding it up where it was embroidered onto the front pocket.

"And you have all these useful little hiding places."

"Pockets."

"That is a very, very good idea." Alice was impressed. "I'd like a puckett too."

"Pocket."

Poppy quickly dressed herself in a long linen shift like a petticoat, a long gown to her ankles in pretty pink linen with a border of embroidered flowers on the bottom of the skirt and the wide hem of the sleeves, and a cloak of oiled blue broadcloth. She had a narrow belt, and a small leather purse tied to it, and a pair of little brown leather shoes. Instead of the woolly stockings sold in the shops for women, Poppy kept her own woollen tights, which Alice said looked like men's hose.

"You don't need to tie up your hair," Alice said, "because you're not a married woman and you're very young." She passed the comb that was shared by the whole group, and watched as Poppy dragged it, wincing, through the knots. "You have nice sun-streaked hair like your brother, all brown and pretty yellow," Alice smiled. "But you should wear a little hat if you want to look respectable." Poppy didn't like the hat, but she wore it to please Alice, with every intention of losing it at some time soon.

Nathan whistled when he came down into the cellar and saw his sister dressed in the simple fashions of the late 15ᵗʰ century. "Wow. Never seen you look like that before."

"Nor you like that."

Hoping to meet up and talk to the smith again, Nathan spent a lot of time walking up and down Bandy Alley, but the smithy appeared to have completely shut down and even the hot wall down in the cellar began to cool off.

Then on the third night, Nathan dreamed once again of Granny October. But this time it was different. Almost as soon as he cuddled up under his blanket and cape, still using his pyjamas as a pillow, Nathan saw Brewster Hazlett in his dream. But this time Brewster was arguing with Granny. She was shouting at him, and he was spitting and screeching in fury. Nathan could not hear one word of what they were saying, until the other Hazlett brother appeared at the window. "Danger," screeched Wagster "He's coming.".

Then suddenly the walls of the Hammersmith house fell away, and a great countryside of cliffs, rivers, ice and clouds swept across the horizon.

Both Brewster and Wagster, staring up, crept into the shadows and their shrill and furious voices faded.

Then the thing appeared and blocked out the sun, the light, and the beauty of the country. Blackness swelled up like two enormous wings, vast as the mountains, but there were no feathers. These were the wings of a bat, leathery and spiked in swooping opaque black, but with a hundred sections, each divided by a thin sliver of crimson bone. Where each narrow bone peaked, it rose in a scarlet point topped with thorns. The thorns curled, reaching down. Clawed feet stretched from beneath, and from the shadow of the wings emerged the head. The narrow eyes were deep glistening red, like bleeding wounds, and the nose was a bat's nose, snubbed with wide flexed nostrils, the mouth was open, dripping pale grey slime between sharp white teeth. The slime coiled, snake-like, and slivered from the twitching mouth to the flat chin and then oozed down to the outstretched claws of the feet.

The creature filled the sky, peering down, and Granny October fled, running towards the distant hills.

No name had been given to the thing, but Granny, Brewster and even Wagster had been terrified. None of them had faced the thing. Nathan, although he had seen it only in a dream, was equally terrified and he heard his heart thump like a drum beat, until it hurt. He woke shaking, as if frozen. It was sometime before he was sure he was awake, and that the thing could not appear again.

He spoke quietly to Poppy. "I dreamed. It was horrible."

"So did I," Poppy whispered, "of Granny in a strange land, and talking to someone who shouted at her. Then it all went black and there was this dragon thing with dreadful eyes and slime in its mouth."

"Same dream," muttered Nathan, taking a deep breath. "Now that sounds dangerous."

Needing a distraction, he was pleased when Alice asked him to accompany her to see her lawyer. "I think we should all go," she said. "I won't be long in there, but I want him to meet you all so he knows we are friends, and he'll recognise you if ever another one of us goes to him, he needs to listen. Then afterwards we can go shopping."

"More clothes?" asked Poppy hopefully. She had fallen in love with her long flowing gown, and little soft shoes, and would have liked a beautiful velvet cloak similar to Alice's. But Alice shook her head.

"I don't think we need more, though John told me he wants a belt. But we needs salad greens and some root vegetables and bacon."

Poppy's smile faded. "Sounds wonderful," she said with a disappointed frown.

"Cheese? Bread, perhaps? And I need a belt too," suggested Nathan.

Sam decided to stay behind with Mouse and the kittens, and everyone else hurried up the steps outside, and began to walk towards the far side of the city.

Poppy stayed close to Alice, feeling glamorous in her new clothes, and Nathan lagged behind a little, still thinking of the dream which had troubled him so much. It seemed to have taken root in his head, like a black shape almost as big as the giant bat of his dream.

But it was a pleasant day with patches of blue peeping through the cloud cover. Only a slight wind made them wrap their cloaks around themselves and shiver. First they walked through the city, cutting up the little alleys and lanes, avoiding the main roads where folk watched them with some suspicion, thinking their faces familiar as thieves and cut-purses from previous months.

"But we don't thieve no more," grumbled Alfie, glaring at a stall holder who was shaking his fist at him, and a shop keeper who took one look, and swung the door shut in his face.

Bright-eyed, Poppy skipped along the cobbles, smiling at absolutely everyone. Peter grabbed at her arm. "You said you didn't like our cellar. But it looks like you're happy now."

"This city is lovely," Poppy insisted. "All those beams and thatched roofs and churches ringing their bells and pretty trees. I love it." Down Water Lane and into Thames Street, they took the open road and wandered the principal avenue towards St. Paul's. Many of the lanes on their left showed glimpses of the river, wharfs where unloading the boats was a heave and sweat from deck to warehouse, and platforms where wherries, the water taxis, waited for business. The river sparkled as the sun blinked out, then dulled again into grey ripples as the clouds closed. The river was crowded and noisy, but Poppy was delighted with how quiet everything seemed after the hectic bustle of the modern city. "Church bells play tunes," she said, "listen. And people chatter. But there's not one single engine, nor a bus nor a car. No one talking to themselves with their phones clamped to their cheeks, and no music blaring out of shops. I can even hear birds. Seagulls. Starlings. Look, there's a flock of swifts, and a row of sparrows sitting along the edge of that roof."

As the great shadows from Baynard's Castle drowned out the light, they turned right into Addle Hill and cut up towards the huge cathedral of St. Paul's. It was not only Poppy who was impressed with the grand building, its marble pillars and magnificent spire. But Poppy said, "Are you sure this is St. Paul's? It's changed."

"It's the old cathedral. Hush," Nathan told her. "Everyone gets confused if we talk about what's different."

Skirting around the great entrance to the cathedral, Alice once again dodged into a side street, and here, amongst a row of two storey houses squashed together, and sharing a slanted roof with many soaring chimneys, she stopped at one very small wooden door, and knocked loudly. When the door was answered, she hurried inside, asking the others to wait for a moment, but soon reappeared and invited them all in.

The room was small with shelves of rolled parchments and books of documents, lists of trials, notes concerning new laws and the duties of judges. Most were covered in dust.

Percival Weeks was a small man in mahogany clothes, a long crooked nose and fingers stained black with ink. His ink pot and a tumbled collection of feather quills lay on a table. Behind the table, Mister Weeks sat, smiling.

"Delighted, delighted," he said as everyone trooped in. "Welcome to all of you. Such friendship and loyalty is to be prized and admired. Now, I know young Alfie and Peter, but not the others. So please introduce yourselves." But they did not stay long. The lawyer had only one thing of importance to explain. "It is very clear that due to the ink blot covering the true intended identity of Lady Alice's proper guardian, Baron Cambridge has been able to claim a position that is not his by right. Although unable to eradicate the ink stain entirely, I've been able to scrape away sufficient to uncover part of the written names Mistress Margaret, the late Lord David Parry's sister and her husband Henry Fallow, the Lady Alice's aunt and uncle, and thus her next of kin. Naturally I have no way of proving that the concealing ink blot was made intentionally, nor by whom, but I can certainly prove that Baron Cambridge is not the proper legal guardian." He tapped his fingers on the little table, looking very pleased with himself. "I have a judge ready to hear this case on Thursday morning, the day after tomorrow, and then he will confirm the situation. In your presence, my lady, and that of your aunt and uncle, he needs to sign and seal the result. Immediately after that, my dear Lady Alice, you may return home and arrangements will be made for the baron to leave."

Alfie was sniggering slightly, since he wasn't used to Alice being constantly referred to as a lady, but he said, "And what if the baron don't leave? What if he makes trouble?"

"We have the law on our side, young man," smiled the lawyer. "No one can fight the law."

Alfie wasn't at all sure about that since he had himself been fighting the law for years, but since nothing else could be done until the case could be officially presented to the judge, trust and hope were the only solutions.

One by one, the group left the tiny office, and hurried out again into the mild sunshine. Clapping her hands, her own long hair flying out from her small white linen cap, Alice was clearly delighted.

"Shopping then," said Nathan. "The old market, or home to the cellar first?"

Alice took Poppy's hand. "Let's go to market," she said. "Let's spend lots of money. Buy hot pies to eat in the street, and smart belts for the boys, and something pretty for the girls. We could buy honey cakes too. Oh, I haven't eaten a honey cake in over a year."

"Never eaten one in me whole life," grinned John. "What's they like?"

"Delicious." Alice was skipping. "Sultanas and raisins all mixed up in honey and rolled with flour and suet into a dumpling ball, and steamed. I used to love them."

"One each then." Alfie was running ahead, calling back. "Pies and raisins and belts and new knives."

Which is when he hurtled straight into a fat man's midriff, who had stepped suddenly out of the shadows. Trying to regain his breath, Alfie panted but found himself caught in a stronghold, both his arms

146

twisted up behind him, which was extremely painful. A group of eight men surrounded them, hustling them together, big dirty hands clamped over their mouths so they could not call for help. Amongst the eight large men were the baron and his brother Edmund.

Edmund gazed down at Alice, who now stood before him, held tight by a bully she remembered as one of the baron's gardeners. Edmund smiled very wide, showing two blackened teeth. "Well now, what a wonderful surprise," he said. "My future wife, looking pretty as a picture. The time has come, my dear."

Half choking with the gardeners hand muffling her voice, Alice tried to shout, but only managed a few short words. "Not – anymore – never – pig – not legal."

"Oh, it will be legal indeed," Edmund smiled. "You'll come back with me now, and we'll be wed within the hour. The priest is ready, and your legal guardian will stand witness as I take your hand."

Alice squeaked, trying to bite the grubby fingers across her mouth. "Never," she managed to say.

Alfie stood next to her, and although he was bent nearly double with his arms feeling as though they were about to break, he shook off the restricting fingers across his mouth, and shouted, "You ain't got no chance of dragging her all the way to Bishopsgate without them market people seeing you and stopping you."

"Fool," said the baron, striding up. "She'll be tied up under a blanket and carried off in a cart with my gardeners, and a load of old bushes on top." He stared, frowning. "But you're not the boy I want. I remember thrashing you already. Well, you can come along and I'll thrash you again. But I want the dangerous urchin who attacked me on the Bridge."

Alice and Alfie were held tight, and it was the Steward Lacey who hauled Nathan up to the baron. "My lord, this is the vile boy, I believe."

Nathan was spluttering and trying to kick the steward's shins, but could only manage a small punch, which the steward didn't seem to notice through his thick velvet padded livery.

But as the struggle continued, it became obvious that although Nathan, Alice and Alfie were captured with no possibility of escape, the others had gone. Poppy had dropped to the ground and crawled between the men's legs, managing to scramble around the corner and out of sight before being noticed. Peter had followed her, doing exactly the same. And John, used to fast escapes, had run like the wind, quickly arriving in the next street with barely a sound of running feet. The three of them met, gazing silently, and nodding at each other. As quietly as any kitten, they slipped away through the deepest shadows, and waited until the grappling noises of the attack had faded into the distance.

CHAPTER EIGHTEEN

With a clenched fist to the right side of his jaw and another shattering blow to the left side with the large wooden hilt of a knife, Nathan was knocked out and collapsed at the baron's feet. With a spiteful grin, the baron kicked the back of Nathan's head as he lay unconscious on the ground. At the same moment, Edmund clamped both his sweaty palms around Alice's neck. He squeezed. Alice closed her eyes, feeling faint. Edmund kept squeezing.

It was the baron who called over, "Don't strangle the girl, idiot. You can't marry a corpse."

"She needs to learn who is the master," grinned Edmund, enjoying himself. He squeezed again and Alice, going weak at the knees, felt first a terrible nausea, and then lost consciousness. She collapsed into Edmund's arms, and he chuckled. "She adores me already – look!"

One of the men punched Alfie four times until his nose bled, his eyes fluttered and then shut, and he also tumbled onto the ground. The steward brought up the cart they had prepared, leading the horse by its bridle. Hauled by the backs of their collars, Nathan and Alfie were slung into the bottom of the cart, and with a lift and a toss, Alice was dumped in after them. Rags were tightly wound around their mouths, their arms were roped behind them, and their ankles tied together. Quickly a large blanket was spread over the three figures, and then, hurriedly arranged over the top was a thorny scrabble of old bushes, looking like a farmer's cartload of hay and plants ready for market. One of the gardeners hopped up onto the front bench, and began to drive the cart over the bumpy ground. The horse, flicking his tail, plodded on towards Bishopsgate.

The baron and his brother, followed closely by Lacey the steward, strolled cheerfully in the same direction, keeping an eye on the cart but pretending to have nothing to do with it. The other men dispersed quickly, making their own way back home.

"I shall whip the two boys until near death," decided the baron, as if discussing the pleasant weather, "and then I shall use their screams to keep young Alice in order, and frighten her to keep quiet. Then I shall finish them off and toss the bodies into the river one night."

"A sensible idea," Edmund approved. "That way the girl will be too frightened to be a nuisance."

It was becoming a fine afternoon, and the piles of straw, hay and plants on top of the blanket, made the bodies beneath swelter in the heat. But they were still unconscious for some time, and when they finally awoke to the trundle of the cart's wheels, and the clop and belch of the horse, they found it quite impossible to extricate themselves and could only lie in the darkness, trying to understand the nightmare that had occurred so suddenly.

Several streets away, John, Peter and Poppy were carefully running together in the same direction towards Bishopsgate. Stopping every now and again to catch their breath, they made good progress but certainly not as fast as the horse and cart.

Poppy whispered, "Can't we go to the police?"

"Who's that?" asked Peter.

"The Constable?"

"'Tis a grand fellow," John explained. "No way we'd get to see him. If we sees an assistant constable in the street, we could try, but they knows us as thieves. Telling one o' them that some grand baron done abducted his own ward – well – wouldn't do much good." He shook his head, the black hair falling in his eyes. "No. We gotta do this ourselves. And if ordinary folks see us running the streets up near the big houses, and if they sees us breaking into that fancy house, then they'll reckon tis us what needs carting off to the Constable."

With a small shiver, Peter said, "I can get past locked doors. But not in that big street. I'd be seen."

"Last time you went round the back pantry," John remembered, "to get Alfie out."

"Won't be that easy this time," decided Peter. "The baron knows what we did. Everything will be watched – kitchen – pantry – cellars."

"Then," said Poppy suddenly, "we'll have to go over the roof."

They stared at her. "Down the chimney? No way. There's fires still burning this time o' year," John said, frowning.

"Attics," said Poppy. "How about it?"

"Brilliant," John said with a sudden dazzling smile. "Totally brilliant. And if we gets up on them roofs pretty soon, there ain't one soul will see us nor try ta stop us."

Having just realised that wearing long skirts to her ankles was not going to make climbing easy, Poppy said nothing, but pointed. "There's a barn. Onto the window ledge, then the roof. Then next to it is a higher roof. We can do it, bit by bit. Are we near Bishopsgate yet?"

"Very close. At the back."

"Perfect."

With a slight blush, Poppy hitched up her skirts, tucking them into the elastic at the top of her school tights, so that both the shift and the gown flapped out just a little above her knees. "No point being shocked," she told both boys. "I wear all my clothes this short in my own time, so there's nothing wrong with it. Besides, with a long dress I couldn't climb at all."

And she began to clamber onto the low window ledge of the barn opposite. The window had no glass, and was open to the air, so the climb was easy enough, both hands to the low planked roof above, hauling themselves upwards. All three sat there a moment, catching their breath and looking further up to the next roof.

"This'll be harder."

But John stood, eyed the exact distance, and jumped. His feet wedged on the mossy wall just below the roof's overhang, and from there he grabbed, and pulled. In moments he was there, and was able to reach down and haul both Peter and Poppy up beside him.

The roof sloped and climbing that slope enabled them all to sit together on the very peak. The tall brick chimney puffed a few little half-hearted wisps of smelly grey smoke. "Reckon these folks 'ave a feeble little fire going on down there," nodded John.

"It's a warm day."

"Them chimneys furver along is nice and dirty," John pointed. "So, who's ready fer the next jump?" It was indeed a dirty chimney, with black smoke oozing from the bricks. "But warm," John grinned. "Ain't no point being clean and dead from cold."

"I have to take my nice shoes off," said Poppy sadly. "I'll slip in these. But I don't want to lose them."

"Best all do the same," said Peter, undoing his ribboned laces. "If we leave them here, perhaps we can come back for them one day."

Poppy giggled. "So we just say, excuse me, I'm just going to climb up on your roof to collect my shoes? I left them there last week!"

"Once we get Alice free, she'll be able ta buy a hundred pairs of shoes."

Three pairs of new shoes sat in a row on the rooftop and everyone climbed down the opposite slope, then jumped the short gap between houses. Arms in the air, taking a deep breath, and then the leap. Landing with a yelp, falling on both knees, panting with the effort and the sudden bang and jolt, then up again and onwards.

Clambering amongst the smoke, up one and down another, slipping and crying out with a yelp, then catching hold of a big hot chimney, feet burned, fingers scraped, and every woollen leg torn, with holes and unravelling wool. Hop, grab, running and scrambling over broken tiles and collected puddles in old corners. The houses had no gutters, and many roofs were mossy, which made everyone slip once more. They grabbed at each other, pulling on hands and sleeves, helping as one slipped or stumbled.

Poppy wanted to cry out, and perhaps even sing, it all seemed so strange. The sense of unreality lessened the danger, and made it all the more exciting. Running over the tops of roofs in a city that no longer existed. But her hands were bleeding, she had bashed her head, feet and elbows a dozen times, and she heaved and coughed from the smelly dark smoke.

"Quick, this way, around this corner."

"Jump. I'll catch you, promise. No way I'll let you drop."

Her dress had fallen, and Poppy found her legs once again caught up in a swirl of skirts. She had to stop and tuck them up again, then laughed, wondering what any decent citizen would think if they looked up now and saw this girl showing off her legs on the top of the roof. Then she realised something else. She had indeed lost the silly hat she had been told to wear, but very much disliked. She patted the top of her hair with pleasure, took another leap, and followed the others.

The climbing and the jumping became exhausting and every new roof had its dangers. Some sloped more steeply, others were thick with soot, their chimneys burning hot. Some tiles were so badly broken that hands were cut, as if by knives, knees ripped, and feet raw. Poppy's tights and the boys' hose were all in tatters. They fell many times, but everyone was determined to succeed with the rescue, and no fall was bad enough to keep them down.

Coughing, wheezing, tears in their eyes and their clothes ruined, they saw how close they had come.

The next roof, tiled in slate, was many peaked and the building was extensive. It was only two houses along from Alice's home in Bishopsgate. So they sat a moment, looking down and catching their breath.

Below them the city stretched huge and beautiful. From that height, they could see some miles, beyond the old city wall, beyond The Tower, beyond the Bridge and beyond the Abbey of the Westminster. It seemed as though London spread its power across all the visible land, but looking only a little north, to where Bishopsgate blurred into green fields, Poppy could see old buildings and a high iron fence, kennels and low sheds.

Watching where she looked, John mumbled, "Bedlam Hospice, for them not right in the head. Locked up, they is, but some goes out begging." Where Poppy now knew the city to be a buzz of buildings and business, here stretched greenery, fields, reedy wasteland and monastery gardens. She pointed, and once again John explained, "That's St. John's Wood. Tis another hospice, fer the lepers, it is, them poor folk sick to die and must be kept away from the rest of us."

But she had no time to feel upset or confused. "Hurry," urged Peter. "Only one more roof to go, and we're there."

There was a larger space between the roofs of the grand houses, surrounded by their grounds, but here was a long stable block, its hayloft high. That gave the perfect access and within minutes they had climbed to the towering chimneys of the old Parry Mansion, Alice's home where the baron and his brother were living in stolen luxury.

Edmund and the baron were already in the cellars, marching past the great tubs of wine and beer, and thrusting into the small stone cell, windowless and airless, which the baron called his dungeon.

"Now then, smirked Edmund, "time to amuse ourselves."

The baron stamped one large flat foot. "No. Leave these two boys here and lock them in. Then get this girl upstairs to the little chapel, and get this marriage over and done with before anything interferes."

Edmund sniggered, then frowned. "What could possibly interfere? Dinner? A visit from the king?"

"I'm taking no chances," insisted the baron without a smile. "What if that fool lawyer turns up? And some of those brats are still out there."

Edmund was complacent. "We have five men guarding the front of the house, and another three guarding the back where they broke in through the pantry window last time. If they show their faces today, they'll be knocked out and hauled off to gaol."

Alfie and Nathan were both slung to the ground, tumbling onto the hard stone with a groan, their wrists and ankles were still tied tightly, and their mouths gagged. Then they heard the squeak of an iron key in the lock, click and clang, and then silence. They were locked in and it was totally black around them. They could not even see each other.

It was sometime before Nathan managed to wriggle his mouth around the gag, and whisper to Alfie. His jaw was extremely painful, and he felt that every bone in his body was bruised or broken. "What do we do now?" he managed to ask.

154

Alfie couldn't answer. In any case, he felt that no answer existed. They would lie there until Alice was married to Edmund Darling, then the men would come down to whip and torture them. Death, Alfie thought, might be a better and easier outcome.

Nathan continued to wriggle, biting his lip to stifle the pain in his head. He had never had such a terrible headache in his life before. But with persistence, he managed to push down his arms behind him, and by squeezing his knees up to his chin, he brought his arms up and over so they were tied in front instead of at his back. Now, although his wrists were tied tight, he could move his fingers and started the careful attempt to untie his ankles. Head pounding and eyes stinging, he continued to struggle until he had succeeded. Now with his legs free, the gag gone, and his arms tied in front of him, he could move and quickly bent over Alfie.

"Look at me," he commanded. "I think I can untie your hands. Then you can untie mine. We'll still be locked in, but at least we can talk and move around."

The little private chapel was on the second storey, and Father Michael, a small and intimidated priest who found the baron terrifying, and was prepared to do whatever he was told, was waiting patiently. The candles were lit, and their wisps of pale smoke twisted up to the beamed ceiling.

Alice was still tied wrists and ankles, but Edmund tugged off the dirty rag around her mouth as he lifted her and slung her over his shoulder. She had regained consciousness, but finding herself suddenly hoisted over one fat shoulder, with the sweaty smell of Edmund's armpit in her face and her head upside down, she almost fainted once again.

"Let me *down*," she shouted, furious and light-headed, "how *dare* you treat me this way!"

"Cheer up, my dear." The baron, walking behind, chortled. "This is your wedding day. Every bride should be happy."

Alice wished with all her heart that she had one of the knives from the next-door smith which Nathan and John had been talking about. Instead, she managed to bite Edmund's ear, as hard as she could. He squealed, dropped her immediately, and slapped her face. He was so angry he seemed to be spitting. "Wait till we're wed," he muttered. "Then I shall have you whipped."

"Where's my friends?" Alice demanded, sitting up and staring at both men.

"Both waiting for their own whipping," laughed the baron. "Now, my dear ward, let's get this marriage over and done with. Then everything you own will belong to my brother, and," and here the baron turned to look challengingly at Edmund, "my brother will share everything with me."

"I refuse to agree to the marriage," Alice said, sitting solidly on the floor, arms crossed as she glared up. "I will not say the words of agreement."

But Edmund laughed. "I don't give a fig, my dear. Both the priest and my brother, your legal guardian, will stand witness and swear that you married me willingly, and spoke the words of compliance. I even have a ring for you. Was my mother's."

'I shall throw it in the river."

"Where you'll probably end up yourself," interrupted the baron. "Now, silence, wench. Or I'll gag you again."

Dropped from shoulder to floor, she was dragged along the passageway, with one brother pulling on each arm. At the far end of the corridor Alice could see the flicker of the candles in the chapel, and the priest standing in the doorway, his hands tucked in his sleeves. She wanted to cry, but instead she called, "Father Michael. You must never agree to this. It is illegal. It is cruel. I hate these men and they want to kill me."

But the priest looked away, as if studying his toes peeping out from his monk's robes, and said nothing.

Alice thought she would be sick and was heaving, coughing, and gasping for breath. Her gown was torn, she had lost one shoe and her little hat, so now her hair was loose and tangled, and she felt very ill and utterly miserable. And then, at the moment of her greatest desperation, she heard an extremely faint whisper from a room just behind her, where the door stood ajar and open to a sliver of black shadows.

"Don't worry. We're here." She recognised Poppy's voice, and blinked, amazed and overjoyed.

The footsteps were so light, as of stockinged feet on tiptoe, that they could barely be heard, but Alice understood. Meanwhile the baron was striding forwards, marching towards the priest.

"Ready, father? This won't take long."

"It is most – irregular, my lord," faltered the priest, stepping back a pace.

"Nonsense man," Edmund told him. "No one will ever question what happened here. The girl is of age, and," he sniggered, "she has her guardian's permission."

"At least let me stand," Alice said, twisting and trying to free both her hands. She was released, and stood, brushing down her torn skirts. But Edmund took a firm grasp on her elbow.

Everyone faced the entrance to the little glittering chapel, except the priest who was flushed and still avoiding Alice's eyes. So nobody saw what was about to happen next as three figures stepped silently from the shadows of the open doorway.

First the sharp-edged roof tile flew suddenly from the darkness into the light, and then, as fast and as heavy, came the rock, hurtling from the gloom behind.

CHAPTER NINETEEN

John threw the broken tile straight at Edmund's head, and amongst his tufts of bright red hair, there appeared a trickle of bright red blood. At exactly the same time, with expert accuracy, Peter aimed a stone at the baron. It hit the back of his head, and with considerable force. John's second roof tile hit Edmund in the middle of his forehead as he swung around to face the attack, and both John and Edmund raced towards each other in anger. Edmund was attempting to pull his short knife from his belt, but the width of his huge heaving stomach made it difficult to un-wedge the hilt, and John, both fists flailing, was able to punch his adversary twice, very hard, on the nose.

"You wanna cut me throat, does ya," yelled John. "Well, take that."

As the baron, rubbing his head, turned to run at Peter, Alice stuck out one foot, and tripping, he tumbled at her feet, and wailed, clutching his stomach.

The priest, in wide-eyed astonishment, scurried back into his chapel and stood before the altar, doing nothing at all.

But Poppy followed him in and grabbed two of the tall flaming candles in their heavy silver holders. In the swirling chaos, she managed to hit Edmund over the head with one, and then, as he bent, cursing, shoved the burning flame into the neck of his fine frilly shirt.

The other candlestick she flung at the baron, and although she missed, the burning wick unexpectedly caught his sleeve and flared into fire, scorching his grand brocade and engulfing his hand.

"There! That's what a woman can do," Poppy shouted, though considerably surprised at her own success.

John moved in, discovered a large earthenware urn on a table beside the chapel entrance, and banged this on Edmund's already very bruised forehead. His knees buckled, as the candle, wedged inside his collar, flared up. His soft fat flesh puckered below his neck, and a trickle of fire singed up to his red hair.

Edmund's eyes rolled up, closed, and he gave a strangled moan, finally collapsing to the floor of the corridor. "Brute," Alice shouted. "Wanted to whip me and kill me, did you? Well, see what your intended bride and her friends can do to you." The licking flamelets on his hair hissed and went out with a sizzle but Edmund lay still.

The urn had broken into a flurry of pieces, each long and sharp, and John grabbed one of these and stabbed out in the baron's direction. But the baron turned and turned again, blood in his eyes, his hand burning furiously as he tried to clamp out the flames with his other fingers. He was still conscious and raging in uncontrolled temper. "Cowardly fool," he roared at the hovering priest. "Call Lacey. Call the guards."

Yet the priest still hesitated. "I must remind you, my lord, that I also owe loyal diligence to the Lady Alice. This is her home, as I understand it, and I owe her my friendship and guidance." His voice took on more volume as Alice smiled warmly at him. So he continued a little louder, saying, "Intending to marry the young lady against her will, did not sit easily on my conscience, my lord, in spite of your orders. Now I fear I must remove myself from this situation. I shall kneel at the altar and pray for your safety and understanding."

The priest shuffled off, Edmund was still lying unconscious on the floorboards, and the baron turned on Alice. Although Poppy ran in and hit him again with the candlestick, he pushed her away and managed to clamp both hands around Alice's neck and haul her backwards against him. He stared at the others over Alice's shoulder.

"Well," he shouted, "want to kill me, do you? So, let me warn you that the girl dies first. I can break her neck with one twist. Back off now, or she dies."

John and Poppy stared at him in disgust and horror, but Peter was no longer there. It was some time previously that he had crept away, and was trying to remain unseen as he searched for the way downstairs, and the cellars where he knew Alfie and Nathan would be locked away. Sidling silently down the huge staircase, Peter kept to the shadows, making himself seem smaller than he was. The stairs seemed to go on forever, but he saw no one. It was on the final flight that a maid trotted past him, and stopped suddenly, staring at him.

With a gulp, Peter muttered, "I'm the new scullion. Just been up to ask the lord's permission."

The maid looked doubtful. "You ain't in livery."

"Haven't got it yet. It's – on order. Coming tomorrow. I've been – collecting the chamber pots."

"You ain't carrying none," she pointed out.

"Done finished," said Peter. "Don't hold me up or I'll be late and get the sack before I even start."

He hurried past her, turned once, and was relieved to see that she was no longer watching him. Pattering through the narrow corridor to the kitchens and pantries, Peter managed to avoid open doorways, and since he knew exactly where the kitchens were, and could hear the noise of cooks and cooking, he dodged again into the darker places at the very back of the house.

Where he had come with Alice to rescue Alfie, had broken a window and climbed in, now the window opening was boarded up. But Peter smiled. That didn't bother him for he was already inside, and now he knew exactly where he was. Slipping through the wine cellars, and hiding behind one of the kegs when he heard approaching footsteps, and stayed, holding his breath, until the steps faded away. He hated the smell of stale wine and strong beer, spilt and trickling across the ground. It stank but there was no time for him to feel sick. Now, quickly arriving at the low locked door to the underground cell, where Alfie had been thrown before, Peter stopped, calling softly. "Are you there? Don't worry. Just me."

He took the little bent nail from his rolled tunic cuff, and began to pick the lock. It took him only a moment, and he pulled the rickety door wide. Its rusty hinges creaked. And there, crouched inside, were Alfie and Nathan.

They leapt up as they saw Peter. "How?" "That's truly wonderful" "You's proper brilliant, Pete."

"No time. Hurry up," Peter whispered. "We're still in danger."

Having already managed to extricate themselves from their gags and ropes, Alfie and Nathan were immediately able to follow Peter as he led them back up to the chapel.

"Shame we can't go into the kitchen and pick up some carving knives," whispered Nathan.

Alfie was in a furious temper, and could hardly wait to get his hands on Edmund and the baron. "We'll manage anyway." He glowered. "Reckon I'm going to kill them both."

"You can try," Peter nodded. "But you both look pretty weak to me."

It was true. They had rope burns around their wrists, bruises and blackened eyes, and their knees buckled and ached as they tried to hurry, feeling as though they could hardly stand, let alone run. First beaten, then knocked unconscious, they had then been carried in a swelteringly hot cart over a thousand bumps, and finally dragged and thrown into the cell. But Nathan and Alfie struggled on, determined to achieve their own freedom and help Alice and the others.

Clattering up the stairs, several of the servants came out to see what was happening, but knowing nothing of the situation, they stood back, confused, and muttering to each other. But the wine steward frowned and said, "Most peculiar. Time to call Mister Lacey, I believe."

Outside the chapel, Peter stopped abruptly, and Alfie and Nathan stared. A dozen candles flickered, the priest stood, a little ashamed and slump-shouldered, before the altar, and standing in front of him were the baron and his brother Edmund, both supporting between them the rigid figure of Lady Alice Parry. It was difficult to see whether Alice was conscious or not, but her head was slumped and had the brothers not been holding her up then she would clearly have fallen.

"Stop," Alfie yelled. "Let her go."

Nathan was looking around for Poppy, but there was no sign of her. One second later, John came rushing from the room opposite, bursting from the shadows with a poker from the hearth. With half a blink at the arrival of Peter, Alfie and Nathan, John aimed directly at Edmund's back and plunged the poker into the sliver of neck showing below his straight cut red hair, and the already singed collar of his shirt.

The point of the poker was raging hot from the fire, and glowed. Edmund howled. He was barely conscious himself, and had only just managed to clamber to his feet at his brother's insistence, ready to complete the marriage at last. But now, releasing Alice, he clamped both hands to the back of his neck and flopped to his knees. John promptly hit him over the head with the poker's edge.

The baron swung Alice in front of him and faced the others. John, Alfie, Peter and Nathan glared back, hesitating.

"You know what I said before," the baron snarled. "Alice dies right now, unless you all back off. This wedding will take place, even if the girl lies dead. Do you hear me? Get back."

"Your vile brother isn't capable of marrying anyone," Nathan pointed out, taking a step forwards. "He's squealing like a sick pig, flat on the ground."

The Baron raised his burned hand. All the flesh was wrinkled and black, and long strips of bleeding skin hung loose. Across one finger, the bone showed through stark white. He said, "You will all pay for this, and so will the girl. But she's not dead yet. And whether my brother stands here or not is of no consequence. This marriage will now take place." He turned to the priest. "Speak those words now, or I shall strangle the girl, and you can carry the blame for that for the rest of your life."

Father Michael quaked, shivering. "But it is hardly proper, my lord _"

"Get on with it, and quick."

162

Edmund knelt on the ground, whimpering, his bottom in the air and his face in his hands. The priest, uncertain, bowed his head. Alice was only partly conscious. Her eyes were half shut and she seemed to be struggling for breath. Around her neck were the crimson marks of the baron's fingers. For one moment more, everyone was still, and waiting.

From the side of the corridor, a faint shuffle could be heard in the silence, but everyone was too absorbed in the urgent danger, and no one appeared to have heard. Then Poppy, who had crawled from the opposite room behind John, when he had rushed out with the poker, was carefully creeping up behind the baron.

As she stood, very quietly and slowly, everyone could see her except the baron, Edmund, and Alice. But no one made any sign. Even the priest, hurrying backwards, kept his mouth firmly shut. Nathan secretly crossed his fingers. Everyone took a deep breath.

John had taken the red hot poker, but Poppy had found the three-pronged fork, used to spear the logs and thrust them into place on the hearth. It was black iron, dripping soot, and Poppy held it straight out like a lance. "Beware," she yelled, trying to look like a crusader, "I am dangerous. And this thing is *sharp!*" She stood on tiptoe in her stockinged feet, and with all her force, plunged the long-handled fork into the baron's back. Through the swathes of velvet, brocade and padded wool, the fork had little opportunity to touch him, but much to Poppy's surprise the prongs hit home and scratched flesh. With one faltering scream, he fell backwards on top of Poppy and Alice slipped to the ground beside him.

Nathan rushed to Poppy, Alfie rushed to Alice, John ran to examine Edmund, and Peter stood, shocked, in the middle of the turmoil.

"Done," said John with a huge and widening smile. "We done it."

Nathan was dragging Poppy out from beneath the baron's enormous weight, telling her how wonderful she was, while Alfie was trying to wake Alice, assuring her that the trouble was all over. Edmund was still conscious, but he was taking no notice of anything else as he whimpered and cried to himself. The baron was out cold, lying flat on his back before the chapel door, his eyes shut and his breathing hoarse.

And then, as everyone was preparing to get out of the house as quickly as possible, there was another voice from the far shadows of the corridor and the sound of two pairs of running feet.

Lacey called, "What is going on here? What appalling attack is this? Oliver, run for the sheriff, the assistant constables, the gardeners, anyone and everyone."

The cook Oliver grunted, "Yes sir," and his footsteps disappeared again while Lacey strode forwards.

"Keep away," Alfie warned. "We're leaving now."

"You'll do no such thing," replied Lacey, and produced the long meat knife he had been holding at his side. "You brats have attacked a lord of the land, and his illustrious brother. You'll hang for this."

But in spite of this threat, Lacey, realising he was now on his own facing six furious faces, and that two of these adversaries were also armed, was too cautious to move against them and the knife remained at his side. John pointed the poker, and Poppy waved the long fork, its prongs now bloodstained. The others stood, glaring. Only Alice still sat, her head back against the wall.

Hoping that some help might arrive before he was attacked himself, Lacey held the knife firmly, and said nothing. Finally, staggering up as she clung to Alfie's arm, Alice looked straight at the steward. "You never worked for my father or myself," she said. "But you know exactly who I am, and you know this house is legally mine. No marriage took place here today, and never will, but I have been imprisoned, beaten, and knocked unconscious. You speak of hanging my friends, but it is the baron and his brother who would be taken to gaol for their wickedness if the truth were known. Let me go now. Both your masters are still alive and neither are badly hurt. We only tried to defend ourselves. I and my friends will leave without any further trouble."

Uncertain, the steward hovered. I must call for the doctor," he said at last. If my lord baron dies, then you will all be called murderers."

"Tis only a scratch," John objected.

164

But Lacey bent over the baron's fat body, turning it gently. Immediately he saw the tiny puddles of blood where the fork had pricked the man's fleshy back. Lacey's face went quite white. "This is dreadful," he mumbled. "I must run for the medic." Still clutching the knife, he turned, nose in the air, and hurried off.

Everyone else looked to each other. "Are you able to walk?" Alfie asked Alice. "I don't think I can carry you, but I can try."

Alice began slowly to climb back to her feet, levering herself against the wall behind her. "I can walk," she insisted. "But I wish I could go back to my own bedchamber now. It's just along the corridor. I could lie down and rest for a little while, and then find myself some decent clothes to wear. These things are in rags." She stood, but leaned on Alfie's shoulder. "Then we could fetch horses from the stables and ride home in comfort."

"Wish we'd brought Pimple," John muttered to himself.

"Too dangerous to stay here any longer," Alfie said. "Lacey called on them gardeners and said to get the sheriff. Could be folk rushing in any moment."

Nathan looked at Poppy. "We have to get out, fast," he said. "But I know the baron left guards both back and front. How on earth did you get in?"

Poppy, her hair in a wild tousle, tried to wipe the baron's blood from her torn skirts. "We ran over the roofs," she said. "Then we climbed in the attic window. There's a nice big one here, and it leads straight down to the stairs."

"The roof?" Nathan whistled. "Well, we can't get out that way. We'll have to risk the front."

Most unexpectedly, the priest now stepped forwards. He looked down, frowning, at the bodies of Edmund and the baron. The baron lay without moving, but his breathing was forced and noisy. Close by Edmund still kneeled, rump upwards, sobbing and cursing.

"I shall accompany you," said the priest softly. "I did wrong, complying with his lordship's orders, but he threatened me, saying he would go to the archbishop and accuse me of heresy. I could have been burned as a heretic and I was afraid. But now I have decided differently. I shall come with you and order any guards to let you pass. Once you have left, then I shall go to the archbishop myself."

Everyone thanked him, a little startled but extremely grateful. They did not think any guard or gardener would risk attacking them while Father Michael walked at their side.

Alfie put his arm around Alice, supporting her, and they began to make their way back to the main staircase, and finally to the ground floor. There was plenty of noise in the house, with Lacey shouting and the sound of people stamping and hurrying, as if running around in circles. "Mind that knife," and "Call for the doctor." "This house is as bad as Bedlam." Then someone falling and a boy crying.

"Excellent," Alfie said. "Theys too busy to take notice of us."

Nathan pushed the front doors wide, and the sun streaked in from behind the clouds. In a group, walking towards the street, they then faced the two remaining guards, large men whom the baron had hired to stop anyone getting in. But no one had ordered them to stop anyone coming out.

Father Michael called them over, as if the authority was his. "You must call for the doctor and the barber-surgeon," he informed them. "There have been accidents and both your masters are injured. Now, hurry, while I help these poor folk home."

Both men nodded and ran off, while the priest smiled at Alice. "My lady, you are free."

Thanking the priest again, Alfie began to lead everyone home, hurrying down Bishopsgate. No one felt strong or energetic, and the walk was slow as they stumbled over the cobbles. People stopped to stare at them, for they were all blood-stained and wearing very badly torn clothes. Four of them had no shoes, and all looked like wounded beggars. Two women called, offering help, and one kind man pressed a penny into Alice's hand. And yet, in spite of the pains, aches, and difficulty breathing, everyone was exceedingly happy. The relief they felt gave them the strength to hobble home.

From Bishopsgate into Gracechurch Street, left into Fenchurch and south towards the Tower, scurrying around the two sharp shadowed corners into Bandy Alley.

They were exhausted. Longing to collapse against the long brick wall and its exuding warmth, to cuddle up beneath their blankets, listen to Mouse feeding her babies, tell Sam every amazing thing that had happened, and close their eyes to sleep, and sleep and sleep every ache away. Even Poppy and Nathan who did not enjoy sleeping on the floor, were yearning for that glorious chance to relax, and perhaps dream of their adventures.

Yet, once again it did not happen that way. As they turned the last bend and hobbled into Bandy Alley, and even before arriving closer to the cellar they called home, they saw something else.

The smithy next door was on fire.

A fury of raging flame hissed and flew, towering into scarlet tongues of hurtling destruction. The blazing heat travelled the length of the lane, crackling like some ravenous dragon.

"Where's Sam," squeaked Alice in horror.

Forgetting their tiredness and pain, everyone started to run. Outside the smithy, a group of people with buckets were attempting to douse the fire. The water barrels which most folk kept outside their doors, were emptied one by one and still the last small flames scattered and reignited as the wind blew the ashes across the little street.

Sam was helping. Poppy and Alice rushed at him and hugged him. He managed a small smug smirk. Yes, I'm alright," he said. "I was asleep but the wall went red hot and woke me up. I ran out and saw the flames."

"Mouse?" asked Peter, white-faced.

Nodding and smiling, Sam said, "She was already running out, fast as me, with her little white kitten in her mouth. So I ran in and grabbed the other two babies. Then we all shouted fire. Well, of course Mouse didn't, but the rest of the street did. Everyone came to help. The ironmonger is mighty good and says we can stay in his cellar for a few days. That's where Mouse is now. Pimple's tether broke and he's run off. Not back yet."

Nathan sighed with enormous relief, though he felt the gulp of fear rise from his stomach to his throat. "It's just one disaster after another," he muttered. "And how did the fire start, when the smith closed up shop three days ago and hasn't been seen since."

"He's been seen now," said Sam. "They found his body inside. Burned, I suppose. Who knows?"

Nathan stared. "Dead?"

"Yes. Said he was found at the bottom of the stairs with his head cracked. Must have fallen down."

"I wonder," whispered Nathan, but only to himself.

CHAPTER TWENTY

A lice murmured, "It's so kind of Mistress Winters. And so much nicer."

"T'ain't," John retorted. "Cos it ain't ours and we can't stay."

"The other cellar weren't ours neither," Alfie pointed out.

"Felt like it."

"Feels like home, cos Mouse is there in the corner, suckling her babies," smiled Sam.

"Yeh," objected John, "But not Pimple. Poor little fellow, he might be hurt. Might be hungry. Might be lost."

Peter, thumb back in his mouth, sighed and nodded.

"I lost my pyjamas," said Nathan.

Poppy said, "And I lost everything. My school shirt and my jumper and my shoes and the school blazer. I feel rotten about that."

"But you saved our lives," said Alice.

They slept well at the ironmonger's, with blankets, pillows and straw mattresses. It seemed like luxury, especially after a hot dinner of bacon wedges, melted cheese, warm baked bread and cups of hot milk.

Mistress Winters had settled them all in comfort, treated them as poor victims of the fire, patted their heads with affection, which embarrassed everyone except Sam, and said she'd be glad if they stayed a few days. "Not too long, mind," she added, "for we really don't have the space. But three or four days while you look for another home."

"Maybe long enough for me to get my own home back," said Alice.

But on the following morning they explored the smithy and the burned out cellar next door, and found only a blackened ruin. Nothing remained, not even a sign of recent habitation, except for one small thing. Scuffling through the soot, ashes and the rancid stench of burning, Nathan had seen something glitter, and had stopped to pick it up. It was a knife, not large but not so small, with a slight curve at its sharpened end, and a beautifully carved hilt. He was astonished, and quickly wedged it into the torn waistband of his woolly hose. At first he thought it might stick into him every time he bent over, but finally he found a way of keeping it sidelong within the wrapped ties around his waist, and it stayed safe. He didn't know why he didn't show anyone else, and at first felt guilty in case it was simply his own greed. But when he stopped to consider later that day, he knew it wasn't greed at all. Something told him this knife had been left especially, and just for him, and that he must keep it secret for now. He had always intended buying a small knife from the smith, and had told him so. Nothing so special and nothing so elaborate, but now he had what he knew he needed, and far more beautiful than he ever could have expected. So he guessed that not only was this a gift, but it had a particular meaning.

Throughout the day, he stared at it often, pulling it out for quiet inspection. The sheen on the blade was utterly smooth but perilously sharp, however it was the hilt that was the most unusual and the most fascinating. It seemed to be made of silver, although Nathan could not be sure, and he thought it might simply be steel like the blade. But its pattern was complicated and showed the dance of three people and a serpent, intertwining and connecting. Yet the two dancing people did not look entirely human, for their hands were clawed, and they appeared to be sprouting wings.

The previous day's beating and the shock of the fire had left

Nathan with a pounding headache, and he wished he was back at home where Granny would have put him to bed with a hot drink and some pills. But here, all he could do was creep around, trying not to think about it. Alfie was in even greater pain, Nathan knew. His bruises and the lash marks on his back from the first beating had not yet entirely faded, and now he had been attacked again. He was weak kneed and shuffled a little as he walked. But he did not complain and when Alice asked him how he felt, Alfie simply shrugged. "Won't die," he grinned.

Alice was also badly bruised, especially around the neck where the baron's finger marks remained like red ropes. "I expect Uncle Henry to return tomorrow," she said, sitting on a small stool in the ironmonger's cellar, with Mouse purring on her lap. "I'll meet him at the Whistle and Wherry inn by the Bridge. Alfie, I hope you'll come with me. We both need to show Mister Weeks how badly the baron treated us."

"Yeh, I'll come," muttered Alfie. "I reckon them two pig-men goes straight to the Constable. If we ain't careful, will be us in the clink. So's your lawyer better see what happened and make sure we ain't arrested."

Without more than a scratch, Poppy was eager to explore the city. "But I might get arrested too," she giggled, "just for walking out the door. Holes in my tights, holes in my skirt, holes in my petticoat, and holes in my sleeves. No hat. No shoes, and probably no brains either. So what happens next?"

Laughing, John nodded. "We all needs new stuff. There ain't nuffing not torn."

"I'm not sure we have enough money left to buy new clothes for all of us," said Alice. "And we can't risk using every last penny until we have a new place to stay. We could end up with no food and no fire and no pot to cook in. Food comes before clothes, and we don't want to go back to stealing."

"Don't care." John was still laughing. "Better than starving, ain't it."

Although more comfortable than previously, the space open to them was somewhat confined than their last cellar, for this one was both a little smaller, and also partially crammed with heaped iron pots, pans, trivets, candlesticks, pokers, spades and other stacked homewares, and great bars of iron ready to be transformed. If not dragged into cuddles by one of the group, Mouse enjoyed wriggling under such irregular heaps as though exploring deep underground tunnels, finding a dark and hidden corner in the shadows, carrying her babies with her, and settling to invisible and undisturbed sleep. Both Sam and Poppy, when they could, frequently stole one of the kittens, adoring the tiny balls of squeak and squirm, their fluffy fur growing thicker each day although their big blue eyes only managed to blink open on rare occasions. Mouse did not object to her friends babysitting, but called her children back to her at frequent dinner times.

Seven straw mattresses, packed into linen bags, lay in a neat row, topped with pillows and blankets. This was truly luxury for every weary and aching body, and the food brought down to them was even more welcome. But this level of comfort did not interest Alice. She was concerned only with regaining her own rightful home, and getting rid of the baron and his brother forever.

The next morning, she and Alfie set off early to the Whistle and Wherry Inn by the Bridge where Uncle Henry was due to arrive later that morning, John stalked off at the same time to search for Pimple. Nathan sat on his bed, stared at the ceiling, which was low brick without light, although wisps of daylight leaked down the stairs. He was tired, not only from the days of worry, running across London, and fighting with the baron, but also with trying to make sense of everything. The one person he had met who might have been able to explain to him, had died, or been murdered, in the fire or before.

But why would anyone wish to murder an aged smith, unless it was for the secret information he had been prepared to divulge?

The knife also puzzled him. There was some meaning to it, Nathan was sure. Expensive, beautiful and extremely unusual, it had come to him for some reason that he could not understand.

There was only one other person that he thought could answer his questions, if he chose. So without saying anything to anyone, Nathan slipped out and climbed the steps to the outside. The smell of the burned out shop opposite was still unpleasant, hanging on the air just like the balloon which he was about to call. So he wandered up Bandy Alley to the great stone wall of the Tower at the end, turned the corner, and stood in the huge slanting shadows. Then he started, very softly, to call.

"Brewster, please come. Come and tell me why you brought me here. Come and tell me who you are. Come and tell me about Lashtang. And why Granny and the smith both get called October."

Nathan did not expect immediate answers, but he had nothing else to do, so he stayed there, muttering aloud. No one else could hear him and no one else walked Bandy Alley. He could not see over the Tower wall, for this was the outer Bastian across the moat. The turn of the alley hid the moat's glinting waters, but Nathan could hear shouted orders, marching boots, and once even the roar of a lion from the menagerie. He had already been told about the great royal menagerie kept at the Tower, and thought it rather strange, but it was something far stranger that he hoped to see now.

Staring up into the sky, Nathan waited, called again, waited once more, and finally called over and over, under his breath, but growing louder.

It was suddenly behind him that he heard the voice. "What on earth are you doing, Nat?"

Startled, he whirled around with a jerk. "Oh bother. It's you," he frowned at Poppy. "You're a nuisance. I wanted to be alone."

"I just saved your rotten life," Poppy glared back. "So why do you want secrets? I'm stuck here too, aren't I?"

Relenting, Nathan pulled out the knife carefully from the torn wrapped ties of his hose. "Look," he handed it to her. "I found this in the burned out ashes. It has something to do with this whole adventure, I'm sure of it. What do you think? And I've been calling Brewster. Just hoping that someone in this whole crazy world will explain something."

With interest and growing wonder, Poppy examined the knife and its hilt. "It's gorgeous."

"It tells a story."

She smoothed her finger over the shapes on the handle. "People with wings. A flying snake. If it's a story at all, then it's one I can't tell." She handed back the knife. "Go on then, call your horrid wizard in the balloon. But make sure it's not the wizard that brought me because he's nasty."

Walking further and turning one more corner, Poppy and Nathan stood directly in front of the Tower moat, its ripples of dark water catching the sudden glint of reflected sun. Across this, the walls of stone rose high, mossy in its crevices, guarding the fortress within. Nathan stopped, staring up.

"Alright," he mumbled. "Come on Brewster. I know some of your secrets. Tell me some more. Or take Poppy and me back home to Granny October and leave us there in peace."

The entrance across the moat and through the wall was closed, although the drawbridge was down, and the iron portcullis was raised. Then, quite suddenly as Nathan and Poppy watched, the massive oak doors swung open, and two guards stood either side. From Tower Street, the wide road leading to the Tower entrance, there was the echo of many hooves and the sound of a bugle call. The noise came closer, a clattering of many riders clearly aiming for the Tower itself.

Neither Nathan nor Poppy had ever seen such a grand and glorious parade. First came four armoured guards, their horses covered in bright swinging and tasselled tapestries. Next rode a group of laughing, talking men, all mounted, turning to each other to speak. Finally two liveried gentleman rode, sitting very straight in their saddles and staring ahead. Last of all came two more guards, their pikes held beneath their arms, pointing upwards as if in salute to the sun. Each horse was handsome as though polished, and the men were dressed in rich velvets, furs and satins.

In considerable admiration, Nathan and Poppy stood back, keeping to the wall as the fine group of men trotted past. But at the last moment, as the parade began to cross the drawbridge, one of the men turned his mount aside, and came towards Nathan. Sure he was about to be in great trouble, he tried to shuffle into the deeper shadows, but the rider stopped in front and he and Poppy, looking down with a gentle smile.

He was a fairly young man with light brown hair, but with a face a little lined with care and worry. Looking directly at Nathan, the man spoke clearly. "Well, young man, I see you have been in some difficulty. I don't mean to criticise your clothes, but it would seem you have no money to spend on mending them or buying a new."

Blushing slightly, Nathan said, "Someone beat me up. And I've nothing to mend them with."

"Then after that, our home just got burned down," interrupted Poppy. "It's not been a lucky week."

"I cannot create good luck," smiled the man. "But perhaps I can help a little. I don't wish the children of my capital city to suffer. Have you no parents?"

Poppy shook her head. "We haven't any."

Nathan noticed that the entire group had stopped, their horses reined in and waiting. He wondered who the grand man was. Saying, "We're living in the ironmonger's cellar, because there isn't anywhere else," he smiled back with a small bow. He had never bowed to anyone in his life before, but he guessed this was a lord of some kind, and unlike the monstrous baron, this lord seemed pleasant and helpful.

The man leaned down across the horse's neck, and, calling back across his shoulder, said, "Francis, give this boy a sovereign." Smiling again at Poppy and Nathan, he continued, "I wish you both well. If you find yourselves still homeless in days to come, you have my permission to come to the Palace of Westminster, and ask for Sir Francis Lovell, saying that you have express permission." He waved to the man behind him. "This is Sir Francis Lovell, a gentleman of great talents and kindness who may order someone to find you work and a warm bed. In the meantime, God speed, and I wish you luck."

The grand man nodded, turned and road on, leaving the man he had called Francis to throw down a small leather purse at Nathan's feet. "Here, boy," he called. "Come to see me at the palace, should you require further help. Tell the guards there that you have a direct invitation from his majesty."

"Who was that man who came over to us?" mumbled Nathan, astonished, as Poppy quickly bent to grab the fallen purse.

Francis Lovell, riding off, looked back over his shoulder, laughing. "Why, the king of course. His royal majesty, King Richard. Surely lad, even a penniless beggar boy should know the king when he sees him. The greatest monarch we've had in many a long century. You've been lucky to meet him. He's in mourning for his queen, but no King has the choice mourn in peace."

And they were gone. The whole party trotted over the drawbridge, rode beneath the mighty portcullis, and disappeared into the Tower's huge courtyards. The sounds faded, the heavy doors clanged shut, and Nathan and Poppy, clutching the purse, were left staring after them in astonishment.

"The king," repeated Poppy, impressed. "I never thought I'd meet any kings or queens. Which one was that?"

"Richard III," muttered Nathan. "Brewster told me he was the king here. But I heard tell he was horrible, like the baron."

"I don't know anything about him, but he seemed nice to me," Poppy grinned, and opened the purse she still clutched. "Look. Three coins, one silver and two gold. But I don't know what they are."

"I know exactly what they are," said Nathan with a large sigh. "Fabulous good luck, that's what. The king said he couldn't create good luck, but he just has."

"But we didn't get Brewster."

"I don't care about Brewster just at this minute," Nathan said, turning quickly. "Let's go back with the money and show the others and tell them we have a special invitation from the king." He chuckled. "John always reckoned he'd end up as Sir John, Knight of the Realm. Now maybe he will."

"Or you will." Poppy was giggling. "I can't wait to tell Peter I've spoken to the king."

With just a few steps and two corners back to Bandy Alley, Nathan and Poppy arrived at the ironmongers to discover Pimple, firmly tethered, standing patiently in front of the shop, munching on turnips.

John was standing beside the horse, pulling his fingers gently through the tangled hair of its short mane. He looked up. "Now don't go telling me off fer buying them turnips," he said at once. "We all gotta eat."

"We can eat whatever we want now, and buy clothes too," grinned Nathan.

"Courtesy of the king," said Poppy, skipping in a circle and clinking the purse.

CHAPTER TWENTY-ONE

"I met the king." It still seemed incredible to him and to everyone else as Nathan told them his story. They clapped him on the back and pretended to bow at his feet. The excitement bubbled through the shop, into the cellar, and up again.

Having found Pimple wandering forlornly outside his own home at the beer carrier's yard, John Ten-Toes had been utterly delighted, bought turnips at the market, and led the small horse home again. Whether it was the sight of John, or the sight of the turnips, it was hard to tell, but Pimple was clearly cheerful again. Although hesitant at the lingering smell of fire, he allowed himself to be tethered outside the ironmongers and continued chomping. Mouse was licking her kittens clean as they rolled into obedient balls, squeaking and blinking. Sam curled content, Peter was busy trying to comb his hair which had blown into long and unkempt knots, and Alice, Alfie, Aunt Margaret and Uncle Henry had arrived back home. While Mister Winters kept the business bustling, Mistress Winters greeted her two eager guests, and showed them into her tiny solar upstairs from the shop. Although there was insufficient space, and also insufficient stools to sit on, everyone crowded in and were smilingly offered a light beer in a small wooden cup.

Poppy shook her head, trying not to pull a face, but Nathan took his with considerable curiosity. He tasted it and the suspicion cleared. He found it very watery, somewhat unpleasant, but easy enough to drink since nothing else was on offer. With no soft drinks in existence yet, and most water highly contaminated, dirty and full of disease, Nathan supposed that sloppy ale was all they had even for children.

"Well," said Uncle Henry, rubbing his hands together, drinking his beer with satisfaction, and smiling widely at everyone, "I believe we have succeeded. The admirable Percival Weeks is convinced that he can present the document, which is the Lady Alice's mother's final Testament, to the judge with every expectation of acceptance. My dearest Margaret is the next of kin named, and not the baron. We can have him evicted, and my dear Alice can move back home."

"Mister Weeks has his final important appointment to see the judge tomorrow morning," Aunt Margaret said quickly, "and I gather he has already hinted that he'll sign and seal an order demanding the departure of the baron. I shall be ready to watch as the wretched creature is hustled out with his tail between his legs. He has been a brute to Henry and myself, and I've lived in fear of him for several years."

"Only a few hours more to wait."

"Just one night more. But how shall I ever sleep?"

"Who cares about sleep when everything is about to go right at long last."

"The greatest good luck, my dear."

"Which is what the king said," mumbled Nathan. "And it's really happening." He was standing by the one little window, and looked across at where Uncle Henry sat. "If the judge says yes tomorrow. How long do you think it will be before the baron gets thrown out?"

"The nobility very rarely get thrown anywhere, I'm afraid," said Henry. "But he will be served with notice to leave, and if he hasn't done so by the end of the month, then guards will be sent to warn him that time is up."

Poppy slumped down again. "That means ages and ages and ages. What if he just won't go?"

Alice stood abruptly. "Then I shall appeal to the courts, the Constable, and the king too if I have to."

"We shall stay this night at the Whistle and Wherry," nodded Aunt Margaret, "and tomorrow we'll accompany the lawyer to see the judge. Alice will come with us too, of course. And," she smiled in a sweeping circle to include everyone, "we'll be back in an hour or two, bringing the wonderful news that we've all been waiting for."

After Aunt Margaret and Uncle Henry had left, with many thanks and kisses to Alice, Alfie hurried back downstairs to tell Sam and Peter. It was over dinner, sitting around on the floor of the cellar, that they all told each other their stories, exclaimed over the excitement of meeting the king, talked about the future, and planned exactly how they would live once they could move into Alice's proper home with her.

"We have to take Mouse."

"Of course we will."

"The king wore black velvet with golden padded bits on his shoulders."

"And the kittens."

"And Pimple."

"Pimple can have the best stable there is, and eat turnips every day until he gets too fat to trot."

"Black. Because the court's in mourning."

"Can I have a bedchamber to myself?"

"No, I don't want to be all alone. I've never slept alone. I want to share a bed with everyone."

"Well, not with me and Poppy."

"You'll have the grandest room of all, and the grandest bed."

"And I," sighed Poppy, "hope to go back to my own room and bed and granny."

Peter grinned. "Bet Alice's house is best. I bet you don't have a hundred candles, nor a big bed with four posts and a feather mattress, and a real garderobe with a painted chamber pot."

"That's true," agreed Poppy with a smirk. "I don't even know what a garderobe is. But I still want my own home."

"Just shows," sighed Peter. "you future folks don't have anything grand anymore. A garderobe is a proper private privy."

"A loo." Poppy giggled. "We have loos in the future, I promise we do."

Curled beneath his blanket, Nathan tried to sleep. He wondered if he was a little drunk after drinking beer for the very first time in his life. But it was the mystery of the Hazlett twins, of Lashtang, and of how he could get home that troubled him. Silently, he called to Brewster. But nobody answered him and finally he fell asleep.

Immediately he found himself back in his own kitchen, with the sun blazing in through the large windows, and the daffodils waving from outside in the garden. Granny October looked up from the kitchen table, where she was busy mixing something in a big blue bowl. "There you are at last," she scolded. "I've been waiting for you all day. Look, I'm making your favourite chocolate cake."

"I want to come home," Nathan insisted, and heard his own voice fading out, as though coming from a great distance. "You have to help me."

"I'm making a very nice cake," said Granny. "What more do you expect?"

"Tell me about Lashtang."

"Don't be silly, Nathan," she said, concentrating on the mixing bowl.

"Alright," Nathan sighed. "Tell me about the Hazlett twins."

"I have no idea what you're talking about, Nathan," she answered, not looking up.

Finally, taking a deep breath, Nathan asked, "Tell me about your name, then. I'm Nathan Bannister. So where's October come from?"

She finally looked up, gazing at him over her glasses. "I am your mother's mother," she told him with a slight frown. You know this. Your father's name is Bannister. Your mother's is October."

"October is a month," Nathan said quickly. "Not a name."

"Ah," Granny frowned, "that's because you assume it is spelled like the month. But naturally it is not. O – C – T – O – B – R. There's no 'e' between the 'b' and the 'r'."

Nathan stared. "Does that make any difference?"

"Of course it does, silly boy," said Granny. "That's the only way it has any meaning at all. Now," and she pointed, "sit down while I put your cake in the oven."

Which is exactly when Nathan woke up.

"Hurry, hurry, I want to look my best, even if I have holes in my stockings and my gown is ruined." Alice was combing her hair, trying to wash her face in a bowl of rain water, and brushing down her skirts.

"That lawyer man understands," Alfie assured her. "'Tis the whole point, ain't it? What wiv that vile step-father o' yourn trying to outright murder you."

"Shall we all go?" suggested Poppy? "It'll be so exciting, waiting outside, to hear the good news."

"T'were waiting near outside when the pig-baron done found us and attacked last time," John pointed out.

"This time," grinned Alice, "It will be the judge's chambers. And there are guards keeping a watch outside."

Alice and Alfie set off for the Whistle and Wherry at the London end of the Bridge, and the others settled to cleaning themselves up, which was virtually impossible, playing with the kittens, although they kept wriggling back to their mother's contented purr and dribble, making some attempt to clean up the cellar, which was even more impossible than cleaning up themselves, talking to Mistress Winters, although she was hurrying off to help her husband in the shop, and pat Pimple, even though the only thing he wanted was a turnip.

Eventually, except for Sam who curled up with Mouse, they all strode off, heading west through the old winding streets, avoiding markets, and making for the judge's chambers. Carter Lane, just south of St. Paul's Cathedral, and the address they had been told. It was a lengthy but not exhausting walk, and although late March had turned frosty, the sun shone low behind the clouds, brightening the rooftops.

Walking with John and Poppy, Nathan asked if anyone had heard about the smith's funeral arrangements.

"Woulda been done by now," John said. "Maybe 'e had no family and the priest done it quick. A bit of a mess, 'e was, after that fire."

Nathan winced. "But he said he had lots of grandchildren. His name was William Octobr and the grandkids called him Grandpa Octobr."

"Don't know nuffing 'bout the man." John shook his head.

"I quite liked him," said Nathan, although this was not entirely true. "I would have attended his funeral if I knew when it was."

Shrugging, John turned to Poppy. "Don't reckon I'll go to no funerals in me life, till tis time to go to me own."

Poppy, grinning, was staring out at the river. "Even the Thames has changed. Look, this is wider and more open. How does a river change?"

"People building up the banks," said Nathan. "But hurry up. I want to hear the good news."

Already the group outside the judge's office was animated, and growing larger. A tall gentleman in his judge's robes, was explaining the seal on the document. Alice, looking flushed, was peeping over his arm, and nodding. Alfie was almost jumping up and down, Uncle Henry and Aunt Margaret were even more flushed than Alice, and looked as though they had just run three times all the way around the cathedral.

Within moments, Alice clapped her hands and rushed to hug her aunt and uncle. The judge nodded to Alice, handed over the document he had been holding, turned on his heel and returned to his chambers. Aunt Margaret squeaked, sounding rather like Mouse, and Alice, laughing, turned to acknowledge the others. Nathan said, "You look as though you've won the lottery," and then apologised because he knew she'd have no idea what the lottery was. "So it all turned out as you hoped?" he asked.

"Better." Alice danced, pointing her stockinged toes. "The order for my horrid step-father to vacate my home will be delivered to him tomorrow morning. I hold the document, signed and sealed, that states I am the sole owner of the property, and that my legal guardians are my aunt and uncle. Everything is – perfect." Her smile was ecstatic. "Oh, Nat – so much is thanks to you. Since you came, and talked about making things happen, and then giving ideas and helping with so much, my life has changed entirely. I can't thank you enough."

Nathan really didn't feel as though he had done much. "That's sweet of you," he said, smiling back at her. But it's only what you deserve, after all. I mean – it really is your house."

"That's what the judge said. You saw him. He even came outside with me to say goodbye and explain a few things. And now I feel as if the whole world is smiling."

"Wish it was." Alfie was looking up to the sky. "Looks like t'will rain any moment."

The clouds had darkened, but the sunshine still managed to blink through in glimpses. Nathan looked up, nodding, and wondering if it would pour just in time for them all to walk home. Then, as well as being dressed in rags, he'd be soaked. But it was as he was staring upwards that he was sure he saw something else peep between the darkening clouds. He thought he saw an unexpected stripe of bright red, and two of gold. So he shook the hair out of his eyes and looked again. This time he could see nothing, only the glowering shadows as the clouds closed, blocking out the last of the sunshine.

"So," Poppy was asking, "what do we do now? Go to your house and kick the mean baron out?"

"I wish I could," Alice said. "But I have to wait until he's been served with the papers tomorrow morning. Meanwhile, all we can do is wait."

"Buy pies," suggested Alfie. "We got the king's money."

"And take one home for Sam," added Peter.

They stood in a cheerful group outside the tall buildings in Carter Lane, and were discussing dinner, how wonderful life was, and what they could take home for Mouse and Pimple, when another, very different, party swept around the corner, stopping in some surprise right in front of them.

One tall and haughty man, wearing a vast scarlet cloak, led the group, his head high, and his hat a wide-brimmed crimson with two long feathers shading his eyes. Behind him a cluster of officials, including two burly men in workman's tunics and heavy boots, stood awaiting the tall man's decision. But behind everyone, peering carefully around the side of the two strongmen, were both the baron and his brother Edmund.

Uncle Henry stepped forwards and greeted the proud Constable in his scarlet cape. I wonder if I might be of any assistance, sir, since I am the Lady Parry's legal guardian."

A somewhat muffled voice from behind, objected with a muttered, "Not true. Not true at all."

The Constable paused, waved one beringed and dismissive hand. "Do you have documents to back your statement, sir?"

He did, flustered but determined, Uncle Henry grabbed the parchment from Alice's fluttering fingers, and held it out to the Constable.

"Take it. Tear it up," said the same distant voice, half muffled.

But the Constable seemed unsure. "This is signed with the seal of Judge Collingwood," he said, tapping the scrawled signature. "A gentleman of the finest ability and utterly trustworthy. But I understand this is a difficult case, and the claim may be false. I require to speak with Judge Collingwood."

"Bother," whispered Alice.

"Oh dear," whispered Aunt Margaret."

"That's not fair," whispered Nathan.

Uncle Henry frowned. "If it pleases you, my lord, I will request the judge to meet with you upstairs. But I have had many meetings with him and my lawyer concerning this, and am assured that my claim is just, and is now certified."

"I shall see, sir." And the Constable opened the downstairs entrance to the chambers and marched in, shouting at a page to inform Judge Collingwood that the Constable himself wished a word with him."

The door shut behind him.

Nathan was momentarily amused to see that both Edmund Darling and the baron stayed carefully at the rear of the two rough men and did not seem at all ready to face Alice and her friends. Having been badly outmatched once, apparently they had no wish to try again. Both had bruised faces, and the baron's left hand was thickly bandaged. The little group of officials stood separate from the others, as if they would not demean themselves by being seen too close to such people. Indeed, the baron was hiding behind those taller than himself, but only Edmund seemed willing to stand close to him.

Talking softly amongst themselves, the officials did not speak to Alice nor her friends. Alice stood, arms crossed, and glared at everyone. Poppy meanwhile was picking daisies from a scrubby strip of grass along the side of Addle Hill, where the slope led down towards the river. Nathan walked over to her.

"Showing you're not frightened?" he asked her, grinning.

But Poppy looked up in surprise. "No. I like daisies." Which is when everything started to change once again.

Firstly the Constable marched from the judge's chambers, holding up the sealed document. He addressed the baron directly. "My lord, I am sorry to have to tell you that your guardianship of the Lady Alice, your step-daughter, is no longer valid. Judge Collingwood is accurate in his findings. We have looked over the situation together. And it is quite clear. The assumption of your guardianship was entirely mistaken."

Ignoring Edmund, who was cringing, the Constable walked over, and showed the document to the baron, who blinked, blanched, and then stood straight. "My Lord Constable, I am sure, indeed, quite, quite positive," he said loudly, as though addressing the deaf, "that this document has been falsified."

"I am not so easily duped, sir," announced the Constable. "Judge Collingwood has only just issued this document, which corroborates my opinion. There will be no arrest this morning of the Lady Alice and her young friends, not unless you have more evidence to bring against them." He looked over, searchingly. "You have cited your injuries, my lord. But I can see most clearly that these young persons have also been severely injured themselves."

"Self defence," muttered Edmund.

"I therefore find," continued the Constable, "that your habitation of the Parry residence is unlawful. You must leave the property forthwith, my lord, and make no further claim. The Lady Alice is now the ward of her Aunt Margaret and her Uncle Henry Fallows until she turns sixteen years of age, or marries."

Edmund went pink and swore under his breath.

Alice thanked the Constable, who bowed very briefly, nodded to his men to follow him, and strode off. Edmund, the baron, and their two swarthy companions watched them go. Alice stared back at her step-father.

"So when are you leaving?"

"Insolent female," the baron stamped one foot. "I've no intention of leaving. Indeed, I may sell the property privately and then leave the country. Or I may catch you as I did before, and cut your pretty throat."

Although, wishing to keep the peace, Uncle Henry put out a protective arm, Alice was furious. "You've no shame, you horrible, evil old man. How dare you flout the Constable and the judge and the lawyers too? I hope they throw you into the Tower and chop your head off."

As usual, the baron lost his temper. He stomped forwards, reached out and slapped Alice with his one bandaged hand, but as he reached to grab her with the other, Aunt Margaret screamed and Uncle Henry marched over and stood threatening the baron, whilst Alfie, John and Nathan surrounded him, punching out. Poppy threw her daisies into his face and yelled. One small daisy hovered on his nose and another had stuck to his eyebrow. Lurching sideways, he grabbed a large handful of Poppy's hair and swung her to face him. Shouting and spitting, he hissed, "If any of you dare touch me once more with your filthy little paws, I shall hurt this brat a great deal more."

Which was when the darkening clouds parted as though a vast black curtain was pulled back, and with a swoop of brilliant colour, the balloon swung down, and Brewster Hazlett leaned out with an echoing cackle.

CHAPTER TWENTY-TWO

N athan, running at the baron to free his sister, was knocked over by the rickety little basket, and instead Brewster, still laughing, poked one very long thin finger at the baron's nose, making him squint, and then snatched up Poppy, who flew through the air like a Ping-Pong ball, landing directly on top of Nathan.

Everyone else was staring open-mouthed at the swaying splurge of sound, colour and confusion. Aunt Margaret staggered, clasped her hands together in prayer, and promptly fainted. Alice screamed. Alfie and John raced towards Brewster, expecting a fight, whilst Uncle Henry stood very still and gazed in unmoving astonishment. Peter, delighted by the magical appearance, stuck his thumb in his mouth and smiled.

While Nathan and Poppy struggled up, Brewster had knocked off the baron's hat and grabbed his hair in a large red clump, much as the baron had tried to grab Poppy. The balloon bounced a little from the ground and rose a few feet into the air, with the baron, grasped by falling tufts of his hair, his forehead stretched in horror, was lifted, feet kicking into nothing.

The balloon managed a neat turn and rose higher with the baron swinging, his arms frantically reaching, his face swollen and puce, and his voice almost suffocated in his throat and just managing some desperate squeaks.

With another cackle, Brewster let him go and the baron landed, toppling and tumbling, into a whimpering heap as he cradled his head, rubbing at the place where now much of his hair had been ripped out.

The two strong men took one look and fled. Edmund collapsed backwards and begged shrilly for mercy.

Realising that it was the baron who had been attacked, and not themselves, Alfie, Alice and John hurried forwards. "Is that a balloon? Is you Nathan's friend? Are you the wizard he told us about?"

Brewster Hazlett stood in the swinging basket, waving both long thin arms as though conducting an orchestra. Laughing and bowing, he looked down on the small crowd staring up at him. "John Ten-Toes," he pointed, "your father has searched twelve long years for you." Cackling, he pointed at Alfie. "You will become a warrior, and a hero of the most unjust battle of the century." Pointing again, "The grand Lady Alice, you know your fate, though not all of it." Then with a mock bow to Peter, "From wizard to wizard, my friend," and as Peter stared, added, "I make no magic. I simply do what you do not understand. But you, Peter Speckson, you'll make magic with lute and song."

The silence around the balloon was so complete, no one could even hear the calls of the boatmen nearby, the rush of the river waters, the splash of the oars or the bump of the boats.

"And me?" whispered Poppy with a hiccup.

The narrow gleaming top hat had slipped over Hazlett's eyes, resting on the thin twist of his nose. No hair showed beneath the hat, but his eyes gleamed out like torches from the brim's shadow. He licked his thin lips, and his tongue suddenly appeared forked. With a slurp he sucked his tongue back into its place, and cackled again. With a smile as wide as his mouth permitted, he pointed at Poppy. His fingernails curled, turning to claws. "You, child of Octobr, wings of a dove, have a destiny I cannot and will not tell."

Poppy stared back at him. "Wings?" Her hiccups had increased. "I'm going to be a pilot?"

But Brewster had turned to Nathan. "Sporrans and spangles. Porridge and parsley. Cobwebs and cowslips. Sorcery and snap, snap, snap."

"You told Poppy October," Nathan said, accusing and defiant. "October with an 'e' or without an 'e'? And snap for snakes? Or is it some silly game you and Wagster play?"

As the balloon bobbed close to the ground, the sky's cloud cover had closed and was now so dark, it seemed like night-time Everyone began to move closer together, staring at the tall thin man, all black below the brilliance of his balloon. Brewster lay back now, his clawed hands clasped behind his head, the tall hat even further down over his eyes and balancing on the bridge of his nose. One leg swung out over the top of the basket ledge. His clothes were tight and gleaming black, but the one tapping shoe was bright gold, as though polished metal.

"Well now, Bumble-Bee Head," he cackled at Nathan, "October with an 'e' would make no sense at all, would it now! But snap is another matter. Snap goes the weasel. Snap goes the Granny clock. Snap go the jaws of the crocadillo, when it finds its dinner."

Shaking his head, Nathan sighed. "You make no sense. I give up. Or have you finally come to take me home?"

Brewster unwound. Suddenly, he stood so tall that he towered like a great black stick, golden feet in the balloon's basket but the top of his hat up into the balloon's rigging. "Now, which home would that be, Bumble-Bee Head?" he demanded, and reaching out like the strike of a serpent, he grabbed both Nathan's wrists.

Hauled to the basket, Nathan yelled, "Let me go," but was dragged closer. Then the balloon began to rise. Brewster's grip on Nathan's wrists was iron tight and did not slip. Kicking wildly, Nathan tried to free himself, but was drawn gradually upwards. Poppy raced forwards, attempting to grab Nathan's feet, but they were just above her reach. Then Alfie, the tallest, ran to help, but by now Nathan's kicking legs were up into the murk of the lower clouds.

It began to rain with a steady cold sleet, falling straight down without wind. Now the balloon was barely a flicker of colour high above, and Nathan looked like a squirming beetle, disappearing into the clouds.

Those below were left staring, although in desperation Poppy ran from Addle Hill into Thames Street, waving and shouting as the rain pelted down over her. Both Edmund and the baron had crept away, and now Alice, Alfie, John and Peter all followed Poppy, trying to reassure her. Peter was skipping through the puddles, but the others were shocked and frightened.

"Did that terrible apparition come to help or to destroy?" whispered Alice.

"Sent the pig-baron running."

"But Nathan?"

Poppy had burst into tears.

Nathan saw none of this, swept ever upwards, the balloon sped through the ice chill of the rain clouds, as gradually Brewster hauled him, hand over hand, into the safety of the little basket. Nathan toppled in as though he had expected never to feel safe again, but he was entirely out of breath. It was some time before he gulped, managed a deep gasp, and said, "You can't take me home and leave Poppy there."

"*Can't?*" demanded Brewster with menace. "I shall do whatever I wish, Bumble-Bee Head."

Trying to make sense of it all, Nathan asked, "So will Wagster bring Poppy home, since that's who brought her out?"

"Wagster?" Brewster forced his head so close to Nathan's, that the brim of his hat cut into Nathan's forehead, and he could see the wizard's eyes like little threatening fires. Hissing like the snake himself, Brewster said, Never say that name. Never speak of him. Never speak to him. And remember *Snap go the dragon's toes. And snap go his teeth.*"

Nathan recoiled, whispering, "Where are you taking me?"

Brewster paused. Then he sat back again, as though happy to begin a holiday. "It's not a long journey, and you'll not stay long either, Bumble-Bee Head. But you'll see what I let you see and you'll discover what I let you discover.

"Lashtang Tower, dark as night with no moon,

191

Lashtang Palace, blazing with flame.
One whispers soft the Hazlett name,
The other roars. Both hide your tomb.

Come taste the flames, come taste the ice.
Nightmare beckons, dreams of death.
Enter. Now breathe your final breath.
Peace at last, but Lashtang claims the price."

Nathan felt his stomach lurch as though the ice, rain, clouds and winds had all blown straight through him. "Lashtang?" he asked.

Brewster was chuckling with a throaty gargle, but he did not answer. They were flying above the rain, although great mists engulfed the balloon, and there was nothing to be seen looking up, or down, or out beyond. No horizon cut through the thick white haze. It was cold, and Nathan pulled his short cape around his shoulders, curling up tight in the basket with his head poking over the edge, hoping to see what was coming. But no landscape was stretched below and no sound permeated the mist.

Then with a sudden cluck, he felt the passing feathers above him, and knew a bird had flown over his head and saw a flutter of white. But they were far too high up for any normal bird, and Nathan peered out, still unable to see anything at all. Only Brewster, sitting opposite with the usual absurd grin, could be seen and even he appeared partially misted.

Yet then after a long wait, the sky cleared above. From his neck downwards, the cloud persisted and the haze made everything else invisible. Bu from chin upwards the bright blue was suddenly startling, fresh and even warm. Nathan stared around, delighted.

A thousand dragonflies danced and wavered in the brightness. Huge or tiny, vividly winged or shimmering iridescence, they soared and twisted, hovered or swooped. Some glittered brighter than the sun and others were the gentle silver of moon-glow. Some were quite black, and although translucent, their wings appeared spun from shadow. Nathan had never imagined so many interweaving creatures, and such a variety of dragonflies. Gaping, enthralled, he turned to Brewster. "Are they real?"

"This," Brewster answered, "is the veil. It divides Lashtang from other worlds."

"A veil of dragonflies?"

"A veil of disguise. Now, we open the wings of the many-winged, and you will be at home." Brewster had stopped cackling.

Standing tall within the basket, he appeared almost weightless. He was so elongated and so thin, that there appeared no space for flesh and bones, but he was energetic, as though pleased to be home. He reached to the flame within the balloon, and with a puff as small as though he snuffed a tiny candle, he blew out the blaze and roar of the fire.

Immediately the balloon began to twirl, gently as if caught in no more than a breeze, and floated feather-light to the ground. The dragonflies, dizzy within their veil, had been left behind. Nathan had entered Lashtang.

The sun shone, and the white glowing tips of the distant mountains were as brilliant as the stars. Sloping up towards the cliffs and the mountains beyond was a valley of deep grass and wildflowers. Peacefully unoccupied, the scene reminded Nathan of a postcard, with *Wish you were here* written large on the back. It was Poppy he wished was there but the countryside was empty except for the beauty of trees, flowers and sunshine. Not only had the dragonflies disappeared, but he could not see so much as an ant, a bird on a branch, or a scurrying beetle in the grass.

He turned to ask Brewster if anyone else lived there, and found that Brewster had also gone. The balloon had gone. There was no sign of life at all. Calling Brewster, Nathan felt a sudden panic. Having no idea where he was, nor where to go, he felt more alone than when he had been dumped back into 15th century London. Brewster did not reappear, nor did he answer the calls, and no balloon floated high in the cloudless sky. But the surge of panic faded. He had survived the previous adventure with all its threats and dangers, and this land was empty, so he was sure he could survive that as well.

Nathan began to wander. He headed away from the mountains, since he did not think he would be able to climb them, having no shoes, only woolly hose with a hundred unravelling holes in the knees and feet. Then, as he walked, he heard a vague squelch, and a squeak as of someone speaking very far away. He still saw no person, animal, nor insect, so he continued walking.

Then he stopped with a surprised jolt. "Help," said the voice. High, shrill and very, very small, the voice repeated its call. "Please help."

A minute green frog, yellow-bellied, large-eyed, but extremely tiny, was gazing up at him from the grass. Nathan said, "You're a frog."

"I'm not," replied the frog, its voice quavering. "Please help me."

Never having been asked to help a frog before, he had not the slightest idea how to do so, and sitting down beside it, mumbled, "How?"

"I smell the knife on you," squeaked the frog, hopping closer with some enthusiasm. "Cut the eternal chain. Cut it and destroy it. Then we shall all be free."

Patting his waist where the knife that he had found in the smith's ruined smithy lay hidden, Nathan said, "This one?"

And the frog blinked, and with a spring of pleasure, hopped onto Nathan's grubby knee. It said, "Indeed yes. The Knife of Clarr."

"I found it," Nathan explained. "I'm not anyone special. This used to belong to someone else."

"If you can carry it," said the frog, "then you can use it."

Leaning back, hands behind his head, on the grass, Nathan gazed at his new companion, smiled, but found he was growing deeply disappointed. His arrival in Lashtang had been puzzling but believable and he had accepted that Brewster, crazed as ever, was taking him on another adventure. But now, talking to frogs he was convinced that he was simply asleep and dreaming. This was not believable. He wondered how he could wake himself up.

"Go on then," he encouraged the dream-frog. "Tell me how. Where is this chain, anyway?"

"In the mountain palace," replied the frog.

"Oh yes," Nathan sighed. "It would be, of course."

The frog was puzzled. "I can lead you there. I know the way."

He wasn't bored, but he wasn't accepting it either. "Maybe later," he said, yawning. "But it's hot. I'll sleep first."

The frog became agitated. "No, no, not here," it squeaked. "You'll wake up as something else. A toad. A lizard. A sparrow."

Nathan wedged himself up on both elbows and regarded his unexpected companion. "So you went to sleep and woke up as a frog. What were you before?"

"A boat builder."

"That's it," decided Nathan. "This is all rubbish and I want to wake up, not go to sleep at all. In fact, I just want to go home."

"You'll never get home from here," said another deeper voice, and Nathan looked around. A cockerel, glorious in his many colours and regal feathers, was looking at him from a small rock. It balanced there, surveyed him with distrust. "Are you a proper human," he asked, "or have you been turned into one?"

Clustered around the rock at the rooster's feet, were six fluff-balls of soft lemon, their round eyes waiting expectantly and their beaks open as they squawked very softly.

"I'm completely human. But you're a cockerel," nodded Nathan. "So why do you have a clutch of ducklings instead of chickens?"

"Foolish boy," remarked the rooster crossly. "Mind your own business." And he stalked off with the six tiny ducklings hurrying after him.

"Who was that?" Nathan asked the frog.

"Stanley Blestone and his wives," said the frog without much interest. "Now, if you pick me up and put me in your pocket, I can tell you where to go."

Nathan didn't have any pockets. He pulled off his cape, since it was warm and sunny and no cape was necessary, tied it into a sack with the ribbons around his waist, hitched it up and doubled the knot, popped the frog into it, and nodded. "Oh very well," he said patiently. "I suppose I might as well play the game until I actually wake up and find out where I really am."

The frog seemed pleased and settled down in the depths of the shadowed cape. While Nathan began, very slowly, to walk towards the mountains. The sun was in his eyes, but the grass was soft, walking was easy, and there seemed nothing to spoil the dream.

Until the flood.

Without warning, it was from the mountains that the water came, booming down the slopes in dark torrents. There was no storm, no rain, and no dark clouds, but as though the barriers of an enormous dam had opened, the water tipped and swallowed the sunlight.

Without lightening but with a roar and vibrating pound of thunder, rushing water pelted towards Nathan, filling the valley and swelling up the sides of the lower slopes. As its black waves cannoned, a wailing of distant voices hung in the sky, like the mournful despair of a thousand drowning souls.

In absolute confusion, Nathan turned and ran. But you cannot outrun a deluge and in moments he felt the splash of spray against his back, then the soggy marsh of wet ground beneath his feet, and finally the strength of oceans lifting him up and hauling him from his feet and into the terrible blackness of an inescapable flood.

Flung up by the waves and then dragged downwards below the surface, Nathan heard the frog crying out, but could do nothing to save either it or himself. Looking down, he saw the frantic swimming of small lizards, fish-like creatures, beetles, and a tortoise with its mouth clamped shut in determination. Looking up, Nathan saw the swirling threat of the deluge, the tiny kicking of webbed feet from the ducks and other creatures attempting to survive, and the sudden eager flight of half a dozen birds freeing themselves from the waters.

It was as though the flood had been directed at him alone, but had carelessly trapped every small creature around him. A vision of tragic desperation swamped him, the panic and drowning surrounded him. The current sucked him deeper and he was dragged ever downwards. He swallowed filth and could not breathe.

Then, with a desperate wish to wake from the dream, Nathan closed his eyes.

CHAPTER TWENTY-THREE

H e woke, exactly as he had hoped, and with every wish granted.
There was his own bed back in Hammersmith, quilt to his
chin, and beneath this he was wearing his own striped pyjamas. Not
the ones he remembered wearing when Brewster Hazlett first took
him time-travelling, but another pair he had owned for several years.
It was warm. It was deliciously comfortable.

Now he knew it had all been a dream, exactly as he had already
guessed. Lashtang had been a remarkably silly one. Perhaps Alice,
Alfie, the baron, Mouse and everybody else had been a dream too.

Blinking, and looking around at his own wonderfully familiar
bedroom, Nathan saw Granny Octobr peeping around the door. His
answering smile was as huge as relief could make it. "Hot chocolate?"
murmured Granny.

Bliss. "Yes please. Absolutely. Yes please."

The mug was hot within his palms as he sipped. And then,
although he knew he must have drunk from this same cup a hundred
times in the past, he suddenly realised that it was decorated with a
large picture of the same knife that he had found in William Octobr's
smithy.

Nathan sat up a little straighter, peered closely at the big china
mug in his hands, drank more of the creamy hot chocolate, sighed,

and was about to snuggle down again into the bed, when a small voice said, "Feeling better, lord?"

A tiny yellow-bellied green frog was sitting on his pillow. Nathan gulped and swallowed so quickly, he burned his tongue. He managed to say, "Ug, u tot nem pobbible."

Granny Octobr sat on the edge of his bed, regarded him over the top of her glasses, smiled, and said, "I see you brought a friend back with you, Nathan. While you were sleeping, young Ferdinand Brook and I have had a highly interesting conversation."

"Really?" Gulp.

"Indeed," she said, with a one finger tap to the little frog's head. "Clearly I've been neglecting Lashtang for far too long. I had decided, you see, that the complications were beyond repair, and that leaving the problems to the Hazletts was the best solution. Now I see I was wrong. The responsibility is ours, and I cannot shirk that any longer. Clebbster Hazlett has turned to cruelty. I must interfere before it's too late."

Nathan had not yet closed his mouth. Finally sinking back against the pillow beside the frog, he muttered, "Am I still asleep?" but knew, now beyond doubt, that he was not.

"Sit up, dear," scolded Granny. "It's time to get involved. There's a good deal to understand first."

"So Lashtang is real?"

"As real as we are."

"And the balloon and Brewster Hazlett and the funny knife?"

"And me," said the frog.

"And Alfie and John and Alice and that horrible baron and his brother?"

"Really, Nathan," frowned Granny. "How can you doubt it after living with them for all that time and helping them so much. I'm sure you'd like to know that Alice has now reclaimed her legal home, and the others have moved in with her. But," she added, increasing the frown, "that doesn't mean the baron won't try to get rid of her again."

"And," this time Nathan asked very slowly, hoping against hope for the right answer, "Poppy's in her bedroom, asleep next door?"

"Ah," said Granny, "no. Your sister is sleeping, just as you said. But not next door. She's in a very large four-poster bed with long green velvet curtains, a lumpy mattress, and a big patchwork eiderdown."

"Oh, bother."

"Wake up, Nathan, and face the truth," said Granny, taking his empty mug from him and standing up. "There is a great deal to be achieved as quickly as possible. I have to go to Lashtang and try to put right all the damage done by that terrible flood. So unnecessary. So inexcusable. Clebbster is a brute."

Nathan had never previously heard of Clebbster. "Another twin brother? I mean – triplets?"

Granny shook her head. "No. Their father. A cruel and unforgiving man." She seemed about to say something else, but changed her mind, and bustled out, turning at the door with a last brief order. "Get up, Nathan. Come downstairs and bring Ferdinand with you."

"Who?"

"Me," said the frog.

The kitchen had not changed at all and Nathan wished he could hug it. Instead, he set the frog down on the table beside the teapot and sat on one of the old wooden chairs. Elbows on the table amongst the crumbs of toast, he put his chin in his hands and tried to make his brain work in straight lines.

Granny was washing the dishes. Over the busy clatter, Nathan asked, "So you actually come from Lashtang?"

"We all do, dear," she answered, wiping the soap bubbles from her fingers onto her apron. "Honestly, Nathan, where do you think your parents have been all these years?"

He had presumed that he could no longer be startled by anything. But he was, and collapsed, burying his head and hands on the table, crumbs in his eyes.

It was after more hot chocolate, two pieces of toast and marmite, a saucer of something that looked repulsive for Ferdinand, and a few more explanations, that Nathan managed to stagger back upstairs and get dressed. His torn and ruined clothes from old London were neatly folded on the bedroom chair, but Granny had suggested that she could make him some new ones. Nathan thought that would help. In the meantime he put on modern clothes including a warm jumper and faced Granny again.

"So you're thinking I have to go back to Alfie and Alice and collect Poppy?" He sighed. "Well of course I want Poppy back, but sometimes I think she's better at things than I am. What makes you think I'm capable of rescuing her?"

Granny paused, stared over her glasses, and then said, "Haven't you realised yet, Nathan, that you are very, very special?"

He thought she was joking and smiled reluctantly. "Could I," he asked, "have a couple of days of normal first?"

"So what do you call normal?" demanded Granny, looking up from her rolling pin. It seemed she was making pastry. "Normal in 1485 London isn't the same as normal here, and certainly not the same as normal in Lashtang."

"Alright." He sat down again. "Can I have a couple of days without any magic?"

She set the rolling pin down on the table with a bang, and the frog bounced, coughing flour. "And what is magic anyway? If you told your friends back in medieval London about electricity, they'd call it magic. And what about television and cars and trains and computers and planes and telephones? They'd be terrified. It would all be black magic to them. Magic is simply anything you don't understand."

Nathan gave up.

After the pastry, Granny got out her sewing machine. More magic, thought Nathan. Within a couple of hours, he had some bright new clothes for his return to 1485 and was ordered upstairs to change.

Ferdinand was fascinated by these developments and tried to follow what was happening, but he preferred to keep close to Granny. "Till I'm myself again, and back with the boats and the rivers and the crabs in the reeds, I shall be safer with the Octobr matriarch," he said apologetically. I would gladly have followed you, my lord, as the holder of the Clarr knife. But you are travelling elsewhere, I believe, whereas I wish to return to Lashtang and claim back my true identity."

Nathan was now eating home-made steak and kidney pie. "So

what does Octobr without the 'e' mean, anyway?" he asked, mouth full.

"My lord, you of all people should know that," the frog replied, shocked. "Each letter stands for the word. *ORIGINAL- CLAIMANT - THROUGH - OFFICIAL - BLOOD-RIGHTS.* The Octobr family are the true rulers of old Lashtang. Deposed by the Hazletts, of course, but they were usurpers without doubt."

On his bed, half in a daze, Nathan spent some time gazing at the Knife of Clarr, holding it up to the light and admiring the intricate beauty of the handle. In the stronger light he could now see that the blade had a goldish sheen and was not plain steel, and on the sharp edge, which curved slightly, the gold was bright. The handle was pure silver, and every wrought detail was stunning. "People with clawed feet, growing funny little wings," Nathan muttered, "and a serpent bigger than themselves," and he had a vague idea just who the serpent might be.

Already he wore the clothes Granny had made for him, a warm tunic, padded inside, in heavy black linen over a neat white shirt. His hose were warm black wool but stayed up far more easily than with the wrap-around ties of his previous pair, for this time they pulled up with strong elastic.

"You have four secret pockets," Granny pointed out. "So you can keep that knife safe."

"Perhaps you should have it if you're going back to Lashtang." Nathan felt a little odd wearing such clothes in his own bedroom, and stared, embarrassed, into the long wardrobe mirror.

"The finder of the knife is the holder of the knife," Granny shook her head. "It goes where it chooses. You can't give it away."

"It came from someone called William Octobr, Was he a relation?"

Granny was straightening Nathan's shirt collar, but looked up sharply. "Naturally. But I never knew him. Five hundred years ago."

"So why did he leave Lashtang?" demanded Nathan.

"Nathan, use your common sense," exclaimed Granny. "It was five hundred years ago that the Octobrs were thrown from Lashtang by the Hazletts during the '85 rebellion. Why do you think you've been sent back to London at that time?"

But he had no idea.

"Can I," he asked very quietly, "just once," and took a deep breath, "see my parents before I go?"

Her gaze was kindly and very sympathetic, but Granny Octobr shook her head, looking down and avoiding Nathan's eyes. "I'm sorry, my dear. That won't be possible. But," and she looked up again, her glasses poised on the tip of her nose, "I can promise you this. You will return to Lashtang one day, and you will eventually meet both your mother and your father. They are very well and there's nothing to worry about. They most certainly haven't forgotten you."

Nathan persisted. "When I was with Alfie and John, sometimes I had dreams when I saw you and you talked to me. Were they real too?"

"Not exactly real," she told him, "but messages. I sent you emails. Naturally you couldn't receive proper ones."

"So send me an email with my parents in." He sat unmoving. "Can you do that?"

"Well," and she paused. "Perhaps. I shall see." And she stood in a hurry, so that Ferdinand the frog had to hop abruptly off her shoulder, and landed in the sugar bowl. "It's time to go. For both of us."

He was surprised that she hadn't changed her clothes, since he had rather expected her to appear in exotic robes or some gorgeous sweeping cloak. Instead she pushed her glasses further onto her nose, and stuck her hands in her apron pockets. Ferdinand quickly snuggled down into one of the pockets, burying himself in flaky pastry and plain flour.

Nathan stood up too, his chair toppling over behind him. He checked his own pockets, knew he had the knife, and a few other things too which he had chosen to take with him. He grabbed up his old cape, and nodded.

The kitchen began to whirl. No balloon and no basket held him, but it seemed as though he would fly through both sky and time as always.

Then, with a slurp of something that looked like black treacle, the worlds began to slip and slide, intertwining, then separating, and finally intermingling like waves on the beach. Nathan saw the old cathedral of St. Paul's and thought he would land immediately, but then it disappeared and he was back in his kitchen again, but with swooping balls of purple mist. Within the mist the dance of the dragonflies appeared, faded, and then glittered in brilliance. It seemed the dragonflies were singing, and Nathan thought they had seen Granny, and were singing to her alone.

He twisted, finding himself once more back in his house, but falling down the stairs as though running so hard he had lost his footing. But then the stairs turned to the cliff side, with snow dripping from the peaks, soaking him, and melting into the ocean below. An earthquake of molten fire rose up from the cliff edge where he was standing, trying to balance himself against the buffeting of the briny wind. He was carried, sitting on a wave of fire and rock, hurtling down the mountainside towards the remains of the floodwaters lying stagnant in the valley.

First peeping, as though the clouds opened into windows, and he could press his nose on the glass and see inside his bedroom.

Then tipping again, sliding on lava, hotter than fire. It rose up in gaping mouths, attempting to swallow him, turning to long fingered grey hands trying to grab and pull him down.

He saw the remnants of screaming things, then knew they were cheering, and not dying but flying high. Nothing made sense.

His own kitchen, and the kettle boiling.

The dank cellar, and Alice stirring an iron pot on a little fire of twigs.

The flood, with small creatures helping each other. Large whiskered fish pushing small scrabbling lizards up to the water's surface. Beetles climbing onto the thick feathered backs of ducks. Ferrets reaching down to struggling dormice, carrying them to the banks in their mouths. Then the gurgle of receding ripples, and a tortoise with two baby hedgehogs sitting on its shell, poked out its head having floated for some time, then waddled onto dry ground as the hedgehogs slipped, squeaking from its back. A sloth sat high in a tree, looking down, and with a cheerful squeak released the clutch of baby geckos it had saved. A lobster retrieved a drowning rabbit and tossed it high, so it flew from the water and landed near the hollow of its own burrow with a grateful bound. A fox emerged from the low water; bringing three bedraggled little owlets with him, desperately fluffing up their feathers, wide-eyed.

Nathan saw Granny, sitting complacent with her hands patiently clasped on her aproned lap. Right before his startled gaze, she whirled upside down, righted herself, and abruptly disappeared. Then he realised that Ferdinand was clinging to his hair, slipped with a gasp, hung onto his ear with webbed panic, and managed to hop onto Granny's nose, where the frog settled on the rim of her purple framed glasses as she made one last obliging appearance.

Zooming in circles like the slats of a windmill, Brewster Hazlett flashed into space, and continued to cackle, his smile as wide as his chin, while licking his sharp pointed teeth with a flick of his long forked tongue.

And then - finally – an alley with wet cobbles and the great stone wall of the Tower closing off the light at the end. So Nathan knew exactly where he was.

He realised, almost immediately, that he felt at home. It amused him, thinking about it, that a place more than five hundred years gone, would be so cosy and familiar to him that he would feel he had come home. But it was true, and he looked forwards to seeing the others.

Walking north, Nathan chose the streets he remembered, quickly up Mark Lane, across Fenchurch Street and into Billiter Lane, and Leaden hall Street to Bishopsgate.

The drizzle was a dreary grey, but as it shone wet over the cobbles, it gleamed and seemed like a welcome to Nathan, encouraging him to hurry. Life seemed safe again. He had his grandmother's word that Alice was back in her own home, and all his other friends too, and he was very much looking forward to seeing everyone again. Even Mouse. Even Pimple. And perhaps even the king.

CHAPTER TWENTY-FOUR

"The Lady Alice," announced the steward, "is at home, sir. But she is resting. I shall ask whether she is able to receive you." This was not the baron's officious steward Lacey. He was a plain man with receding hair, and a forehead of frowns.

"Tell her Nat Bannister has returned."

"I shall inform her ladyship."

Alice jumped the last four steps of the grand staircase, raced from the shadows onto the doorstep, brushed the drizzle from her eyes, and dragged Nathan into the warmth.

"You're back. You're back." She danced around him. "I'm here in my own grand house, as you see, and so much of that is thanks to you. We were all terribly upset when you went away. And it was all so frightening, and Poppy cried and cried and John went to church to ask for your safe return. I don't think he's ever been to church before, but now he got a 'yes,' so he'll have to go again to say thank you. Come in, come upstairs, and show yourself to everybody."

Nathan followed her, taking the stairs two at a time. "So, no more Lacey?"

"He left when my vile step-father got kicked out. I expect they're together, but I haven't asked where. I got rid of the assistant cook Oliver too, and three of the gardeners. "

As she spoke, Alice flung open a door immediately at the top of the stairs, and a dance of candlelight sent the shadows flying.

Everyone looked up, and then jumped up. It was Poppy who reached Nathan first, throwing her arms around him, and then Sam, who was unapologetically excited. Nathan had never been so emotionally welcomed in his life. It made him feel surprisingly overwhelmed, and he hid the slight sniff.

Poppy screeched, "At last. I was so frightened. Where have you been?"

It wasn't a story he felt he could tell everyone, and so Nathan just nodded, smiled, and said he had magically returned to his own time and home for a few short days. "As I have," Alice said, beaming. "But more than just a few days. It is weeks since you left, and both my uncle and the lawyer have helped me so much. The baron was forced to leave after a very public meeting with the judge, who threatened to take the case to the king if my step-father didn't leave at once. He went bright red like his hair, it was so funny. I wish you could have seen it."

"I wish I could have too."

"But I've been back here for just over a week," Alice explained, "and we are all nearly settled in. My aunt and uncle are here very often but they like going back to their cottage in Hammersmith, so I don't see them all the time. It's exactly the way I like it."

"John and me, we shares a bedchamber," said Alfie with pride. He was looking very smart in a proper doublet.

"And Peter and me," said Sam.

"But I have a little room all to myself, which is beautiful," Poppy said, "because of course Alice, as lady of the house, has her old bedroom back. And there's space here for everyone, it's so big."

"We eat every single day." Taking his thumb from his mouth, Peter spoke in a voice of astonishment as if eating daily was virtually unheard of.

"And so does Mouse."

"And I reckon Pimple does an 'all," interrupted John, "though we don't see him every day. Reckon he's resting."

Eating, as Nathan soon discovered, was favourite past time, he had never been offered so much food, on so many different platters, and could never have tried them all. "But that doesn't matter," Alice explained, "because whatever is left over goes to the servants if they want it, and to the poor who come to the kitchen doors." This didn't sound ideal to Nathan, but it was, he realised, the habit of the times and it was not about to be changed just because he didn't approve.

It was a beautiful old house, with three storeys, many casement windows with their leaded mullions, a principal hall with a dining table that could seat twenty, and a high vaulted ceiling, a hearth that stretched almost the length of one wall, and a staircase sweeping upwards. The grounds were not extensive, but there was a gravel walkway that wound between short hedges, and here the sunshine, on a bright day, turned the foliage to emerald. Within the house it was shadowed, but a candelabra of candles was lit each day, and there were many other candles, braziers and torches throughout the corridors and bedchambers.

Nathan sat on his new bed, gazed around him, and grinned to himself. The room was neither tiny nor huge, and more than half the space was taken by the great four-poster bed. Sleeping in one of these was something else that Nathan had never imagined doing in his life, but he found it extremely comfortable. The base swung a little on knotted rope, but he liked that as he curled each night. Wooden shutters blocked out the moonlight, and as he blew out his little bedside candle, Nathan felt safe, enclosed, warm and cosy.

Mouse stalked the corridors, peeping into each bedchamber for a last goodnight before slipping off into the gardens for moonlit hunting. Her babies were growing bigger, their huge blue eyes regarding the world with wonder, their whiskers twitching. They shared the bed with Sam and Peter, who looked after them until Mouse returned to take over in the morning.

But it was in private that Nathan told his story to Poppy. She sat on his bed, leaning back against the carved wooden headboard, listening in amazement to his tales of Lashtang, the dragonflies, the small creatures turned from human to animal, and then the catastrophic flood. But she listened in even greater wonder to what Granny Octobr had admitted.

"Octobr means queen?"

"Well, not exactly."

"Our very own granny is a sort of witch?"

"I don't think she'd want to be called that either."

"We've been living all our lives without knowing all these strange things?"

"And without knowing who, what and where our parents are."

Poppy flopped flat out on the bed, stretched out her arms, shut her eyes, and breathed deep. "Crazy."

"Perhaps we both are."

"So," Poppy opened her eyes again and stared at Nathan, "when can I go to Lashtang?"

Sighing, Nathan shook his head. "I don't know how to go anywhere. Not home. Not Lashtang. No idea. Granny can do things. Of course, the Hazletts can do things. But me – nothing!? Poppy laughed at him.

The weather, now early May, had improved. Although winds whistled around the chimney pots, the sun glittered on the river and peeped in through the windows. Alice and Poppy went shopping in the markets, and even John, now clothed in dark red velvet and a short brown cape lined in lamb's fleece, could not be recognised as a cut-purse and thief, or chased from the shops.

But there were some things that could not be bought in the market, which Nathan had brought back with him. And they seemed as magical as Lashtang did to Poppy.

"Chocolate." A bar of different type and flavour chocolate for each of them.

"A ball-point pen." Four of them, in fact. And four little note pads to write on.

"Tights – I mean hose – for everyone. With elastic waistbands. Really comfy and they won't fall down. And they'll fit because they stretch."

Astonishment, applause, delight.

The chocolate lasted almost two days because each of them wanted the miracle to continue forever, and they sucked slowly, nibbling only a little as they drew the bars reverentially from within their doublets. Only Poppy ate hers quickly, then looked around blank-faced as everyone was staring at her in horror at the lack of appreciation.

Although only Alice, and of course Poppy, could read and write, the pens were treated with equal delight, and the notebooks with their little pages, each decorated with the picture of a rose, were considered absolutely beautiful. The elastic wasted tights, black wool, of fine quality, were such a joy that it seemed John would play with his more often than wear them.

Other thrills abounded. Nathan had brought a pocket torch, complete with four spare batteries. Everyone took a turn clicking this on – admiring the light – and then off, with a sigh of wonder.

Lastly was the most magical of all. Nathan had found, and brought with him, a miniature Rubik's Cube, which everyone thought amazing, loving its colours as each played, spinning the different squares one after the other. Nathan explained the aim, which he had never been much good at himself. He was somewhat surprised to find that after five attempts, it was Alfie who solved the puzzle with a grin.

"Magic," said John, with a whisper of awestruck wonder, "has done entered our lives. I ain't never gonna be the same."

Having left his home in some haste, there were many other things Nathan wished he had brought with him, but had not thought of at the time, yet he hoped one day to learn how to pass through the barriers himself, and come and go at will. Then, he laughed to Poppy, "I could start my own medieval chocolate shop in the middle of Eastcheap."

But the one other thing he carried in his hidden pockets was the Knife of Clarr, and this he did not show to anyone.

Wearing his sturdy black leather school shoes with the clothes Granny had made him, and the oiled cape he had bought before, Nathan decided that he looked more like Alfie and John's servant than their companion, so he bought himself new clothes, as had all of them. He felt over-dressed in the deep blue doublet with its padded sleeves slashed in pale blue. A doublet was only a sort of closed jacket after all, but men liked fancy materials and decoration, which Nathan did not like at all. Poppy, he thought, looked like a princess in flowing pastel pink velvet, and Alice had passed on the fur trimmed cloak that John had stolen for her. Alice now had all her own clothes back, and a maid to help her dress in them each morning.

Uncle Henry and Aunt Margaret came regularly and stayed two or three nights every week, but much of the time they left Alice alone. "She's only thirteen," Nathan told Poppy. "No way she'd be left to run her own life in our world."

"All she has to do is smile and wait for the staff to do everything for her," Poppy giggled. "It's an easy life for ladies with titles and money, even if they are only thirteen years old."

"Except for those with horrible step-fathers."

The first time Nathan saw the baron, it was not a surprise. He had gone alone to the riverbank, watching the little boats row across, taking their passengers to the wooden planked piers where the wharfs offered easy unloading.

"Taxi ranks," Nathan said to himself. But as he watched, one boat was heading upstream with two fat gentlemen sitting together, somewhat unbalancing the boat since the wherryman rowing hard opposite them was small and thin. The little boat definitely had a backwards tilt.

The baron was clearly angry and was shouting at his brother, but Nathan could hear no words over the busy thud and splash of the river traffic. Then they were out of sight, and Nathan thought no more of it.

He was equally unsurprised when he saw both Edmund and the baron on the following day when he accompanied John and Alice to market. This was a covered warehouse on the southern corner of Bishopsgate, which Alice called the Foreign Market. No one appeared to be speaking in a foreign language, but Nathan soon realised that foreign simply referred to anyone who was not a Londoner.

The sun was shining and the east wind was blowing, the market was buzzing and the stall's awnings were flapping for although the market was roofed, there were no enclosing walls. The tooth-puller, pliers and string already blood-stained, stood at his usual corner. Behind him were six stalls all selling root vegetables. John, buying turnips for Pimple, peered at each one.

"How much?"

"Penny a large bag, mister. Fresh and crunchy."

"Bit much. Do a deal?"

"I'll throw in two more turnips. Now tis worth a penny and more."

It was a large bag, but John didn't seem to mind the weight, and marched cheerfully on. He aimed for the corner where the market stalls edged back, making space for the entertainers. One man was juggling three wooden cups and two platters, dancing as he threw these into the air, one after the other. Next to him stood a man playing a reed pipe with one hand, and beating a small drum with the other. There were chickens for sale, a young goat and some pigs scrounging in the earth, cabbages, herbs and spices, tortoise-shell combs, fresh baked bread and freshly cooked pies.

No tomatoes, potatoes, pumpkins, tea, coffee or chocolate. Nathan had realised some time back that these things had all been discovered in America, and Christopher Columbus had not yet sailed.

John's hat was blowing off as he hurried to catch Nathan up, after watching the piper and the juggler. "I just seen that horrible baron and 'is revolting bruvver," John said under his breath. "They was talking to some nasty big wrestling fellow, what fights folk fer money and wagers."

"I saw them yesterday," Nathan nodded. "I suppose they still live somewhere. But they don't seem to recognise us now we're all smartly dressed."

"I reckon they both lives in the bruvver's house," said John. "Up near Cripplegate it were."

"I don't care," smiled Nathan. "They can't hurt us now."

An elderly scribe sat at a tiny table, his quill and ink beside him, parchments spread before him on the table top. "Show him yer funny quill wiv the ink all sucked up inside," suggested John. "Poor fellow would faint, I reckon."

Alice wandered back to them, her basket overflowing with herbs, and the perfume rising fresh and sweet. Nathan immediately carried her basket for her, John carried his turnips, and they walked up towards the London wall, and Alice's home. The spring wind rattled the window frames and on the opposite side of the road, a brick toppled from a chimney pot. "Sometimes them whole chimneys fall over in strong winds," John said, pointing. "We better get inside."

It was that evening after supper that Nathan smelled burning.

He told Alfie. "Just the kitchens, I reckon," Alfie decided, stretching out his legs to the empty hearth. Too warm for fires, it was only in the kitchen that the flames blazed, for without fire they could not cook.

"But," Nathan said slowly, breathing in the distant stench, "it doesn't smell like food. It's a dirty smell."

"You reckon them kitchens is all scrubbed and spotless?"

"Well, no," Nathan decided, "but we only had a light supper and most of that was cold cheese and smoked sardines."

"Don't like them sardines. Reckon tis the smoking what smells rotten."

Nathan walked first down to the kitchens, and startled all the cooks, scullery boys and pages as he walked in and asked if anything was burning. The two hearths were indeed alight, but there was no raging blaze and the logs were burning low. From there Nathan hurried to the pantries but found only the usual dark shelves, lightless tubs and jars, and the aromatic scent of spice.

He checked the cellars, including the tiny stone cell where once he had been tied up and imprisoned himself. Now it was used to stack beer kegs, and it was cold. Back upstairs, Nathan darted into every room, and when the others saw him, he explained and they began to follow, sniffing for any threat of fire.

"No chimneys fell, and not much smoke neither."

"Ain't nuffing in the hall. No candles done fallen and no torches nor ashes."

"I have looked in every single bedchamber, and both garderobes, there's no sign of fire, Nat, but now I can smell it too." Alice was running up the stairs.

"So do I," said Sam suddenly. "Where's our babies?"

"I got them," said Peter, the three kittens bundled up in his arms. "Mouse is out, but I can save the little ones."

"I shall inform the servants," said Alice, a quiver to her voice. "We need buckets and water barrels and I'll send the scullery boys down to the conduit." She turned to the others. "It may be dangerous. Until we know where it is and how big, then we ought to leave."

"I can help fight it," Alfie said at once. "Reckon I'll stay."

"Me too," John said, standing beside him.

"Well, get the younger scullery boys and pages out, and the two maidservants too. They're all too young. We can't risk anyone being hurt."

The stink of it rose up around them, like unseen smoke or a mist descending from above. Now they all hurried through the rooms, and in a rush of desperation, the servants explored each corner. Scullery boys raced up and down the stairs, the cooks, waving huge wooden spoons, leapt behind. The pages, nimble in and out of cupboards, could find nothing.

"I know," muttered Nathan, and disappeared up the stairs once more.

On the top floor, instead of turning back again, he found the tiny steps which led from the end of the dark and narrow corridor, ten black wooden blocks, going seemingly nowhere, but which stopped at the trapdoor to the attic.

Smoke, noisome and dark, billowed downwards, and the trapdoor was askew.

He yelled, "I found it," but no one heard. Heading immediately back downstairs, Nathan began to wonder how a fire had started in an unused attic, where nothing was stacked, where no one went, and where there was nothing except the roof above. He hurtled the last steps and bumped into Alfie. "Attic," he gasped, breathless.

His explanation was no longer needed. The flames had followed him.

The heat raged against his back as the fire took hold, and the smoke whirled in dirty clouds that made everyone cough, feeling nauseas. A long rug which covered the corridor floorboards was alight, and added to both stench and smoke. The steward, his frowns multiplying, organised the relay of buckets, but although the water doused the smaller licking flamelets, the larger blaze continued, rushing from one corner to another. Window shutters flickered, changed from brown to scarlet and gold. Tapestries on walls singed, then leapt into flame. A bunch of dried flowers sitting in an earthenware vase within the empty hearth, became a small heap of hissing ashes.

Nathan could see running shapes, but through the darkening smoke and scattering scarlet, it was impossible to see who anyone was. The steward threw water, which soaked him, turning heat to freeze, but only for a moment. Then he thought he saw Alice, but her skirts were on fire and when he rushed to extinguish them, he found her gone. Desperate to help and terrified that someone might die, and that the beautiful house might be destroyed forever, Nathan stood tall and shouted, "As the bearer of the Knife of Clarr, I demand the powers of the Octobrs."

Reaching, ready to pull out the knife as the flames mounted around him, he heard first the clatter, then saw the flash of silver light amongst the raging red, and realised the knife had fallen, and lay now at his feet. He picked it up, surprised since it had never before dropped from its hiding place, and pointed it, feeling a little frightened and even slightly foolish, at the flames. Nathan did not expect a magical reaction, but within a blink. It came.

The change was immediate.

CHAPTER TWENTY-FIVE

I t seemed, incredibly, as though everything moved backwards.

The points of each flame, the flickering crescendo of each blazing pinnacle, suddenly turned back into itself, as if it had decided not to burn after all. The roaring of oncoming threat was silenced, and turned quite suddenly to a whisper of retreat. Where items had been burned away, where walls had been scorched and furniture singed, the stains of heat faded back and everything glowed again, untouched. Even the ashes, where something had been utterly destroyed, twisted again into their rightful shape, and with a faint and tentative crackle, thrust up as bright as new. Flicker by flicker, each flame, whatever its size, cringed as if terrified to continue. Slowly and carefully, the blaze ebbed and was gone.

Along the passageway and back up the stairs, the flames hissed, went out or hurried into shadowed oblivion. Scurrying backwards, the fire not only went out, but was as if it had never been. There was no burned echo, no damage, and no smell. Everything was fresh as though washed. And Nathan stood in the middle of it all and stared around him in complete wordless astonishment.

As if it never was," he whispered, still holding the little knife with its beautiful and unusual hilt, pointing towards the disappearing fire.

Alice crept up behind him. "Did that really happen?"

Nodding, Nathan turned. "You saw it too? Then it really happened."

"You didn't just put it out, Nat. You made it go backwards and disappear."

"I think," he said, "you should send someone up into the attic, because that was where it all came from. There might be some signs left."

She sent the steward. But it was John who came running up the stairs, shouting, "How? Wot? And who were that big fellow out the back running away?" Neither Alice nor Nathan had seen anyone, but John was entirely convinced. "It were the wrestling fellow I seen in the market wiv the baron yesterday. I knows it. And I reckon the baron paid him ta start a fire."

They stood looking both at each other, and at the last traces of fire as it fled up the stairs to the attic, and was gone. For one brief moment, the traces of the smell, and a swirl of condensing smoke told the story, but then even those signs had entirely vanished.

"Not even a little scorch mark is left." Alice was shaking her head as though entirely confused.

"Never mind 'bout that," John objected. "Wot about the rotten baron? I reckon tis all his doing. The pig-man wanted to burn us out and the house down."

"We could have been killed."

"So best go back ta that lawyer fellow." John was furious. "Tis not only us. Coulda killed all them poor boys in the kitchens. Coulda caught in this wind and ended up burning half o' London."

"It's true." Alice put her hands over her face. "It was a wicked thing to try and do. But how can we prove it was my step-father?"

"Catch the wrester fellow," said John. "Make 'im talk."

The others had gathered around, shaking their heads in shock. The steward returned, reporting that the attic had been searched and there were no signs of fire, nor of damage. However, the trap door was askew as though someone had climbed up there, and a tinderbox lay on the floor.

"But," Nathan pointed out, "how can you accuse the baron of

starting a fire, when there isn't the slightest sign of any burning at all. The lawyer and everyone else would think we were mad."

"How true." Alice stared around at the clean and polished corridor. "I'd be sent to Bedlam. What fire? Clearly there never was a fire."

"We'll have to deal wiv the baron ourselves," said Alfie. "And wiv that magic knife o' yourn, Nat, I reckon we can do somefing proper awesome."

Nathan was still holding the knife. He looked down at it, running his finger over the smooth glowing metal. It worried him a little, that he owned something with such astonishing power. He also wondered what more it was capable of. Could it act without his orders? Could it make decisions on its own? Although it had achieved exactly what he wanted with the fire, he had not spoken those words, and the results were far better than he could have imagined. He only wished for the flames to stop and go out. Yet the magic had exceeded his hope. That was wonderful. But it was also a little frightening.

"I think," he said, "I'd sooner not use this knife too often. I don't know what you want to do to the baron, but I just want to hide the knife away for now. I'll try to think of another plan."

He looked down, and realised that Poppy was standing at his elbow, waiting for him to finish. "Don't be a coward," she snapped, "I bet that thing can do whatever you want."

"What if it can do things I don't want?" Nathan answered her.

"We need to practise," Poppy decided. "Come on, let's go into the big hall and sit together like we used to in the cellar, and find out the secrets of that magical knife."

Nathan paused. He would have liked to refuse, but the whole group was looking back at him with such wild excitement, he surrendered. "Come on, then," he said. Holding the blade close. "Let's make a magic circle." He was laughing, but he wasn't at all sure if he was doing the right thing.

Although there were comfortable chairs and a long cushioned settle in the hall, they all chose to sit on the floor, just as they used to in their warehouse and then their cellar. But one thing was very different, for this time they had a large platter of marzipan biscuits and a big jug of light ale warmed with spices, cloves, and nutmeg. Although Nathan did not like the few tastes of beer he had tried in the past, this spiced ale he found very pleasant. Poppy, however, pulled a face and said it was disgusting.

"Right then," started Poppy, eyes glinting in the candlelight, "point your knife at my cup of ale, and make it turn into Coca-Cola."

Chuckling, Nathan did as she asked. The knife reflected Nathan's smile, but nothing else happened.

"So turn the marzipan biscuits into chocolate cookies."

With the knife pointing, Nathan called loudly. "Make these biscuits different. Chocolate, not marzipan." The knife, with suitable contempt, went dull. "Look. It's asleep," said Nathan.

The candles were burning low, and the shadows drew in. Alice shivered. "Make me nice and comfy and warm," she said.

But Nathan shook his head. "I won't risk pointing this knife at anyone," he said. "I don't trust it. Not yet. Ask something else."

"There's cobwebs right high up on them beams," Alfie pointed. No broom would ever reach, for the ceiling was very high and vaulted. "Tell your friend to get 'em down."

"My friend?" Nathan laughed again. "Perhaps that's what's wrong. I'm thinking of it more as an enemy rather than a friend."

"Crazy," Poppy said, with a pout. "That knife's the greatest friend you could have. It did a miracle. It saved all our lives. It's *wonderful*. I *love* it."

"So, come on friend," smiled Nathan. "Bring down those cobwebs,"

But once again, nothing happened.

It was quite sometime later that everyone trooped up to bed, a little disappointed by their attempts at magic, but enormously relieved at the disappearance of the fire. The steward regarded his mistress with enormous respect. He had certainly never before been employed by anyone who could produce such astonishing magical results. But it was Nathan who was more puzzled than anyone else.

"Good night, Nat. Golden dreams, and thank your beautiful knife from us all."

"Good night, Nat. Good night, knife."

"Sleep well. I just hope the fire doesn't start again in the night. Better keep that knife handy, Nat."

Nathan lay on his bed, the knife lying across his lap. He had not closed the shutters over the window, and the starlight was a creamy studded gleam from the sky outside. The moon was almost full, a glorious silver light peeping out from behind the clouds. The wind had not yet died down, and it blustered around the rooftops, whistling a little through the blackness. But it was the knife which interested Nathan, and he watched as it caught the starlight as though ingrained with diamonds.

"Now I wonder," murmured Nathan to himself, "why you were so incredibly powerful against the fire, but not for any of the funny little things that other people asked." He stroked the knife and its intricate hilt. Then suddenly he had an idea. Everything he had asked the knife to do that evening in the hall had been requests from other people. There had been nothing he wanted himself. So now, pointing the knife at the window, he said softly, "Put up the shutters."

It took only a moment. The shutters themselves, big slatted wooden boards which sat on the floor, resting against the wall under the window, did not seem to move. But one moment the window was clear mullioned glass showing the sky outside. And the next moment, it was closed off with the shutters clicked solid into place.

"Wow," said Nathan, "now that really is magic. Incredible. And all mine. It really is a friend after all." And he leaned over, and kissed the blade, just as if this was his greatest friend, or perhaps even a member of his family. He almost felt as though his mother and father had returned to him.

And that, of course, gave him another idea.

He held the knife upwards, pointing at nothing in particular. And then he started to twist it. Gradually turning it faster and faster, he whispered, "Show me my mother."

It seemed as though nothing happened, and this time Nathan was bitterly disappointed. He waited, rubbing the blade of the knife as though polishing it. Then he asked again. "Please. Show me my mother."

With the window shuttered, no light entered the small room. Complete blackness surrounded Nathan, except for the sliver of silver gleam which came from the knife itself. So Nathan closed his eyes with a sigh. He hoped that perhaps his mother might make a brief appearance in his dream, and so he settled to sleep. He pulled up the eiderdown to his chin, kept the knife in one hand, curled up, and waited. But the excitement had been too much, and he could not sleep. He felt more like leaping out of bed and turning somersaults.

Tossing, trying to get comfortable and resist the restlessness, Nathan turned and found the knife scratching his leg. He hurriedly moved it to his pillow, but was then frightened that it might stick into his face while he slept. With a deep sigh, he tucked it beneath his pillow instead. Once again he closed his eyes, and tried to think of sheep jumping a low fence. One. Two. Three. Four, but one ran in the opposite direction. Five, but a farmer started shouting from the field behind the sheep, calling them all to come home. Six, but the sheep refused to jump. Seven, but a sheepdog was running in circles, and the sheep all got confused.

Nathan opened his eyes and sat up.

And then he heard a strange noise, as of someone tapping on the outside of his window. Assuming it was simply the wind, Nathan tried to ignore it, but the tapping grew louder.

Finally, shaking his head in disbelief, he crawled out of bed and went to the window to see what was tapping. He thought it might be a loose nail banging in the wind, or a broken slat. But when he lowered the shutters and looked out of the window, he could find nothing wrong. So he opened the window.

The wind blew in with a whoosh and a tumble, a bump and a whole armful of white feathers. He shut the window again as fast as possible, clunk. But the whoosh continued. Then a voice behind him said, "Passage to Lashtang. Was it you who asked for a lift?"

With a jolt as sharp as the knife blade, Nathan turned.

It was a Goose. Large, smart, tall as Nathan's shoulder, pure white as snow and fierce-eyed, the Enbden goose stood beside the bed and regarded Nathan, who stared back with considerable confusion. "Did – you say something?" he asked with a hiccup.

"Certainly," said the goose. "I received the usual message. Someone needs a special lift to Lashtang, payment already negotiated. So here I am."

"But," mumbled Nathan, "who sent the message and who negotiated the price? I'm not sure where I want to go. Well, I suppose I did ask – but I didn't expect anything like this." He thought a moment. "I'm not sure I want to go," he ended on another hiccup.

With a sort of feathery shrug, the goose settled itself on the little Turkish rug at the end of the bed. "Oh well," it said with a hint of irritation, "I'll just have to wait here until another message comes in."

"So where did you get the first message from?" Nathan wasn't used to sharing his bed with a goose.

"The Tower of Clarr, of course," replied the goose. "I am, after all, the special Clarr envoy. Hermes by name. I presume you have a name, sir?"

Having flopped down on the little cushioned window seat, Nathan tried to think, and finally made up his mind. "My names Nathan," he said, "Nat for short. And I'm the Holder of the Knife of Clarr." He paused, then added, "The Lord of Clarr, I suppose. And I do have a job for you after all."

Unfortunately, the goose appeared suspicious. "Forgive me for doubting, my lord," he said with a very noticeable wink, "but you are rather young for the Lord of Clarr. He was a tall gentleman with muscled shoulders and arms, last time I saw him."

"William Octobr," Nathan nodded. "But he died and passed the knife on to me," and he hopped up, pulling the knife from beneath his pillow. "Look. Here it is."

Now that the window was unshuttered again, the moonlight beamed in, and the knife sprang to reflect the light. Suddenly the entire room was brilliant with silver, brighter than any chandelier of candles. The light glittered, seemingly alive.

Nathan blinked, falling backwards onto the bed with a plop. The goose stood, and bowed. "Forgive me, my lord," he said immediately. "That is indeed the Knife of Clarr, and the holder is the lord. I am honoured to serve you, sir. May I take your orders?"

Nathan knew where Poppy's bedroom was, being just two doors away from his own. "Can you carry two people," he asked, "if one is small? My sister and I both wish to go to Lashtang tonight. But we both want to come back too. So one quick trip there, and then back here again. Is that possible?" Personally he rather doubted it, but thought it worth a try.

"Easily, my gracious lord," said the goose, "as long as you carry the knife with you. That would give power to a sparrow."

Imagining himself and Poppy trying to climb onto the back of a sparrow, Nathan gulped, and was glad this was a goose, and a very large one." So wait a moment," he said, "and I'll get my sister."

Trying to be as quiet as was possible, Nathan crept from his room and into the dark passageway. Tiptoeing, hardly daring to breathe, he counted two doors along, stopped, and listened at the keyhole. He could hear a slight grunt, as of someone sleeping and not quite snoring. So he turned the handle and slipped into the room.

"Is this your sister, sir?" asked the voice behind him, and once again Nathan jumped and whirled around.

It was worse than he had imagined. Not only had Hermes followed him, but John and Alfie, who slept in the room between Poppy's and Nathan's, had been awake, had heard the footsteps and flutter of feathers, and had peeped out to see what was going on. Now they burst into Poppy's room, and she woke up with a squeak.

"Horrid boys," she said rubbing her eyes, and then saw the goose and squeaked again.

Next room along, Sam and Peter heard the noise and came running in with the kittens under their arms. The goose took one look at the kittens and squawked, flapping its wings wide. The kittens rushed from the boys' arms and raced beneath Poppy's bed. Sam looked first at the goose, then at everyone else, and kneeling down, began to crawl beneath the bed, calling gently for the terrified kittens.

"Oh, goodness gracious," said another voice from the doorway, and Alice, wrapped tight in her bedrobe, was standing wide-eyed in the doorway.

"That's it," said Nathan. "I give up."

Poppy, still both alarmed and puzzled, stared from the goose back to Nathan. "But what did you want, Nat? And where did that thing come from?"

"I was going to take you to Lashtang," sighed Nathan. "And Hermes was going to take us."

Everyone spoke at once. "What's Lashtang?" "Who is Hermes?" "Where did that goose come from?" "We want to come with you." "Take us too." Is Lashtang in the country?" and finally, "Did you get the goose for dinner?"

Hurriedly, Nathan glared at Poppy, who had spoken of dinner. "This is Hermes," he announced, patting the ruffled back of the goose's feathers. "Lashtang is a magic country and that's where I was when that Balloon carried me off. It's where my magic knife comes from. Poppy wants to go there with me, and this very kind and courteous goose was going to take us there tonight for a very quick visit."

The answering silence was very brief, Then the five voices rose in unison. "Take us with you. Please. Please. Please. Please. Please."

"Sorry," Nathan mumbled, "but there's no way this poor goose can take us all."

Hermes, who kept one eagle eye on any possible movement in the shadows under the bed, looked up at once. "Ah, but I can, my lord, I definitely can. How many passengers, my lord? Two humans per goose is the normal load, as long as the Knife of Clarr leads us through the veil. I shall call my flock."

CHAPTER TWENTY-SIX

P oppy hugged the goose. "Tell about Lashtang."

The goose looked down its long golden beak. "The Lord of Clarr will explain more, my lady."

"Humpf," declared Poppy with a smirk towards Nathan.

Hermes's voice deepened, and he recited the verse Nathan had heard before, speaking slowly.

"Over the horizon, to where the mountains soar,
Wander Lashtang snow and ice,
Explore the forests and the fields,
But see your world no more."

Nathan sighed. "Alright. Let's all go. It doesn't sound very safe, but you know about it now so you might as well know the rest too. We'll be back by morning."

"But we can't take Mouse or the kittens," said Sam with a small sniff.

"Certainly not," said the goose.

The fluff balls were found and tumbled into the bedclothes, hidden beneath the eiderdown, to sleep until Mouse returned. Hermes turned away in distain, bowed his head, and hissed softly. It appeared that he was calling his flock. Within moments three other geese, each looking remarkably similar, had landed on the window sill and hopped down, splay-footed, into the room.

"Message received," said goose number two.

Number three was busy grooming beneath one wing, where he seemed to have found an errant feather, while goose number four sat down with a flop, looking exhausted.

"We have passengers," Hermes informed them. "And are to follow a direct route for Lashtang. We follow the Knife of Clarr, and this is the Lord of Clarr, who will be flying with me."

There was a slight shuffle of feathered excitement.

The four geese trotted the floorboards, ruffled their wings, nodded to each other, managed a little quick grooming, and then obediently lined up, webbed feet flapping.

"Hurry, hurry."

Alfie, being the largest, had a goose to himself, while Alice and Poppy scrambled onto the back of another. Nathan and Sam held on to Hermes's neck as they sat astride, and John and Peter sat aboard the last one.

"We're off."

Hermes, feet to the window sill, launched himself into the dark air, and the stars scattered as though their flickering light was trapped in his feathers. He looked back over his long white neck. "Comfortable, my lord?"

Sam sat, squeezed up to the goose's neck, both his arms hugging tight. Nathan sat just behind him, one arm around Sam's waist and the other holding his knife high. It was brighter than the moonlight. They soared over the uneven rooftops, the many tall chimneys, the little peaked attics with their casement windows, the thatched cottages with their tumble-down roofs and the grand houses with their pillars, tiled peaks and spreading gardens. The moon pooled its halo in a polished silver sheen, spinning rippled glitter across the river, and a thousand pearly reflections in passing windows. Way beyond the Tower the Thames wound to a dazzling twist where the estuary split into a dozen threads, each a tiny silver serpent, as a froth of mist rose up from the night's chill.

The geese flew in arrow formation, Nathan, Sam and Hermes at the point. So it was Nathan who first saw the veil before them, and knew they had arrived.

The dragonflies shimmered, dithering without focus, flying like tiny stars of many colours, as beautiful as any starlight. The curtain parted, and the geese entered Lashtang.

It was serene. The flood had drained from the land which sat bathed in dawning sunshine. The snow-tipped peaks on the distant mountains gleamed pastel pink and lilac as the sun, huge and glorious, peeped up from behind the mountain range. They had left London in the middle of a cold but peaceful night in May, but had arrived at the start of day during an eternal summer.

Landing on the rich green of grass and shrub, the geese overshot their aim, ran a little, slid a little, slowed down a little, and stopped.

"Well done," said Nathan with a pat to Hermes's neck as he hopped from the soft white back. The goose clucked with faint satisfaction.

"Good grassy plain," said goose number two. "Time for breakfast."

"I prefer wheat, said goose number four with a disappointed look at the grass.

"And I prefer potatoes," said goose number three with a sniff.

Alice climbed off, kissed her goose's nose, and thanked him. "But," she said," I'm afraid I have no idea what a potato is."

"Ludicrous," said goose number three. "The younger generation have no proper education these days."

"Don't you insult my passenger," said goose number two, its beak in the air as it waddled off to feed.

Hermes stood before Nathan, bowing again. "My lord, the first part of our mission is accomplished and we have delivered your noble self and your party to the plains of Lashtang. When you are ready to return, please raise your knife and call me. I and my companions will come immediately to take you home."

"But," Nathan frowned, "I want to be back home by early morning."

"My lord," explained the goose, "I shall arrange that. However long you wish to remain here, I will guarantee that you are back in your bedchamber by dawn. Time there does not correspond exactly to time here. Please feel free to leave whenever you wish."

"Useful," muttered Nathan. "But I don't want to stay here too long anyway. Anything could happen." He looked up and spoke to the others, who were all grouped at his back, staring around in bemused astonishment, muttering about magical dreams. "Please don't wander off," Nathan told them. "We can't stay more than a few moments." He paused, then quickly added, "And please try not to stand on any little crawling things or animals."

But Poppy's excitement was infectious. She danced, spreading out her arms and whizzing until dizzy. Alice joined her, interweaving and laughing. "It's so exciting, like a whole new world. Look. And so warm." Alice was still wearing her flimsy bedrobe and nothing else.

"It *is* a whole new world. It's a magic world."

"It's a dream."

"No. It's real."

Nathan sat on the grass, wondering what he would do if small frogs, beetles or other creatures approached him, but it was Poppy who approached him first. She asked, "Where's Granny?" And, with a whispered excitement, "Where's our parents?"

He had no idea. "We're not likely to see them this time around," he said, shaking his head. "And I can't risk staying too long. Everyone could wander off in different directions and get lost and we'd never get back together. Then even worse things could happen. I told you about the flood. We could even get killed." He lowered his voice. "I'll bring you again one day, just you and me, and we'll look for our mother and father."

"And Granny."

"She may have gone home by now. But the Knife of Clarr is brilliant. It seems to do all sorts of clever things."

"And I liked the geese."

"They'll take us home again," explained Nathan, "as soon as I call them. So let's just sit here a few minutes and let everyone run around and think it's all magic, and then we'll get the geese and fly home. I mean the medieval home, not ours. We can go back to ours afterwards."

Disappointment seemed to shadow the sun. "Can't we have some fun first?" asked Poppy. "Just a very, very little, little, little time more?"

"But," said Nathan, and got no further.

Having been worried about the arrival of frogs, tortoises and beetles which might start speaking and beg for a rescue which Nathan had no idea how to achieve, he was unprepared for the tiger. Mouse had been a cat of snuggles and her kittens had been adventurous delights. The tiger was none of those. Huge, elegant and ferocious, it walked, long-legged, from the rocky crest of the foothills where the mountains began.

Everyone watched its approach, as it padded slowly from the distant stones and crevices, unhurried and head high. Its markings were almost luminous in the sun, its colours blinding, its eyes golden and black, surveying them as though curious rather than hungry.

Nathan, although unsure, supposed this was another of the talking creatures which had once been human. He waited. The geese had disappeared. Alfie stood, watching, and carefully pushed Alice behind him as though ready to protect her. John, Sam and Peter stared with interest. Never having seen a tiger before, they now considered this creature as a cat of unusual magnificence in a country of fantasy and magic.

It was the largest tiger Nathan had ever seen, its back legs thick muscled and its high back arched in gold. Poppy, however, whispered, "Nat, get your knife out." And Nathan did exactly that, holding up the Knife of Clarr before him.

The tiger, however, took no notice whatsoever. Having slowly padded to within a few feet of the group, it stopped, and with elegant majesty, sat, front paws crossed, and licked its lips. "Just as well I'm not hungry," said the tiger.

Heaving a sigh of relief, Nathan asked, "Excuse me, but are you one of the poor people bewitched into animals? I wish I could help, but I'm afraid I can't. I believe my grandmother is here trying to help at the moment."

The tiger raised an eyebrow. "As it happens, your pity, charming though it is, seems sadly misplaced, Master Bannister. Indeed no, I am not one of those poor unfortunate souls trapped in the form of some small creature, with whom you so kindly sympathise. On the contrary, I am the power and the one who organised the trapping and changing, and with considerable pleasure arranged the delightful results." The tiger once again licked its lips. "How do you do? I am pleased to meet all of you. I have waited some time already in the hope of meeting the Octobr heir and was, let us say, ecstatic when alerted to hear of your arrival. Waiting can be so," and the tiger's eyes gleamed suddenly with a sheen of menace. It opened its jaws and yawned, and the ripples of its throat glowed crimson, "tedious," it continued, closing its mouth with a snap. "And how intensely thoughtful of you to bring other humans with you, as a gift, no doubt, for me to play with. I have some creative ideas of how to transform you into shapes far more attractive. Caterpillars, maybe. A little too easily squashed, perhaps. Or would you prefer squirrels? A life of collecting nuts might seem appealing to one of little brain." Its eyes hooded, narrowing, as it looked at each of those watching. "The slim girl – a millipede I think, with a thousand legs wriggling in desperation as the fox walks by. The dark boy – a rat, snuffling and sniffing and loathed by all, running for its life as the bear sniffs its sweat." Into the absolute silence which followed this statement, it added, "As for your grandmother, meanwhile, she sits forlorn in the Tower of Clarr. Her mission was sadly mistimed, for I was patrolling the Clarr boundaries on her arrival."

"She's in danger?" Nathan gulped.

"By no means," said the tiger. "She is neither in danger, nor can she be a danger to anyone else. The wretched woman is quite safe. And so am I, from her."

"In prison?" whispered Poppy, clinging to Nathan's arm.

"Naturally. The ice prison of Clarr."

Poppy had started to cry. Nathan kept a tight hold of the knife, and pointed it at the creature before him. "Who are you?" he demanded. "Wagster in disguise? Brewster?"

The tiger stood, once again seeming even larger and grander than it had before. The ruff around its head was almost as wide as the mane of a lion, and its mouth opened to teeth so enormous and so sharp, they seemed like tusks. Then it opened its mouth even wider and snarled. The snarl turned to roar, and the sound vibrated until the ground shook and the echoes swirled around their heads like a vast storm of flies.

As the last echoes faded, the tiger looked down on the quivering humans before it. "I am the mighty Emperor Clebbster's principal warden," it roared. "I am Yaark, the holder of the great Key of Clarr."

In a voice as tiny as a whisper, Nathan mumbled, "As the Lord of Clarr, I have power over the key. I command you –" and the tiger disappeared into the dazzling pink sunshine.

Everyone gasped, rushing to Nathan and hugging him, trembling and cheering in a mixture of fear and relief.

Between sobs, Poppy kissed Nathan's cheek, and said, "We have to rescue Granny."

"I know," sighed Nathan. "But everyone else has to go home. It may be really dangerous."

The geese had returned, having been quietly hidden behind rocks while the tiger spoke. Now Hermes slapped one webbed foot on the grass, and declared, "I shall volunteer my services, my lord. I am more accustomed to the ways of Lashtang and have considerable knowledge regarding the Tower of Clarr. I am a servant of Clarr, and I have met with the magnificent Lady Octobr. Permit me to help you, my lord."

John nodded violently. "Well, I ain't no servant and I ain't got no knives nor keys nor titles. But I ain't going nowhere neither, lest I comes wiv you now. Wake up, Nat. We's in this together."

"I'm coming too," said Sam. "I'm good with cats. Though I prefer them a bit smaller."

"That beast was talking about keys," said Peter. "That means me. So I'm coming."

"You know I won't leave, Nat dear," Alice smiled. "You helped me when I was in desperate need. Would I desert you now?"

Alfie stood his ground. "Don't you go talking to me of running off," he said, looking grim. "Cos I ain't leaving. If you finks I's a rotten coward, just reckon you'd better keep it to yerself, for I ain't afraid o' nuffing."

Nathan hung his head. "None of you know how dangerous a tiger is. And even I don't really know how dangerous this country can be."

It did not look dangerous at all. The sun continued shining the pink and lilac dawn having turned to a golden morning, and the treetops fluttered in the light breeze. The snowy peaks of the mountains were a long way off and the grassy slopes led for many miles across the peaceful land. But there was no bird song.

Poppy said, "No birds? Are they too frightened?"

But Nathan had no idea. He turned to Hermes. "My friends want to help," he said, frowning and worried. "But I don't want them hurt. Is it too dangerous?"

"Well, naturally, my lord," replied the goose. "But you cannot go alone. Even the Lord of Clarr cannot approach Clarr with no one beside him."

"It's my grandmother too," said Poppy between gritted teeth.

"We's all coming," John said, pushing in front. "Stop wasting time, Nat. D'you knows where ta go?"

"My lord, we geese know the way," Hermes assured Nathan. "We will take you, if you take up your previous positions. Passengers, please board at once."

They scrambled on, legs behind wings, arms around necks, excited, flustered and a little frightened. Nathan had never before imagined himself obeying a goose, but nor could he ever have imagined any single thing that had happened to him for the past few months. The breeze was in his hair, cooling the flush on his face. Only one small thing reassured him, and that was the tiger's abrupt disappearance as soon as he held up the knife and claimed lordship, commanding the right of Clarr.

Once again Hermes led, with the other geese fanned out behind him. Nathan was able to look down with considerable interest and watch the changing countryside below. At first there were no buildings. There were no farms, nor fields of crops, no roads and not even animals. The grass stretched onwards over a considerable distance, but then it began to rise into rock piles and craggy mounds of pale stone. The foothills of the mountains beyond were flecked with ice, and then Nathan began to see buildings, although many lay in ruins. Within high roofed caves in the mountains' sheer rises, there stood the debris form palaces, temples and buildings that had once been vast and beautiful. Through the tumbledown walls, their painted ceilings, mirrors and marble arches shone like sad reminders of the glory of the past. Even some tattered loops of furniture remained, but there were also blackened and burned out piles of rubble.

Peering in as they flew, Nathan saw pits and marks of fire. These were the signs he knew well, and wondered what battles had occurred here. The destruction spread wide, until throughout the lower slopes there were old books, armour and clothes piled up, and mossy heaps of broken marble statues, walls and gold hinged doorways.

Poppy called out, and pointed. "Look. There's smoke."

It was Alfie who called from behind. Ain't no way smoke. Tis wot you gets when steams hits ice."

"Condensation," murmured Alice. "And an avenue of icicles, stalactites, and frozen waterfalls." She twisted around. "Look through there. It's a road, leading into the mountain. A road of ice."

The geese flew higher, and the air began to cool. Where there had been warmth and the glimmering gold of the sun, now there was a bright blue sky shimmering with frost, clouds that hung in pendulous drops of white freeze, as though even the sky above echoed the ground below."

"How can clouds turn into ice?"

"This is Lashtang," murmured Nathan. "I suppose anything can happen."

There was a ledge hewn into the mountainside. It was narrow and slippery with iced puddles, but here the geese landed, breath harsh.

"We can go no further," Hermes said with an apologetic sniff. "We cannot fly through the ice of Clarr, even with the knife to guide us, unless the curse is lifted. It fights against us and we are forbidden to pass. We cannot either breathe, nor stretch our wings." Several of the birds were plucking tiny icicles from their feathers. Already their flat feet slipped on the icy ground.

"Then stay where you're safe," Nathan said at once. "Just tell us where to go." He was finding it difficult to breathe himself, for the air was not only bitterly cold, it held a barrier within it, as if he was being pushed back. His clothes were warm enough, but he wished he had his medieval eiderdown to wrap around him. Then he realised that Alice wore only her bedrobe, which was far lighter than a dressing gown, and he hurried over. "It's too cold for you. Stay with the geese. Cuddle up. Their feathers will keep you warm."

"I've fought the baron and his ugly brother. So I can fight a tiger."

"You can't fight ice." He turned to Alfie. "Make her keep warn."

Immediately Alfie wrapped his cape around her, and tucked her up beside the geese, half hidden beneath their feathered wings. "Stay here," he ordered. "Now, I reckon I's ready. Lead on. Tis a dream I want to finish." Too cold to argue, Alice stayed with the geese as the others stared forwards, ready to march the ice paths.

CHAPTER TWENTY-SEVEN

"Follow the road," the goose had said. "When the road is closed by rock and wall, then climb. And when you can climb no more, you will find the entrance to the tower. But remember this," and he stretched up his neck, as though indicating power, "Enter, and search for the eternal chain. You hold the knife. It is only the Knife of Clarr which will cut the chain, and release us all."

They grouped together without any clear leader, but Nathan kept the knife tight clasped. The road they had been told to follow wound from the rocky outlet where Alice and the geese remained tucked against the cliff to lessen the wind and cold, Onwards into dark shadows it continued, winding like a narrow throat between clenched jaws. The chill increased. Although now sheltered from the wind, the ice seemed to grow out from the walls, shedding slivers of white ooze, as though the pathway itself was creating the freeze. There was no roof and above just a thin slice of sky showed, pale and clouded. Then even that disappeared and the ground became dangerously slippery. After Sam had fallen three times and Peter four times, John laughed.

"Reckon this ruddy mountain is trying ta spit us back."

And Nathan realised that this was exactly what was happening.

Abruptly they stopped, and before soared an uneven wall of rock, a great cliff face of dripping stalactites and mossy ledges.

"We have to climb," Nathan sighed. It looked challenging, and he had never been much of a climber before.

"Easy," said Poppy, pushing in front. "But not in a long skirt and funny cloak."

"Too cold to take them capes off."

"Tie them around you. And Poppy, tie your skirts up."

The climb was tedious and slow. There were many places to grasp and step, but most were slippery with ice, suddenly melting water, or wet weeds and lichens. Fingers could not hold tight enough and toes slipped. The tumble from one grasp back to the previous one below was repeated over and over and everyone, except Alfie, was soon covered in aches and bruises.

Alfie smiled at them all. "You ain't right good at this, is you lot."

"No." Peter looked up, having landed with a bump on a ledge of soaked pebbles, each falling beneath him with a scatter of gravel. "It's too cold and too slippy."

Nathan, attempting to keep a safe grip on his knife, found it almost impossible, but his school shoes had rubbery soles, and held well to the ice, and although his fingertips were numb he was managing better than some others.

With a sigh of relief, Poppy pointed upwards. "It's a doorway. That's what Hermes said, isn't it? When you can climb no more, that's when the door to the tower shows. Or is it a trick? How many doors can there be?"

This had not actually occurred to Nathan, and he paused, both feet steady, wedged into a crack in the stone, and both hands to another. The knife was safe in a hidden pocket. "I'll risk the first door, and hope for the best."

The scramble to the doorway was immediate, and everyone breathed deep. Only Alfie dared look back down the steep cliff to the way they had come, and he shivered, looking quickly away again. The precipice fell sheer and frozen below, and to fall now would surely have meant death.

The doorway was high arched and decorated with patterns of mosaic, closed off with a door of carved wood, dark and battered, and an overhang of icicles. There was no handle on the door, but in the centre was a very large keyhole. Surrounded by plates of iron, there was neither key nor any manner of peering through the opening. Squinting, John was attempting to peer inside, but shook his head saying, "Tis so dark. Can't see nuffing."

"Let me." Peter pushed past.

Nathan held up the knife. "I'll see if I can help." The knife was gleaming, as if it recognised its home. "Open," called Nathan. "Let Peter in."

The door shuddered. It did not swing open as Nathan had hoped, but instead the keyhole began to squeak and creak, the iron surround groaned, and very slowly the entire keyhole enlarged.

As the door hinges squealed as though their metal was stretched beyond breaking, the keyhole magnified again and again, widening until it cracked, then widened more. It no longer resembled an actual keyhole, but more like a small dark tunnel.

Peter stared. "I think I can climb in."

Nathan, astonished, looked from the door to the knife and back again. "When I said to let Peter in, this definitely isn't what I meant."

"No matter." Peter was smiling. "Look. It's big enough if I squeeze and squeeze. And big enough for Sam and probably Poppy too. Then we can either unlock it from inside, or find another way to open the door."

With a hoist up from Alfie, Peter was already climbing into the keyhole. He lay on his stomach, wriggling bit by bit. Laughing, Sam followed. "Look," he called back. "Just like Mouse."

Before Poppy had a chance to follow, the door swung open. "There's a handle on the inside," Peter told them. "Easy."

They rested first, catching their breath. It was still icy cold, but they were able to rub feeling back into their fingers, stamp their feet, and prepare for the next exploration.

Alfie looked at Nathan. "Now reckon you goes first, Nat, he said. "Hold up that knife o'yourn. But I's not mighty sure wot we's looking for."

None of them knew. The Eternal Chain could be anything. "A real iron chain perhaps. Wound around a pole."

"Or wound around a cage with Granny in it."

"Could be a rope, I reckon."

But, Nathan thought, it might not be anything visible at all. It might be a symbol, an invisible barrier, or something even more difficult and dangerous. Meanwhile Poppy was calling, "Granny, where are you? If you can hear us, please answer. Where are you?"

There was no answer but her voice began a journey of echoes as though the sound alone started to search, sliding upwards and downwards, slipping around corners, and rebounding from ceilings. As they all stood there, uncomfortable, puzzled and fearful, the voice came back to them from a hundred directions until it shouted and screamed, and they all held their hands to their ears.

Finally, as the echoing voice faded and the last thrum died, they stared at each other, not daring to speak. Eventually, holding the knife up and out before him, Nathan began silently to walk from the open doorway into the tower.

The entrance was circular, high roofed, and windowless. The ceiling was painted with intricate designs, too shadowed to see clearly, arched and domed but without beams. The walls were stone and around their base were six open arches, and no windows, In the centre of this circular entrance was a many faceted mosaic, incorporating an arrow pointing to each of the six openings, but without any clear indication of where they led.

Poppy hopped from one to the other. Carefully keeping her voice to a virtual whisper, she said, "Look, this one has a picture of a flame and a sort of spoon. Perhaps it's the kitchen."

"Reckon this is a bed," pointed John. "Like a plumped up mattress wiv coloured blankets."

Guesses, possibilities, and Nathan shook his head, whispering, "Not sure. Those pictures don't look like beds and spoons to me. If it's a bed, then all the blankets have fallen off."

"'Tis a puzzle."

Poppy looked up with a sudden smile. "That's exactly what it is," she said, risking a voice just a little louder than a whisper. "We have to solve the puzzle."

It was John who promptly sat on the polished mosaic floor in the midst of the strange patterns, and looked closely at each. "Don't

237

reckon this is a spoon," he decided, pointing to the arrow which Poppy had guessed as the kitchen. "I reckon tis a spade. Burning and digging."

"And that ain't no bed," pointed Alfie. "Tis a trap, wiv curtains."

"Maybe that one's a throne." Nathan remembered the throne Brewster had claimed, sitting on the velvet chair with his cackle and top hat askew. Crimson and gold, he remembered it well. "What do the rest of you think? If this points to the throne room, then that's where we could go first."

"Six arrows and six arches," nodded John. "So – mighty lucky – six of us. Reckon we try one each."

"No. We keep together, Too dangerous."

"So let's sit down and work out these puzzles," said Poppy. 'This is all streaky and white. Like icicles. Or stalagmite's."

Nathan was staring, but he saw nothing. It was his memory that clicked in, and suddenly he started to chant in a voice that did not even sound like his own.

"Lashtang Tower, dark as night with no moon,
Lashtang Palace, blazing with flame.
One whispers soft the Hazlett name,
The other roars. Both hide your tomb.

Come taste the flames, come taste the ice.
Nightmare beckons, dreams of death.
Enter. Now breathe your final breath.
Peace at last, but Lashtang claims the price.

"We mustn't choose any door that says fire, or ice, or that throne. They are all traps. And the curtain, well, that must be the veil. It's the way out of Lashtang, which would be a great escape, but we're not ready to leave yet."

"So it ain't that way." John, still sitting in the centre of the mosaic, banged his fist down where the arrow pointed to flame and spade.

"Reckon it means we'll be burned and buried. And not 'ere, neither." He pointed to the curtain. "Nor all them ice things, whatever you calls them. Icicles. Nor that mighty big chair, you says. So, four out. Two ta go."

"That one," wondered Peter, "might be a wind. Look. Whizzing around and around."

"Perhaps Brewster's balloon."

"No," Peter insisted, jumping on the edge and following the whirlwind with his foot. "There's a key in the middle. It's a key flying, and it's in the shape of that strange tiger, with black and red stripes. A tiger key."

"Then it's the last doorway we want to take. That only leaves one," said Nathan. "But what does the last one say. It's almost empty. Just the arrow with something around it."

"Reckon I knows what that is," said Alfie. "I seen enough of them when we done helped Alice get her house back. Parchment it is. Documents. Them legal things what I can't read."

Nathan clapped his hands. "Brilliant. So that's Octobr, which means the claim, and just what we want." He looked from one to the other. "Are we sure? Shall we go?"

Only Sam looked troubled, mumbling to himself about prisons instead of parchments, but he nodded, not wanting to be left behind. But even with agreement, no one was eager to hurry. Bunched together with the knife glowing as Nathan held it up before them, they crept through the archway and into the shadows beyond. The darkness engulfed them and it remained bitterly cold, but there was no ice. It neither hung in icicles, nor dripped from walls or ceiling. The ground was dry, flat, and wide, much like any passage in an unlit house. Nathan heard his own heartbeat as if it was as loud as thunder, and his breath caught in his throat, but he led the way, testing each footstep before moving onwards.

Gradually the light from the knife began to shimmer and grow until it dazzled like a star, and they could finally see around them. Not that there was a great deal to see, for the walls were stone, the ceiling low beamed in heavy wood, and the ground was also stone, unpolished and undecorated. A draught blew behind them from the outside door which they had intentionally left open, but it was not as freezing as it had been before.

Continuing to whisper, they reassured each other, and kept close enough to feel and see, knowing that not one of them had fallen, or been lost. Then their shuffling and careful distrust proved both helpful and necessary, for as they saw another opening before them, indicating a room or new corridor with increased light in a reddish glow, they began to hurry, taking less hesitation over each step.

"Stop," Nathan yelled, turning around. "There's a great open strip, like a pit, and wide enough to fall into."

They peered down. "Heaven help us," mumbled Peter. "It's all ice and cliffs and it goes down and down and down."

"Can we jump it?"

Alfie considered. "Reckon I can, and John too. Nat surely can. Not so sure 'bout the rest of you."

"Of course I can," said Poppy crossly. "Look." Nathan reached out to stop her, but she took a running leap, easily sailed over the huge crack, and landed with a dance of pride and success on the other side. Then suddenly she stopped, gazing ahead into an angle which the others, still on the other side of the pit, could not see. Very slowly and sadly, she turned back and spoke directly to Nathan. "We're here," she said softly. "It's Granny."

Nathan jumped quickly and joined his sister. Then they stood together and stared.

In the vast circular chamber before them, once again the floor was patterned in multi-coloured mosaics, but this time there were no arrows. The ceiling was high, and arched, too shadowed to see clearly. But it was the walls that held the attention. They were made either of glass or of ice, and frozen within them were many people, standing paralysed as though frozen both in place and time. They did not move but stood staring out at those that stared back. Their eyes were open and glazed, their hands stretched out before them as though pleading, and their clothes as still as themselves.

Alfie and John had jumped the pit and had helped Sam and Peter across. Now they walked into the room of horror and gazed around, shocked.

Sam stepped forwards and stretched out one hand, smoothing it along the wall before him. For a moment, he snatched his fingers away, saying, "Too cold. It's ice. All ice. Solid." But then he pressed his palm once more to the ice, as if to wipe away the vision. "Are they real?" he asked.

"Yes," said Nathan, his voice very small. "And one of them is my grandmother."

Granny Octobr stood, golden hazel eyes wide, still in her blue checked dress and white apron, her grey hair in a short cut, pulled back behind her ears, and her purple rimmed glasses on the end of her nose as though about to slip off. Her expression was puzzled, and disappointed, as though the sudden end to her life came unexpectedly when she had, instead, been expecting something pleasant. Her hands, like those of the other figures, were stretched before her as though in supplication. Her mouth, just slightly open, seemed to be speaking, but no words could be heard. Nathan felt the tears hot on his cheeks. Beside him Poppy dropped to the ground and sobbed loudly.

It was Alfie, with one sympathetic hand to Nathan's shoulder, who said, "We ain't given up, is we? You got the knife. Reckon we could try breaking through this."

John tapped the ice wall. "I counted," he said. "There's ten, just like me toes. Four is females, 'cluding yer granny. Six is men. You start wiv yer granny, and me, I'll start wiv the fellows, for once they's free, if they comes alive and don't just crumble away, then reckon they can 'elp." And with a huge kick to the ice wall, he began to hammer, finally hurling himself at the wall, his shoulder to the barrier. But nothing happened, not even a faint shudder nor a vibration. Alfie had started trying to release a tall woman, gazing out from beautiful hazel eyes, and wearing a long white gown, and both Sam and Peter were punching and kicking as hard as they could. Nathan and Poppy were furiously attacking the ice that imprisoned Granny Octobr. Using feet, fists and elbows, they both continued in desperation, and Nathan attempted using the point of his knife. Afraid of blunting the blade, he soon stopped and admitted that not one tiny crack nor split had been caused.

"Tis not working," John glowered.

Nathan held up his knife again. He pointed it towards the ice wall, and spoke loudly. "I am the Lord of the Knife of Clarr, and I command this ice to melt and the prisoners to be released."

Everyone stood back, excited, waiting for what might happen. Poppy wiped her eyes, and gasped. But it appeared that nothing was happening at all. Nathan and his group were as unmoving as those trapped in the wall, waiting, and hardly daring to breathe. Eventually a few drops slithered down the ice, slopping into tiny puddles, but this was no major melt.

Bitterly disappointed, Nathan believed that the knife had been unable to help, but then he realised that a haze had begun to swirl in the very middle of the room. Puzzled, he waited. The haze thickened, and it felt as though the whole room began to tremble. Staring into the mist, Nathan began to see shapes, as though watching a television through a blurred window. Then he saw himself. He could see the whole group quietly and carefully exploring the long dark passage, with only the light of the knife to guide them.

Poppy, standing beside him and clutching the hem of his doublet, was watching with equal fascination. "Look," she whispered, "that's the big crack in the floor just outside this room. Why are we being shown that? We don't have to climb into it, do we? That would be terrifying."

Nathan knew he would do anything to rescue his grandmother, but certainly climbing into a bottomless pit was the most horrible possibility. Then he realised he was being shown something else. Right in the centre of the wide open hole was stretched a fine red cord. It was so thin it could hardly be seen, but as he stared, Nathan saw that this was red from blood. Blood dripped from the cord down into the abyss, and where it landed could not be seen at all. The cord itself could barely be noticed, so fine and thin, and so dark, clotted with blood. He blinked, testing his vision. Then he blinked again, and the whole haze and the pictures he had been shown had all totally disappeared.

Hurrying quickly back to the doorway, Nathan, with Poppy close behind and everyone else behind her, stared down into the actual pit which they had managed to jump. And there, exactly as the picture had shown them, right in the centre and stretched tight across its length, was the red cord, clotted with dark dripping blood. Nathan felt sick, but he looked up, saying, "We've found it, haven't we? The Eternal Chain."

"Quick, quick," yelled Sam, jumping up and down. "Cut it with the knife."

"It's what Ferdinand said," Nathan mumbled, just as excited. "This could free everyone and turn the frogs back to humans." No one except Poppy understood what he was saying, but this worried nobody. They watched with avid interest.

Nathan reached out with the knife. The cord was so thin he believed it would cut easily, but as the blade came close, the cord fell away. Looping downwards, it flopped into the centre of the pit, spinning like a guitar string. So, waiting until the cord settled once more, Nathan lay down flat on the ground, with his arms outstretched across the pit. "Hold my feet," he begged the others. "I'd hate to fall in."

They ran to grab his ankles, and Nathan reached out again, extending the blade towards the cord. But once more, with a slight buzz as though laughing, it dropped from sight.

"Sneaky," said Alfie. "But tis attached both ends, ain't it? So don't cut the middle. Cut one o' them ends."

Nodding, Nathan crawled to the edge of the pit beside one of the walls, and once again leaned down and over while Alfie and John held tight to his legs, Sam and Peter grabbed at his waist, and Poppy grabbed at the neck of his shirt.

With a deep breath, Nathan sliced at the cord where it was firmly knotted to the ice wall. For just one brief moment he thought he had succeeded, but then saw the cord spring back and knew it had once again evaded him.

"Too clever by half," complained John. "Try t'other end."

Nathan was furious with himself, the cord and the knife too. He didn't think the other end would be any easier, and he wondered what he was doing wrong. But he shuffled to the opposite wall, ready to attempt another cut.

But this time the failed attempt was caused by something entirely different. As Nathan knelt and prepared to lie down by the great open crack in the floor, there was a triumphant hooting, a cackle of laughter, a whizz as of something flying above, and a jab of pain in his back where something with sharp nails had poked him hard.

"Well now, Bumble-Bee Head," laughed the shrill voice, "can't cut one little bit of string, eh? What a shame, what a mess, what a failure."

CHAPTER TWENTY-EIGHT

"Fools," screeched another similar voice. "Didn't know you were all tricked, did you?" Both Brewster and Wagster leapt and hurtled, knees bent to spring into the air as though on motor-powered stilts. With persistent shrieks of laughter and repeated flying jumps, both on the ground and above in a whizz of erratic speed, they raced around Nathan and his friends.

'Tricked. How tricked?" demanded Nathan, "I was stopped from cutting the eternal chain. But I hold the knife. How did you stop me?"

"It's not the real chain," chortled Brewster. "We knew you were coming and so we changed it."

Alfie, John, Sam and Peter, utterly dismayed and completely confused, stepped back and pressed against the ice wall. Poppy ran after the Hazlett twins, attempting to hit them as she jumped and tried to pull their long thin noses but she could not jump high enough and didn't catch anyone.

Nathan stood still, pouting. "How did you know I was coming?"

Wagster scratched behind his ears, dislodging his hat. "What a flea-brain, Bumble-Bee Head. Poor topsy-turvy waspy-tottle. Can't do a thing right. What a shame. Got it all wrong as usual."

Annoyed, Nathan glared. "You're cruel and you capture people and put them in ice prisons and that's far more stupid than anything I've ever done. So," he said, "how did you know I was coming?"

"The great Yaark, Warden of the Key of Clarr" said Brewster, coming to rest beside Nathan, "told you where your silly little granny is. Then, when you fluttered that useless knife of yours, he pretended to disappear, leaving you oh so eager to come and rescue the poor old woman. We changed the eternal chain, and waited for you to get your little heads around all these sticky-wicky puzzles. You managed in the end, though it took you long enough and most of them you got wrong anyway. And here you are, trying to cut the cord of destiny. And no one can ever cut that. Not until they die, of course." Still cackling, he pointed to the pit. "You cut the cord of destiny, and you drop oh so very dead, without any more destiny left to live. So think yourself lucky the cord refused to be cut."

"Stuff him with rice pudding," called Wagster from the ceiling, and, "strangle the little pest," from back on the ground as his leap landed, bent kneed, beside them, spider-like. Curling their fingernails, both stabbed out, and Wagster scraped his thumb along Nathan's forehead, laughing with delight as the cut started to bleed. He leapt again, zooming like a helicopter around Nathan's head.

Alfie and John both ran forwards, now infuriated and determined to rid the tower of these two dangerous creatures threatening their friend. Wagster lashed out, pointing his claws and jumping over their heads. Disorientated, it was impossible to know up from down, and where to expect the next spring.

"Stuff them down the privy," Wagster cackled. "Rip their ears off and make them eat the gristle for supper."

Laughing with the echoes of an emptying drain, Brewster settled and stood, leaning against the ice wall in front of Granny Octobr, pointing and sniggering at her frozen prison. But Wagster was changing once again. From the high ceiling, he gazed down, gone from human shape to shadow, and from shadow to serpent. The coils swelled, fat as tree trunks and long as rivers, wrapped around Nathan's feet, holding him utterly still. The snake eyes were scarlet slits, its mouth an open jaw that spread wider and wider, extending its throat into a fathom of gnashing teeth as sharp as splinters, and a black gleaming tongue as long as an arm, forked into dark curling prongs. Within the throat, crawling through bubbles of thick slime, were the exploring bodies of fat maggots and thin white worms.

Watching the transformation of his brother, Brewster turned to Granny behind the ice wall. "Say goodbye to your heir, queen of failures," he laughed. He had watched Wagster, Nathan and Granny. He had not watched Alfie nor John.

Peter yelled, "Get out the knife," and as Brewster's attention was snatched back, the other two ran at him from opposing sides, each with a closed fist, punching at the same moment, one to Brewster's left temple and one to his right. More in surprise than injury, the wizard blinked and slid down the ice wall, tumbling at Granny's feet.

The serpent hissed and reared. Nathan held up his knife and called, "From the Lord of Clarr to the Knife of Clarr, send flames to burn the serpent and set me free."

The vast snake's scales were interlocking and luminous in purple and black, but now fire rippled through them as though it had ignited within and was burning outwards. The huge flames could be seen rippling from inside until they licked every coil.

The serpent howled.

But it was as the fire burst around the rearing scales, and as Nathan jumped from the remaining coils, that everything shrank back into the shadows once more, the fire blew out in a tiny hiss, the arched doorway seemed to shiver, and the tiger Yaark padded slowly into the chamber. Already freezing, the chamber now turned arctic.

Brewster woke, crawling quickly aside. Wagster's tongue was alight. With a suck and a grimace of pain, he swallowed the flames, and was himself again, cringing against the ice wall. "Put your knife away, fool," Yaark told Nathan. "It has no effect on me, for I hold the key, and the key opens, closes and locks."

"The lord must out rank the warden," whispered Nathan, shivering.

"The warden guards," Yaark said, solemn as a statue. Even his whiskers seemed solid as ice. "While the lord plays, travels far, fails to learn or to stay at his post, so the warden remains, guarding what is precious to all the land. I do not claim lordship as the Octobrs do. I claim power, and that is what I hold. And my power, discover at your own peril, is greater than any other."

Face to face, the tiger's head reared over Nathan's, its eyes like hooded halos, and Nathan could not look away. "But the lord commands," he mumbled, trying desperately to summon his pride and his courage. "When the lord orders the warden, then the warden should obey."

Yaark sneered. "Not when the warden knows the lord to be a fool. And if I disobey, how do you retaliate, lord of fools? How do you dismiss me? How do you snatch back the key? You know nothing at all."

Alfie, John and Poppy stood close to Nathan, supportive and protective. But still dancing behind them and whizzing overhead, the Hazlett twins continued to cackle and snort. Yet they avoided Yaark's sinuous ambush, and did not come too close. Nathan noticed this, and turned to Brewster. "The tiger frightens you?"

But it was Yaark who answered. "With my own feline power, I can kill any one of you. I can leap, and in an instant death will snap your cord of destiny. Before I leave the tower, I shall take my feast. One of you will suffice. The little tow-headed child at your back, perhaps? Or the plump girl, her hair almost as striped as I am in the colours of the sunset." Standing in the doorway just beyond the great pit, the tiger seemed to grow and its fur dazzled without light. Its back was arched high. "I am the lord of beasts and master of the jungle," it continued, voice calm and expressionless. "I am the cat which takes what it will, 'But,' and its eyes once again narrowed, "as the great tiger I may choose to eat a human, and tear it limb from limb, rip out its belly and crush its skull. Or I may choose to change that human into a pleading worm, a pathetic string of flesh which I can pierce with one claw until it writhes in agony, awaiting death."

No one answered. They stared. Then Poppy whispered, "I loved the tigers – in the films."

Yaark raised its head. "But," it continued, "I am more than cat. I am the great Yaark. You do not yet know me for I am the beast of hellfire. With the Key of Clarr I have even greater powers. I can hurl any one of you into the ice and keep you imprisoned there for evermore."

"And so you can also release anyone already there," mumbled Poppy, glaring.

"Naturally," said the tiger. "Or swap one for the other. And easy skill."

"Then swap Wagster for Granny," muttered Poppy.

As the pounce of the predator from ambush, the tiger leapt the pit without warning, coming to the inner chamber, and gazed back at those trying vainly not to tremble at its feet.

"So," said Yaark, and the deep gravelly voice became harsh, "who sacrifices himself – or herself – for the others? Which human do I feast on first? Or shall I devour you all?"

Nathan stamped, and marched forwards. "If you try to kill your own lord, you'll be cursed," he said, as loud as he dared. "And all my friends are under my protection. You will not touch any of us. And I demand you free my grandmother. She comes from the ruling house, and you do not."

The shadows moved back, as though cautious and fearful. Even Brewster and Wagster quietened and shrank against the ice wall. But Yaark snarled, curling back his lips over his huge yellow stained canine teeth. "Free the Octobr queen? Offer yourself in her place, then. As a free sacrifice, I shall release the old fool, and send you to the ice grave in her place."

It was John who spoke, very softly, into the following silence. His voice quavered, saying, "Reckon I could offer, Nat, if you likes. I ain't got naught ta lose and me life ain't worth a scrape o' salt. Take me and get yer granny back if you wants. I ain't afraid of a few years asleep in the ice."

Poppy gulped and Nathan nearly cried, knowing that tears were silently collecting and his eyes were moist. He turned and clasped John's hand. "I won't lose you for anyone," he muttered. "But that's the greatest offer – kindness – bravery – incredible. I'll never forget it." And he turned back to the tiger. "See how brave my friends are. You're cruel and stupid and you want to hurt people so much better than yourself."

Yaark roared, and even the Hazlett twins shrank back. The roar reverberated as Poppy's shout had in the outer chamber. The sound swept around the walls like an engine, the stone floor shook beneath their feet and the ice trembled. Each tone of the roar increased, encircling and repeating. No one moved. Even the tiger himself stood tall, majestic and furious, unmoving, until the endless echoes had faded. Then the golden eyes narrowed, heavy-lidded with menace, and Nathan knew the beast intended action.

With a disguised shiver, Nathan stepped forwards. He held up the knife and pointed it directly into the tiger's face. 'I command,' he began, "that you take the place," and then, shocked, he stumbled forwards and the knife dropped with a metallic clatter. Wagster had pushed him from behind, the clawed hand vicious into the small of his back. Both Alfie and John jumped on Wagster to stop him grabbing the fallen knife, and Poppy knelt as Nathan staggered, clasping the knife in her fist, and passing it immediately to Nathan. He thanked her turning, as she held out her hand.

"It burned me," she whispered. "So what you said is true. Nobody but the Lord of Clarr can hold the Knife of Clarr."

The tiger, pushing between Nathan and Poppy raised one paw, it claws outstretched, but as Poppy screamed, the tiger stopped, looking up quickly.

Wagster and Brewster no longer zoomed around their heads, but a great white bird was circling, the draught of its wings like a curtain of chilled wind.

"Tis Alice," yelled Alfie. "And Hermes."

With a swoop of triumphant feathers, a call of greeting, and a squawk of exuberance, they encircled the chamber, and the shadows fled. Instead of the darkness of threat, gloom, misery and fear, now the ceiling was a fluff of white and a whoop of joy.

"Look," called Alice, her arms around Hermes' neck, "this beautiful goose tried and tried, and eventually we managed to fly high enough to enter the tower. None of the others could make it, but here we are. And dear Hermes felt sure there was danger, so we wanted to help."

Looking down she saw the huge shape of the tiger standing motionless, and called, "is that Yaark? "

The tiger reared up, his claws almost catching Hermes' breast feathers and Alice's toes. "Yes, I am Yaark, fools," he roared, and once again the echoes began to reverberate. "Beware the Warden of the Key." Its roar turned to snarl. "But I am more than you can know. Do not challenge the lord of hellfire, or hellfire will swallow you all."

Hermes continued to circle the room, the great outspread wings battering against Wagster and Brewster, who kept their distance. Alice had a handful of sharp stones collected from the ledge outside where the geese had landed, and she threw one fast and hard at the zooming and the cackling twins. One hit Brewster on the nose, and he snarled like the tiger, rearing and turning. Alice looked down, calling urgently to Alfie and John, Nathan and Poppy. "Jump on that thing's back. Throw something. Pull its tail. Kick. Get together and attack while Hermes distracts its attention."

Forewarned, the tiger snarled again, bent forwards, back legs high, as though to pounce. Nathan, deep breaths and unquenchable determination concentrated, attempted to jump on Yaark's back, and his leg touched the rough vibrant fur. He fell backwards. The fur was fire as the tiger began its own transformation.

Alfie kicked out and jumped, but the tiger leapt around. Alice threw another stone but it missed. Poppy picked it up from the ground where it had fallen, and threw it straight into Yaarks eyes. But before the stone touched, it rebounded, lifted high into the icy air, and clattered to the ground.

"Ignorant creatures of the grasses," spat the tiger. "You think you can touch the Warden of the Key, and the Lord of Hellfire?

The striped fur began to spike, and with a shiver, the tiger's eyes went dark. Its face began to change. But while they yelled, fought and dodged, Nathan remembered something which had intrigued him at the time. Although Yaark claimed that the knife had no power over him, and for most of the time this had proved true, when Nathan had held it out and said certain words, Wagster had stopped him immediately, as though those words were dangerous. So now, moving back away from the scrabbling ferocious fury of the tiger, Nathan held up the knife, pointed the blade directly and spoke as loudly as he could.

The echoes began to spiral and rebound. "As Lord of Clarr and master of the Knife of Clarr, I command you to take the place of Queen Octobr. The queen shall be free of the ice, and the warden Yaark will take her place within the ice prison."

And he stopped, took a deep breath, trembled, and watched, waiting, with the knife held firm with its point to Yaark's face. The fading sounds of his voice flooded out and then fell back into whispers. A sudden spring of shadows, like the engulfing leather wings of a giant bat, turned the room black. A last whispering scratch of wingtips, and then silence fell like a shroud, no one moving. Hermes had landed and Alice had clambered off, groping in the dark for Alfie's hand. Brewster and Wagster could be heard wheezing in the background. Nathan stood in the centre of the room, blinking.

Yaark's transfiguration was halted. The shadow blooming from its yaws became a halo of ice crystals. Where giant black wings had started to form, now they shrank back. The thin crimson lines of skeleton bone turned again to the stripes of tiger fur, and a freezing and stagnant force pushed everyone, even the Hazletts, back against the walls.

Then once again he held up the knife.

Its light blazed out. The gold and silver gleam strengthened and spun its webs up to the ceiling and around the ice walls. And there, suspended within the wall where Granny Octobr had been, was the rearing form of a great angry tiger, on its hind legs as it leapt, its front paws extended, and its lips curled back in a snarl. Encased in the freeze, it remained utterly motionless. Yaark had indeed been taken by the ice grave.

Everyone stared. And then a very small voice said, "Is that you, Nathan?"

Whirling around, Nathan saw, and rushed into his grandmother's arms. Poppy raced close behind him. But as they both clung to her, and her to them, shaking as though still frozen, another sound reverberated.

Both Wagster and Brewster were standing, mouths open, gaping and shouting, their knees trembling and their long fingers pointing at the vast slithering sheen of barely rippled ice which encircled the entire room beyond the arched doorway. They were horrified and desperately unbelieving. Their long skinny legs were bent and unsteady, their tight black jackets heaving as they tried to catch their breath, their top hats half slipping over their noses, and their little green button eyes wide as glass.

Hermes, standing proudly next to Alice, was bobbing his head in approval and respect, as Nathan stared back at Yaark, hardly able to understand what he had achieved. The others, crowding around, began to clap. The sound echoed. Granny, speechless, stood with her arms around Poppy, and she joined in the clapping.

And then, quite suddenly with a startling yell of fury, Wagster attacked. Nails curling into claws, he leapt. As his long legs sprang like sprinted stilts from the ground, he began to change and once again his body narrowed, twisted, and became dark coils of scaled power. His head expanded, the forked tongue flicked out and his jaws slit.

Dodging and running, Nathan raced around the room as the huge serpent swayed, ready to hurtle down, entrap, and contract its body to squeeze, strangle and kill. Hermes flew up at once, flapping violently around the snake's head, its feathers in Wagster's eyes and its webbed feet slapping against the back of his head. Brewster jumped to save his brother.

But he jumped too high and without stopping to look or think, Brewster Hazlett leapt straight into the long open pit.

As he fell, Brewster wailed, and then was gone.

With a screech, only half human, as he saw his twin disappear, Wagster fell back into his old form and scrabbled to the side of the pit to save his brother, He reached down his long arms into the shadows, but found he was slipping, his scales still clinging to his body and sliding on the icy stone.

Nathan knelt, and looked. Brewster, frantic and voiceless, was hanging onto the cord of destiny, his fingers entwined with rope and oozing blood, his face in open-mouthed panic, his hat disappearing down into the bottomless fall below his scrabbling golden feet.

But the cord was as fine as any invisible destiny, and Brewster, his attempts to climb up quite useless, was slipping and his fingers were unable to grip securely.

Beside Nathan, Alfie, John and Peter looked down.

"Leave him," said Alfie. "Vile creature."

"He wanted to kill you," whispered Alice from behind them.

John looked dubious. "Those shrieks is mighty hard to hear," he admitted, and it was Sam who began to sniff, as though about to cry. Hermes had trapped Wagster against the far wall, half man and half serpent, frantic and confused in scales and jacket, top hat and coiled tail. It was Poppy who came beside Nathan, peering down, and hurried away back to Granny's sheltering arms.

Nathan shook his head. "I can't leave him there."

"Save the wretches' life, and reckon he'll try to kill you instead," said Alfie gruffly.

But Nathan knelt again, and stretched down his arm, saying softly, "Brewster was the one who brought me to you. I wouldn't have met any of you without him. And now you're my best friends. The only really wonderful friends I've ever had. And all these most incredible adventures. All thanks to him."

With another stretch, he grabbed Brewster's failing fingers and pulled them up into the tightest grasp he could manage. Brewster finally released the cord of destiny with his right hand and clung to Nathan. Then Nathan grabbed Brewster's left hand. It was coated in dried blood, put gradually Nathan managed to hold tight and slowly pulled. Brewster's grip was now so desperately tight it was painful, but Nathan clung on and hoisted the skinny wizard, bit by bit, back onto the wet floor.

They sat together, collapsed and gasping for breath, staring at each other. Behind them Wagster had stopped struggling and watched quietly. Without his top hat, Brewster's head was half bald with straggles of black tufts here and there, dropping over his ears but quite bare on top. He had never looked so vulnerable, and he was not laughing at all.

Everyone was watching and it was sometime before Brewster could speak. When he did, it was quiet, and only to Nathan. He murmured, "I owe you, boy. And a Hazlett always pays when called."

Then, with a sudden turn, Wagster, more serpent now than man, snatched his twin brother up in his coils, hugged him safe and tight, swung across the pit, and within a blink was gone into the shadows. The faint sound of a slither on wet stone echoed back, and then quickly disappeared.

CHAPTER TWENTY-NINE

The small plump woman pushed back the thin grey wispy straggles of hair behind her ears where they got entangled with the purple frame of her glasses, leaned back with a breathless gasp against the ice wall, then realised what she was leaning against, glimpsed the motionless leap of the springing tiger directly behind her, and hurried away into the middle of the room.

There was no one left except Nathan, Poppy, Alice, Alfie, John and Sam, except for the goose. But Granny did not seem in the least perturbed by a talking goose, and smiled at everyone, pushed her glasses back up to her eyes, and sighed.

"I am most exceptionally grateful," she said. "And so is he."

"He?" asked Poppy. "You mean Brewster?"

"No, no," said Granny, and drew out a tiny green frog with a yellow belly and huge black eyes from the dusty pocket of her apron. "Ferdinand," she introduced him, brushing some self-raising flour off his head with her fingertip. "I'm not sure how long we were imprisoned, but it was most unpleasant."

Nathan said hello again to Ferdinand, who bowed and muttered never ending thanks and loyalty, and then he regarded the other frozen figures encased in ice. "How do I get the others out?" Nathan asked.

"Sadly," replied Granny, "there is no one to replace them. Without the key, you cannot unlock the prisons. And you well know who holds the key."

"So how do I release Yaark and get it?"

"Without the key," she repeated, "you can only swap one with another, and cannot simply release them all, nor even any one of them. Which is," and she took both Nathan's and Poppy's hands in hers and walked very slowly over to another part of the wall near the doorway, "a great sadness for us all. For these, my dears, are your parents."

"I should have kept Brewster, and swapped him," whispered Nathan, staring, awed, at the motionless figures before him. He could not look away, and beside him Poppy was staring mesmerised as he was.

With a twitch of his fat stumpy tail feathers, Hermes waddled to Granny Octobr and bowed with reverence. "My lady," he said, "I would be honoured to offer myself in exchange for one of our great imprisoned monarchs."

John looked up. "And me. I reckon I wouldn't mind. Go to sleep, maybe. Wouldn't know the difference."

"It's not right." Sam was crying again. "Take me. Just as long as you promise to look after Mouse."

"Certainly not. None of you." Granny clapped her hands and smiled. "You are heroes, each and every one. But the people trapped here must be freed by the great Key of Clarr. Every one of these are important men and women, and outside there are a thousand innocent souls turned to tiny creatures at the mercy of bad weather and the predators of the forests. Poor souls transformed into beetles, shrews, moles and turtles, the farmers have been unable to look after their crops. The craftsmen have had to abandon their businesses. The builders and carpenters have had to abandon their work. Lashtang has simply become the ruined plaything Clebbster, the tyrant, the wizard father of the Hazlett twins. Not only these people must be saved, and those outside, but Lashtang itself must be rescued. It has been too long."

Nathan heard little of this speech. He and Poppy were staring at their parents.

The woman was tall, and her eyes were hazel with golden streaks, as was her hair. It was long and thick, and sun streaked just like Nathan's and Poppy's. Bumble-Bee Heads, all of them. She wore a long white dress to the ground, and there were pearls in her hair and around her waist. "Mother," whispered Nathan to himself.

"How beautiful," whispered Poppy. "Will we ever meet her properly, do you think?"

"I swear it. I promise it," Nathan mumbled back to his sister. "I will come back here over and over until I find out how to help them both, and everyone else too."

The man was unusually tall, and his hair was light brown, as were his heavy-lidded eyes. He wore a dark cloak which surrounded him, and there was a large square emerald ring on one thumb.

"I love them both," said Poppy. "You have to let me come back with you, Nat. I want to fight the wizards too."

Alfie had been listening. "Don't leave us behind. Reckon this is a fantastic country. You better bring us all back."

"Tis more than adventure," John said suddenly, staring at Nathan. "Tis a duty, I reckon. And them puzzles to sort. Fire and ice, you says in that poesy. Well, this tower is ice. That be clear enough. And Yaark, tis the fire. The ruddy Hellfire tiger is trapped in the ice, but I don't reckon the ice can keep him forever."

"And we need the key back," Poppy sniffed.

"But now," said Granny, "it's time to go home." She nodded vigorously. "You have already achieved something wonderful on this visit. Oh yes – rescuing me of course – and thank you very much indeed. But more important, you have Yaark trapped in the ice. That is a great blessing."

"But we have to rescue all those people trapped there," said Poppy, shaking her head. "And that means Yaark too, doesn't it?"

"May I," Hermes bowed once again, "offer my services, my lady? If you wish to return to the human worlds, I can transport at least two of your illustrious selves."

"There's the puzzle," said Nathan suddenly, remembering. "One of the arrows leads directly to the veil. We can leave altogether."

Holding up her hand, Granny stood in the doorway, smiling. "You have all been heroes," she said, "and people I should like to know better. I offer an open invitation for all of you to return to my land. But Lashtang is under great threat and needs warriors. One day, we will be at peace and will welcome everyone to our shores."

It was Alice who stepped forwards, and bowed, as if to a queen. "My lady," she answered, "I come from a time when war and great battles are fought all over the world, threat, invasion and danger are what we expect to face every day. We have been fighting a powerful and cruel man, and Nathan and Poppy have helped us beyond all expectation. We would like to help them in turn."

Granny Octobr took Alice's hand. "My dear," she said, "I thank you and all of you brave people. Now I must return to England in my own modern times, and the life I adopted many years ago. I will take Poppy with me, if she will come, and hope to see Nathan soon. For we need to plan and get ready for the great fight."

Nathan was still staring at his mother. He could hardly remember her from his childhood, but he recognised the kindness and love in her face and wished he could kiss her cheek. Now he turned back to his grandmother. "I want to go back with Alfie and John first," he said. "I'll come home soon."

"Then we take the arrow towards the veil," said Granny, "and I shall explain the different tunnels after that."

In virtual silence, they returned to the entrance of the Tower, where the door still stood wide open, and beyond it the mountains soared, snow-topped, with their deep ravines, cliff sides, frozen waterfalls and precipices of ice and ruin. The wind howled, scattering icicles and whining through the slits in the rock. Everyone shivered, crowding together, and Hermes ruffled his feathers. The sky was grey, but there was daylight behind the clouds, and a glimmer of sunbeams on the higher slopes where the snow glittered bright.

In the circular entrance hall, the mosaic patterns on the tiled floor shone. Everyone trooped to the arrow that pointed towards the curtain of colours.

"Who leads?" whispered Nathan.

"You, my dear," Granny told him, "and I shall bring up the rear."

"And I," announced Hermes, "shall walk beside my Lord of Clarr, and protect him from all dangers."

It was a longer corridor than Nathan had expected, winding so frequently that it seemed to him that they might be going in circles. Sometimes there were windows, but each was black, as though shuttered, or closed against the night and the wind. Having an idea that they were locked against him, Nathan once again wished he had the secret of the Key of Clarr, but clutched his knife tight, knowing he had the most magical gift of all.

He had asked the key to show him his parents, and although it had taken both time and danger, the knife had done exactly as he had asked. And, with incredible power, it had released his grandmother and trapped the terrible Yaark in the ice.

But there was very little Nathan yet understood about the knife, and some things it seemed unable, or unwilling to do.

His thoughts were interrupted. "My lord, here is the veil," Hermes said, stopping before the opening and the dazzling curtain beyond. "We have arrived. Command me, lord, and I shall do as you wish."

Nathan was certainly not accustomed to giving orders. He looked back to his grandmother, her hand in Poppy's, as they hurried to catch up. She came to Nathan, a little out of breath. "It seems we have to part again, my dear," she said and looked around. Everyone had crowded close. "Walk straight through there," she said, pointing. "Think only of where you wish to go. Think of your homes, your towns and cities, your families and your friends. You'll find yourselves right back at home."

"And how do I get back to you later from 15th century London?" asked Nathan.

"Don't you worry about that, my dear," Granny told him. "I'm sure Hermes will bring you when you're ready."

"I'll miss you." He looked down. "And Poppy."

"I don't think you'll be away long, Nathan dear," answered Granny. "I'll put the kettle on. Poppy, Ferdinand and I will be waiting. There's a lot to do once you come home."

She stepped back and the others moved forwards. The veil was translucent, and in constant movement. It appeared to be fashioned from dragonfly wings, but every dragonfly lived and fluttered, spinning, hovering and flying in bewitching patterns. Every wing seemed different and every flight individual. Some were magnificent, huge and glittering, others small, hesitant and luminescent. Nathan moved closer and stretched out his hand. The veil parted. He could not feel the touch of wing, antennae or flight, but each creature flew aside, and the way through was opened in blazing light. The sky made its own tunnel of sunshine. And as they passed, so then the veil closed behind them.

Nathan rested his hand on the goose's neck, where Hermes' feathers were short and soft. "I'm thinking of London," he muttered to himself. "Medieval London and the cobbled streets and all those old buildings."

He found, almost without intention, that he had shut his eyes. He had felt, rather than seen, all the others crowding around him and the warmth of their hands, their whispers of excitement, and their hesitant steps. But then, when he opened his eyes again, he was all alone except for Hermes, standing in Bandy Alley and staring up at the ancient walls of the Tower.

"From the Tower of Clarr to the Tower of London," he muttered. And stood still, staring. This was where Brewster had dropped him, long before, and where he had lived in the now burned out cellar. The ironmonger's shop where they had all stayed after the fire, was still open and looked busy. Nathan decided not to go there. He wanted to hurry off to Bishopsgate and Alice's house, where he knew all the others would be.

A fine drizzle had turned the chilly air to a steel grey, and although it was light, it seemed to soak through and he began to shiver. But it wasn't a long walk, and with a nod to Hermes, he pulled his cape tight around him and set off at a quick pace. Then, as he turned the top end of Bandy Alley where the Tower rose dark to his right, he had to dodge aside to the wall, avoiding the long parade of riders and their prancing and highly decorated horses approaching the drawbridge and portcullis.

The shining bridles jingled, and the horses' hooves clattered on the wet cobbles, their ears alert and their manes twitching in the rain. The riders were grandly dressed and seemed unconcerned with the drizzle, though some had raised the hoods of their cloaks. One man, who rode near the front of the procession, turned to call to someone behind, and immediately Nathan recognised the bright face and the deep brown eyes, light brown hair, and air of regal command.

Smiling to himself, Nathan bowed, for it was King Richard, who had spoken to him once before. But then, as he looked up, Nathan was shocked to recognise two other faces. At the very end rode the baron and his brother Edmund. Their bright red hair was wet and plastered in dripping streaks to their heads, and they bumped, both a little too fat for their saddles, as their horses clomped over the cobbles.

About to step further back into the shadows, Nathan was even more surprised when his majesty the king, turning again, noticed Nathan standing bareheaded in the rain. He paused, then beckoned, and sat waiting until Nathan walked quickly towards him, bowed as low as he dared without putting his knee to the slippery wet road, and tried to shake the rain from his hair.

King Richard laughed. "I see you have bought a goose," he said, smiling. "Was that with the money I gave you? But one goose will not make you a living, nor buy even a cape with a hood to keep that sun-kissed hair of yours dry."

Nathan could hardly reply that the goose was a friend, and certainly not for sale. Instead he stuttered, saying, "Your majesty, I am honoured. I was, that is, intending to look for an – apprenticeship. As a – tailor."

"An excellent ambition, young man," the king said, "come to the palace once the training has begun, and I'll give you work." He turned again, facing the outer walls of the Tower, and rode on across the moat and its murky grey ripples, the flat waters busy with the cascade of rebounding raindrops.

As Nathan stood back, he realised that the baron and his brother, peering in blatant fury, had both seen and recognised him. Waiting until the cavalcade had passed into the Tower, and disappeared within the great walls, both men, looking down from their saddles, came to

Nathan, blocking him as they edged one either side. Nathan was squashed between the two horses, their flanks and the nervous swish of their wet tails enclosing him so he could hardly move.

"You," spat the baron between gritted teeth, "ever since the first time I saw you, you've brought only trouble. You've spoiled every plan I had, you've ruined everything. Without you, you nasty little thief, Edmund would have been married to Alice Parry by now, and we'd all be living the high life in Bishopsgate."

"And," snarled Edmund, "somehow you put out the fire."

Nathan looked up angrily. "So you admit paying someone to light that fire. That's disgusting. You could have killed a hundred people and burned that beautiful house to the ground. I'll tell the judge."

"As if anyone would believe you," hissed Edmund.

"I could tell the king."

"You'll be dead before you can open your mouth to his majesty or anyone else," roared the Baron, and snatching up his riding crop, he lashed out at Nathan standing, barely breathing, below. The crop was woven leather, and it slashed across his cheek with a pain so violent, that Nathan would have fallen had he not been held upright by the horses. Again the baron lashed out with his riding crop, but the end of it caught one horse's neck, and it reared, neighing and frightened.

Freed, Nathan ran. But he could not outrun two horses. "Come here, you scum," roared Edmund.

The great Tower doors were still open, and Nathan made one mad dash for the drawbridge. The baron, he thought, could not attack him with everyone watching, and he managed to scramble beneath the portcullis and into the great courtyard beyond. Both Edmund and the baron thundered after him, and Nathan could also feel the draught of the goose feathers over his head and knew that Hermes was with him too. This was some consolation, and he knew he had a loyal and faithful friend, but he didn't see how a goose could battle against two murderous men with riding whips, and two huge horses with hooves like anvils.

The white-washed Keep rose enormous before him, its battlements in the low rain clouds. Clearly the king and his entourage had already entered, climbing the exterior steps to the Royal

Apartments within the Keep, and their horses were being led away by the Tower grooms. Nathan whirled around, looking for guards or anyone who might help him. Hermes now stood beside him, neck stretched and head held high, but this seemed to confuse anyone watching, who appeared to think he might be a servant, come to deliver a goose to the kitchens. The guards patrolled the walls, but they took no notice of Nathan and the grooms and stable boys were too busy with the lords' horses.

Then Edmund and the baron were on him again. The Baron raised his crop, and Edmund slashed out with his whip, which caught Nathan around one arm, making him stumble. He straightened immediately, now extremely angry and he did the first thing that came into his head. He lifted the Knife of Clarr from his pocket, held it up into the drizzle, and as its light grew strong like a swirling golden sheen, he called, "Brewster Hazlett, you owe me a favour. Come now and rid me of the two wicked men who want me dead."

The Baron paused, surprised to see the knife and its luminous light, but then he raised his riding crop once more. "You think to use a knife on me, you vile urchin?" he shrieked. His hair was now like red straw in his eyes, and the eyes themselves were bloodshot. Edmund, close behind, rode his horse directly at Nathan.

But Hermes spread his wings, rose up, and pecked, hissing and squawking, at both Edmund and the horse. With a snort of panic the horse reared again, throwing its rider from its back. Edmund lost saddle, stirrups and whip, and came crashing down onto the wet paving of the Tower courtyard.

Nathan fled. All around him the winding alleys ran between the huge stone buildings, on from the Gatehouse, past the great keep and dodging, one eye over his shoulder, managed to find those places where shadowed passage was too narrow for two screeching fat men and one terrified horse. But Nathan heard them behind him, and kept running.

All too quickly he raced out once more onto open ground and unless he could enter the Keep itself, which was well guarded, he did not see where he could go. Edmund, on foot with his hose wrinkled and soaked, had managed to keep hold of his whip and was lumbering towards Nathan from one side. The whip cracked. On the other side was the baron, still astride his horse, his crop in his hand and his mouth wide open in a shout of rage.

And then, sweeping down from the sky, were two long thin black shadows, seated on something equally long, thin and black, whizzing in ever tightening circles. One of the swirling shadows wore a tall top hat. The other wore a small golden cap, its peak decorated with a scarlet tassel. They were, to Nathan's confusion, riding broomsticks.

The baron fell off his horse and the mare bolted. Two guards rushed after the horse, but no one was prepared to help the men, for clearly they were being attacked by witches, and not even the guards were prepared to face black magic. Both the baron and his brother stood, knees trembling, and watched, growing both dizzy and terrified, as the strange apparition encircled them. Brewster and Wagster were cackling and wheezing, enjoying themselves, and manoeuvring their brooms down, around, between, and finally up again. Knees tight to the sticks they rode, the Hazlett twins flew faster and faster.

Inspired, Hermes rose up again, large flat feet waving in the breezes from the wizards, squawked into the baron's face, pecked at Edmund, and dived down at both, one after the other. Clearly delighted with his own speed, it was some time before Hermes settled.

Brewster waved at Nathan, calling, "Well, Bumble-Bee Head, I always pay my debts and here I am, with Wagster to help." Then, broomstick parallel to the ground, he hovered just above Nathan's head. "What shall we do with these fat lumps? Drown them in the moat? Tie them up with their own belts? Strangle them with their own soggy hose?"

"I don't know," Nathan gasped, completely out of breath, "but thank you for coming. Now you've rescued me so it's a rescue in exchange for a rescue."

Cackling and waving his golden cap in the air, Brewster was practising aerobatics, spinning his broom in somersaults and, end over end, coming back to the baron and his brother Edmund. He reached over, pulling their hair, kicking them in the back of their necks with his little golden boots, then soaring up again with a cheer of exhilaration.

Wagster pointed down fiercely at Nathan. "Make your decision," he called, his claws unsheathed. "I come only to help my brother pay his debt. Where do we take these two fat imbecile humans? Quick, or I leave."

The answer came suddenly and without any doubt, Nathan immediately knew what he had to do. He stood firm and called back to both Brewster and Wagster. "Take them to Lashtang," he said, "and then to the Tower of Clarr. And although I will stand here, and not there, I will order my knife to do exactly as I wish. Take them to the chamber of frozen ice walls. Then leave. You will be free, debt paid."

With a whoop of delight, both twins aimed directly down at Edmund and the baron, grabbed them by their bright ginger hair, and with a grip like iron, carried them up into the sky. Nathan watched as the figures became smaller and smaller, the two fat men struggling, their legs kicking out wildly, screaming until their voices were hoarse. As they all disappeared behind the clouds, the drizzle a silver mist, Nathan could still hear Brewster cackle, and Wagster swear.

Nathan turned, and without looking at anyone, nor meeting any of the horrified and shocked eyes of those watching, he walked silently to the Tower gatehouse, crossed the drawbridge, and hurried into the shadows of Bandy Alley's wet cobbles. There he stood, catching his breath and smiling to himself. Once more he held up the Knife of Clarr and it seemed that the shadows fled.

"I am Lord of Clarr and the holder of the Knife of Clarr," Nathan said speaking loudly and clearly. "I therefore order that the two humans about to arrive in the Tower of Clarr, be taken to the chamber of ice. There they will be exchanged and taken into the wall in place of their Majesties, the Octobr Sovereigns. The king and queen will be free of the ice wall, and their places will be taken by Hugh Darling, Baron Cambridge and his brother Edmund Darling, who will be kept there until their eventual release."

He felt it. There was a click, as if the words had been heard and accepted, and he knew, as he had never known before, that his wishes would be followed exactly.

With a satisfied smile, Nathan turned north and began to walk towards Bishopsgate. Beside him walked the large and proud white goose, flat feet slapping on the wet cobbles, his wings tight folded against the rain, but his great golden beak held high.

The rain stopped and the sun came out, shining its light in the reflections of the puddles. Then, as brilliant as the sunshine and as iridescent as a dragonfly's wing, a rainbow arched over the roadway, its vivid foundation firmly descending within the roof of the large house in Bishopsgate where Nathan was heading.

It was sometime that Nathan did not stop smiling.

CHAPTER THIRTY

I t was Mouse who saw him first.

She raced down the main staircase like a wild tangle of streaky fluff, and behind her, jumping and bumping down step to step on minute legs not long enough to walk, came the three tiny kittens, one white, one black and one grey.

Then Mouse saw Hermes, and stopped, with a squeak. The kittens fell over backwards.

Hermes raised and outstretched both wings, lowered his head, thrust forward his beak and hissed, waddling full pelt towards the cat. "Begone, predator," Hermes squawked. As Mouse pelted back to a position of strength halfway up the stairs, glared down, she hissed back with a warning yowl.

"Oh dear," sighed Nathan. "Life is never simple."

By now everyone else had appeared, leaping the steps and bombarding Nathan with questions. Sam, with a sudden grin, hugged first Nathan, which he really wasn't used to, and then Mouse, who was exceedingly used to it, cuddled up and purred with a gaze of smug satisfaction at the goose.

They sat in the main hall, draped over chairs and settles, Sam, the kittens and Mouse on a cushion on the floor, and Hermes guarding the door. Peter plugged his thumb back into his mouth and sat on one of the wide window seats. Spots of rain still slithered down the windows, but the drizzle had stopped and the sun was a sparkling reflection throughout the city.

"A natural mistake," Nathan said. "I came through the veil straight into Bandy Alley. I was thinking of the old house, I suppose. But as it happens, it was a lucky mistake."

They demanded to know how.

"Well," said Nathan, pleased with himself, "I don't think you'll be having any trouble from that horrible baron and his revolting brother in the future."

They all leaned forwards. "What did you do?" asked Alice and Alfie at the same moment.

"Sent them to Lashtang," said Nathan with a grin, and watched the open-mouthed astonishment with pride. "I'll explain later. But it's true. They've gone. And," with another grin, "I met the king again. He actually remembered who I was."

"O'course," John sniggered, "You're the Lord of Clarr."

Shaking his head, Nathan lay back in the deep cushioned chair. "Doesn't seem real, does it. So strange – so crazy – and so exciting."

"And you're taking us back with you?"

"One day."

He had, he hoped, although he could not yet be sure, released his parents. He had every intention of returning to Lashtang to find and meet them, to see the Darling brothers trapped in ice, and to discover more about who he was. But first of all he wanted to go home to Granny, Poppy and his own comfy and familiar bedroom. Even the hope of meeting his parents again didn't seem real. Sometimes he still thought he must be dreaming.

"Reckon you better stay right here fer a day or three," John said, nodding with determination. "Can't go just yet, I reckon."

"Maybe a day." Nathan accepted the ginger biscuits which Alice was handing him, and a big pewter cup of heated apple cider. "It's hard. I want to be here. I want to be with my sister and grandmother in my own home. And I want to be in Lashtang too."

"And I reckon I got me own adventure to chase after," John said, leaning forwards, elbows to his warm woollen knees. "T'was one o' them Hazletts what told me I still had a father. Bin looking fer me fer years, he said. But it's hard believing that, after them monks. I were brought up in that monastery cos they said I were found on a rubbish dump. Best place fer me, they reckons. So where were me Pa hiding, then?"

"Wiv a proper Pa," objected Alfie, "how can some little brat what can't walk yet end up on a dump?"

"So," nodded Alice eagerly, "we're all going to help John look for his real father. We'll go back to the monastery first, and keep searching from there."

"I'd love to help," said Nathan, wondering if his knife might be able to solve puzzles like that. "But tomorrow I really do have to leave. I'll be back. That's a promise. But I don't know when. Time doesn't run smoothly, does it?"

"T'ain't nuffing smooth, never."

"I dreams o' tigers."

"And me of ice."

"I shall dream about all of it," Nathan sighed. "I believe Yaark is the greatest danger. We haven't discovered his real powers yet. And Clebbster, the Hazlett father. We haven't met him at all. But he must be terrible, with sons like the twins. What is still out there to discover?"

"More danger."

"More excitement."

Alice ordered a feast. Everyone chose a favourite meal, and each one was served at the long table. Hermes sat on the table in the middle with a platter of grass, mashed parsnip, cabbage and wheat. He declared that he had never eaten better. Mouse kept her distance, suckling her kittens beneath the table, while being secretly fed with anything and everything by Sam.

Nathan looked at Hermes. "I could take one of the kittens home with me," he said softly, "if you help me look after it."

This was a slight shock for Hermes, who nearly choked on a cabbage stalk, and had to hiccup. "I am not," he said regretfully, "what you might call a natural mother, my lord. I fear I might fail in such a task. I am a warrior, and a messenger of Clarr."

"Which kitten?" asked Peter.

"The white one," after a pause. "It would look more like a baby goose."

"A Gosling, my lord."

'Yes, indeed. "Nathan swallowed the mouthful of apple pie and custard and smiled at Hermes. "And, Hermes, you would have the honour of giving it a name."

"In that case, my lord," Hermes ruffled his feathers and stuck out his breast, "I shall swear to do my best, my lord, and since my best is, without doubt, better than most, then this gosling should thrive, and I will undertake to be both mother and father."

Hiding the grin, Nathan said, "Think of a name and tell me tomorrow. He looked over at Sam. "You don't mind, do you?"

"'Course I do," admitted Sam. "But they've been weaned and poor Mouse, she can't look after them forever. At least this one will go to a better home. Do they have special food in your time, Nat?"

He thought a moment. "Absolutely yes."

Sam muttered, "I called the white one Beauty, and she's a she."

"As the servant of the Lord of Clarr," Hermes declared, "I shall think of a more suitable title."

"Humph," said Sam to his cup.

It was in bed that night when Nathan brought out his knife. Hermes was outside in the corridor, guarding the bedchamber, and Nathan was alone with the shadows. He had slipped the Knife of Clarr beneath the pillow, but now he brought it out and held it up, squinting into the brilliant light that flooded out.

"If it's true," he said carefully, "that John Ten-Toes has a father who's looking for him, please help them find each other. I want to come back and help, but I want you to help first." For a moment, Nathan wondered if he had failed to make himself clear, since the knife's brilliance appeared to fade a little, as though in doubt. So he held up the knife again. "We don't know what the father is called and we don't know where he is. But he's here. Not in Lashtang. Unless Brewster was lying and there's no father at all."

The light glimmered with a copper tone that Nathan had not seen before. He was accustomed to a silver and golden dazzle, but this time the glitter was hesitant. Nathan once again ran his fingers over the hilt, tracing the intricate pattern, the two figures with their budding wing feathers, and the dragon serpent between. He had seen Wagster transformed in serpent form, but he could not see why such a thing should be represented on a knife of power and service, kindness and intelligence.

Shaking his head again, he pushed the knife back beneath his pillow, lay down and closed his eyes.

He woke to the sound of pelting rain outside, groaned, rolled over, and waking slowly. Then with a sudden burst of happiness he sat up and smiled at the rain, remembering that this was the day he was going back to Granny, Poppy and his own home. He would arrive with a talking goose and a very small fluffy white kitten which would no doubt be known as a gosling, and would hopefully not try to eat Ferdinand. He would tell his grandmother that he might, just perhaps, have miraculously released his mother and father from the ice, and he would undoubtedly begin to learn more and more about Lashtang, Clarr, and himself.

There was a great deal to discover, but since Granny Octobr was some sort of royalty in Lashtang, she would certainly be the one to tell him everything he wanted to know. Then Hermes would take him back. He would try and take Alice, Alfie, John, Peter and Sam with him, but they might be too busy looking for John's father. And there was still a lot to learn about medieval London too.

The goodbyes were warm, loving, and difficult. Nathan almost decided to stay another day, but He looked at the rain, shook his head, called Hermes, and insisted that he had to leave. Climbing on the goose's back, he smiled deeply, sighed with contentment, and put his arms around the soft feathered neck. The white kitten was in one of his pockets, already asleep.

"Alright," whispered Nathan. "Let's go."

Within a heartbeat he found himself falling onto Granny Octobr's kitchen floor and was sitting in self-raising flour which had blown from the table.

Granny looked up and over her glasses. "About time," she said. "I'm making raspberry crumble for dinner."

THE END FOR NOW…

So what will Granny tell Nathan about their ancestry? Did his parents escape the Ice? And what did happen to the Baron and his brother?

So many questions still to be answered, and so many adventures still to be had. Find out what happens next in 'Snakes & Ladders'

AFTERWORD

I hope you enjoyed reading this instalment of Nathan's adventures. I would love to hear your thoughts on anything to do with Nathan and his friends.

You can contact me through either the Bannister's Muster website at https://bannistersmuster.com. or the Bannister's Muster facebook page.

If you could leave a review on Amazon, that would be wonderful and so very helpful, and gives me a happy face!

See you soon in the next instalment...

Made in the USA
Monee, IL
12 December 2020

52550792R00166